Summer on Highland Beach

ALSO BY SUNNY HOSTIN

Summer on the Bluffs
Summer on Sag Harbor
I Am These Truths

Summer on Highland Beach

A NOVEL

SUNNY HOSTIN
WITH SHARINA HARRIS

wm

WILLIAM MORROW
An Imprint of HarperCollins*Publishers*

HarperCollins books may be purchased for educational, business, or sales promotional use. For information, please email the Special Markets Department at SPsales@harpercollins.com.

FIRST EDITION

Designed by Bonni Leon-Berman

Library of Congress Cataloging-in-Publication Data

Names: Hostin, Sunny, author.
Title: Summer on Highland Beach : a novel / Sunny Hostin.
Description: First edition. | New York, NY : William Morrow, 2024. | Series: Summer Beach ; book 3
Identifiers: LCCN 2023056563 (print) | LCCN 2023056564 (ebook) | ISBN 9780062994257 (hardcover) | ISBN 9780062994271 (ebook)
Subjects: LCSH: African American women—Fiction. | African American families—Fiction. | Self-realization in women—Fiction. | Family secrets—Fiction. | Summer—Fiction. | Highland Beach (Md.) —Fiction. | LCGFT: Novels.
Classification: LCC PS3608.O837 S84 2024 (print) | LCC PS3608.O837 (ebook) | DDC 813/.6—dc23/eng/20231228
LC record available at https://lccn.loc.gov/2023056563
LC ebook record available at https://lccn.loc.gov/2023056564

ISBN 978-0-06-299425-7

24 25 26 27 28 LBC 5 4 3 2 1

This book is dedicated to those who have come before. Thank you for your excellence, for finding and grounding joy, respite, and community despite it all. And for leaving the legacy of Black Beach Communities so that others can find the same. Joy is resistance.

Summer on Highland Beach

PROLOGUE

MAJOR CHARLES DOUGLASS'S LETTER TO HIS
FATHER, FREDERICK DOUGLASS

Bay Ridge, March 12, 1893

Dear Father,

I received the money to help us purchase the land from the Blackshears, which Laura and I are very grateful for. Our attorney has drawn the papers, and we have deeded the land to Joseph, as our attorney advised us to protect ourselves from my position at the Pension Office. Now the twenty-six and two-thirds acres are ours.

As an investor, you deserve an update. We surveyed the property and divided the remaining land into eleven blocks and 129 lots. Our surveyor, Mr. Charles P. Calvert, says this place is excellent for fishing, crabbing, and boating. I've also filed the land with Anne Arundel County. We are well underway to making this place a resort.

Also, I want to address a question you asked me in your last letter.

You asked: What makes this place so special?

I thank you for the question. It is not just the location by the Bay Ridge Resort and the Queen Resort of the Chesapeake. But after they refused to let us sit down and eat at that resort, I knew we needed a place where we could sit by the water and keep our heads lifted high without worry. I had enough of that in the Fifth

Massachusetts Calvary. They tried to starve us with dry bread, made us sick, and threatened to harm us.

The character of a white man determined how we were treated, whether with respect or like animals. And though there are good ones out there, I think we need a place just for us. Not just for our family, but for our friends, too.

Laura, Haley, and I came for the summer, and Laura liked it so well we wanted to stay for a few weeks. We walked around and it felt like home. Then a bus driver came around, told us about property owned by other Black folks. Heirs, he said, and it used to be a slave plantation.

We never would have guessed that the place, just a few miles from where they refused us, had land owned by Negroes.

I did not want to believe it at first. Nor did I want my wife to become disappointed. But she wouldn't hear of us not trying. So we tried, and the land is ours, for now.

Once we get our feet under us, Laura and I will build our cottage. We've made a list of friends and family who may want to own a place here.

We found a nice spot for you near a creek. It has the best views of the water. I hope you find you can slow down here. You and Mama did not have a chance to rest together, but I hope this is a place where you can be at peace.

This place is special—I know it is just as sure and solid as our feet on the ground we own. The white folks across the way may not like it, but we bought it proper, thanks to you. We'll teach our children to keep our land protected, so they'll always have a place to call home.

Your Aff. Son
Charles R. Douglass

CHAPTER ONE

May 2022

THE WICKED WITCH
OF THE BEACH

Olivia stood on the serene shore of Highland Beach. Though quiet, it buzzed with the same thread of energy as her other favorite places—a delicate silken cocoon filled with pride and history and safety.

A place carried out by the ancestors, a place to lay your head down and let your soul rest. The founders made Highland Beach, a Black resort town near Annapolis, into a haven like Sag Harbor and Oak Bluffs.

Its very existence was revolutionary, spurred by discrimination. The founders—Major Charles Douglass, the son of Frederick Douglass, and his wife Laura—didn't go low or high but headed for the middle path, working around racism, carving out a new path of their own by purchasing and developing beachfront property south of Bay Ridge.

Olivia felt proud looking at the sandy beachfront where famous Black figures like Booker T. Washington, W.E.B. Du Bois, and Paul Laurence Dunbar once rested. They needed the calm waters of the bay to wash away the poison of racism. It was their refuge.

At least for a little while.

She inhaled, and the salt in the air soothed. Shoots of grass surrounded the edge of the beach. Wooden planks stood high in the bay, creating a safe buffer between man and water.

Olivia could feel the tension in her body release as the salty water kissed her toes. She'd been in Highland Beach for only forty-eight hours. The entire time she avoided people, quietly watching from the house as neighbors strolled by, walking their dogs and greeting each other.

They were entirely too friendly. Too social. She didn't mind it normally, but she planned to visit here for only two weeks.

And she had absolutely no plans to reveal that she was the mayor's secret love child.

Which was why she'd quietly crept out of her father CJ's home at dawn to give her restless body a sweet boost of adrenaline by jogging a few blocks around the neighborhood of not only Highland Beach but also its sister community, Venice Beach.

Now she glanced at her Apple Watch, walked away from the shoreline, then slipped on her sneakers and resumed her run before anyone stopped her for a friendly chat.

Even through her self-imposed seclusion, Olivia could still feel the special beat to Highland Beach. It wasn't noisy, like a busy city with a symphony of horns. It wasn't quiet and isolated. But there was a constant thrumming, something that felt communal and intentional and steady—like a mallet on a bass drum.

The sound was faint, like a well-kept secret, but it thrummed throughout her body, pulling her in.

She didn't understand the yearning.

Or rather, she did not want to know. She had only one mission— to get to know her father. A man she didn't even know existed a few months ago.

Breathe.

Throat tight with tension, she massaged her neck without breaking her stride. The air flowed through.

She ran away from the water, breathing in the salty air, creating her own chaotic rhythm with her pink sneakers tapping impatiently against the pavement. The sweat soaked her shirt as she sailed past rows of beautiful cottage homes and turned the corner of Douglass Avenue. Highland Beach homes gave visitors a snapshot view of early and mid-twentieth-century architecture. During her first jog around the neighborhood, Olivia took her time getting familiar with the historical beach town. She noticed a mix of steep roofs, spacious porches, and dormer windows—perfect for getting a private view of the neighbors. Now, on her sixth loop, the homes had become a blur of blues and whites and grays.

Olivia stopped her sprint in front of the house of her father, Charles "CJ" Jones, which stood a few feet away from the curb. Stretching her arms overhead, she smiled, knowing she had hit her personal best in speed.

When she noticed a white BMW idling by, her smile slipped, dropped, and plopped onto the pavement. The passenger window zipped down while the car slowed to a creep to match Olivia's cooldown pace.

Olivia lowered her hat, which did nothing to obscure her face but at least made her feel better. She had a strong resemblance to CJ and not wanting to risk a neighbor taking notice of her, Olivia picked up her pace. If she hadn't been trying to avoid perfect strangers, she'd have laughed at the way her speed-walk gave her the look of a marching soldier.

The woman in the BMW laughed and tapped the gas pedal to adjust. She leaned her head out of the window. Her hair, pressed to perfection in an impeccable bob, slid to the side but did not move otherwise. "Who are you?" she said in a tone that demanded obedience.

The audacity, besides the tone, nearly made Olivia stumble.

Who is this woman?

Red-hot sparks shot throughout Olivia's body. She wasn't mad at the nosy old woman, but rather at herself. Although she was an early riser and had begun her jog at five a.m. to avoid neighbors, the historic beach town was only 0.06 square miles long. Sag Harbor was a little over twice its size. She realized it was ridiculous to expect to keep her identity hidden. Not only that, but she also had nowhere to go. If she ran inside the mayor's home, the woman could make dangerous assumptions.

This was why she had tucked her hair under her hat and worn oversized sunglasses on her runs the past two days.

Olivia stopped walking and turned to face her stalker.

"And who are you?" she snapped.

The woman's eyes went wide, and she let out an awful scream. She must have punched the gas pedal because her car careened into CJ's mailbox.

Her head rocked forward, just missing the steering wheel.

Olivia ran to the passenger side. "Oh my God. Are you okay?"

The sweet adrenaline she felt from her run had now transformed to terror.

"I . . . Indigo?"

"No. I'm . . ." Olivia swallowed her name. She'd nearly forgotten about her low profile. "That's not my name."

"Of course you aren't." The woman's words were clear, but her eyes were not.

"Are you okay, ma'am?"

"I . . . I'm f-fine."

"Are you sure?" she asked, opening the woman's door. She scanned her form. Outside of shaking hands, the woman looked uninjured.

"I said I'm fine! Close my door this instant."

"What's going on?"

Olivia's attention flipped from the old woman to CJ. He was jogging to the end of his paved walkway, hopping over the toppled mailbox. The gold plate that once sat beneath the mailbox to denote the historic significance of the home swung like a broken pendulum.

Wood slats covering the living room window shook. She couldn't clearly make out the figure lurking behind them but knew it had to be her mother, Cindy.

"She's okay." Olivia's voice carried a light, dazed note.

"I'm doing just fine, Charles. Seems like you left a few things out the last we spoke." The woman's voice was hard and sharp.

Olivia flipped her attention to CJ, noticing that the grooves in his forehead were as wavy and deep as sand dunes. He stared down at the woman in the car.

"All okay over there?" An older man walking a gray Newfoundland dog edged toward them. It was the same man who had stopped her when he walked his dog yesterday.

Damn. The nosy woman had really blown Olivia's cover.

"We're fine, John," the woman quickly replied. "Now, don't come over here with that gigantic beast. You know he doesn't react well to my perfume."

The old man raised his bushy white eyebrows. "I don't know if that's it, but . . . if you're sure."

"We're sure." Both CJ and the woman replied simultaneously.

The old man didn't budge despite his large dog tugging him in the opposite direction.

CJ gave him a friendly wave. "Just a neighbor running into my mailbox. I guess I'll have to charge her."

The old man threw his head back and laughed. "Make sure she pays every penny, too."

"I'm good for it." She twisted her peach-tinted lips into a pinched smile and offered a stiff wave that seemed more like a shoo than a sincere goodbye.

Once the dog and the owner turned the corner, the woman snapped her lively brown eyes back on Olivia.

Letting out a slow, calming breath, Olivia returned the woman's direct stare with a fierce look of her own.

The woman's scowl dropped. Her hazel eyes softened, and her pinched expression relaxed by a full millimeter. Now staring at the woman, Olivia noticed she was as beautiful as her beloved godmother, Ama, her short bob accentuating sharp cheekbones.

"I'm, um, a cousin—"

"I know who you are," she hissed. "Olivia Jones, daughter of . . ." She laughed, but was clearly unamused. "Who is Cindy claiming is the biological father these days? Is it Chris . . . or is it you, Charles?"

Her cruelty, aimed with sniper precision, struck hard and deep, leaving Olivia with a mess of memories from last summer at her home in Sag Harbor. Olivia had finally adjusted to the idea that Chris Jones, who was going to raise her with Cindy, was not her biological father. Then someone murdered him while he was serving as a witness to police corruption in his department. It was just last summer when CJ, Chris's twin brother, barreled into her home armed with the truth—that she was his biological daughter.

"You know I am, Mother," CJ growled. "You're the one who ran Cindy out of town all those years ago."

Goosebumps plumped Olivia's sweaty arms and spread like a rash across her chest.

Ama, her godmother, had warned Olivia about Christine.

"Watch out for that one, cher. She will do anything and everything to protect what's hers. Lie, cheat, steal . . . but she won't kill."

"Well, that's a relief." Olivia snorted. *She couldn't imagine a seventy-something-year-old woman killing someone.*

"No, she'd rather drag out someone's misery, and delight in the fact that she's ruined that person's life."

"But—"

"Don't ever, ever let your guard down with that one. I don't know what happened to her to make her act how she does, but there's something else . . . something that I don't want you around. I may sting, but she . . . she devours."

The heat of Christine's gaze pierced through Ama's warning. "I expect you both over for dinner tomorrow night." She pressed the ignition button, shifted gears to back off the curb. The car teetered until the front tires slammed against the road.

"Tomorrow. Seven o'clock sharp. Be on time." She pointed at CJ, and then her attention settled on Olivia. "I abhor tardiness."

She zoomed away.

Olivia slowly turned to face CJ. "Am I in the *Twilight Zone*?"

CJ stared at the car, his flexed fingers digging into his waist. "That's your grandmother, Christine." His eyes met hers. Eyes like that woman Christine's.

Eyes like Olivia's.

The storm cloud grew inside of her chest, making her heart thunder, her pulse quicken at lightning speed.

"And I guess we have dinner plans."

"With Christine," Olivia whispered. The woman who'd paid her mother, Cindy, to abort her pregnancy. The woman who, for twenty-nine years, had pretended that Olivia didn't exist.

What exactly does she hope to accomplish by forcing us to come to dinner?

Olivia shot her father a defiant glare. "I'm looking forward to it."

The red door to CJ's home whooshed open. Cindy leaned forward, her head just outside the doorway. She looked from the left to the right.

"Was that Christine?"

"Yes," CJ answered. "And she wants us for dinner tomorrow."

"Dinner?" Cindy's lips flatlined.

"Dinner," CJ confirmed, walking into his home. Olivia followed him to the living room. He sat on the beige overstuffed couch and Olivia settled across from him.

Cindy stood in the entrance of the living room. "Does she know I'm here?"

CJ crossed his legs, his arm slung over the top cushion on the couch. "I didn't tell anyone else you were coming, just as you both asked." Despite his relaxed stance, his tone snapped like a whip.

"We're only staying for a week. Maybe two." Olivia defended her position for the third time since they arrived. Her father should be happy that she and Cindy agreed to come to the very place that had rejected them.

"Well, I don't think you should go to dinner." Cindy sat beside Olivia on the love seat facing CJ, crossing, then uncrossing, her arms. She finally settled on recrossing them again. "You know Christine is up to no good."

"She's changed over the years." CJ's voice was politician smooth. Olivia expected no less from a mayor.

"I highly doubt that." Cindy huffed. "Do you really want to subject Olivia to her cruelty?"

"I'll be fine," Olivia assured her.

"I thought we had a plan?" Cindy's questions, hissed through thin lips, served best-in-class for suspicion. "In and out, get to know your father, keep a low profile, and—"

"If we don't face Christine, she's just going to hound us. The woman ran into a mailbox to figure out who I am. She doesn't strike me as someone who easily gives up."

Cindy shook her head, her hands balled into fists in her lap. "I know you've learned from the best, and you're quick on your feet, but Christine is different." She nibbled on her lips, flicking a glance at CJ.

"She . . . she reels you in and . . . and then next thing you know she's spewing words that cut deep and leave you in tatters," Cindy whispered. "Or she's doing things . . . things you can't pin on her, but you know aren't a coincidence. I just think it's best if we stick to CJ's home for now."

"It's important we let Christine know that we aren't afraid." Olivia gentled her tone. "But there's two of us now. This time, she won't run us out of town."

Her mother had been only twenty years old, left alone at a bus stop, waiting for the love of her life, CJ, to come to his senses and believe that Olivia was his daughter and that Cindy had never betrayed him.

Christine had shown CJ photographs that made it seem as if Cindy had cheated on him. Then Cindy's best friend, Chris Jones, picked up the pieces of her broken heart, and they built a life together. That is, until Olivia's godfather, Omar, had unwittingly blown his anonymity.

"There's *three* of us now," CJ added. "But Olivia is right. My mother won't give up until she's talked to all of us."

Cindy closed her eyes and raised both hands in surrender. "Fine. If you both insist, I'll be in attendance as well."

She snapped her fingers. "But I'm giving you a warning, Charles Jones . . . we are leaving immediately if she tries to dig her claws into me or Olivia."

"You two are my top priority." The smooth tone disappeared, replaced with something tougher and more battle-ready. "This time I'll protect you."

Cindy avoided his direct gaze. Staring at her shoes, her arms slid tighter around her torso. "I believed you years ago." Her voice shook. "I can't afford to do that now." Then she hurried upstairs to the guest room.

CJ stared after her like a man starved.

Olivia looked away, tucking away the knowledge that her father still had feelings for her mother.

After a few awkward seconds, Olivia cleared her throat. "My mother told me all about Christine last summer. But why don't you tell me about her? About your family?"

Olivia wanted to be as prepared as possible.

"Of course. But to understand Christine, you need to understand our family and where we come from. Maybe . . . maybe with time you'll want to get to know us better. I'll show you some pictures if you're up for it."

When Olivia nodded, CJ left the room to retrieve the photo album.

While she waited for her father, she gave in to curiosity and explored a bit. When she and Cindy had arrived, the masculine warmth of the house had surprised Olivia. The first floor had a nautical theme, but the second floor, where both the primary suite and the guest bedrooms were located, featured bold colors like burnt orange, gold, and black, with Black art from the likes of Leroy Campbell. Then there was CJ's study, which boasted a hundred-plus titles ranging from fiction to biographies of great minds such as Frederick Douglass. On his dark oak desk was a thick map of Highland Beach.

Someone had clearly designed the first floor for guests, and Olivia imagined that CJ often entertained Highland Beach residents. Careful displays of his family included the indomitable Christine Douglass-Jones, whom she now recognized, with another man around his mother's age. On a coffee table in the living room stood a picture of his entire family, including his late father, Olivia's grandfather, when he and Chris were young boys.

CJ returned with a leather-bound photo book. He sat beside Olivia and placed the book on the low table. He took a quick breath, then slowly opened it, revealing a mixture of faded and glossy bright photos.

"I've made some updates, since I knew you'd be interested." He leaned back while Olivia scooted closer to him.

There were names and a caption under each photo. "You've made a scrapbook."

"Yes. I figured it would be easier for you to look, take in the names, and maybe ask some questions along the way."

Olivia skimmed her shaking fingers over the plastic-covered photo, wonder and sorrow swirling like a cyclone in her chest.

My family.

Olivia had known, in theory, that she had a family out there somewhere. Her extended family may as well have been oceans and miles away, though, and it was too late to make any meaningful connection with them. But flipping through the photos gave her a sense of belonging among people who shared her DNA. As much as she had hoped and prayed and dreamed in her childhood, she wasn't related to Ama. Only Billie, Ama's granddaughter, had the distinction of being a blood relative of Ama.

The first picture she took notice of was the family photo—the twins Chris and CJ, about four or five years old, were flanking their parents. She could tell them apart now. Not just by CJ's scowl and Chris's wide grin, but she saw that CJ's ears protruded just a little more. As CJ grew up, his jawline became more chiseled and angular, with a dimpled chin, giving him a mischievous look.

Chris's face was a bit more rounded. The dimple was there but barely perceptible, despite his constant smile.

But it was the little baby girl who grew up into a beautiful teenager who caught her attention.

Olivia's eyes zeroed in on her name.

Indigo. The name Christine had called her after she'd crashed into CJ's mailbox.

Oh. She looks like me. She wasn't as dark-skinned as Olivia, but her face was the same.

Indigo had been an athlete. Track and field, swimming, and basketball, and there were multiple pictures of her clad in a one-piece swimsuit with medals around her neck.

"I have an aunt?"

He exhaled and squeezed the bridge of his nose. "Had. She died before you were born. Right after I went to college and Chris enlisted. Both my siblings are gone. Dad too."

CJ leaned over and flipped the page. The plastic snapped from the force, his hands splayed across the picture of his relatives' faces. Olivia looked up, witnessing his expression shut down—the fading light in his eyes, the forlorn gaze, the downturned curve of his lips.

He'd lost so much. Too much. His father, his brother, and his sister.

Me. My mother.

Olivia covered his hands, hoping to bring warmth to the numbness of grief. He looked down at their hands, giving her a relieved, albeit brief, smile. "A lot more pictures to come. Why don't I give you some time alone without me hovering?" CJ jumped up from his seat and strode to the kitchen before Olivia could respond, so she followed him with the scrapbook in hand.

He rubbed a hand across his face and grew still when he noticed Olivia's stare.

"How about a mimosa?" Olivia suggested, settling on the seat tucked under the kitchen island. "It's a little early, but you're off duty, right?"

He glanced at his watch, nodding. "For the next twelve hours."

"Good. Then we'll have a drink," Olivia said, smiling.

"I don't have any orange juice, but is just chardonnay okay?"

Olivia laughed. Wine in the morning with her father would just have to do right now. "Yes, please." Olivia turned away, her back facing her father. From the way he jumped up and left the room at the mention of his sister, she knew CJ needed space to process his feelings. Meanwhile, Olivia returned her attention to her family's photographic history. Some pictures dated back to the early 1900s. According to the caption, an older man with snow-white hair and wearing a white shirt, a short-striped tie, and khaki pants was the mayor in the 1940s.

"Wow."

"What's the *wow* for?" CJ asked, then handed Olivia a glass of wine.

"I'm impressed by the long lineage of mayorship, I suppose."

"Between the Jones and Douglass families, we've had four mayors serve Highland Beach."

"It runs in the family."

"Are you interested in politics?" He leaned forward.

Olivia shook her head. "Oh God no. The furthest I've gone into civic duties was serving as class treasurer in high school."

CJ grunted.

Olivia couldn't quite believe he could charm his constituents with grunts.

"If you don't mind my observation," Olivia began, "you don't strike me as talkative."

"Am I boring you?" CJ raised an eyebrow, though his eyes crinkled at the corners. She assumed he found her observation amusing.

"Not at all." Olivia waved a hand. "It's just that politicians usually have the gift of gab."

CJ nodded. "When I ran for mayor, the previous one had been in office for eight years. Highland Beach needed new blood. With only forty-six households and—"

"So few?" Olivia gasped.

"Yes. We're a strong-knit and well-connected community. But we have our sister neighborhood, Venice Beach, so it doesn't feel small at all."

The neighborhood ran parallel to Highland Beach, with some homes perched right on the bay waters.

"And, well, they needed new ideas. The elders were passing down their homes, just as their relatives had done before them. Now, if the younger generation can't keep up the homes, we just tap our network and use our local realtor, Nancy. So far we've been able to keep the Beach secluded. There's only one house that's a rental, and they asked for permission. We don't allow Airbnb or anything commercial out here."

"I suppose the sellers don't make as much money that way."

CJ shook his head. "We aren't shortsighted. If someone needs to sell, it's not about making the most money. It's about sliding the right pieces into place and ensuring that our prospective neighbor respects the history and the beach. We can't just trample over how this place came to be."

"Still, it's a marvel how you've been able to keep the community protected."

Olivia was strategizing a protection plan with her business partner, Whitney, with whom she ran a nonprofit that sought to preserve historic Black neighborhoods. When it was all said and done, it boiled down to capitalism. Permitting a coffee shop, chain grocery store, rental properties, or any other profitable business in a neighborhood was a sure sign that the area would soon be gentrified. And although she, Whitney, and the rest of the Sag Harbor neighbors had run out a major developer just last summer, they still had their work cut out for them. Developers were like a bug infestation—smash one and more seemed to spawn out of nowhere.

"We've got some of the brightest minds living here, descended from exceptional people," CJ stated, his tone matter-of-fact.

Olivia gave him a brilliant smile, happy that they had finally landed on a topic they were both clearly passionate about. Studying more pictures and reading the captions, she noticed there were quite a few pictures of the Douglass family.

"So we are the family Jones and Douglass."

"That's right." CJ put down his wineglass. "My mother, your

grandmother, is a distant relative of the founders of Highland Beach, Charles and Laura Douglass."

"I suppose you are his namesake."

He nodded. "Mom is very proud of her lineage. The story goes that Major Charles and his wife Laura were turned away at the Bay Ridge Resort because . . ." He held up and waved the back side of his hand. "You know why."

"I do," Olivia agreed. In her excitement about spending some time with her father in Highland Beach, she'd read the history, though it was better to hear from a relative of the founders.

"Well, ole Charles fought fire with fire. He bought up real estate—beachfront property south of Bay Ridge. Then he developed the property as a summer resort, sold it to some of his friends . . . powerful friends like Congressman John Mercer Langston, Judge Robert Terrell, the first Black judge in DC, and Mary Church Terrell, who played a quintessential role in women's suffrage."

"He created his own Black oasis," Olivia said with a dreamy smile.

"Indeed. Built a summer house called Twin Oaks. I'll show you. It's a museum now. It was supposed to be a retirement residence for his father, Frederick Douglass, so he—"

"Wait. The Frederick Douglass, as in abolitionist and civil rights activist Frederick Douglass?"

"The one and only."

Olivia put down her wineglass. "So that means that I'm related to Frederick Douglass!" Olivia squeaked. She wasn't a squeaker. The very noise would appall her godmother Ama, but this was a squeak-worthy moment.

"Don't forget ole Charles. He was a retired officer in the first Black regiment during the Civil War."

"Wow." Olivia's chest swelled with pride.

"Look at me earning two *wows* in one day," CJ said in a teasing voice.

"That's right. And I stand corrected. You do indeed have the gift of gab. That was quite a story."

"No, it's quite the history. We have a lot to be proud of in Highland Beach."

"Does everyone else who lives here also have an impressive Black elite lineage?"

"Oh yes. We are a proud and accomplished community. We do a lot to protect our land environmentally, and we make sure to take care of each other. Which is why you should rethink hiding out in my home. Get out there, get to know our neighborhood."

CJ's phone rang. He glanced down at the screen. "Excuse me for a moment."

While CJ answered his phone, Olivia digested the news of her famous relations. In high school, she'd written an essay on Frederick Douglass. She'd even researched his wife, Anna Murray Douglass, and read *My Mother as I Recall Her*, by their daughter, Rosetta Douglass Sprague. She'd read how Anna supported Frederick's escape from slavery and how, in the background, she supported his abolitionist work. But a year and a half after her death, Frederick Douglass married a white woman . . . and, well, it left an incredibly toxic impression on Olivia at the time. She'd even read some sources that insinuated he may have had affairs prior to Anna's death.

Her teacher hadn't appreciated her adding "gossip" to what was supposed to be a well-researched paper, and for the first time she'd gotten an A- instead of an A+ grade on a school assignment in high school.

CJ walked to the corner of the kitchen. "Mother."

Olivia couldn't discern any of her grandmother's words, but she could hear a distinct trill through the phone speaker.

"Yes. We'll be there tomorrow."

More chatter on the other end. Loud, angry, panicked. Olivia stood and moved closer to CJ. She wouldn't pretend to not be con-

cerned. After all, her grandmother was reacting to her very existence.

"No, not—" He snapped his mouth shut. He shook his head and
mouthed "Sorry" to Olivia.

More animated chatter came from the speaker.

"No." His voice went deep, his tone annoyed. Like his face, his
voice held a frown. "If you pop by, I won't answer. Don't make me
regret my decision about dinner. We have an understanding, yes?"

"Good." He clicked off.

He took a deep breath. This time Olivia didn't move her stare
away from CJ.

"Christine, I presume?"

He nodded. "Are you ready for your grandmother?"

What a loaded question.

Her throat, coated in chardonnay, suddenly went prickly and dry.
This was the woman who'd attempted to pay off her mother with
thousands of dollars to stay away from her precious twin boys. The
woman who, after Chris died, left her widowed daughter-in-law and
grandchild in the cold. Olivia had a lot to say to this woman, and she
wouldn't hold back. Hours of therapy had helped her recognize her
worth. And if Christine thought she could get away with disrespecting Olivia or her mother, well . . . she'd be in for a rude awakening.

She was one of Omar and Ama's girls, after all.

CHAPTER TWO

May 2022

BON APPÉTIT

Olivia tried relaxing against the lounge chair, her eyes closed, head tilted toward the sun, heartbeat rabbit fast. In a few short hours, they would have dinner with Christine. She'd called her boyfriend, Garrett, to get a boost of serotonin, but he was out crabbing with his daughter, Zora, and the signal had been poor. She missed him and could have used his powerful arms right about now to hold her body—and sanity—together.

CJ's backyard had given her ideas for her own yard in Sag Harbor. The heated square-shaped pool was surrounded with natural stones. A few feet away stood a large picnic-sized wooden table with long benches. Her backyard was close to the bay waters; if she had a pool, she could have the best of both worlds.

"Olivia, it's about time to get ready for dinner."

She jumped at the voice, although she recognized who it belonged to before she opened her eyes.

CJ made confident strides down the steps and sat on the lounger closest to Olivia. Something like worry or fear clouded his eyes.

Does he think Christine will run us away again?

"Where's my mother?"

"She's getting ready for our family dinner."

Family dinner? Olivia wouldn't have labeled it that just yet. She would meet her grandmother, but it wasn't going to be some kind of cozy affair.

"You mean the *meeting* with Christine and Alan." Olivia pushed up, straightening her posture as much as she could in the curved lounger. She glanced at her watch. "It's not for two hours, correct?"

"I know, but I . . . just wanted to make sure you're okay. You've been out here all day. I hope you applied sunscreen."

Olivia twisted her lips at this man who barely knew her, taking on the tone of a concerned father. They weren't at that point just yet. "It's beautiful here. Quiet."

"It's just a backyard. But if you really want to be impressed, why don't I take you to Black Walnut Creek sometime this week? We can take out the kayaks."

"That sounds lovely." Olivia reclined into the chair and stared at the pool. "I guess I'll take a shower," she said before reluctantly rising from the lounger.

CJ nodded and led her back inside. He stopped when they entered the kitchen, pivoting to face her. "Are you nervous?"

"I'm ready." Still, she was nervous.

Stopping short of buying a pair of binoculars and hiring a private detective, Olivia had done all she could to prepare for dinner with *the* Christine Douglass-Jones, her grandmother. Between online research and primary resources—namely her mother, CJ, and Ama—there seemed to be a tale of two Christines.

The online Christine Douglass-Jones persona had been edited, filtered until it was ultimately flawless. Philanthropist Christine supported children by donating to hospitals and various charitable organizations. Civil rights activist Christine was quoted and interviewed in newspapers like the *New York Times* and the *Washington*

Post. Ebony, Black Enterprise, and *Essence* magazines had interviewed her about Black wealth and political participation.

On paper, she exuded perfection. Despite a desire to hate her grandmother, Olivia found herself admiring her activism.

But to her mother and Ama, Christine was a fire-breathing dragon who had no qualms about burning anyone who crossed her.

Earlier in the day, her mother sat Olivia down and gave her a rundown of all the "wonderful attributes" of Christine that she wouldn't find online.

"You must be in a certain tax bracket to be important to Christine," Cindy schooled Olivia while tossing salad in a bowl. "She despises anything she perceives as less than. Christine graduated top of her class at Spelman, then went to Yale Law. She wanted to be a corporate lawyer, but she met your grandfather in law school, got married, and had the twins. Daniel, your grandfather, convinced her to stay home and take care of his boys. Together they would create a little dynasty in their hometown, Highland Beach."

"Why does she do all the charity work if she's mean to her own family?" Olivia asked.

"Clout. Prestige. You're an accomplished businesswoman . . . have you never met someone who donates to various organizations but has the morals of a jackal?" Cindy asked, raising her eyebrows.

Olivia knew this was the story of many millionaires and billionaires.

"I've seen the worst side of Christine. And she has plenty of minions to spread dirty rumors, though I don't think they realize that they're tools. Like once she lied about her husband's opponent for public office, said they'd cheated their way through college. Oh, or that time she blocked a young woman from getting a recommendation to a prestigious college because she dated Chris without her approval."

Olivia's mouth dropped. "She really ruined someone's chances of going to college because of her son?" The woman was quoted in *Ebony* about the critical importance of education in socioeconomic mobility.

Cindy tsked. "Yes, but to be fair, the girl broke his heart. That was before he dated another girl. That one Christine approved of, and she paid the girl's tuition her first year of college. She clearly has control issues."

She stopped whisking the salad dressing and stared at Olivia. "I think she'll like that you graduated from Yale and then went to business school at UPenn's Wharton School. Whether she wants to admit it remains to be seen," she muttered to herself. "And there's no denying your career accomplishments on Wall Street." Cindy gripped the handle of the whisk. "Better than a single mom and public school teacher." Insecurity shook her mother's typically measured tone.

"I received an excellent education, thanks to you and your public school teaching job. And besides, I'm not interested in impressing Christine."

Cindy's downturned lips shifted into a stilted smile. Her mood bothered Olivia. She didn't recognize the anxious woman in front of her. Cindy should be proud of ensuring that she raised Olivia in a stable environment. As a widow and mother, it couldn't have been easy. It was what she admired about her mother. Olivia also admired her godmother Ama, who faced difficult odds in climbing the corporate ladder on Wall Street in the 1960s.

Facing hardships yet having the resilience to overcome them was the unsung story of many Black women.

But Ama and Cindy had taken different paths. Ama hadn't allowed children to stop her dreams. She'd given up her daughter Edie for adoption, knowing that she would face difficulties raising a child alone as an unwed teenager. Edie later gave birth to Billie,

Olivia's godsister. Though Ama stood by her choices, Olivia knew her godmother also held some regrets.

As for Cindy, until last year Olivia had thought she'd hated being a mother. She wasn't loving, but she'd made sure Olivia did well in school and had every advantage she could afford. Now Olivia had learned that her mother was guilt-ridden and broken-hearted while raising her. Cindy had just now begun the journey to mend her broken parts.

"Don't let Christine or anyone make you question your worth," Olivia said in a firm voice. "It's even more impressive for all the things you've accomplished without a silver spoon."

Cindy smiled, though it didn't reach her eyes—it rarely did. Cindy murmured her agreement and fixed their plates for breakfast.

After eating eggs and toast, Olivia dashed to her room, ready to find the perfect outfit.

She hung two options on her closet door: an emerald summer dress and a pink vintage Chanel blazer with matching pants.

Olivia lifted the summer dress in the air. "Casual?" Then she raised the pink blazer. "Or business?"

"I'll ask the girls," she decided. Olivia put on each option, snapped pictures of herself, and sent them to the Omar & Ama's Girls group chat, which included her godsisters Billie and Perry.

Meeting my grandmother tonight. Which one should I wear—business casual or springy elegance?

Olivia attached the pictures and sent the text.

Billie: I never thought I'd live to see you ask me for fashion advice but . . . I'm saying yes to the dress. Dulce says you look hot in anything . . . and I'm processing my feelings right now with ice cream.

Olivia laughed at Billie's reaction. Being pregnant and having a child had brought out what their godsister Perry called "Big Feelings" in the normally aloof Billie.

Just as Olivia sent a wink smiley, her phone dinged with Perry's choice.

Perry: Go with business. That hag doesn't deserve cute and approachable Olivia. As far as I'm concerned, this is a business meeting.

"Business it is," Olivia decided. Perry was right—she needed to be all business with that woman. Her new grandmother would not welcome her with open arms and warm apple pie. She likely had an agenda—to get the illegitimate child far away from her family as quickly as possible.

A little seed of nervousness bloomed in the pit of her stomach. Olivia clasped her hands over her flat abdomen, closed her eyes, and imagined the seed fizzling into oblivion. The prick of worry disappeared, and she mentally infused herself with strength. After a quick breathing exercise, she showered, moisturized from head to toe, and then artfully applied her makeup. With the pink power suit on, Olivia twirled in the full mirror installed near her door.

"I'm smart, capable, and independently wealthy. Thank you very much."

She thought about who her mother had been thirty years ago. Young, pregnant, scared, and poor. She imagined how big and intimidating Christine must have looked to Cindy in her small apartment. That check probably felt like a million dollars instead of a few thousand.

"May I enter?" Cindy asked and then followed with a soft knock on her door.

Her mother looked gorgeous, and her deep red lipstick popped against her bronze skin. Her stylish bob had grown just past her ears. She wore gold stud earrings, a paisley gold-and-black blazer, and wide-leg pants. Olivia noticed with delight that her mother wore a gift she'd given her last Christmas—red Louboutin pumps that tied at the front with a bow.

"You look—" they spoke in unison.

Cindy gave a rueful smile. "Beautiful," she finished.

"Stunning," said Olivia, adding her own compliment.

Cindy dropped her smile. "Now remember to keep your wits about you. Christine is . . . a lot. She's a master at finding weaknesses and then exploiting them."

"Mom." Olivia placed a comforting hand on Cindy's shoulder. "I'll be okay."

Olivia dealt with both top executives and spoiled young millionaires. Each type required handling with finesse, and Olivia had it in spades. Besides that, she was schooled in the house of Amelia Vaux Tanner. And Ama never suffered fools.

Cindy exhaled. "I forget how competent you are."

Olivia didn't think she forgot, only that Cindy had had limited interactions with Corporate America Olivia.

"You know, before we left, I snapped a few pictures of your awards and achievements in storage to share with CJ. You've always been a high achiever."

"You kept my awards?" That bit of news surprised Olivia. Cindy had cleared out her room the summer after she graduated from high school and turned it into her reading room.

Cindy nodded. "I couldn't bring myself to throw them away. But it's all packed and stored in the garage if you ever want it."

"Th-thank you."

"Oh, it's the least I could do." Cindy stepped back into the hallway.

CJ walked toward them wearing a navy blazer, light blue shirt, and dark slacks. It looked like the entire Jones family had the same thought—this dinner was all business.

"Are we ready to go? I promise you I'll make sure no one makes you uncomfortable tonight," he vowed.

"Even your mother?" Olivia's tone dripped with cynicism. And she had every right, as Christine had clearly sabotaged their relationship.

"Especially Christine," he answered in his confident mayoral voice. "I won't ever let her or anyone else disrespect my girls again."

Girls? Olivia opened her mouth to correct, or rather tease, CJ, but her mother looked gobsmacked. Moved.

And much to Olivia's dismay, turned on.

"All right." Olivia clapped her hands to snuff out the sexual tension. "To Grandmother's house we go."

CJ opened the passenger doors to the Audi and ushered in Cindy and Olivia. "I'll give you a tour on the way there."

He partially rolled down his window.

"Our founder, Charles Douglass, the son of Frederick Douglass, named each of the six streets at the time after Black leaders. We live on Douglass Avenue—"

"*You* live on Douglass," Cindy quickly corrected.

He exhaled, seeming to lose steam for a bit, but then continued. "Then you have Langston Avenue. Many visitors think it's for Langston Hughes, but it's named after John Mercer Langston, the US congressman from Virginia and founder of Howard University." While CJ talked on, Olivia noticed a small white banner wrapped around the street pole with a picture of Frederick Douglass.

"Can you slow down?" Olivia interrupted CJ's street history lesson. "I'd like to read that sign."

"Of course." CJ pumped the brakes and backed closer to the banner. A quote was centered under the picture.

ONCE YOU LEARN TO READ, YOU WILL FOREVER BE FREE.

"We have lots of banners honoring our famous residents and frequent visitors. Next time you go running you should bring your camera and take pictures."

And have the neighbors stare at her and ask for her name? No, thank you. Olivia mentally shook her head. Only forty-eight hours in and she could already tell Highland Beach was as intimate and tight-knit as Sag Harbor. And from her experience, whether people were kind or not, tight-knit neighborhoods gossiped.

CJ slowed as he pulled up to the sidewalk in front of a rather sizable white cottage with black shutters.

"We're here." Cindy's voice shook, though not with fear but partly with weariness and partly with sadness.

Olivia had forgotten that the house CJ now lived in had been given to him by his father. However, Christine's house was the one in which he grew up. CJ bent over and slid the lock on the white picket fence that surrounded the two-story white cottage. The lush yard just to the left of the three-step porch, with a garden bursting with bold colors, was well maintained.

"It's beautiful." Olivia couldn't hide the admiration in her voice. She could see herself lounging on one of the rockers that flanked either side of the door on the wraparound porch, which was adorned with window boxes full of beautiful flowers.

CJ's childhood home.

She imagined that her mother remembered the last time she was here—when she gave her ultimatum to CJ about her pregnancy. A lump rose in her throat just thinking of her father's rejection.

CJ must have sensed the rising emotions because he reached for a hand from both of them. Olivia flinched, surprised at the quick and sure way he held it, but she didn't let go. In fact, she squeezed.

Cindy huffed and strode up the pathway, marched up the three steps, and then stood at the side of the door. CJ and Olivia walked close behind.

After letting go of Olivia's hand, he pulled out a key and unlocked the door.

Once the door opened, Olivia heard a voice.

"Welcome." Olivia's attention traveled to the top of the stairs. While Olivia, CJ, and Cindy were all about business in their clothing, Mrs. Christine Douglass-Jones made a splash. In her ensemble— a black lace pantsuit paired with a matching jacket that flared out like a ballroom gown and fell to her ankles—she could easily have glided into a five-star restaurant, a debutante's ball, or an intimate family dinner and outshone everyone.

Christine Douglass-Jones was a diva, and by design, not because of age, the diva took her time descending the stairs.

"Still a flair for the dramatics, I see," Cindy said.

CJ cleared his throat, but Olivia didn't need reminding to keep her cool. Christine's growing smile at Cindy's visible irritation was reminder enough.

A full ice age later, Christine had finally descended all twelve steps. Her sharp, light brown eyes landed on Olivia.

"My oh my. You look just like our Indigo."

Christine came closer and lovingly cupped her cheeks. Where was the woman who pushed her mother away? The woman who savagely cut Chris Jones out of her will when he didn't get in line with her plans and instead married the woman he loved?

"Doesn't she, Charles?" Christine asked her son.

"I rather think she looks like me."

Christine chuckled. Her nude nails scraped Olivia's cheek.

"Her skin is darker than mine and Indigo's, but she has the same almond-shaped eyes. I haven't seen it yet, but I bet you have a beautiful smile. You're a Jones all right."

Olivia flinched. She'd never put much stock in her last name. The possessive way Christine said it, the name felt like a brand.

Olivia stepped away from Christine's icy hands. "Nice to meet you." Olivia softened her lie with manners.

"You as well. I've been looking forward to this day for a long time."

A snort sounded from behind her, but Olivia didn't turn away from her grandmother—she couldn't.

Perhaps it was because of the strong family resemblance. Had she known as a child that there was someone who was her spitting image but who had fair skin, she wouldn't have felt so alone. And maybe she wouldn't have ever questioned her appearance because Christine Douglass-Jones was drop-dead gorgeous. Olivia had quickly done the math, and this woman did not look her age, but rather perhaps a decade younger. The mirror image stopped at the nose.

That she got from her mother, Cindy, who had an upturned nose. That upturned nose tipped even higher as Olivia stared at Christine's antics.

"Come." Their host broke into Olivia's silent reverie with a smile that highlighted her sharp cheekbones.

"Welcome home, son." She pivoted to CJ to give him a quick kiss. "Oh." She patted his face. "You need to shave."

Cindy cleared her throat. Christine pivoted on her heel to face her. Her curved eyebrows, which were not sharply pointed but rounded, enhanced her almond-shaped eyes. "Well, hello, Pumpkin. You look well."

"Don't you *ever* call me that name again." Cindy's nails curved into her palm. Her jaw seemed welded shut.

The heat in her tone worried Olivia and made her step in front of her mother.

"I . . . okay." Christine clutched her pearls. "I thought that was a nickname."

"It was." Cindy's voice rasped. "From a beloved person, and that person is *not* you."

"Fine." Christine's fingers fluttered, as if shooing an errant butterfly. "I'll refrain from calling you a lackluster vegetable whose only importance is in October."

Olivia's mouth dropped open. She wondered if she should've worn chain mail instead of a pink pantsuit.

Cindy shook her head. "What a shame. I hoped you'd grown up by now, but you're just the same evil woman."

Christine's eyes glittered like a pair of Swarovski crystal earrings. "Hm. Perhaps a *tramp* is more befitting—"

"I ask that you stop disrespecting my mother." Olivia's tone held a do-not-proceed warning, the kind she'd use for a misbehaving but important client. Patient, but willing to walk away, because not all money is good money. "We've been here for less than five minutes, and you aren't off to a great start."

"Mother." CJ's voice was hard-edged. "Embrace civility or we will leave."

Christine nodded. "Of course." She turned to face Olivia, who stood in front of Cindy with an arm outstretched in front of her mother.

"My apologies. Sometimes old habits die hard. We'll dine in the formal room today. Leigh has prepared a delicious seafood linguine for us."

Christine led them to a long black lacquered table with upholstered emerald chairs. The walls were a dove gray, and the art took center stage, from miniature black bust statues by Woodrow Nash to a vibrant colored portrait of Christine in a white flowing gown with pink, green, and yellow flowers surrounding her.

"Is that . . . a painting by Kehinde Wiley?" Olivia whispered in awe.

"Yes." Christine looked at the painting of herself with pride. "And I'll have you know I had this commissioned before President Barack Obama's official White House portrait."

On the opposite wall, a black-and-white oil painting titled *Generations*, by Olivia's good friend Kara Warren, caught her attention. The painting featured grandmother, mother, and granddaughter.

Although Olivia loved the picture, it was certainly an interesting choice. Christine hadn't exactly claimed her own granddaughter.

A table against the back wall held platters of food, including linguine tossed with scallops, shrimp, and mussels; crusty bread; and a colorful salad. A woman, Leigh, Olivia presumed, stood near the narrow table and plated the food on the bone-white dinnerware. "Where's Alan?" CJ asked, pulling back seats for Cindy and Olivia.

"Alan is finishing up a business call and should be along shortly."

"He's not working the campaign at this hour, is he?" CJ asked. His stepfather had come on board as his campaign manager.

"Of course. You are running against a respected elder and experienced contender. You best not rest on your laurels, or you'll find yourself jobless."

CJ rolled his eyes like a teenager. "Surely my law degree isn't useless."

"Of course not. Best money I ever spent at Yale School of Law."

Cindy flicked a look in his direction. "You did it?"

"Yes, I graduated from Yale Law." CJ smiled at her. He leaned in close and whispered, "So you don't have to worry about my gainful employment. I'll always find a way."

They soon heard Christine's husband marching down the creaking stairs. Alan Easton waved at the group, then made a beeline for CJ and gave him a hard pat on his back.

"Hey, son. I just got off the call with Tim. He's going to host the fundraiser at his hotel. With him on our side, I think we'll finally be able to shake that nonsense regarding Riley for good."

"And good riddance to her," Christine muttered.

Her? Olivia wondered if Riley was another woman Christine ran off, like she'd done in the past, according to Cindy.

"Who's Riley?" Olivia leaned over and whispered while Alan and Charles continued their conversation.

"No one of importance." Christine swatted her hand in the air, then pivoted her attention to her husband and son. "No business talk, gentlemen," Christina said with a syrupy glaze to her voice, "this is a family dinner." She glanced at Cindy. "Plus guest."

Cindy's harrumph was overtaken by Alan's boisterous laugh.

"Of course, dear. I know you love your rules." Alan pulled her close and kissed Christine's cheek. She slapped his chest lovingly and laughed. The sound tinkled like bells.

He turned to face Cindy. "Well, you are a sight for these old sore eyes." Alan smiled from ear to ear. "Welcome back, Cindy." He opened his arms, and Cindy stood to step into his embrace.

"Thank you, Alan. I almost forgot how kind and hospitable you can be." She cut her eyes toward Christine, who offered a strained smile.

Alan pivoted toward Olivia. "And you look just like your father."

Olivia smiled. "Christine told me I look like my aunt Indigo."

He tilted his head, squinted a bit, as if to focus on her face. "I suppose so."

"You suppose so?" Christine's voice pitched high. "She's Indigo's spitting image. No offense, Charles. She's just darker." Christine's lips turned down at the corners. "That's why I got rattled when I saw you, dear. You gave me a fright." Christine waved toward the table. "But no matter. Olivia, why don't you sit to my right? I'd love to get to know you."

Cindy, now seated across from Olivia, stretched her eyes as if mentally conveying, *Don't forget the plan.*

"Certainly," Olivia complied. "But I would love to know more about you and the family. I'm told you're related to Frederick Douglass?"

The diversion proved effective. For the next thirty minutes, Christine reviewed their family tree. Olivia couldn't pretend she wasn't fascinated. She took occasional bites of salad as she listened to Christine.

"We are cousins, twice removed. Once Charles and Laura Douglass established the resort, they invited family and friends. Naturally, my family transitioned here, and what began as summers became year-round. It was my grandmother, Lucilla, who decided that Highland Beach would be our forever home. I was born here. Your grandfather Daniel's family lived in Washington, DC, and had a summer home here. It's the one CJ now owns."

Olivia nodded. "Did you date as teenagers?" Olivia asked.

Christine smiled and released a soft sigh. "We'd known each other all our lives. You know, same church, at least when they stayed for the summer. Our families were quite close, but we didn't really become romantically involved until college. He attended Morehouse, and I attended Spelman. We were well matched." She exhaled, and a brief smile flitted across her face. "Once our friends and family pointed that out to us, well, things really clicked."

"Daniel was a good man," Alan agreed. "We met each other at Morehouse."

"You met me, too," Christine teased.

"That I did. But Daniel and I became close. Your grandfather was a special man. A man anyone would want to follow. A natural leader, like your father."

"Did you have a home here growing up?" Olivia asked Alan. As she understood it, Christine and Daniel had lived in this home, which Christine had inherited.

"My aunt had a home here, so I'd visited a handful of times before I moved to Highland Beach. But when I became Daniel's campaign manager, I would drive from DC on the weekends and camp out at my aunt's home."

"Oh, what was your trade?"

"I thought I wanted to become a lawyer, like your grandparents, but I quickly found out that wasn't a good fit. So I put my law degree to good use, and with the full support of my parents—"

Christine's tinkering laugh cut in. Alan looked at his wife and joined in on the laughter.

"Oh, okay. Not the least bit of their support, but I successfully pivoted to communications in the government sector. And the rest is history." He forked a shrimp, swallowed, and smiled. "Now I'm mostly retired, but I help CJ here and there with his reelection and communication strategy. Besides, this is the last hurrah."

"Until the Senate," Christine quickly added.

"Right," Alan nodded. "If you run for Senate, you'll need to have all your ducks in a row. No vices. No *more* skeletons."

The delicious seafood linguine thwapped like lead in Olivia's stomach.

I'm the skeleton.

Olivia grabbed her wine and swallowed. "Well, I certainly don't want to impede your future. We can keep this quiet. I won't confirm our association."

"Association?" CJ said in a gruff voice. "I'm your father and I'm the one who messed up. If I run for Senate in a few years—and that's a big *if*—we'll take a proactive approach, as I've discussed with both of you more than enough times," he said, pointing at his mother and stepfather, "and focus on the messaging before the spin can happen."

Christine dabbed the corners of her lips with a white linen napkin. "Of course, dear. You're a proud father and Chris—"

"Is a hero." Cindy cut in. "I won't stand by and let you slander his name or mine."

"I would never insult my son."

"You insulted your son," Cindy jerked her head toward CJ, "when you offered me a check to stay away from your boys."

Christine's fork clacked against the dinnerware. "And yet the check cleared." Christine's voice went haughty and high.

"Instead of worrying about who Chris or Charles dated," Cindy retorted, "you should've been a better mother to your daughter."

Christine's shoulders jerked back as if she'd been shot. Tears deepened the hazel in her eyes.

"I can't believe I stooped down to your level again," Cindy whispered harshly to herself. "I need to get out of here." Cindy sprang up from the table and rushed out of the room. CJ threw his napkin on the table and followed.

At the sound of the slamming door, Christine became unstuck and glided upstairs.

Watching his wife like a hawk, Alan waited until Christine had made it upstairs, then turned his attention to Olivia. "For what it's worth, welcome to the family." Alan stood, moving away from the table. "If you'll excuse me, I need to check on my wife."

For the first time in over an hour, the house was quiet. Olivia unclenched her jaw and hands and let her shoulders slump. She wanted to follow her parents outside, but she knew Cindy and CJ needed to talk about those early days when Chris had died.

Cindy never let on how lonely she'd been. That would've required her to acknowledge her feelings and let them flow. And Cindy Jones rarely, if ever, emoted. Until now. If Olivia could find her mother's therapist, she'd give her a gold medal.

Alan returned to the table. "Christine is retiring for the night."

Olivia stood. "I wanted to give CJ and Cindy some time to speak, but I'll check on them now."

"Please sit for a while. Christine . . . she's been through a lot. But there is no excuse for what she said. I don't blame Cindy for her feelings. For saying the things she said."

Olivia nodded.

"Christine lost so much. Daniel, Chris, your . . . your father. And Indigo. Is she a proud woman? Yes, and that's what I love about her. But she bleeds like the rest of us."

Everyone from Ama to Cindy had advised her about Christine's witchy ways. But she'd witnessed the blood draining from Christine's face. She was a mother with a broken heart who'd had not one but two children die before her.

"How did she . . . how did Indigo die?"

"She drowned." Alan removed his glasses with shaking hands. "Can you do me a favor?" Alan asked out of nowhere.

"What is it?"

"Can you allow Christine to make amends? To get to know you? I think she would like that very much."

"I . . ." She thought of her mother and hesitated. Exhaustion had already overtaken her from just one hour of dodging Christine and Cindy's crossfire.

"You don't have to do anything special. Just come over and have lunch."

"O- . . . okay. Maybe next week?"

"Yes, of course." Alan pulled out a piece of paper and pen. "Could you write down your number and email? I'll give your information to Christine."

Olivia took the paper and pen and wrote her number.

"I'll see you later, Alan."

She walked outside and exhaled. The dinner weighed heavily on her soul.

She found CJ and Cindy near the sidewalk. Cindy was staring at the moon.

"Are you okay?"

Cindy shook her head, her attention shifting to CJ. "I won't stop either of you from seeing Christine, but I never want to come back here again."

CJ and Cindy stared at each other, a silent communication Olivia could not decipher.

CJ broke the silence. "I should have listened to your concerns earlier today. I'm sorry."

Her mother gave him a sad smile. "You should have listened to me a long time ago. Now look at us, walking around and still hungry."

They'd stuck it out for only a third of the meal, never mind dessert.

"I can fix your hunger," CJ answered in a hoarse voice. "I'll order some takeout. If you're craving seafood, I can order something from Boatyard and pick it up."

They nodded their assent and moved toward the car.

What a day.

But the hardest part hadn't been the war of words between her mother and grandmother. It was Indigo who stayed in Olivia's mind and heart. She recalled her aunt's image, the picture of her dripping in gold medals from swimming meets that she'd seen in CJ's photo album earlier that morning.

"Huh," she said out loud to herself. Not that it wasn't possible, but it was quite unsettling to learn that a Junior Olympian swimmer had drowned.

CHAPTER THREE

May 2022

FAMILY TEA

A week had passed since the family dinner. Christine phoned twice, but Olivia couldn't bring herself to answer. The first time her mother had been in the room. This time Olivia was in the middle of a run. But even if she hadn't been, Olivia wasn't ready to speak to Christine.

For now, she wanted to get to know the beautiful resort town, though her heart still belonged to Sag Harbor. Her home in Sag Harbor, along with the community, had been multiple gifts rolled into one from her godfather, Omar. A place where she could slow down from work and hear her thoughts. And after she slowed her pace, she changed her hair and her job and ended the relationship with her ex-fiancé, Anderson. It had seemed impossible to overcome so many obstacles and changes in such a short time over one summer, but she'd done it.

As Olivia jogged past the Highland Beach houses, a few residents outside gave her curious waves. She pivoted from her usual path and ran the street that led to Black Walnut Creek.

A familiar man jogged toward her. He was just as fast as Olivia and sped toward her as if he were in an invisible race.

He raised a hand, halting as he wheezed, "Olivia!"

She stopped and turned. "Alan?"

"Hey you." He inhaled and exhaled. "Christine mentioned she called you a few days ago."

"She . . . she did. It just wasn't a good time. I was with Cindy. And she called a few minutes ago, but as you can see . . ." She waved a hand over her sweaty body.

"I'll let her know we bumped into each other," he said with a heaviness to his voice that gave Olivia the deep impression that she should call her grandmother.

"I'll call her today."

He nodded, looking down at his feet. All went quiet except for the rolling bay waters.

Olivia could tell he had something else on his mind. "Is everything okay?"

"I truly am sorry about the other day. I hope you give Christine another chance to explain her actions. She's been really looking forward to getting to know you."

Olivia thought about Cindy's accusation that Christine encouraged her to have an abortion. Though her mother had been hard on her growing up, she thanked God Cindy had kept her. Still, the thought of her own grandmother saying those things, not wanting to give Olivia a chance at life, speared her heart. Olivia knew she shouldn't care about the woman's opinion, but deep down she wanted Christine to be proud of her granddaughter.

Olivia exhaled, shaking her head. She would have to unpack her feelings with her therapist, Dr. LaGrange, later in the week.

"I will. But I must be honest, the way she treats my mother is . . . disturbing. It makes it hard for me to want to try building a relationship with her."

"I understand, and—"

"But does *Christine* understand?" Olivia would argue that she didn't. Or rather, that she didn't think it was important enough to reform her ways.

"She does, most definitely. Look, she and Cindy will never be friends, but she can be cordial."

Olivia nodded. "If she treats my mother with respect, then we can move forward. I'll return her call later today." She stretched her arms. "Right now, I plan to do a cooldown. Would you like to join me?"

"Yes." Alan walked the shoreline with Olivia.

"If you don't mind my asking, what are your plans for the summer?" he asked.

Olivia shrugged. "I'm not sure. It's unlike me, but I don't have a solid plan. I'm committed to staying through the Fourth of July weekend. After that, I'm unsure. Just taking it week by week."

"Well, hopefully between your family and the community, we can convince you to stay."

"Oh, I don't know about that."

Alan laughed. "Why not?"

"I'm not sure if I'm ready to reveal my identity just yet. That's why I've been avoiding people. I dislike scandals."

"So does your grandmother."

"I can see the headlines now: 'Mayor's Love Child Spends Summer in Highland Beach . . . Is She a Gold Digger?'"

"That's quite a long headline," Alan quipped.

Olivia threw her head back and laughed. "True, but let's be honest. I will be the talk of the town."

"Yes, you will. But it's not the first time the Jones family has been under fire. Not by a long shot." He sighed. "Trust me, we can overcome a little chatter."

"What's the point if I'm only here for a short period?"

Alan nodded his agreement. They walked in silence until Olivia broke it. "I'm just worried about CJ's career. How will this impact his reelection?" Olivia nibbled her lips.

"What's CJ's take on this?" he asked.

"He's Mr. Honesty Is the Best Policy. He wants us to announce our relationship and move on. Simple as that, damn the consequences."

From her periphery, Olivia noticed a smile spread across Alan's face.

"Why are you smiling? As his campaign manager, you of all people should be concerned."

"I'm not just his manager . . . I'm his stepfather."

Olivia rolled her eyes. The man was heavily invested in CJ's campaign, from what she could tell. "Still, I ask . . . why aren't you concerned?"

"Of course, I'm worried. And I won't lie. This will affect his reelection. And he's already getting over another hump with . . ." He stopped walking, stopped talking. "Maybe it's old age, but life is too damn short for regrets. And CJ has regretted his actions regarding you and your mother for a long time. I want him to be happy." He swallowed, clasping his hands behind his back. "I want him whole." Nodding, Alan added, "I know a little something about regret and as his stepfather, I'd rather he be happy as an ex-mayor than unhappy as a mayor."

"But is he really happy now?" Olivia winced at the doubt and insecurity dripping from her tone. "I can't tell. I don't really know him."

"You don't know him . . . yet. Just know that he's been under an incredible amount of pressure with the reelection campaign. He's made some mistakes, but he's owned up to them. But take my word for it. He smiles more. He laughs, and he looks at you and your mother as if you two hung the moon."

Olivia couldn't vouch for how he looked at her, but her mother . . . oh yes. He looked at her like he wanted to be everything to Cindy.

Yet her mother seemed undecided. And after all she'd been through, Olivia didn't quite know how to help. If she had been a friend of her mother's, Olivia wouldn't encourage her to take a chance on a man who abandoned her and his child all those years ago.

"As his consultant, I'll smooth things over once the news breaks. It's what I do." Alan shrugged.

"*If* it breaks." *I'm not sticking around*, Olivia thought.

"Trust me, these things get out. Everyone knows everyone. And soon people will talk." He lifted his arms in the air to stretch. "Well, young lady. Thanks for the talk and cooling down with me. I'll see you soon."

Alan turned in the opposite direction and slowly jogged away.

Olivia's phone rang again, and she sighed, hoping it wasn't the persistent Christine. When she looked at the screen, she smiled.

"Olivia." The way her boyfriend Garrett said her name sent delicious sparks up her spine. It'd been too long since she'd seen him.

"You never called me back about the dinner. How did it go?"

Olivia laughed, but without humor. "It was fairly terrible."

"F-fairly terrible?" Garrett chuckled.

"Yes. You know those *Real Housewives* shows on Bravo?"

"Addy is obsessed with them."

"Yes, it was like being on set. But of course this was unscripted, which is even more stressful because you don't know what to expect."

"So is your grandmother everything Ama and your mother said she would be?"

Olivia exhaled. "Yes and no. She hates my mother for sure, and she is controlling, but there's a soft side to her. I suspect her daughter's death as a teenager shattered the family. I think it's obvious she wanted her sons to stay as close as possible and toe the line. It's her version of keeping them safe."

"How did she treat you?"

"Christine treated me nicely. She even seemed . . . happy to have a granddaughter." Olivia remembered the affectionate way Christine had compared her to Indigo.

"She'd better treat you nice," he growled.

Olivia laughed. "You sound very threatening, Mr. Brooks."

"Threats are a waste of time. I'm more about promises. And I promise I won't allow anyone to hurt you."

Olivia's heart melted at his words, though she didn't show it. "You've been watching too many superhero movies. What are you going to do to a seventy-something-year-old lady?"

Garrett laughed. "I'm not going to lay a hand on your grandmother. But I'll stand in front of you, let her know you aren't to be insulted."

"Don't worry, I can handle Christine. Besides that, I get the strong impression she's living with some regrets from the choices she's made. It couldn't have been easy losing two children."

"I can't . . . don't want to imagine losing a child. Zora is my everything."

Olivia smiled. She'd come to love Garrett's daughter, who was also her goddaughter, like she was her own daughter.

"So I suppose softhearted Olivia will give her a chance to make amends."

Olivia told him about the conversation she'd had just minutes ago with Alan and the predicament with her father's reelection.

"What would make you happy?"

"Seeing your face," Olivia quickly answered without thinking.

"Done."

"Done?"

When she heard a familiar robotic noise through the phone's speaker, she lifted the phone and smiled at the FaceTime request. After a loud *zoop*, Garrett's face appeared on the screen.

Even on a six-inch screen, the man was the definition of fine. His dark brown skin was now peppered with a shadow covering his jawline.

"You know what I mean. I want to see you in person," Olivia said with a pout.

"Well, then I can visit you, or you can come back home."

Olivia smiled. "Soon. I promise."

"Fine. I'll just tell Zora that her favorite person said she'll come home *soon*. You know she wants something more specific. Anyhow, back to my question." Garrett smiled. "In this entire situation unfolding, what would make you happy?"

"I don't know. With CJ's campaign around the corner, I just don't want him to—"

"You keep basing your decision on others' reactions," Garrett interrupted. "So I ask again: What do *you* want?"

"I don't like keeping secrets. I want to walk around town with my head held high."

"There you go. Sounds like your father wants that, too." Olivia had told him CJ had protested about keeping her identity a secret.

"Yes, but it's easier said than done." Olivia shook her head. "You know, I just want one summer of peace. One summer when I can just relax."

Garrett nodded. Olivia told him everything, including the deadly secrets about her father Chris that her godparents had kept hidden since her childhood.

"I think the peace will come once you've faced everything head on."

Olivia scrunched her nose at his words. *Face everything head on?* Hadn't she done that by uprooting her life and spending weeks with her father in his beach town?

"I'm here, aren't I?" Then, muttering under her breath, "With my mother no less." While she and Cindy were well on their way to mending fences, there were still miles of hurt between them. Luckily, it was a distance both were willing to bridge.

"You are there. But you're hiding. Whispering." His voice boomed loud over the phone. Olivia looked over her shoulder, wincing when she realized the truth in his words.

Olivia sighed. "I'm out of my comfort zone. I admit it." She walked and stopped once she stood in front of CJ's house.

"You told me once that Zora was incredibly lucky to have a father like me."

"She is."

"And I'm lucky to have a wonderful daughter. Look, there is no excuse for your father. He didn't step up, and he let his brother do it for him. But he's there now, and you said you wanted to get to know him. And part of getting to know him is looking at how he takes care of his town. How he interacts with his family and constituents. You don't have to forgive him, but you owe it to yourself to fight for your peace."

"Fight for peace?"

Garrett nodded. "Yes. Even if it doesn't work out. Even if you don't want anything to do with your father, you'll leave Highland Beach with peace of mind, knowing that you tried."

Olivia swallowed the groan that crawled up her throat. She wasn't a groaner, and she wouldn't start now. But she could start with the truth.

"I miss you."

"I miss you more," Garrett quickly replied. "I can't wait to see you again. In person. In my arms, underneath me."

"Shh!" Olivia giggled and then looked around. "Fine, I was going to wait for a few minutes, but if you really miss me, check your bottom drawer in the nightstand."

"I'll check now."

"You don't have—"

"I'm checking now." She could see he was on the move.

He opened the drawer. "It's a bag."

"And you should open it," Olivia teased.

"Okay, let me put down the phone." He propped it on the nightstand and then rummaged through the bag.

"I love it."

She beamed when he found the picture of the two of them with

Zora at the Labor Day weekend race last year. Zora sat on her father's shoulders, and Garrett's head was bent low as he spoke to Olivia. Her partner Whitney had shared the picture after they made their relationship official.

"It's my favorite picture of us."

"And before we were together. You could see how crazy I am for you."

Olivia's smile grew wider. "There's more."

"I see, I . . . wait, my watch. Didn't Zora lose it? I thought I'd never see it again." He grinned.

It was the same watch she'd admired the day they ate ice cream together. When she asked for the model, he refused, stating that he didn't want her to buy Anderson, her fiancé at the time, the same watch.

"Well, good thing I figured out where you got it from, hmm?"

"I know how much this cost, Olivia." He looked troubled. "You didn't have to do it."

"Two more things."

"Olivia."

"Very inexpensive. I got it on sale."

He sighed and searched the bag, pulling out two tickets and then grinning.

"Two tickets to the Caribbean festival."

She smiled. "You asked me out last summer, but I . . . I couldn't. I'd like to go with you this year if the offer still stands."

Garrett chuckled. "Woman, I'll go every year with you for the rest of our lives if you let me."

"I . . ." Olivia didn't know how to respond. *Did he somewhat propose to me?*

"Olivia, close your mouth." He smiled and seemed oddly amused at her shock. "We'll take it one step at a time, okay?"

"Sure, yes. O-of course."

She was somehow elated and disappointed by the quick dismissal. Was she ready to get engaged or even married at this moment?

Yes?

Maybe?

Her heart thwacked against her chest, as if silently demanding that Olivia make up her mind right then.

"Thank you for the gifts." Garrett broke the silence. "They mean a lot. You mean a lot to me."

"Y-you mean a lot to me, too. I'll call you later." Olivia blew him a kiss and ended the call.

When she walked into CJ's home, she stopped at the noise.

She leaned her ear toward the sound and heard it again. A giggle. A genuine giggle from Cindy Jones.

"Hello," Olivia said, greeting her parents in a loud voice before she rounded the corner. She didn't want to walk in on any surprises.

"We're in here watching a movie," CJ answered.

As Olivia walked into the living room, her father grabbed the remote, then pressed Pause.

Olivia stared at the screen, but she couldn't place the movie. "What are you two watching?"

"Oh, it's *Poetic Justice*," Cindy replied. "It was our . . . I mean, we watched this a long time ago. Brings back memories." Cindy's smile faltered. She looked down and then away from Olivia.

Olivia nodded. "Well, don't let me stop you. I'm going to take a shower."

"You had a longer run than usual," CJ replied. "I was about to go out and check on you."

"I ran into Alan."

"Alan's running again?" CJ said in a high, disbelieving voice.

Looks like Alan wanted to run into me, Olivia thought. *No wonder he heaved and ho'ed.*

"I suppose so. He wanted to check in on both of you. Then we talked about your reelection."

CJ grunted again.

"I'm not sure what your grunts mean just yet. Translation?" Olivia asked.

"I'm not sure if I want to be reelected."

"Why?" Cindy straightened her shoulders.

"Because the life of a mayor is no joke, even for a small beach town. Everyone wants a piece of you—your mind, your time, your power. And everyone has an opinion of who you can and cannot date. Years ago, it was fine when I was . . . unattached. I slowed down this week, but I'll be at full speed next week."

"And you still *are* unattached," Cindy noted, with starch in her voice.

"I don't *want* to be," he replied, staring at her mother.

They held each other's stare while Olivia awkwardly observed them. She felt like an interloper.

"I'll . . . just go shower." Olivia pointed upstairs.

"You don't have to leave." CJ stood. "I've got nothing to hide. And I don't want to hide you two."

"You had no problem doing that for nearly three decades." Cindy's words held spite.

"No, I've always had a problem. But back then, I felt like you chose Chris over me, and I acted like a coward. Then after my brother died, I . . . thought about you and Olivia all the time, but then I was afraid that if I pursued you, you'd construe my actions as insincere."

Cindy let out a weary exhale, then put the popcorn bowl on the table. "I'm going for a walk."

"Mother . . ." Olivia followed Cindy outside.

Cindy paused at the front door. "I'd like to be alone." Her voice was as sharp as a shard of ice. Pivoting around to face Olivia, she exhaled. "I'm not running away from you."

"It's okay. I understand." Cindy needed to distance herself from CJ. Olivia couldn't blame her.

Cindy nodded once, then strode down the steps.

Inside, CJ leaned against the refrigerator, a bottle of beer in hand.

"I suppose it's five o'clock somewhere," Olivia said, trying to lighten the mood.

He took a sip, a miserable look etched on his face. Olivia remembered the stories her neighbor Mr. Whittingham told of him as a boy. He was determined, straightforward, loyal. But the man in front of her didn't seem that way.

"I'm not sure how to approach your mother. She's so different. We're so different."

His level of honesty caught Olivia off guard.

She took some time before answering, staring at her father for a long time, taking him in, assessing his intentions as if she were trying to smell them. Then she broke the silence.

"I'm not sure if I want the two of you together, not that you want my opinion."

Brown and intense, his eyes held her captive. "I want your opinion," he finally answered.

"Then maybe give her time. You were friends before dating, right?"

He nodded. "Yes, but there's always been something between us. We settled for friendship at first. When I was too stupid to see how she felt about me."

"Well, you're right in that you aren't the same anymore. So instead of trying to win her back, just get to know the woman she is now. Stop playing on memories with that old movie."

CJ chuckled, but without humor. "It's not *that* old. Janet Jackson is timeless."

"Yes, she is. But you know what I mean." Olivia smiled. "Make fresh memories."

CJ nodded. "Speaking of making memories, how about we have a drink on the patio and order takeout for lunch?"

Olivia smiled. "I'd like that."

"I left a few menus in the kitchen drawer. You can choose a few restaurants you want to try."

"How about we go out soon? Maybe we can drive to Baltimore." Olivia knew she couldn't hide away forever. And she was getting cabin fever.

CJ's eyes brightened and a rare smile spread across his face. "I'd like that a lot. Just the two of us sound all right?"

"Perfect."

Olivia showered and then afterward lingered in her room. She grabbed her phone and made the call.

"Hello, Christine."

"Olivia. I'm so glad you called me back."

"Yes, of course. My apologies for not calling sooner. I've been busy."

"I would love to take you to lunch." Christine's voice was soft, almost shy.

The effect on Olivia was dizzying. She couldn't believe this was the same woman who called her mother a tramp and a pumpkin.

Olivia's heart pounded. Could she? Should she? She thought of her mother, striding the house with a storm cloud over her head, largely because of her grandmother.

"Hello?" Christine's question roped her back into the conversation.

"Oh yes. Sorry. I'm just processing."

"What was I thinking?" Christine sighed. "You're right, it would be too much to ask of you, especially after my poor behavior."

"W-wait, no. I'd love to have lunch with you." She didn't realize until Christine had backtracked her invitation that she really wanted to get to know her grandmother. She wanted to get to know the woman—her mother's enemy. The mother to her father and uncle.

"I'll pick you up tomorrow at noon," Christine rushed, as if she thought Olivia would change her mind.

"That's okay." She did not want to walk outside to Christine's car under the prying eyes of Cindy. "I'll walk to your house. I'll be there at noon. See you then."

"Yes, of course. Bye for now."

Olivia ended the call and tried to shut down her chaotic thoughts, all racing to the same conclusion—Christine was up to no good.

But as with every other lesson she'd learned in life, she wouldn't rely on the feedback of others. She would give her grandmother a chance because not a lot of the Jones family was left. Her grandfather was dead. She no longer had her aunt Indigo and her uncle Chris—the man who'd had every intention of raising her, until he died.

This family had lost too much. Now it was time to heal.

CHAPTER FOUR

May 2022

FAMILY TREE

Since the family dinner had baptized Olivia by fire in Christine's style, she didn't worry about what to wear to lunch. It was already 85 degrees, and her white eyelet romper with capped sleeves was the perfect summer outfit. She paired it with her white Hermès heeled espadrilles with a braided detail on the wedge.

Olivia checked the living room. Seeing that her parents weren't there, she walked out the front door. She didn't want to sneak around, but she wasn't ready for the conversation with her mother about Christine.

She walked for ten minutes and found her grandmother waiting in her pearl white Lexus. Christine rolled down her window. Over-sized Gucci sunglasses nearly covered her pale elfin face.

Olivia opened the passenger door and slid into the seat. The smell of new car and leather teased her senses.

"We're going to go a little farther out today and drive to DC. I've made reservations at Ocean Prime. You like octopus, scallops?"

"I do." Olivia's voice was brighter than her feelings. Instead of dining closer to Highland Beach, they were going deep into Washington, DC. Maybe Christine was ashamed of Olivia?

"Excellent. Their food is divine."

Dr. LaGrange's voice entered her mind.

Don't assume. Just ask.

Olivia cleared her throat. "Is there a reason you selected this restaurant?"

"Now, I know you're in Sag Harbor, but I'd argue the way we prepare our seafood in DC and Baltimore is even more delicious."

"I hear the restaurants in Annapolis are very good, too. Not as far as DC."

"I see." Christine gripped the wheel, then glanced at Olivia.

"It's just that—"

"Alan told me yesterday that you aren't sure how long you are staying. And that you've been avoiding engaging with our neighbors."

"I have."

"Why?" Christine stopped at a red light and then stared at her. "Why?" she repeated her question, this time softly.

"I worry that once the news of my existence breaks out, it will negatively affect CJ's career."

"So I have an altruistic granddaughter." Christine harrumphed. She tapped her pale pink fingernails against the leather steering wheel. "Surely CJ, a man you've only just met, isn't the only reason you want to lie low."

Ah, there she is, Olivia thought to herself. The woman Ama and Cindy warned her about. The woman who wanted to know everything about family, friends, and foes.

Olivia swallowed. "I don't want to be known as the love child of Cindy and CJ. I've done a lot of . . . of growing this past year, but I don't want to go to that place of insecurity again. I won't tolerate anyone who makes me feel unworthy."

Olivia exhaled when the light turned green, and Christine returned her attention to driving the car. She changed the music station to smooth jazz until they arrived at the restaurant.

Christine already had a table reserved in the back of the restaurant, away from the bathroom, away from prying eyes.

After they ordered oysters, goat cheese ravioli, sautéed shrimp, and wine, Christine launched into a series of questions. Olivia noticed a pattern to her questions. She started off safe, with rather disarmingly charming inquiries, like her favorite toy as a child. Olivia had forgotten about a beautiful rag doll named Suzy that Omar and Ama had bought for her.

Olivia could've sworn she saw a flicker of annoyance on Christine's face. And maybe it was her imagination, but jealousy, too. The Black elite circles were small, and Christine had met Ama a handful of times, according to her godmother.

Hoping to bridge the uncomfortable divide, Olivia jumped in to ask Christine's favorite color, but the woman soon took back control, launching more personal questions. "Are you dating, dear?"

Olivia did not share that she nearly married Anderson, but did divulge that she and a neighbor had been dating for a little less than a year. She also gushed about Garrett's adorable daughter, Zora, who was also her goddaughter.

"You have many ties to Sag Harbor."

"I do. I love it there." Olivia found Sag Harbor charming, but it was the spirit of the people that had captured her heart. People there understood they needed to fight unapologetically to keep their homes away from greedy developers. And what's more, she'd discovered herself in Sag Harbor the previous summer. She'd fallen in love with the confident and beautiful woman she was today.

"Have you visited before?" Olivia asked. Though she knew the answer, she needed a reprieve from Christine's curious yet pointed questions.

"Oh yes. My sister and her husband lived there for a long time."

Christine tipped the deep red merlot into her mouth and then cleared her throat. "Tell me your favorite place to visit."

"Italy."

"Favorite city?"

"Florence."

"The shopping!" they both exclaimed.

When she was a teenager, Omar and Ama had taken the god-daughters to Florence when fall break came during the same time frame for all three of them. They'd sampled delicious treats like lemon and pistachio gelato while walking the narrow, cobbled streets within the old city walls. They'd each chosen a gift. Olivia had gone with a Prada purse.

"What was your favorite purchase?" her grandmother asked.

"My favorite purchase was from Ferragamo. A sheer, off-the-shoulder blue-and-lime dress." Olivia had bought that dress on her second trip to Florence, during her third year at Goldman Sachs. She'd also gifted herself a matching purse, stilettos, and an amazing lover.

"You must be having some memory." Christine's syrupy voice and lifted eyebrow snapped her back to attention. She could just imagine her grandmother's thoughts.

"It was an unforgettable experience." Olivia's cheeks warmed. "I can't wait to return."

This time she'd love to see Paris, Rome, and Florence through Zora's and Garrett's eyes. An Italian summer, just the three of them. She could feel their hands holding her own. Her heart raced from the fantasy. Shaking her head, she focused on the shrewd woman in front of her.

"Where's your favorite city to visit?" she asked her grandmother.

"Singapore." Christine rested her pointed chin on her hand. She smiled idly, as if reliving a beloved memory. "Talk about shopping—just pure opulence. Spas and the food . . . incredible. It's the best I've ever had. Have you been?"

Olivia shook her head. She'd had a trip to Singapore planned about five years ago until work got in the way. "I haven't been to Asia at all, but I would love to visit."

They continued chatting, and soon Olivia broke the vow she'd given to her mother about avoiding personal topics and sang like a canary. However, when Christine asked about past hardships, Olivia talked about food, travel, and shopping instead.

Not life, death, money.

After a few hours of eating and drinking and talking, Olivia looked around and realized the staff had changed over to prepare for the evening rush.

Christine noticed as well. She glanced at her rose-gold Gucci watch. "Goodness. It's a quarter to four."

After they walked to the car and got in their seats, Christine pressed the ignition but kept the car idling.

"You know, there's a wonderful boutique a little closer to home in Annapolis. It's no Florence, but they have the most brilliant colors and patterns in the area. Would it . . . would you mind extending our day a bit?"

Olivia's smile spread so wide her cheeks stretched. "Of course."

Christine smiled and then shifted gears to Drive. "You know, my Indigo wasn't much of a shopper. But she had a distinct style. Polka dots, stripes, sometimes at the same time."

When Christine shuddered, Olivia laughed.

"I can't say that I miss the '80s style," Christine explained. "Give me '50s, '60s, skip the '80s and '90s and early 2000s." Christine waved her hand. "But now . . . now is good. It seems like we've returned to our fashion senses."

Christine drove deeper into Annapolis and pulled into a cute shop off the corner of Main Street.

They entered the shop, and Olivia soon found a few items to add to her summer wardrobe.

Christine clapped, sipping champagne that they'd been given

upon arrival, as Olivia modeled a strapless midi dress from the Sergio Hudson collection.

"You look beautiful, Olivia."

"Thank you."

"I insist on buying this for you."

Olivia twirled again, meeting Christine's eyes in the mirror. "I appreciate the gesture, but I like to pay my own way."

Christine stared, her eyes blazing with something Olivia couldn't identify.

"Believe me, I know I can't buy you, nor do I want to. But if I'm being honest with myself, this is the best time I've had in a long while. Alan is a dear, but he has no patience for shopping. Charles is . . . he enjoys his alone time. And my dear sister Sandra is taking care of her husband, Jeff. She won't be down for a visit for some time. So this," she waved her hand with the champagne, "is all the girl time I have."

"What about your friends?"

"The friends my age live here part-time. They're here for a few weeks, and then they are raring to go back to their children and grandchildren. I'm not one to beg, but . . ." She exhaled. "Please let me commemorate this special day."

Olivia shook her head. "I really couldn't—"

"I saw you eyeing those earrings near the counter. So was I. Why don't I buy those instead?"

Olivia remembered the price. It wasn't as steep as the dress, and her mother wouldn't look twice at pearl and silver studs.

"I suppose that's fine."

Christine lifted her glass in the air as if toasting to her good fortune and then downed the rest.

As the sales associate wrapped the earrings, a beautiful woman who looked to be in her early forties walked into the store.

"Well, hello, stranger!" She greeted Christine like an old friend.

"Lauren, hello!" They leaned forward, but instead of the hug Olivia had expected to see, they air-kissed. "How's work been treating you? Charles told me you could barely come up for air."

The woman tossed her long brown hair over her shoulder and gave Christine a smile tighter than her skirt. "Did he now?"

Christine cleared her throat and shrugged.

"Well, work is going well. I had a tough case, but that's been over for *weeks*." Lauren's voice trailed off when she turned her attention to Olivia. Her tight smile morphed into an open-mouthed stare.

"And w-who is this young lady beside you?"

"I'm Olivia."

"Olivia?" Lauren offered her hand. "I'm Lauren. Lauren Miles. It's very nice to meet you."

"Likewise," Olivia replied, though she couldn't get a beat on the woman. Lauren looked at her without malice, but certainly strangely. While Lauren studied her face, Olivia swore she could see the woman's pulse throb at the base of her throat.

Olivia tried to remove her hand, but Lauren didn't let go. Then, as if she were coming to her senses, she shook her head and finally released Olivia's hand. "S-sorry. You look like . . . you look familiar." She laughed to herself and took a step back.

She dragged her gaze from Olivia back to Christine. "Well, Mrs. Jones. I would love to have lunch or dinner soon."

"Yes, of course," Christine replied. "You're always welcome in our family."

"Well, that's a relief." Lauren laughed. "I wouldn't want to be on a Jones's bad side." She tapped Christine's shoulder with affection.

Christine looked at the spot on her shoulder, then back at Lauren. Her smile, a little less wide now. "No indeed. I'll see you soon."

"I'm looking forward to that invite." Lauren gave Olivia one last smile before leaving the shop.

When Lauren walked away, Christine slipped to the other side of the store. Olivia trailed her grandmother, eager for details about Lauren and CJ's relationship. Christine pulled a pale-yellow blouse from the rack. "Now this would look absolutely amazing on you."

But Christine didn't say anything about Lauren, and after they left the shop, she deftly maneuvered to keep the conversation focused on fashion as they rode back to Highland Beach.

"I love what you're wearing today," Christine complimented Olivia. "Who is the designer?"

"Feben. She's a Black designer based in London and a veritable genius at her craft. I . . ." Olivia bit her lip. She had almost confessed what she loved most about the designer—that she explored and redefined feelings of displacement. "I'm a big fan," Olivia finished softly.

For miles, she'd waited for an explanation from her chatty grandmother about the woman they'd met at the store. But after they hit the city limits, Olivia dropped the pretense. "Christine." Olivia turned in her seat for a clear view of her grandmother's expression. "Is Lauren a friend of yours?"

"Oh, Lauren is more like an acquaintance. She and Charles date."

"Date? As in presently?" If Olivia had had antennas, they'd have risen to the moon.

Christine shrugged. "Who knows with Charles? But they attend events together, and she's been a huge help during the campaign when . . . when things got sticky for Charles. I like her, and honestly . . ." she cut a look at Olivia and then sighed. "They're well matched."

Olivia's mouth went dry. She didn't want to believe that CJ had his perfect, well-hidden family at home and ran around with the incredibly beautiful Lauren Miles during the day. And what exactly happened before she and her mother arrived? Not only Christine but Alan had alluded to some troubles with CJ's job.

Olivia's heart hurt for her mother. *I'll just have to ask about his intentions*, she told herself.

Lying in bed that night, Olivia found she couldn't relax enough to fall asleep. She didn't know what to say to her mother. Her phone was on Silent, but she heard it when it chirped. Ama's name flashed across the screen.

She accepted her godmother's call.

"Hello, Ama."

"How was your day, cher?" Ama's voice instantly soothed Olivia's anxiety. She wasn't at all surprised by her godmother's phone call. She'd told her about her plans for the day.

"It went well."

"Really? How so?"

Olivia told her the truth. That Christine had been charming—so charming that she gleaned information regarding her childhood, like her favorite toys.

"Maybe old age has softened her," Ama seemed to mutter to herself.

"Maybe it has, she really—"

"Or maybe she's playing the long game. Fattening the cow to slaughter, so to speak."

"I'm a cow now?" Olivia's voice pitched high.

"Now, cher. I would never call you anything so vulgar. I just know her game. She wines and dines you, and then lets you down."

Olivia swallowed her sighs because Ama did not tolerate sighs. To sigh was to lose hope, to give in audibly to weakness when one only needed silent strength.

"I know about Christine's checkered past, but it seems like she wants to get to know me."

"And what do you want, cher?"

"I don't want the locals whispering behind my back."

"Everyone knows everyone, just like Oak Bluffs and Sag Harbor. Yes, there will be talk, but guess what?"

"What?"

"You won't die. It'll run its course."

Olivia didn't answer. She didn't want to be on a "course" to begin with.

"You don't think I've had rumors about me? A Black woman in the '60s who bossed over those white boys?" she huffed. "They didn't just call me the Witch of Wall Street. I can't tell you how many times I heard those god-awful rumors about sleeping my way to the top."

"I didn't know about that." Though the rumors didn't surprise Olivia.

"Because rumors eventually lose their steam. They fall away and the person's character and reputation remain. And that's what you'll do, my beautiful girl. You will weather whatever storm blows your way."

"But what if it blows *me* away?" Olivia realized she had voiced that fear out loud only when Ama replied.

"Then I'll pull you right back." Then Ama chuckled. "But something tells me Charles and Cindy won't let their girl fly away."

Olivia soon said goodbye and hung up. For once, a call with Ama hadn't cleared her mind or heart.

What needled Olivia the most was that she wasn't sure if Lauren was CJ's girlfriend. And even more disturbing—she wasn't sure how serious he was about her mother.

It took a special woman to be the wife of a powerful man. After almost three decades as a widow, Cindy deserved to be a man's sole focus.

CHAPTER FIVE

May 2022

THE OTHER WOMAN

"We need to talk." Olivia's low voice broke the morning quiet. She'd walked in on CJ, who was reading the *Bay Journal* at the kitchen island.

It was far too early for Olivia to lecture anyone, let alone her biological father. But if she'd learned anything the previous summer, it was how to exhume *seemingly* dead feelings and bring them to the surface.

He straightened and then waved toward the open seat at the kitchen island.

"No." Olivia shook her head. "Let's take a walk. What we need to discuss won't take long, I promise."

CJ glanced at his watch. "I've got to get going in the next fifteen minutes. I'm sorry, but today I'm in back-to-back meetings."

"Fifteen minutes will be more than enough time," she assured him. "But I would like to take this outside."

"O-kay." He lifted his eyebrows, but she didn't give anything away. Wordlessly, he stood and opened the front door. Together they walked down the quiet street to the shoreline.

Sometime overnight a rainstorm had paid a quick visit, amplifying the smell of salt in the air. The normally smooth, dry sand, now damp, sucked the soles of their shoes, leaving memory-foam footprints in their wake.

Olivia exhaled a few seconds later. "I think we're far enough, so I'll get right to it. Yesterday, when Christine and I had lunch, we ran into Lauren Miles."

CJ stopped walking, looked around, sighed—not toward Olivia, but to the sky. "I hope Lauren wasn't rude—"

"Lauren was fine." Olivia rushed on. Never mind that the woman didn't let go of her hand and stared as if she'd seen a ghost. "But Christine confirmed that you two are dating."

They're well matched. Her grandmother's words had pinged and ponged around her mind all night.

A frown formed on his face, deepening the grooves on his forehead like bulked-up biceps.

"We dated, but we aren't anymore."

"Since when?"

"I broke it off weeks ago, just before you arrived."

Olivia rolled her eyes.

"And let me be clear, we were more partners than friends. She offered help when . . . when my character was questioned."

"How did she help?"

CJ looked at the sky. "I was hoping to never have this conversation, but I don't see it going away. Honesty is best, right?" He seemed to speak to himself more than to Olivia.

"Right. It's best not to lie to us," Olivia advised.

He cleared his perfectly dry throat. "I was in a relationship with someone on my staff. Only a few months."

"People who work together often date." Olivia summoned a magnanimous tone.

"She was young."

"How young?"

"Twenty-four."

"Oh God." The magnanimous tone fled the scene. "She's half your age . . . younger than me."

"It wasn't about age . . ."

Olivia held up her hand.

"No. You want the truth and I'm giving it to you. I was lonely. She was . . . is . . . a bright young lady who was eager to make a big splash."

"Are you saying she seduced you?"

"No." He shook his head. "No. It was consensual. I liked Riley, and I hadn't been with anyone in a very long time. All I can say is that we had mutual respect. But she's the niece of one of our long-term residents, who wasn't pleased about our relationship. So Riley told her side of the story, which made it seem like I took advantage of her."

"Was that before or after the summer you found us?"

"Before. It's been nearly two years, but people have long memories. And I won't lie. I lost the trust and respect of many people."

Olivia guessed. "So now you're using Lauren to—"

"No. Lauren offered help. She has her own goals and agenda, to be sure, but there is nothing romantic there. She's more like staff than anything else."

"Like Riley was staff?"

"Lauren and I are friends who occasionally have dinner or escort each other to industry events. Nothing more." His tone remained even and matter-of-fact, with just a hint of annoyance, as if Olivia were a pestering reporter at a press conference.

"And does Riley live here? Is there a chance either Cindy or I will run into her?"

"No. She's back in DC, and I haven't spoken to her in over a year."

"Do you love her?"

"No, I don't. The only woman I've ever loved or missed is your mother. I don't love Riley or Lauren. That's the truth."

Is he telling the truth?

Olivia examined his body language. He hadn't crossed his arms and turned away—gestures that could confirm his guilt. Olivia remembered Lauren's surprised response when Christine assumed that Lauren and CJ hadn't talked much lately because she was too busy.

Olivia cleared her throat, nodding, though she wasn't 100 percent convinced of his innocence. "Are you sure Lauren feels the same way? That you're just acquaintances who occasionally serve as dates?"

He opened his mouth, shut it, then placed his hand on his chin. "I . . . well . . . I don't think so. She didn't want to be physical with me."

"Are you sure?" Olivia challenged.

"Very sure. Lauren once said that she viewed me more like a cousin or big brother. We'd known each other for five years prior to our agreement."

"Was she ever jealous of other women? What about Riley?"

"No, not even Riley." He shook his head. "The only time I felt a spark of jealousy was when I left unannounced last summer to visit Sag Harbor. We'd just started our fake relationship, so I found that odd." He stroked his chin. "Maybe she wanted something more."

Olivia shrugged. "People's feelings can change." Just two summers ago, she wanted to marry Anderson. But now she couldn't imagine her life without Garrett.

"Regardless, I told her that some things in my life had changed, and I wouldn't make a suitable partner. She said she understood and took the news in stride. She didn't seem particularly hurt or upset, but asked that I keep her in mind if I needed a partner for future events."

Olivia channeled the spirit of objectivity and refrained from rolling her eyes. There was no way this woman suggested they date seriously, got rejected, and did not feel a modicum of hurt or embarrassment. "I know I've no say in your personal affairs. Not to mention you are an adult who runs an entire town. That's no easy feat," Olivia began diplomatically.

"Thank you," he replied, in a get-to-the-point tone.

"You and my mother have spent lots of time together. Quality time. You seem to like her."

"Without a doubt," he confirmed quickly. "I want her in my life."

"Then I suggest you square things up between my mother and your mother. Then you'll need to tell her the truth about Riley and tie up loose ends with the beautiful Ms. Miles."

"Beautiful?"

"Yes." Women, especially Cindy, would home in on her beauty. And what was more, Olivia did not want her mother to question her own looks or self-worth.

"You have my directness," CJ said, inclining his head toward her. "I like that."

"I think it's best to lay all the cards on the table this time around. Don't you?"

There would be no more missed connections. No misunderstandings because of meddling mothers. And absolutely no driving off with someone else in the rain—not on Olivia's watch.

"I agree that it's best to be up front. And I'll handle things with Lauren and Christine because I want to spend all my free time with you and your mother. You two are the most important people in my life."

Olivia turned around and looked away to hide her blooming smile. "Very well then." She gave him an awkward thumbs-up. "Our fifteen minutes are done now."

He glanced at his watch to confirm. "It is. You're dressed up. Are you meeting with Christine again?"

"No. I have a conference call with my partner Whitney today, but otherwise, not much else."

"How about you come to the office today? You can see me in action."

"Wouldn't people ask questions? Especially with another young woman around. They wouldn't want a repeat of the Riley scandal."

"I'll tell them you're a relative. There are a lot of us Joneses around the world," CJ said with a hopeful smile.

Lots of Joneses, huh?

He said it easily, unaware that his words detonated an emotional earthquake. Olivia wished she had known the Jones family earlier. When she received the governor's award for academic achievement in middle school, she wished she had family to cheer her on like the other students. Or at fifteen years old, when she delivered a winning argument for her debate team.

"Lots of Joneses . . ." she whispered. That's why she was here. To get to know her father. Her family. She couldn't allow the past to get in the way of what she was doing now.

CJ's smile morphed into concern. "I know you're still getting to know my side of the family and our history. The best way to do that is to explore Highland Beach and meet people."

She shook her head. "I just don't want all the questions from strangers. Maybe I should—"

"I know this sounds cliché, but the people here are friendly and accepting. Just give us . . . give *me* a chance." CJ swallowed. "I would really like to get to know you, Olivia Charlotte Jones."

"You know my middle name?"

"It's a matter of public record." He smiled slowly. "Hey, I just realized . . . did your mother name you after me?"

She laughed at his dumbfounded expression. Something that felt like the sun warmed her chest. "I don't know. I guess we'll have to ask."

"So will you come to the office with me, Olivia? I promise I won't let you down."

Somehow it was the silliest yet most profound conversation she'd had with her father. He was trying. She would go with him. It was time.

"I . . . yes." She lifted her hands up in defeat. "I'll grab my purse and laptop, and then we can be on our way."

On the way back she had the oddest feeling of being watched. She quickly glanced over her shoulder but found no one behind them.

When they returned, Cindy stood in the kitchen making a veggie and ham omelet.

"Well, hello." Cindy greeted her daughter and CJ with a wave of the spatula. She then pointed the utensil toward Olivia. "You got in late last night," she said to Olivia.

Olivia could hear the question in her mother's voice. She'd told her mother in passing about her plan to meet with Christine. *Did it go okay? Did Christine frighten you away?*

"We had lunch, and then I went shopping after."

"Oh?" Cindy whisked eggs and a few other ingredients into a bowl and then poured it all into the hot skillet.

"Yes, but all is well. We'll talk later, okay?"

"Why not now?" Her voice was calm, but she flipped her omelet so hard it smacked the skillet.

Despite Olivia's little white lie—implying that she'd gone shopping alone—her heart galloped as though she were a teenager who'd missed curfew.

"I'm going into work today with CJ."

"Oh . . . that's a change." Cindy didn't sound concerned, but curious.

"I traveled all the way here to get to know CJ. So . . . if he's busy with his reelection and job, I should go to where he is."

"And what about the good people of Highland Beach? I thought you were worried about the rumors."

"We're going to say I'm a distant relative for now."

The stiffness in Cindy's shoulders relaxed. "Keep it simple and as close to the truth as possible. That's your style, CJ." Cindy nodded at him. "Hit them with the truth and let them deal with the rest."

Olivia just barely covered her snort. If only Cindy knew about him covering up the truth about Little Miss Half His Age.

"Sometimes I don't get to do the things that I want, but I try to stick to the truth." CJ leveled his attention at Cindy.

Cindy gave him a weak smile and then swung her attention to Olivia. "Have fun."

"I won't be out all day, so maybe—"

Cindy shook her head. "I've got plenty to do here . . . reading, relaxing by the pool. Don't worry about me."

Olivia smiled. Her mother had never experienced the luxury of unwinding. Even during the summers, she usually taught school or tutored English to incoming middle schoolers.

"Good for you."

Olivia grabbed her purse and laptop. While CJ was in meetings, she could work on the proposal to the government of Sag Harbor to add more homes and buildings to the National Register.

"There she is," CJ said when they parked on the road in front of a small gray-and-white clapboard house. The drive to Town Hall had taken less than five minutes.

A stone column stood just before the building, bearing a brown placard. Gold lettering etched in an epigraph read:

HIGHLAND BEACH
INCORPORATED 1922
FOUNDED 1983 BY CHARLES R. & LAURA A. DOUGLASS

Though a part of her was ashamed of the history surrounding her birth, another part of Olivia wanted to shout the news from the rooftop that the founders were her relatives.

They entered the building, crossing over the square gravel pit that surrounded the front wooden steps. On each side of the steps stood a planter filled with colorful flowers. Beyond them, Olivia quickly recognized the flowering begonias, thanks to all the hours she and Mr. Whittingham had spent in Bea's Garden and Apothecary.

Just under a window hung a bulletin board encased in glass. After getting a closer look, Olivia noticed a mishmash of flyers, including local community events.

CJ pulled out a key, opened the door, and let himself in. Olivia found a few others milling about at their desks with their mugs of steaming hot coffee in hand. A fifty-something woman with a small crowd around her was animatedly telling a story about her weekend. She turned to face Olivia and CJ.

"Good morning, Mayor Jones." She smiled, revealing deep dimples in her cheeks. She nearly spilled her coffee with her enthusiastic greeting.

"Good morning, Janice." He turned to Olivia, though Janice already had her attention fixed on the young woman standing next to the mayor.

"Janice, this is Olivia. Olivia, Janice. Janice is a local and has been kind enough to volunteer with admin work on Mondays, Tuesdays, and Thursdays."

Olivia stretched out a hand and shook the admin's hand.

"Janice, Olivia has a nonprofit that helps historic Black neighborhoods fight those developers that like to eat up our land and drive up our property taxes. Olivia has already done some great work in Sag Harbor. She'll be observing how we run things around here to see how she can replicate our success in other historic neighborhoods." He looked down at Olivia with a proud dad smile. "She's a Jones, and she's good people. It'd be great if you could be a resource if she needs anything."

He's quick. Before rumors could circulate, he had clearly sought out Janice first, confirmed their familial connection, and validated Olivia's reasons for visiting the office.

"You've got it, Mayor Jones. Olivia, I love that you're focused on protecting historic Black neighborhoods. I'll give you access to anything you need."

She pointed to CJ. "Oh, and I'm sorry, but I had to add another meeting to your schedule to discuss the beach erosion project with that marine scientist."

CJ pumped his fist. "Thanks for getting that back on the books."

Janice shook her head. "I can't believe we have to start over again."

CJ nodded. "Everyone's feelings were valid. We just need to figure out a compromise to contain the beauty of the bay and protect our shoreline."

Janice, who looked positively forlorn, seemed to brighten at his words.

While Janice ran down a list of to-dos for CJ, Olivia examined the tight quarters. Though it was small, with four offices and a wide-open space with several desks lined up along the wall, it wasn't confining. Olivia thought it might have been all the bright smiles and coffee that made the place seem open and welcoming.

Janice, who'd just finished her conversation with CJ, touched Olivia's hand to get her attention. "Come swing by my desk after the morning crush, around eleven a.m. I'll get you anything you need." The admin pointed to her desk in the corner, near the back office.

"Thank you, Janice. I'll do that."

The woman nodded and returned to her desk.

"Olivia, you're welcome in my office, though I'll be on calls most of the day," CJ reminded her.

She patted her laptop bag. "I've got all I need to assist," she replied, keeping up the pretense as Janice listened from behind her desk.

On the way back to his office, he greeted his team and briefly introduced Olivia.

True to his word, as soon as he had sat down at his desk and booted up his computer, he dialed into his first meeting.

Olivia listened in on the conversations. CJ met with the volunteer fire department about being up to date on codes. He spoke to a representative at a local hospital about easier access and improvement in triage times. Occasionally he'd look up to find Olivia staring in fascination, flash her a winning smile, and then resume his conversations.

He was straightforward and honest, with an earnest delivery, as he smoothed ruffled feathers and navigated critical conversations. And most of all, she could tell that his constituents trusted him.

CJ didn't have the larger-than-life personality common among politicians, but people still gravitated toward him. His team squeezed in five minutes here and there between calls to catch up or pitch something that could have been relayed in an email.

He was also a creative problem-solver, a skill that was important to Olivia and one she continued to refine herself.

She added that trait to the list of what she and her father had in common. It seemed she really was a Jones. She and Christine had even more in common—they were both in Greek organizations, they both loved shopping, and judging from a text message Christine had sent the night before, they enjoyed the same books.

Olivia's stomach sank at the thought of being so like the woman who'd terrorized her mother.

What would Cindy think? And a more terrifying thought—what would Ama think? Before her thoughts jumped off the deep end, Janice, who'd at some point lightly knocked on the door, waved at Olivia.

Olivia glanced at her watch and saw that it was a quarter past eleven.

"Sorry," she mouthed and quietly stepped out of the office into the main room.

"My apologies. I was just fascinated by CJ's conversation and time got away from me."

"Oh, that's fine. It's fun to see the mayor in action. CJ is exceptional at his job."

"That he is," Olivia agreed.

"Did you get any ideas so far?"

"No." Olivia shook her head. "But I am getting a sense of what makes Highland Beach special. He's got a meeting at noon with the Anne Arundel County Chamber of Commerce about new business coming in nearby, and I think that meeting will give me some ideas on how to translate your town's strategy to other neighborhoods."

Janice sucked her teeth. "Now I told him to stop taking lunch meetings. He never eats on camera." She sighed. "I'll get him a sandwich."

"I can get it," Olivia offered.

"No, ma'am. That's my job."

"I guess I'm looking for an excuse to explore."

"Oh, that's a must. How long have you been here?"

"A few days," Olivia answered with a tight smile.

"And how are you and Mayor Jones related?"

Olivia nibbled her lips. She wanted to say they were cousins, which was easy enough, but she didn't want to take away from CJ's honest approach, especially if the truth got out. Olivia stuck as close to the truth as possible.

"I just discovered this side of the Jones family last summer. Once we connected, he invited me to learn more about our history. So . . . here I am."

"Oh, that's so lovely! Like one of those online family tree things, huh?" Janice nodded, as if answering her own question.

Olivia took the brief reprieve to pivot the conversation away from the personal to the professional. "Now, the best way I can help other cities is to understand the history of this city as well as how you approve your real estate developments."

Janice snapped her fingers. "I know just the thing. Give me a minute." She stood and marched over to a small bookcase that stood opposite CJ's office, then pulled out a slim volume with a glossy cover.

"Here's everything you need to know about our history."

Highland Beach on Chesapeake Bay: Maryland's First African American Incorporated Town.

Janice also provided Olivia with some old newspaper articles. "But if you stick around town a few more days, we have a nice Memorial Day event at the Pavilion and on the beach. You can ask our residents about how they came to inherit or purchase their home here. Honestly, it's the best way to learn about how we operate. It's not just something you'll find in books and articles."

Memorial Day was only a week away, and Olivia would probably be around. Still, she didn't want others to know her plans. "If I'm still here, I'll try to make it out."

"I'm on the planning committee for our holiday celebrations, and this year our Labor Day weekend celebrates 130 years for Highland Beach. All of that is to say, if you end up sticking around even longer, or if you want to come back to visit, let me know."

"Of course."

Olivia pored over the documents and found out a few more new and interesting things about the family and the history of Highland Beach. The residents obviously loved this special gem of a town, and its history was one that Olivia felt should be widely known and celebrated. Even Harriet Tubman had visited Highland Beach.

Janice had been spot-on about the publicity side. Awareness of the historical significance of places like Highland Beach might discourage residents from selling to the highest bidder. But it was more than that. Olivia knew the younger generation wanted a place to socialize and party. They wanted to walk from a bar to their resort. Even on vacation, many people wanted the noise.

It was quiet here, even in the summer. And perhaps it was a testament to Olivia's nearly three decades on the earth, but she now preferred quiet and peace.

She hadn't known peace like that until Sag Harbor—or rather, she hadn't appreciated peace and quiet until adulthood. Martha's Vineyard certainly could be very peaceful in the fall, but during the summer the Vineyard was party central, especially in August.

She stared at Janice, a busybody for sure, but she seemed to care about CJ's success—and about the residents of Highland Beach.

Would Janice be so understanding and welcoming to Olivia if she found out she was CJ's secret daughter?

Over the lunch hour, a few employees—or rather volunteers—introduced themselves, each clearly curious about her and focused on her every word. Meanwhile, Janice had bought CJ a sandwich and ordered Olivia a Cobb salad.

CJ stuck his head out, searching the room until his eyes landed on Olivia. He waved at her to come into his office.

"I didn't know you would be out there for so long," he said once she closed the door behind her.

"Oh, well, I had a delightful conversation with Janice. She's given me great resources about the town."

"Anything you can use?"

"You all have truly protected the town to remove commercial development, which keeps the property taxes from skyrocketing. The next step is talking to the elders in the community to fill in the gaps." Olivia tapped her chin. "By the way, what's the average household income here?"

"A little over $130,000. We have a low poverty rate. Under 4 percent. Still work to be done, but we're under the national average by eight points."

Olivia nodded. "What's your goal for Highland Beach?"

"On a local level, I want our residents to keep homes in their family. It's not that we don't want new blood, but it's hard to see someone I've known all my life being forced to sell something so precious to their ancestors. I also want to figure out a sustainable way to protect our beach against natural disasters. On a national—hell, an international—level, I want the world to know our history. I want Highland Beach to be revered, and its history held dear. I want to seek advocates who'll protect and invest in the neighborhood. And I want those damn redevelopers to stay far away from us."

"Yeah, get in line," Olivia agreed.

"So how did you get them out of your hair, anyway?"

Olivia's face grew warm as she recalled all that had transpired. She wasn't quite ready to confess that her ex-fiancé was related to those developers—the CEO of ASK Developers was Anderson's father.

"We, umm . . ." Olivia cleared her throat and tried again. "We knew the owner, and we gained certain information that dissuaded him from further development in the area."

CJ lifted an eyebrow almost as high as his hairline. "So you blackmailed the man?"

"Not exactly," she replied slowly. "He just found out that he had his hands full with other things in his life." Olivia's voice nearly squeaked.

She bit her lip. She did not want her father to think she used strong-arm tactics.

The grin on CJ's face spread slowly and wide, like the Grinch's infamous smile. "I look forward to learning more about you, daughter."

Olivia put up halting hands. "I assure you our strategies were legitimate."

CJ chuckled. "I'm taking all the advice. We could use a little innovation for sustainability."

"It's not in my wheelhouse, but I'm always willing to try."

"Oh, I think one of the *Forbes* Top 10 Rising Financial Analysts will knock it out of the park."

"You . . . you know about that?"

He nodded. "Now, I didn't have you investigated, but I did my research." He looked down at his hands. "I know this doesn't mean much, but I'm so impressed and I'm so proud of you. Cindy did a great job."

Hands clasped in her lap, she acknowledged his praise with a tight smile. "Thank you." She looked out the back window.

"It's the truth. Christine tells me you had a great time shopping."

"We did."

His lips turned into a frown. "Did she—"

"She was a perfect angel," Olivia answered. "We connected well and had great conversations."

"Really?" He didn't wear that Grinch grin anymore. He looked uneasy.

"Yes, really. We have lots of things in common, and she's . . . somewhat agreed to be cordial to Cindy. It's really all I can ask for."

CJ sighed. He opened his mouth, but a ping dinged from his laptop. "That's my next call. Sorry, but someone added a last-minute meeting that won't end until five, maybe later. Please take the car if you want."

"No, that's okay. I'll just walk back to the house."

"No, no. Take the car. There's a coffee shop about five miles down the road called Main & Market. I noticed you're a caffeine fiend, so you'll enjoy the coffee."

Olivia laughed. "Okay, I'll do that."

CJ reached inside his desk, then handed over the keys.

"Now, I know I'm about a decade late. But be careful."

Olivia rolled her eyes. "Yes. You are much too late for that, CJ."

He winced, but quickly recovered. "Am I? Well, I know you New

Yorkers are aggressive drivers. Don't scare the old folk around here with all that beeping."

Olivia laughed and grabbed the keys. "I'll do my best. See you at home."

"Knock, knock!" Before CJ could beckon her into the office, Lauren stepped in.

"Oh, hello." Her smile tightened. "Olivia, right?"

"Yes. Right." Olivia swung her attention to CJ, who frowned at Lauren.

"What are you doing here, Lauren? You don't have an appointment."

"I didn't think I needed to make one." She glanced at Olivia, hesitated, then pivoted her attention to CJ.

"We should talk."

"I have a meeting."

"Then you can move it," she nearly growled. "Or I can wait."

"The conversation is confidential, so you can wait outside." He motioned to the door.

Lauren, with balled fists, turned on her green Louboutin heel and stormed out of the room.

"Seems like you and Ms. Miles have some unfinished business."

"Olivia."

She raised her hand. "I'm going to repeat my advice from this morning . . . tie up those loose ends."

Before he could say anything further, Olivia shut the door. At a quarter past five, most of his staff had already left, except for Janice, who clacked away at her computer. She was surprised when she didn't see Lauren stewing at one of the desks.

Olivia walked to Janice's desk and asked about Lauren. Janice harrumphed. "The one and only? Oh, she sashayed out of here." She shook her head and continued typing.

"If you don't mind my asking, how long have they been dating?"

Janice paused and gave Olivia a who-wants-to-know look. "A little under a year. But CJ told us they were no longer an item. Imagine my surprise to see her here."

"Maybe it's a business meeting."

"Hmm. Maybe. Our mayor needs to focus on town issues, not another . . . not her," Janice mumbled under her breath. "Anyway, are you heading out?"

Olivia walked to her desk. "Yes, and it was an absolute pleasure to meet you. Thank you for taking some of your precious time to help me today."

"Of course! I'll see you tomorrow?"

Olivia shook her head. "I'm not sure about tomorrow, but I'll definitely return to review those records again."

She stopped typing and waved. "Headed home? I guess you're staying with Mayor Jones."

Olivia nodded before she could think through her answer. "I'm headed to the coffee shop."

"Oh good. You'll meet lots of residents there, and I'm sure they'll recognize that you're a Jones," she laughed. "Whew! Y'all have some strong genes. If I didn't know any better, I'd say Christine had a child later in life." Janice laughed at her joke.

Olivia choked.

"Anyway, have fun!" Janice wiggled her fingers.

"I will. Thanks again." Olivia hurried to open the door, walk out, and close it shut behind her.

She smiled, relieved to be outside of the scrutiny of the office. And best of all, the sun was still shining after a long day.

But when Olivia clicked the alarm and opened the door to the Audi, she had that same weird feeling she'd had that morning. She hurried into the car, locked the doors, and checked her surroundings.

A couple walked a few feet away, engrossed in their conversation. But no one seemed to notice the woman who jumped into the mayor's car.

Then a fleeting thought occurred, a fear no bigger than a mustard seed. What if someone recognized her and remembered Cindy and Chris?

What if someone figured out that she was the mayor's daughter?

CHAPTER SIX

May 2022

BREAKING NEWS

Olivia whispered a quick prayer that all would go well for her first public outing. She pressed the ignition, laughing when she recalled CJ's joke about New Yorkers' aggressive driving.

It simply wasn't true. Most car owners lived in the suburbs and rarely burdened themselves with the bumper-to-bumper grind in the city. And those who lived in the city took the subway.

Growing up in the suburbs of New Jersey, she'd had a typical suburban driving education. When Cindy tried to teach Olivia how to drive, she quickly realized her nerves weren't up to teaching her headstrong daughter. Olivia was embarrassed when she was forced to use a class credit for Driver's Ed, since the class was for students who couldn't learn from their parents or who failed their license test.

The teacher, Mr. Giovani, did not tolerate what he called a "rude driver." Decorum had been part of the overall score—no rolling eyes or cursing or blaring of the horn was allowed, not even when it was justified.

But if CJ ever drove with one of her godsisters, Billie or Perry, at the wheel, he'd be scared out of his mind.

Olivia quickly found the coffee shop, using her father's directions rather than her phone app. She parked the car and found the small square building sandwiched between a barber shop and a nail salon in a busy plaza. Olivia craved a piece of Ghirardelli chocolate with sea salt after smelling the dark roast, chocolate, and salt.

She pushed open the door and immediately slid into the short line in front of the counter. Toward the back of the room sat six women of varying ages, books either clutched in their hands or scattered on the low table. Olivia immediately recognized the distinct royal blue with a gold hair pick comb on the cover of *The Other Black Girl* by Zakiya Dalila Harris.

Olivia placed her order and then drifted near the book club, pretending to look around the coffee shop.

"I liked the book and all, but now I can't use grease or drink tea."

An older woman who sat in the center of the group, near the wall, raised an eyebrow. "Now what are you talking about, Kelli?"

"I mean, I can no longer trust those products after this book and after watching *Get Out*. These social justice–slash–thrillers need to choose something I don't care about. Like a macaron."

One woman clutched her nonexistent pearls. "Speak for yourself. Those French almond cookies are delightful."

Olivia's lips twitched at her reaction, though she'd have to agree with the stranger. She fell in love at fourteen years old when Ama took her, Billie, and Perry to London's Louis Vuitton store, where they were served tea and macarons while they waited.

"Is that why you switched to coffee?" another woman asked.

"Yes!" Kelli responded. "I just can't bring myself to stir in cream," she said with a shudder.

The other women laughed at her joke.

While crocheting a scarf, a woman with salt-and-pepper hair said, "That's why you can't use random hair grease."

Olivia smiled. Crocheting a scarf was an interesting choice given the season.

"Ladies," tsked the woman in the center, who looked to be the leader of the book club, "let's stay on topic."

"This *is* on topic," argued Kelli, the conspiracy theorist.

"Our questions." The book club leader slapped a piece of paper with the back of her hand. "I put a lot of effort into pulling these together."

"Google is free," Kelli muttered.

"I'm this close to kicking you out." The older woman pressed her thumb and index fingers so close together that Olivia was sure there was only an infinitesimal space between them. "You better be glad your mom is my friend."

Kelli stood and gave her a hug. "You know you love me, Aneesa."

"I suppose, since I'm your godmother and all."

Kelli patted her shoulder and returned to her seat.

"Okay, now back to my questions." Aneesa opened a gorgeous aquamarine-and-gold notebook and clipped the printed page inside the folder.

"I found it interesting that the author chose hair grease instead of a chemical relaxer. Do you have any theories on why the author made that choice?"

The women were quiet for a moment. Some of them picked up their mugs and sipped. Olivia leaned in closer. She wanted to hear their perspectives, especially since she stopped her relaxers and went natural just the summer before.

"Come now. I told you we were going to be an actual book club this summer." Aneesa scanned the faces of her lackluster book club members. "We have to read the book and answer questions. Not just drink tea and coffee and gossip."

A woman who sat next to her raised a hand as if she were in school.

"Yes, Dana," said Aneesa.

"I think it's the lower barrier of entry, right? No one's going to put something chemical in their hair, especially when Black women are moving away from relaxers."

Kelli removed her fingers from across her closed mouth. "But wouldn't it have been an interesting choice?" She pursed her lips. "You straighten your hair to fit into a certain standard? No one's asking you about your *interesting* hairstyle. No one wants to touch your hair if it looks like theirs."

There were no comments after Kelli spoke her piece.

Aneesa's attention drifted toward Olivia, who quickly pivoted on her heels and turned to face the counter. Surely it didn't take this long for a salted caramel macchiato.

"Hey you," Aneesa yelled.

Olivia wasn't sure if Aneesa was addressing her, so she didn't turn around.

"The pretty young thing in the yellow blouse," Aneesa sang in a yoo-hoo voice. "Turn around, please."

Okay, so she is speaking to me.

Olivia slowly turned around, tilted her head, and then pointed to her chest.

"Yes, you who's listening over there." Aneesa waved at Olivia to come closer.

"You seem like you have something to say, and as you can see, no one is answering my very thought-provoking questions."

"Hey!" Kelli protested.

"I'm Aneesa Wilson." The woman gave Olivia a wide smile. It may have been the freckles smattering her chestnut brown face, but she seemed open and friendly.

"This is Lydia, and Carol." She pointed to the women seated beside her. "The one with the big mouth over there is Kelli. Beside her is Dana. We are the members of the Highland Beach Bookworms."

"Working title," Kelli muttered.

"It's decided. We've already voted," Aneesa snapped. She reapplied her smile when she turned to focus again her attention on Olivia. "Anyhow, what's your name?"

"I'm Olivia J . . . Olivia." She stopped herself from saying her last name.

"Olivia J. Sounds like a DJ." Kelli mimicked scratching a record.

"I assure you, I have no talent for spinning records."

"Olivia J . . . oh!" Aneesa's eyes stretched wide. "Janice mentioned an Olivia at the mayor's office today. She, um . . . popped by earlier for coffee."

Wow. Janice really got the word around.

"Yes. I'm working with the mayor to see how we can replicate the strategies you've used for Highland Beach to protect other historic Black neighborhoods."

"And you're related to the Jones family," Aneesa surmised.

"Hmm, yes. Well, I'd better get my—"

"So back to my question. Using a natural product is an interesting choice, right?"

Olivia nodded. "*The Other Black Girl* was actually one of my favorite reads. It's deliciously subversive. I think using hair grease, something we are familiar with and grew up with, is a brilliant choice. Especially when many of us now view natural hair care as a way to reclaim our natural beauty. It's insidious . . . and genius."

"Very astute, Olivia Jones." Aneesa smiled. "You want some wine?"

"Oh, I . . . didn't realize they sold wine."

"They don't." Aneesa lifted a bottle from a red tote bag. "We bring our own. You should join us next time. Next up is *Island Queen* by Vanessa Riley."

"I'll do that," she agreed. *Though by the time they meet next, they may not want me to join.* She shook off the melancholy and exchanged phone numbers and email addresses with Aneesa.

"Olivia! Salted caramel macchiato," a young man shouted from behind the counter.

"That's my order. I'll see you later."

"Oh, please sit. You haven't had any wine yet." Aneesa pointed to the bottle of Catena Zapata malbec.

Olivia leaned over and whispered, "That wine won't force me to smile more or make me 'not see color,' right?"

The women laughed, but Kelli responded, "Oh, it'll make you smile, all right."

Olivia took a glass, and the women moved on from the book to chatter about their families.

"The Nelsons will be here next week. You know Selene had that surgery, so they had to delay it."

"Oh, that's good. She deserves some rest, poor thing, after her husband died."

Dana turned to face Olivia. "How's our mayor doing? I haven't seen him out and about as much."

"I . . . think he's doing fine, I suppose." Olivia shrugged. "N-not sure why he isn't as social."

"Oh, now, I wouldn't call Mayor Jones a social man." Dana shook her head, but her straightened bob never moved a strand. "He can carry a conversation, but he's more action oriented. Which is good, because we need someone to fight for us."

"Hmmm. He's social enough. Saw him out a few months ago with Lauren Miles," whispered Lydia, a short woman with even shorter hair. "Then last year it was that young girl."

"Wait a minute. Back up to Lauren." Kelli leaned closer. "I feel like I've been out of the loop. They're dating now?"

Lydia shrugged. "I saw them at a few events together. Once at dinner in downtown Annapolis. I'm telling you, Lauren is smitten."

"And CJ?" Aneesa asked. Olivia noticed she was the only one who addressed him without the honorific.

"Seems like he's biding his time. Now, don't get me wrong, I don't think our mayor was in love with Riley either, but he and Lauren have no chemistry, if you ask me." Lydia shrugged. "Meanwhile, Lauren is buddying up with Christine. You know how she is about her son."

Carol sucked her teeth. "Intimately."

Lydia looked around and then leaned forward. "Well, seems like she has Christine's blessing and—"

"Ladies, are we going to talk about the book or gossip?" Aneesa cut in.

Kelli gazed at the ground as if she were thinking. Then they all looked at each other and grinned. "Gossip!" They clinked their glasses together and chattered more about the good residents of Highland Beach. Thankfully, the conversation drifted from the mayor to other people who were coming in for the summer.

"Do you have any little ones, Olivia?" Dana's voice boomed, grabbing everyone else's attention.

"You have kids?" Carol asked. "How old? Which chapter of Jack and Jill are they affiliated with?"

"Oh, I . . . no kids just yet." Though she thought of Zora, who would do well in Jack and Jill, an organization run by Black mothers to shape future leaders in the African American community. "But I have a goddaughter, and I think I'll talk to her father about joining the nearest chapter."

"What about her mother?" Kelli asked.

"She passed away when she was a baby." Olivia smiled. "She's such a sweetheart. If you have any recommendations for affiliations near Sag Harbor, I'll be sure to pass that along."

Carol took her contact information and promised to email her details. After about another hour, they ended the meeting. Before Olivia could leave, Aneesa tapped her shoulder.

"Do you have a few minutes to talk?" Aneesa asked once the other women had filed out of the building.

"Sure . . . of course."

"Okay, good." Aneesa waved at the sofa. She looked around and then finally settled her warm, chocolate eyes on Olivia.

"I know who you are."

Olivia stiffened on the oversized sofa. After absorbing Aneesa's shocking news, she stood to leave, but when the older woman reached out to touch her knee, she settled back down.

"I'm not here to threaten you, and I don't gossip. Well, not in a bad way," she amended.

"I know Cindy," Aneesa went on. "I was her best friend growing up. In fact, I helped her choose your name. We kept in touch for a few years after she left the area, but then, when your . . . when Chris passed away, she and I fell off. I should've tried harder, but I—"

"You know my mother?" Olivia repeated in shock. She should've known someone would know Cindy.

"Yes. How is she?"

"She's good. Really good." Olivia wasn't sure if she should share the fact that her mother was back in Highland Beach.

"I'm glad. I miss my friend." She shook her head as if she were disappointed in something. Herself, maybe? "I should have been there for her." Aneesa's words confirmed Olivia's guess.

"I should've . . . insisted she come back home after everything. We would've taken care of her . . . and you."

"We?"

"Me, your grandmother, God rest her soul. This community. We take care of our own, even if Christine would've had a conniption."

Olivia tilted her head, recalling her mother's words, though she couldn't remember how Cindy felt about Highland Beach. She'd grown up nearby in Annapolis. Cindy once told her that to travel to the exclusive beach town, she either borrowed her mother's car or asked CJ and Chris for a ride. She'd been clear about Christine and CJ, but the community itself? Olivia couldn't say. But knowing

Cindy, Olivia thought she would've assumed that the community, since she technically did not live there, would side with Christine.

"Does anyone else in Highland Beach know about my mother's pregnancy?" Cindy had shared that although some people might remember her, they didn't know about Olivia, since she stayed away from Highland Beach during her pregnancy.

Obviously, that wasn't true. Aneesa was living proof.

The woman shook her head, leaning forward. "She knew tongues would wag, so she stayed away," she answered, lowering her voice. "If she's worried about coming back, those who would recognize her would remember her only as the girl who dated CJ for a few summers.

"I hope this question isn't too intrusive," Aneesa added, "but I thought about you and Cindy often over the years." She nibbled her bottom lip. "Were you both okay back then?"

Olivia's defensive armor slipped away, and she wondered what it would have been like if Cindy had stayed in Highland Beach. "We did just fine in New Jersey. We had some amazing people who helped us. They were like family to me." She thought back on all the things Omar and Ama had done for them. For Omar, that generosity was born out of guilt: he'd made an honest mistake and revealed Chris as a whistleblower while working for the police force. But over the years his guilt was transformed into love, as Olivia knew now, and remembering that filled her heart with comfort.

"What is Cindy doing now?"

Olivia internally debated. She'd like to confirm Aneesa's purported best friend status before she divulged more details about her mother.

When Olivia didn't respond, Aneesa pointed her finger. "Okay, Fort Knox. I'll let you keep your secrets. Just give your mother my number and tell her she had better call me. We've got twenty-five years of catchup to do."

The drive home had been quiet and contemplative. Olivia had

been shocked by Aneesa's immediate recognition of her. She was also shocked by the conversation surrounding Lauren Miles. CJ really needed to make sure his slate was squeaky clean before pursuing her mother. She didn't want her mother labeled a pariah, or "the other woman." And no matter what Aneesa had said about benign gossip, it was never fun being on the receiving end.

She parked the car and found her mother seated at the table alone, eating a salad. Cindy wiped her mouth and greeted Olivia, while looking over her daughter's shoulder. Olivia knew who her mother was waiting for, though she would never admit it.

Olivia glanced at her watch. It was just past eight o'clock, but she didn't really know the mayor's hours.

"He had to stay a bit later." Olivia answered her silent question. "I actually went into town, grabbed a coffee, and I . . ." She walked to the table and sat across from her mother. "I ran into one of your old friends."

"A friend?" Cindy looked genuinely confused. Olivia's stomach dropped. Was that woman a charlatan?

"Aneesa."

"Aneesa!" Cindy clapped a hand over her mouth. She let out a muffled cry.

"She claimed you two were best friends."

Cindy nodded, with her hand still covering her mouth. She rocked in her seat, as if someone had tugged a thread that unraveled her balance.

Olivia reached into her purse and pulled out the folded sheet of paper. "She wants to reconnect."

Cindy lowered her hand and grabbed the paper with shaking fingers. "I'll call her." Her lips pulled down into a frown. She looked worried, sad.

"For what it's worth, Aneesa really wants to talk to you. I don't think she'll give you too hard of a time. She just misses you."

"I shut her out." Cindy licked her lips. "I . . . I knew if I contacted her, if we talked like we used to do, that she'd call me out. I know she wouldn't recognize me."

"You changed a lot?"

Cindy laughed. "A little. Now, I've never been what you'd call a warm person. I've always been a little closed off." She huffed. "I am an open-and-shut case of having daddy issues."

"You do?" Cindy rarely talked of her mother and hadn't said a peep over the years about her father.

"Your grandfather left me and your grandmother, Eileen, high and dry. He had an entire other family somewhere in Virginia, and I guess he loved them best because he left us. Told us he had to make a choice and that he was very sorry, but he couldn't handle two households."

Deep down, Olivia had known there was something awful about her grandfather. And now, learning this about him, she had an even better understanding of why CJ's actions were so painful for her mother.

Once, in the natural curiosity of a ten-year-old, Olivia had asked about her grandfather after Cindy shared a sweet memory about Olivia's grandmother during Christmastime.

"Your grandfather is dead. And good riddance," Cindy said, with so much venom in her voice that Olivia was too afraid to speak for the rest of the day.

Still, Cindy's revelation was shocking as it rolled over her. Taking a page from Dr. LaGrange, Olivia simply waited for her mother to share more at her own pace. Cindy laughed—a pitiful and small laugh. "I became a woman that day. After that, I trusted men as far as I could throw them, and at twelve years old . . . it wasn't very far," she said, shaking her head. "But Aneesa . . . I trusted her. She made me believe in goodness again."

"You'll call her?"

"I will," she answered in a decisive tone. "Tomorrow evening."

Olivia was happy for her mother and Aneesa. They'd have so

much to catch up on, and Aneesa would be excited about Cindy being at Highland Beach. But she'd want to meet up, of course, and then . . . Olivia's stomach dropped. Then maybe her mother would run into Lauren, or maybe Aneesa would mention her to Cindy.

She glanced at her mother, who stared at the paper with Aneesa's phone number.

Olivia cleared her throat. "I think you should know that there is a rumor going around that CJ is dating another woman," Olivia blurted out. "Her name is Lauren Miles. And he was in a relationship about a year ago with someone on his staff. She was . . . younger. But she's out of the picture now. As is Lauren Miles."

Cindy flinched at this news, but then seconds later her face went blank.

"Same old CJ." She shook her head. "Yes, I didn't trust men, but that didn't mean I wasn't attracted to them."

"I spoke with CJ," Olivia began, "and—"

Cindy waved a dismissive hand. "Did you know Aneesa and I met him and Chris on the same day?"

Olivia shook her head. Of course, she didn't. Her mother rarely, if ever, spoke of Chris and CJ. It was as if she'd jammed all her hurt feelings in a mason jar and tossed it to the bottom of the ocean.

"Aneesa and I lived in the same apartment complex in Annapolis. We were in eighth grade, called ourselves 'grown,' and went down to Venice Beach to see some boys we met at the mall. That's when we met Chris and CJ." Her mother wore a dreamy smile on her face.

She didn't know her mother could be so soft and so loving. A year ago, she would've argued that Cindy was too practical to dream. Shame chased that errant thought away. Olivia, of all people, understood the hidden emotional depths of a Black woman. Why share the pain when the world had shown little care for your feelings?

"Chris was running around with friends and stopped in his tracks. Then he introduced himself as if I was supposed to know who he was or be impressed." Cindy laughed.

"He was friendly, chatting away. He bought me a popsicle and introduced me to CJ, but he didn't have to. I saw him . . . *felt* him staring at me," she whispered, more to herself it seemed, and so low that Olivia wondered if Cindy realized what she'd been sharing.

"That's how I spent my weekends that summer. Me, Aneesa, Chris, and CJ. Some other friends, too. Chris was dating some stuck-up girl at the time, but they broke up when she went back home for the school year. Then Chris and I became closer. Best friends. He'd often drive to see me when he got his license.

"Christine loathed me. I think she knew what I didn't realize back then." Cindy looked up from her salad at Olivia with wet eyes. "That Chris loved me, but I had my eyes, my heart, fixed on CJ." Cindy's voice hitched. "Stupid me. I could've been loving Chris the entire time instead of falling for a boy, for a *man*, who would break my heart time and time again."

"Mom . . ."

Cindy reached out and squeezed Olivia's hand. "Thank you for telling me about Lauren."

"We don't know anything concrete just yet. It's just gossip. Hearsay. CJ himself told me they aren't anything serious." Olivia's heart thumped. Maybe she should've waited. She'd done this before with Perry and royally screwed up. She'd done it with her friend Kara, too.

Would she ever learn to just shut her mouth?

I can fix this.

"Mom, listen to me." She squeezed her mother's hand.

Cindy shook her head.

"No, please listen to me. This is important, okay?"

Cindy's dark and weary eyes focused on Olivia. "Okay."

"I didn't tell you about Lauren so you'd retreat. I told you so you could be prepared for the whispers. You should be fully aware when you eventually go into town."

"It doesn't matter."

"It does. Because you matter to me and to CJ. He doesn't know how to reconnect with you. He's made it abundantly clear to you and to me what his intentions are. He stood up to Christine and left when she disrespected you. If he could, I'd bet he would shout how he feels from the rooftops." Olivia sighed, realizing her own role in this.

Olivia didn't want him to acknowledge their existence because she was afraid of the backlash.

I'm tired of secrets.

Secrets had a shelf life. What's more, it became so much worse when the owner of the lie didn't bring them to light.

CJ wanted to own that he abandoned his family, but Olivia wouldn't let him. And now, the shame Olivia harbored around her birth created distance between them.

She hated the distance, and she wanted to get to know her father openly, without restrictions.

"I have to give him permission to talk about us," Olivia said slowly, accepting what she must do.

"I'm scared," Cindy admitted.

"Me, too. But we must be brave."

Cindy surprised her with a quick hug. "You have a good heart, Olivia Jones."

Olivia sat frozen at first, but then finally squeezed back when Cindy didn't let go.

"It takes a lot of work. A lot of . . . therapy."

"Well, I hope it helps me. I feel like I'm just unearthing a lot of old and painful memories right now."

"It is working," Olivia assured her mother. "A year ago, you wouldn't have shared about your past. You couldn't speak about Chris without shutting down."

"So we're going to do this? Strut around Highland Beach and tell the world you're the mayor's daughter."

"And Cindy's daughter, too." A rush of nervous energy made her entire body shake. She drummed her knees with her fingers to relax her nerves. "We'll need to talk to CJ and Alan to see how they want to handle the communications."

Cindy nodded, and then finally she smiled wide and slow like the Cheshire Cat revealing its presence to Alice.

The change of heart surprised Olivia. "You're happy about this?"

"Oh, I just thought about Christine's reaction." Cindy widened her smile. "I'm looking forward to it."

They both laughed. Her mother stood. "If you're hungry, there's salad in the fridge. I think I'm going to get in some rest." She stretched her arms overhead. "Tell CJ I'll talk to him early tomorrow morning. I think we should craft a plan as soon as possible."

Olivia agreed. "I'll let him know if he's here before I go to bed."

By the time Olivia ate the salad and showered, she was drooping like an unwatered plant left in the sun. It had been a long and emotionally draining day, and she just wanted to nod off. CJ texted to let her know he was still at the office, catching up on paperwork that was due in the morning.

She let him know that she and Cindy wanted to catch him before work the next day. He replied with a thumbs-up.

Olivia slept, but not without strain and worry. She didn't know what to expect from Highland Beach, but she hoped the community would be accepting.

She woke up the next morning to a hurried knock. Opening the door, she found CJ's frowning face, heated eyes, and clenched jaw.

"Good . . . morning?" Olivia greeted him with a question in her voice.

CJ grunted.

"I still don't understand your grunting."

"It means . . ." she heard Cindy's voice from behind CJ, "that someone beat us to our announcement."

CJ tapped his phone and showed it to Olivia. She recognized the Highland Beach newspaper's Facebook page. Her attention snagged on an anonymous comment.

There was a picture of Olivia laughing with the Highland Beach Bookworms. The poster had circled her face in red with the comment:

This is Olivia Jones, Mayor Jones' child. @Highlandbeachmayor Why hide your daughter? Are you ashamed?

Olivia's eyesight went blurry. This was a nightmare.

"Oh my God." It had to be Aneesa. Olivia shook her head. No, Aneesa was in the picture, though the poster had been kind enough to blur her face. It was someone else. Someone had suspected her identity and followed her into Main & Market. The same someone she thought she felt following her to CJ's job and watching her when she used his car to drive to the coffee shop.

Her body went cold with the realization. Someone really had been following her.

"What do we do?" She lifted her head and met CJ's heated stare.

"How do you feel? Are you okay?"

Olivia stepped back into her room and sat on her unmade bed. She shook her head, gathered herself close, and curled into a ball. She wasn't ready to reveal her identity—not like this.

"I'm fine." The lie tumbled out of her mouth with ease. She was not okay. Not even close.

CHAPTER SEVEN

May 2022

RUN AWAY

Hi. I'm Olivia Jones and I'm a coward.

She repeated this to herself for the umpteenth time during her drive to Sag Harbor. After the infamous social media post heard 'round the world, or at least in Highland Beach, Olivia did not, in fact, face the music. Instead, she muted it and ran away from the beautiful beach town and into the welcoming arms of Sag Harbor.

She did not want to endure the stares. The whispers. The judgment. As if she could control the messy situation surrounding her birth. She thought she was ready for the world to know the truth, but it had to be on her own terms. Not like this.

She would spend an entire week, or maybe forever, with Garrett, Zora, and the rest of her beloved neighbors.

But before she connected with her friends, before she even went home, she had an emergency appointment set with Dr. LaGrange.

As soon as the psychiatrist opened the door, Olivia jumped straight into conversation.

"Everything is horrible. Just horrible. We've got a lot to cover in the next hour." Olivia nervously adjusted the wide bangles that bracketed her floral Gucci watch.

"I can carve out more time if you need it."

"Oh, I need it." Olivia snatched the offer of more time like extra stock in Disney.

While Dr. LaGrange told her assistant to block off the next two hours, Olivia made herself comfortable on a plush sofa.

The doctor returned, and Olivia noted her new aquamarine tortoiseshell glasses and hairstyle. Her hair, formerly a big, beautiful Afro, was now braided into smaller plaits.

"I like the new look, Dr. LaGrange."

The doctor tentatively patted her hair, as if to reassure herself that she'd made the right choice.

"I'm finally making the jump to sister locks. I've been wanting to do so for years, but it was hard to let go of my 'fro."

"What made you decide to change your hair?"

"I finally forced myself to accept that it's just hair. If I don't like it, I can always shave it off and start over."

Olivia stiffened her body to stop her shudder. She wasn't interested in starting over in any aspect of her life. She'd done enough of that in the past year.

"Enough about me. Where's the fire?" Dr. LaGrange waved at Olivia.

"I've been outed."

"You're expanding your sexual preferences?"

"Oh no. Not that type of outing." Olivia waved her hands.

"Hmm. Well then, that's an inaccurate word choice."

"Sorry." Olivia took a deep breath. "The good people of Highland Beach know that CJ is my father."

"Oh. Ohhh." Dr. LaGrange's thick eyebrows rose so high her eyeglasses rose onto her forehead. "What happened?"

Olivia crossed her arms and rubbed at the goose bumps that marched along her forearms. "Someone anonymously posted on the town's newspaper Facebook page. They even snapped a picture of me."

Dr. LaGrange looked alarmed.

"I didn't even notice, but someone was following me. I'm so . . . so embarrassed by everything."

"What makes you embarrassed?"

"The entire situation!" Olivia's voice pitched high. "My mother had a baby with one brother and married the other. I didn't sign up to be in a soap opera."

"I can understand. But certainly the town will understand that they don't know the full story. Context that either your father or mother can fill in if they feel they need to explain themselves to the town."

Olivia massaged her forehead. Before she had fled, Christine and Alan came to CJ's house to discuss a plan of action. CJ didn't feel the need to explain anything, but Alan had all but insisted they do so. Christine had yelled, had even snapped on Olivia for not lying low until they could figure out a proper strategy to reveal her existence.

That had hurt. A lot.

It had taken everything in Olivia to stand still and adopt a cool, unaffected look, even though she was shaking inside by Christine's sharp accusation.

She had excused herself from the room, gone to her bedroom, and locked the door, ignoring several rounds of insistent knocking as she set about packing her bags.

So yes, Olivia fully embraced her cowardice. Though she felt guilty for leaving her mother unprotected.

"Alan, that's Christine's husband—"

"And Christine is your grandmother?" her therapist asked.

Olivia let out an ugly laugh. "Not sure who she's claiming these days, but technically, yes, she's my grandmother. Her husband, Alan, insists we host a town hall meeting to explain the post. They plan to keep it at a high level: Cindy and Chris formed a relationship and left Highland Beach. Chris died a few years later in the line of duty. CJ later reconnected with us, and here we are."

Dr. LaGrange tsked.

"I know. It's an awful plan, right? No matter how we craft it, my mother will look like an opportunist."

"Yes, she will." There was a tinge of anger in Dr. LaGrange's voice. She rarely let her emotions roam free.

"CJ wants to admit fault. Alan and Christine disagree."

"And your mother?"

"She's calm." Olivia remembered her mother's serene face. She hadn't raised her voice. She had only one demand, which she relayed in that even, cool tone of hers. "Don't you dare disrespect Chris," she had warned.

"Why do you think she's calm?" Dr. LaGrange asked.

"I don't . . ." Olivia huffed, shaking her head at her epiphany. "I don't think she expects much." Or maybe Cindy was relieved the cat had been wrenched out of the bag?

"Now, how do you feel, Olivia?"

"I already told you . . . humiliated. I feel like Hester in *The Scarlet Letter*, but instead of an **A**, I'm wearing a **B**, for Bastard."

Dr. LaGrange shook her head. "You're being incredibly disrespectful to yourself and your family."

"Do you not remember what happened last summer? Not only that, but how I found out? By CJ barging into my home, no less."

"I do, Olivia. I still think you shouldn't judge them so harshly."

"I'm not." Olivia waved her hands. "Don't get me wrong, I've always wanted a family. I just wish everything hadn't been so complicated. Why couldn't they just talk to each other? Why couldn't CJ just fight for his family?"

When Cindy shared the news of her pregnancy with CJ, he hadn't believed her mother. Christine had shown CJ pictures of Cindy with another man while he was away at college and lied about their relationship.

"I don't disagree with you," Dr. LaGrange said, "but it must have been a shock for him to see your mother kiss his brother after he did in fact try to fight for his family."

"Well, he didn't put up much of a fight," Olivia argued. "He could've confronted his brother right then. And then maybe . . . maybe Chris could still be alive. And I'd have had an actual father growing up."

"But it didn't happen that way. And you must give them time and patience to work through their past. They were, what, in their early twenties?"

"Just barely," Olivia whispered. Although studious and career-focused, Olivia had made plenty of mistakes at that age. "Okay, fine. They deserve a second chance."

"They do. We're only human. And we make mistakes . . . daily. Some small, some gigantic, but it's our capacity to love and forgive that makes us special."

Olivia exhaled. "So I should go back. Be brave."

Dr. LaGrange smiled. "What do you want—"

Olivia covered her face and groaned. "I'm too tired to think, Dr. LaGrange. Just tell me what I should do."

When the doctor laughed, Olivia dropped her hands.

"You should return when you feel it's best. I think you should take care of yourself, too. Take a few days or a few weeks and then return to Highland Beach. Now, it's not up to you to fix their mess. I simply ask that you not judge your parents too harshly."

By the end of the session, Olivia had stopped calling herself a coward. She wasn't weak, just incredibly exhausted.

After she left Dr. LaGrange's office, she texted her parents to let them know she would no longer hide and would be back by next week, but that she had no plans to show up for the town hall meeting and put herself on display, as Alan had suggested.

As Olivia drove down her street, the anxiety from the past forty-eight hours rolled away like the tide. She couldn't wait to see Garrett, though she had to wait because he was chaperoning a field trip with Zora's kindergarten class.

When she parked her car, she noticed another car pull in just behind her. She didn't recognize the electric blue Range Rover.

They both stepped out of their respective cars. The woman was around her age, with long braids that brushed the middle of her back. Olivia gave her a friendly wave and a smile.

"Hello. I'm Olivia Jones."

"O-oh." The woman's smile faltered.

Oh no. Did she hear something bad? Olivia thought she'd fully redeemed herself by driving the ASK developers away, but maybe that rumor lingered?

"I don't believe we've met." Olivia held her smile steady.

"I'm Francesca McCoy. I bought the house next to you from the Larsons."

"Oh! I heard they were selling." Olivia smiled brightly. She was glad Whitney had found someone nice to purchase the home. "Well, I'm a bit late, but welcome to the neighborhood."

"Thank you so much. I've been here for a few weeks, and everyone's been so welcoming."

"I must have just missed you then. So sorry I couldn't have welcomed you sooner."

"Oh, that's fine," Francesca responded, her voice distant. Not rude but distracted.

Francesca glanced past Olivia's shoulder.

Turning to see what was distracting her new neighbor, Olivia noticed she was staring at Garrett's doorway.

He'd opened it, stopped, and grinned like a loon when he saw Olivia. His long legs quickly covered the short distance between them. "Olivia."

"Hey, you." Olivia wrapped her arms around Garrett's waist and gave him a long hug. "I thought you were on a field trip with Zora?"

"One kid got sick, so they ended a little early."

"Oh no. Is Zora okay?"

"She's perfectly fine, and she can't wait to see you. She almost threw a tantrum when I left her at school."

A delicate throat clearing pulled their attention away from each other.

"Oh yes!" Olivia turned and found the lovely Ms. McCoy batting her bright brown eyes. "I was just introducing myself to our new neighbor, Francesca."

Francesca smiled at her. Her smile was a bit too wide. In fact, Olivia couldn't tell if she was smiling or baring her teeth, but decided to ignore it.

"Thank you for your help the other night." Francesca's eyes focused on Garrett, as if Olivia did not exist.

Help?

Olivia swiveled her attention to Garrett.

"Oh, it was nothing." He looked down at Olivia. "Mr. Whittingham and I fixed her faucet."

"Oh, that's very neighborly of you."

He winked at Olivia. "You know me. I aim to please." He looked over Olivia's head. "Well, Francesca. We've got to get going. We've got lots of neighborly things to catch up on." He pulled Olivia's hand and set off toward his house.

"Garrett!" she laughed as he nearly dragged her across the yard and into his home.

"Bye, Francesca!" She waved at the unblinking woman.

Undeterred by her wave, Garrett pulled her close to his side.

"Now, Garrett—"

"Sorry. I'm starving," he said once they were inside the door. He kicked it shut, cupped her face, and kissed her deeply. Desire hit her hard and fast.

She was burning up—sparked by fire, lit by joy. She'd forgotten how delicious spearmint tasted on his lips.

As if a gun had gone off at the start of a race, they hurriedly pulled off each other's clothes.

"I miss you," Olivia gasped between kisses.

"Me, too. You were gone for too long."

It had only been a week, but she didn't have time to tease him.

He lifted her and moved them to his bedroom, then tossed her down on his soft king-sized bed. "Put me in," he growled.

She shivered at his demand. Sometimes Garrett could be so incredibly gentle she felt like crying.

But today he was in a mood. A mood to dominate.

"Do it, Olivia," he demanded in a dangerous whisper, pulling her legs apart. He nudged at the opening, daring her to give in. She stared at him, a living work of art, raking her fingers across the sprinkling of hair that covered his broad chest.

"Do it," he said between soft kisses along her collarbone.

Her fingers dragged down his long, muscled back to his thick thighs.

"Olivia. Now."

She finally honored his demand, cupped his ass, and guided him inside.

He hissed as if she burned. He paused for a moment and then thrust deeper.

She squeezed, gasping, overwhelmed by his strength.

He groaned in her ear, rocking back and forth with ferocity.

"Garrett, I—"

"Miss your smile, your taste . . ." He was breathing heavily, as though he'd run a marathon. "Miss you . . ."

Olivia kissed his throat until the first wave of her orgasm hit. Locking her legs around his waist, she clenched his shoulders and held on until they crashed in bliss.

"Wow." She gasped between breaths. "Wow."

He rolled off her body and pulled her close.

"Been thinking about doing that all day. Nearly killed me to go on the field trip."

Olivia laughed into his chest.

"I'm serious. I hope little Gabby is okay, but I've never been so happy to see vomit."

Olivia slapped his chest. "I need to go back home and shower."

"Shower here."

"I have my things in the car." Olivia moved to the edge of the bed.

"Please. I just want you close."

"I suppose I can continue to grace you with my presence."

Garrett laughed and tugged her back to his chest. "Good of you to do that."

They held tight to each other.

Garrett sighed. "I don't know how I'm going to go the entire summer without you near."

She pulled away, staring into his eyes. "It's tough for me, too, but I want to—"

"Get to know your father." The tips of his fingers brushed her chin. "Trust me, I get it. You deserve time to get to know him."

"It's your fault, you know," she whispered.

Garrett laughed. "How is this my fault?"

"Seeing you and Zora just . . . made me want to try. You don't just provide for her financially, you really are her best friend right now."

"Oh, no one's taking my spot for best friend. Ever."

"If you say so." Laughter bubbled inside her like spring water. She dipped her nose into his chest, attempting to smother her laughter.

"Maybe I'm in denial. I mean, she's already replaced me with her new friend, Iman." He frowned as if the other six-year-old had wronged him.

"Bring that smile back." Olivia pressed her fingers into his dimple.

He shook his head. "No, it's too late."

"Fine. I can be your best friend."

"That's a huge step from best neighbor."

"Well . . . if you don't want to be my new bestie—"

Before she could finish, Garrett kissed her, thoroughly and deeply. And so, so sweet, she could cry.

"I want to be everything to you, Olivia Jones. Do you know what I'm saying?"

She shivered at his confession. Without a doubt, she felt everything in that kiss. She could only nod. The words he said, *without saying*, were too important. And if she opened her mouth, she would undoubtedly make a mumbled and jumbled mess of a response.

"Am I scaring you?"

"Not by a lot." She put two fingers together with a tiny space between the digits. "Just a little."

"Don't be afraid. I'm a patient man." He kissed her nose. "I'll get your things. You just stay here." He stood and then put on his underwear, jogging pants, and shoes. He started for the door.

"Where's your shirt?" Her sharp voice made him pause at the doorway.

"Somewhere on the floor?" He shrugged. "I'll just run out and—"

"Oh no you don't. Francesca McCoy does not get to see your bare chest." The woman would probably break everything in her house so Garrett could come over to fix them.

"I'm pretty sure she's already seen me."

"What? When?" Olivia pushed up from the bed.

"We live on a beach, Olivia."

She pouted. "I don't care. Besides, you need to take care of your skin."

"I wear sunscreen. And I have melanin."

And lots of it, Olivia thought, smiling. Garrett's skin was as chocolate as her own.

"A shirt offers better protection."

"Are you jealous, Olivia Jones?"

"No. It's just painfully clear that fixing her faucet is a double entendre for Francesca."

"I don't care what she wants." He dipped his knee into the bed and bent his head low. "I only want you," he whispered against her lips. "I'm *your* boyfriend. Not hers."

She shivered at the feeling of his lips against hers. "Good." She cupped his neck and kissed him. "Very good."

Olivia tried to forget about Francesca, but then recalled Anderson's jealousy toward Garrett. Hugging her boyfriend tight, she could only hope karma skipped her this time around.

CHAPTER EIGHT

May 2022

JUST A FRIEND

Even though Garrett wanted her to stay at his place, she convinced him that she needed to briefly check on her home.

Olivia opened her door, expecting a stale smell to hit, but the smell of lemon greeted her.

A note sat on her table, along with a vase of flowers. Olivia smiled, leaned over, and smelled the surprise gift. A small placard bore familiar handwriting.

> **I'll be waiting for my invitation to play chess.**
> **—Mr. Whittingham**

Olivia immediately picked up her phone.

"Hello, neighbor." Her friend's familiar deep voice came through the speaker.

"Mr. Whittingham. Thank you so much for the flowers." She stroked the mixture of daisies, tulips, and sunflowers.

"Of course. You deserve beauty." He cleared his throat. "Your father called. He told me what happened."

Olivia sighed. "I'm sure he's upset that I left."

"Your father is upset, but not because of your actions. He's upset with himself. CJ promised to protect you and your mother, and now you're being followed. Be careful. Check your surroundings, you hear?"

"I hear," Olivia replied softly. Then she pivoted the conversation. "How about we go for a walk and play a game tomorrow?"

"Of course. I'll meet you at eight a.m.?"

"Sounds like a date, Mr. Whittingham."

"All right. Garrett tells me you're having dinner at Whitney and Charles's place?"

"Yes. Along with Kara, Rich, and Addy." Olivia had met her Sag Harbor neighbors only last summer. Their bond had been quickly solidified, however, when they came together to defend their neighborhood against gentrification. Now they'd become sounding boards and very dear friends.

On Olivia's drive to Sag Harbor, she had given Whitney the *Reader's Digest* version of what had happened in Highland Beach, and her friend had insisted on catering a dinner for Olivia when she got home. She let Whitney give the details to her other neighbors, and now friends, Kara and Addy, but had made it clear that Addy had to keep it a secret from others. Though her friend was a huge gossip, Addy had a code that she wouldn't share if explicitly asked.

Garrett knocked on her door and then together they took the fifteen-minute walk to Whitney's home.

"I forgot to ask about your appointment with Dr. LaGrange. How did it go?" he asked.

"It went well." Olivia nodded to reinforce her words, but her tone conveyed uncertainty.

"Are you sure?" Garrett walked backward, studying her face.

"Yes. It was productive." Dr. LaGrange had surprised Olivia when she agreed with her running-away strategy. Well, as her doctor had framed it, Olivia didn't run away so much as prioritize her mental health and safety.

"What?" Garrett's eyes narrowed. "You know, you can talk to me about the hard things."

Olivia stopped walking at his words. "I know, Garrett. But I'm a processer. I like to . . . mull things over and weigh the pros and cons. Trust me, I'm not shutting you out."

"Good. Because I'd just have to pry you open."

"Pry me open?" Olivia smiled. "How would you do that?"

"Seduce you with all of your favorite things."

"Like?"

"A foot massage. Prawns with sweet chili sauce. I'll take you out dancing. Drinks and music on a rooftop bar in New York City. Or maybe I'll just pull together a picnic by the beach. Give you a nice . . . thick . . ." He raised his eyebrows.

"Garrett!"

"Book." He laughed.

Olivia chuckled. "Bah. You don't know me."

"Yes, I do. And if you're feeling *really* stressed, I'll bypass the non-fiction that you have lined up in your office for optics. Something contemporary, maybe a thriller or a beach read." He looked up, as if contemplating the choices. "A thought-provoking beach read."

"Did I tell you CJ's neighbors invited me to join a book club?"

"See? You were already making friends."

"Well, we'll see when I get back. They'll either welcome me with open arms or tar and feather me."

Aneesa, her mother's friend, was likely to be understanding. She knew the history of the Jones family, after all.

When Olivia and Garrett arrived at Whitney's home, their host opened the door and immediately pulled Olivia in for a hug. "Girl, do I need to travel out there and kick somebody's ass?"

Olivia laughed, but she didn't pull away. She hadn't realized just how much she needed a friendly hug.

"No ass-kicking services are necessary. I just need some time away with my people."

Whitney pulled back, a wide grin on her face. "That's right. We are your people."

She stepped back from the door, hooked Olivia's elbow, and guided her to the formal dining room, where the table was set with gleaming polished silverware.

Olivia sat in the middle, and Garrett settled in the seat across from her.

Before Olivia could open her mouth to make a request, Whitney returned with a half bottle of rosé in an Olivia Pope–sized wineglass. If she attempted to toast anyone, the wine would slosh over the table.

"Ummm . . . how many ounces did you put in here?"

"I don't count ounces." Whitney shrugged. "And hurry and drink it before Addy arrives. I am not in the mood to hear her disrespect my wine choices."

Olivia followed directions and quickly sipped the wine. Garrett grinned from across the table.

The doorbell rang, announcing Kara, Rich, and Addy. When the trio entered the room, they exchanged more hugs. Olivia briefly wondered if Kara and Rich still maintained their open marriage, especially now that Kara was traveling again.

Olivia shook her head and smiled. *Not my business.* Besides, her friends looked happy, and that's all she could ask for.

Addy immediately went into nosy mode, wanting all the details.

"Girl, I joined that little Facebook page and saw your picture. It's fuzzy, and it looks like they snapped it through a window."

"I hadn't . . . I only looked at it once." Olivia couldn't recall the post's specific words. She just remembered how she had felt— violated. Like she'd been slapped.

While they caught up, Charles and Whitney started the first course, a creamy summer squash soup.

"Bea sends her love." Kara took a sip of wine. "She couldn't make it tonight. She's in New York with her boo."

"Who, Mike?" Olivia asked, though she knew the answer. Billie still wasn't quite used to her father being in a relationship, let alone with her mother, the woman who'd abandoned them over twenty years ago.

"Yes. They are hot and heavy. She's like a new woman," Kara said before she began to scoop up the delicious soup. "Their PDA is on ten. I saw them last weekend holding hands."

Olivia lowered her spoon. "Our prickly Bea held Mike's hand?"

"Yes." Addy's eyes sparked. "With a smile on her face."

"Wow. The world *is* changing." Olivia shook her head. She'd be sure to call Billie to tease her. Her godsister needed a good laugh these days, what with her limited sleep thanks to life with a newborn. "What else is new around here?"

Addy glanced at Kara, who then looked at Whitney, who then zeroed her attention on Garrett.

"More like who's new in town." Whitney lifted her eyebrow and cut a glance at Garrett.

Olivia immediately knew who they were referring to. "I've met my new neighbor. Francesca McCoy, right?"

Whitney nodded. "She's got her eye on Garrett."

Garrett groaned. "No, she doesn't."

"Yes, she does, best friend," Addy responded. "Get this," she added, leaning forward, her eyes glittering with mischief. "She asked me for his number yesterday."

Olivia's mouth dropped open. "No, she didn't."

"Yes, she did! With claims that she needs more help around the house. I recommended Thumbtack for a maintenance worker, since Garrett has his hands full with Zora and his beautiful and accomplished girlfriend."

Olivia couldn't help but laugh at the smirk on Addy's face. "You didn't."

"You're welcome. Also, I took it upon myself to get the scoop on Francesca. She's an architect for a big firm in New York, and I hear she's very good. And your lovely neighbor got divorced a little over a year ago. Her ex-husband was well off, one of the managing partners at the architecture firm, and she received a nice settlement—"

"How do you know all of this?" Kara interrupted her friend.

"Some things she told me, and some things I found out through my contacts in the city."

Whitney sighed. "Look, she's not a bad person. She just needs to fix her eyes elsewhere." Then she stood, saying she was going to get the shrimp cocktail.

"Well, enough about Francesca," Olivia said, in an attempt to end the conversation about the woman who most definitely was interested in her boyfriend. "She hasn't done anything wrong." *Yet*.

Addy shrugged. "Okay, then. Let's talk about your plan of attack when you return to Highland Beach."

"Or we can just talk about something else." Kara smacked her friend's shoulder. "You aren't going to change, are you?"

Addy looked genuinely confused. "Why would I?"

Kara sighed. Olivia took advantage of the small reprieve to ask about Kara's latest work.

"I'm doing an art show in New York in December. Right now I'm working on pieces for the exhibition. I hope you can make it."

"Of course. What's your theme?"

"The world is a gift. The intention is to showcase that life can be complicated and messy, and so the themes will encompass both light and dark as well as shades of gray elements." She looked at Rich without judgment, but with love. "But life can also be beautiful. I just want to remind people to enjoy the journey."

Rich leaned over and kissed her. Addy, to her credit, looked unbothered. No, Olivia would never understand their arrangement, but she reminded herself again that it wasn't her place to judge.

Garrett grabbed her hand and attention, giving her a gorgeous smile. An army of butterflies stormed her stomach.

Will it always be this way with Garrett? Or would time diminish our feelings and allow someone else to step into the relationship?

Francesca wasn't the only woman who would find Garrett attractive. Olivia didn't want to feel insecure, but the thought of someone taking her place in Garrett's heart was terrifying.

CHAPTER NINE

May 2022

THE SHIFTING TIDES

The following morning, she woke up early, but not nearly early enough. Mr. Whittingham was sitting in his spot below her raised deck, ready to play chess at a quarter to eight.

"Mr. Whittingham." She smiled down at him from her porch.

"Hi, neighbor." He smiled and waved. "Sorry I'm a bit early. I was too excited to sleep in."

Olivia laughed at his excuse and was glad to note that nothing about Mr. Whittingham had changed. He still arrived early for any event or appointment. He wore his summer uniform: a white polo shirt, khaki shorts, and a hat for his long walks.

"Never change, Mr. Whittingham," Olivia muttered under her breath. She smiled and said out loud, "Would you like water, coffee, or tea?"

"I'll have some of that infamous coffee your godmother Ama created. Garrett goes on and on about it."

"I've got a fresh pot. I'll be right back."

Olivia returned with two cups of dark roast with chicory and whipped cream—Ama's recipe—and placed the hot beverages near the concrete chessboard.

Mr. Whittingham waved at the board, and they immediately started playing. For once, they started the game in silence. Each held victories over the other, and what had started off as pure fun had transformed into a battle of minds. When Olivia made a strategic move that nearly guaranteed her win, Mr. Whittingham winced.

"Care to make a wager?"

Olivia lifted her attention from the board to her friendly opponent. "On this game?"

"Yes." He nodded.

"The one you're about to lose?" Olivia grinned. He could handle the smack talk.

He nodded again. "The very one."

"All right. Name your stakes."

"If I win, you will go home in two days."

"This is my home."

He lowered his chin and eyebrows, and Olivia just knew he'd given his children the same disapproving look when they smarted off.

Olivia sighed. "Did CJ put you up to this?"

"No." Mr. Whittingham shook his head.

"Then why do you want me to leave? I thought you missed our neighborly chats and beekeeping."

"And I do. Miss it even more now that Bea's back with her husband."

"Then why?"

Mr. Whittingham leaned back in his chair and crossed his legs.

"Young lady, when I met you, you were incredibly sad and lost. And respectfully, you were with a young man with whom you were not well matched."

Olivia gasped. "Anderson wasn't poor. And he had lots of potential."

"When I say 'well matched,' I'm not speaking of money. His family has millions. I'm not even speaking of class. What I mean is that you did not love him. And Anderson . . . he loved the idea of you. And that simply cannot sustain a relationship."

"We aren't together anymore, so I don't understand why we are having this conversation."

"Because you focused so much on that relationship, you couldn't see the possibilities of your future. You didn't see that you could have neighbors turn into friends who adore you. Or being a godmother to a motherless child. You wouldn't . . . stop running long enough to see the beauty of growth." He furrowed his eyebrows. "That's why I wanted you to slow down. Walk with me, play a game. How else could you appreciate things when you're always running?"

Olivia held her breath. She wouldn't interrupt him. Mr. Whittingham rarely had an unkind word to say, and something told her to hold her words and listen.

"And now you're running again, aren't you?"

Olivia shook her head. "No. Even Dr. LaGrange said I needed to give myself space to process. It's a good thing."

"That's baloney."

"It's not baloney. It's me, slowing down, my way."

"You ran, young lady. I've seen for myself that your spirits are high and your eyes are clear. It's time to go back and stand beside your mother and father."

"For what?" Her voice went high. "CJ's never stood beside me. Not when I was born, not for any graduations, not once over the years when I've had my heart broken. Why should I care?"

"You aren't afraid of chatter, Olivia. You're mad. And you have every right to be. But this self-care that you speak of includes letting go of that anger and hurt, letting the poison inside of you clear. It's about embracing adventure and saying yes to the quest."

Olivia crossed her arms. The pep talk had soured her mood, but she wouldn't be disrespectful to her neighbor. "I'm not in the mood for adventure."

"But aren't you? I believe you once told me you wanted to get to know your father. You wanted to understand why he never came back for you and your mom. Well, there's more to the story than hurt feelings."

"Like what? If you know something, tell me."

"The reason CJ stuck around Highland Beach, the reason he became mayor, was that he wanted to understand what happened to his sister. He thought there'd been a cover-up."

Olivia nearly cracked her chess piece. "Did someone murder her?" Olivia was under the impression that Indigo had drowned.

"He doesn't know. Never did find out. But something happened between him and his sister the night she died, and . . . I don't know, he decided if he couldn't be a good big brother to her, or to Chris, he couldn't be a good father."

Olivia shook her head. "Still, that's no excuse. After what happened with Chris, he should have reached out."

Mr. Whittingham shook his head. "Now, Chris, he didn't want—" He sighed, shaking his head.

"He didn't what?"

"That's not my place to say. You've got to have your own conversations."

Olivia clenched her jaw and quickly moved her piece. "Checkmate." She stood up from her seat. "I'm sorry, but I'll need a rain check on our walk today as I'm suddenly not feeling so well."

"Of course, and I'm sorry I came down on you so hard. Olivia, I've enjoyed watching you blossom, but you still have more growing to do. I don't want this situation to make you shy away from the sunlight."

He handed Olivia his empty mug and, with sad eyes, walked away from her yard. Olivia stomped back inside her house, fuming.

She couldn't believe her sweet, genial neighbor had said those things to her. "I'm not running. I'm pivoting," she said to no one.

So what if she hadn't answered Cindy's or CJ's calls? She'd communicated on her terms and told them she'd be in touch.

Olivia massaged her temples.

"I mean, someone snapped my picture and posted it on the town's Facebook page, for goodness' sake."

She'd bet the image had gone viral. Olivia opened her laptop, searched for the group, and saw that it had been taken down. But a few comments caught her eye.

Who posted the picture of that poor baby?

That comment had gotten over a hundred likes.

I've seen her jogging! She certainly looks like a Jones.

Whoever posted that picture should be ashamed! I know almost everyone in this town, and we don't tolerate paparazzi.

There were a few more comments. Some rather benign about her looks and a purported run-in. Some were mean-spirited, but mostly they berated CJ about having a child in secret.

None had been about Cindy. For her mother's peace of mind, she was grateful.

Olivia needed advice, but not from Garrett, who she knew wanted her to stay. And not from her parents—they obviously wanted her back at Highland Beach.

She took a shot in the dark and sent a text to the women she trusted most in the world.

In need of some advice. Can you all talk this afternoon while Libby and Isabel are napping?

Ama was in France, so the timing would work.

Over the course of two hours, Billie, Perry, and then finally Ama texted to confirm their availability. Ama had tried calling, but Olivia diverted her call. She didn't think she could relive the humiliation more than once in a day.

The FaceTime ringtone trilled at the agreed-upon time. Perry had been the first to dial in, then Ama, and finally Billie, whose face was flushed red.

"Hi," Olivia greeted her godmother and godsisters.

"Hello yourself, young lady." Ama sat regally at what appeared to be a table in a vineyard.

"I've called you twice today." Ama lifted two fingers. "And I do not appreciate being ignored. I have been on pins and needles all day, imagining the worst, when I need to focus on developing my special wine. Now what is going on?"

"Sorry, Ama. But where are you?"

"I've bought a vineyard in Provence. Discussion for another day."

Billie suppressed a smile while Perry looked alarmed.

"Someone discovered that I'm CJ's daughter. They posted a picture of me on the town's Facebook page. And so . . . now I'm in Sag Harbor. I ran away, and I'm unsure if it was the right thing to do."

"Who posted it?" Ama narrowed her eyes. Her pale skin flushed red.

"It was anonymous. They likely created a dummy account."

"Everything has a trace. I'll find out who the culprit is, don't you worry."

"How are you feeling?" Perry whispered fiercely.

"Embarrassed by both the post and my actions. Mr. Whittingham told me this morning that I keep running away from things."

Perry bit her lip, but she didn't respond.

But Billie sang, "She's a runner, she's a track star."

"Billie," Olivia snapped.

"What? It's just a song."

"I want advice, not jokes."

Billie sighed. "Listen, you've grown by leaps and bounds ever since you've been to therapy. So I don't say this lightly, but in the past you have walked away. And then when you walk away, you just sit on your feelings until they fester. But given the situation, I totally understand why you would want to get out of town for a few days."

Olivia nodded. She wasn't offended by Billie's assessment. "But if you were me, would you go back?"

"Hell, yes. No one is going to run me out of town. I leave on *my* terms."

"Language, Billie," Ama admonished.

"Yes, Grandmother." Billie rolled her eyes. "I thought being part of the moms' club gave me a pass."

"To use unbecoming language in front of your elders?" Ama harrumphed. "Absolutely not.

"Now, my darling Olivia." Ama gentled her tone. "You aren't some wilting flower who shrinks under adversity. You've faced tougher odds, you've gone head-to-head with the worst of the worst. Go back to that place, hold your head high, and if they dare disrespect you, put them in their place."

"Amen." Perry clapped.

"Now, tell me how Ms. Thing responded."

"Ms. Who?" Billie asked.

"Christine, her biological grandmother." Ama narrowed her eyes. "What did she have to say?"

Olivia's eyes widened. She wasn't ready to talk about Christine. But Christine's words were like jet fuel to a rocket. "She wasn't pleased by the reveal."

"Not pleased? What do you mean, *not pleased*?" Ama's voice rose. "Was she upset that someone followed you and posted your image without permission on their dinky little page?"

"Well, no."

"Not pleased?" Ama sniffed. "She should be not pleased about how she treated you, her son, and the mother of her granddaughter." She shook her head. "Do I need to pack my bags and visit Highland Beach?"

"No." Olivia shook her head. "Absolutely not."

"Now, Ama," Perry tutted. "You were telling me how much fun you were having with Carter in France. It'd be a shame to cut your time short."

"We'll be in the Bluffs in a few weeks."

"Really?"

"Yes. I want to see my darling goddaughter Libby and I'm looking forward to spoiling Isabel. She hasn't seen my face nearly enough. And I will bring samples of my wine from my vineyard. It's called 'Ama's Blend.'"

Billie, for once, had nothing to say, outside of the huge grin on her face.

"Are you still not allowing any visitors for Isabel?" Ama asked.

"Affirmative." Billie nodded. "Well, except for you, Ama. Just be sure to wait a few weeks after you return and test."

"Of course I will. I would never harm my precious grandchild."

"Olivia, did we help at all?" Perry thankfully brought the conversation back to the subject.

Olivia nodded. Their words had not only helped, but she appreciated their confidence in her to face the fire.

"For what it's worth, I think you did what was best for you," Perry said. "There's nothing wrong with leaving and resetting. It worked wonders for Damon and me and our marriage."

Billie snorted. "'Resetting'? Is that what the kids call it these days?"

Olivia wanted to laugh, but then remembered her own resetting between Anderson and Garrett last summer.

"Hush, Billie," Perry hissed.

"What did you do to reset, dear?" Ama asked.

"O-oh, nothing," Perry mumbled.

Ama opened her mouth, seeming likely to press the issue. Olivia quickly jumped in. "So you all agree I should return?"

They all quickly agreed.

"Sooner rather than later?"

"Absolutely. Olivia Jones does not hide away and lick her wounds," Ama reminded her, her voice determined. "She faces things and sets her own terms."

"All right. I'll stay for another day, and then I'll go back to Highland Beach."

Before ending the conversation, Olivia thanked them all. Then she called Garrett to let him know that she'd soon be leaving. They agreed to takeout dinner since Garrett couldn't secure a sitter during the week and at the last minute.

She was grateful that Garrett had taken off from work so they could spend the day in bed, in each other's arms. Later, instead of going home as usual at the end of the evening, she planned to stay overnight.

She and Garrett had another round of lovemaking and finished just before Zora's school bus arrived. Garrett ran outside to wait at the stop.

As she started to get dressed, her phone rang. She immediately recognized the number and growled into a pillow, then took the call.

"Hello, CJ." She covered her torso with a blanket.

"Olivia?" he asked, as if he hadn't called her. "How are you?"

"I'm . . . okay. Just taking some time away to think."

He grunted in that way of his, which was not endearing now. "What is it, CJ?"

"When you came to visit again, you said you wouldn't run back to Highland Beach. I thought you were made of tougher stuff."

"What did you say?" His words were like a lighter to charcoal, and she was ready to burn. And how in the world would he know what she was made of? They were running off merely months of knowing each other.

"I'm not running." Her words were cool, despite her temperament. "Someone is literally stalking me. Taking photos of me. Do you know how dangerous that is?"

"I can protect you."

Olivia laughed. "Sure you can."

"I will."

She snorted. "You can't even protect your own image," she said, thinking about what she'd heard about Riley and Lauren.

"Do you ever let your guard down?" he whispered. "You're just like your mother. Tougher than the earth's core. How is it even possible for that young man, the one Mr. Whitt told me about, to dig deep with you?"

"Garrett knows the score. He knows I'm not . . . in a place where I can give more than I am."

"Not according to Mr. Whitt. He says he wants more. He wants to—"

"I don't care what Garrett wants," Olivia yelled. "Or . . . or what *you* want. And I don't need your opinion."

"I'm just trying to help. And the only way I can do that is if you come back . . . get to know me as your father."

Oh God, how she had wished and prayed for a father as a child. But then CJ came along. The man who denied her existence. The womanizer who didn't have sense enough to separate business from pleasure. He was not the dad she'd longed for.

"Let's get one thing straight. You and Christine love to tout all the amazing things about you and the Jones family. But you know what? You're just a goddamned deadbeat dad."

"Are you a deadbeat daddy?" Olivia heard a wounded, tiny whisper from the door.

"Oh . . . oh God." Olivia scrambled to cover herself. "I'll talk to you later, CJ." She immediately ended the call.

She felt Garrett's stony gaze as she scrambled to cover herself.

"Oh, baby, of course he isn't a deadbeat! We . . . I was just talking to someone about big people's stuff. I'm so sorry."

Zora jumped into bed and hugged her tightly. "You're here."

"Of course! I told you I'd be back." Olivia smoothed her hair.

"Forever?"

"I . . ." She looked at Garrett, who hadn't moved a muscle from the doorway.

She hadn't expected such a pointed question from her goddaughter. Or expected to be caught half naked in Garrett's bedroom, in a heated argument with her father. "Sweetie, can you give me a second to finish getting dressed?"

"Okay, Olivia." Zora happily bounced off the bed and skipped out the door past her father.

Olivia stared at her boyfriend, scared of his expression, the cold, the hurt.

"Garrett, I'm sorry. How much of that did you and Zora hear?"

"You don't care what I want." Garrett stared at Olivia, as if daring her to deny it.

"Of course I care. It was just . . . I was caught up in a heated moment."

"In my house. With my daughter, who heard you curse at your father. She looks up to you, and you showed your ass when your dad told you some uncomfortable truths. If this is . . . is how you react to having critical conversations, then . . ." He shook his head and waved a tired hand.

"Why don't I go home for now? We can discuss what happened after Zora goes to bed." Her tone was hopeful. "I promise I didn't mean it how I said it."

"Fine. But yes, I think it's best you go home for now." Her heart tumbled to her feet. She hadn't thought he would agree so easily that she should leave.

"What will you say to Zora?" Olivia had looked forward to their afternoon together.

"That you're sick and you need to attend to your *issues*."

When Olivia nodded, Garrett shut the bedroom door with a bang.

Olivia slumped over, cradling her forehead in her hand. Something soured and curled inside her stomach.

I am sick.

How could she do that to Garrett? And in front of Zora, no less. She swallowed down the bile that threatened to shoot like a rocket up her throat.

After Garrett had tucked in Zora, Olivia sat across from him at his dining table. A bottle of his favorite wine and silence stood between them.

Garrett's gaze seared her—and not in the electrifying way that his attention usually did. It felt like angry bees stinging her all over.

"I'm so very sorry for saying that I didn't care about your feelings," Olivia said. "And of course, I'm sorry for how careless I was when Zora was home."

"I know you are," he replied simply, without relinquishing the heat of his gaze.

"Out with it," she invited.

"With what?"

"With your feelings, Garrett. You're obviously mad at me."

He leaned back. "Fine. I think you're still lost."

"I'm not lost."

"You are. And I think you still don't know when love is staring back at you."

"Y-you . . . you never said you loved me."

He cracked a crooked, sardonic smile. "Maybe that's a good thing." His deep, blasé voice hollowed her heart.

"You don't . . . you don't really mean that, do you?"

"You know what Zora asked me when I put her to bed?"

"No." Olivia had arrived back at Garrett's precisely ten minutes after Zora's bedtime at eight p.m.

"She wanted to pray for you. She wanted you to stop saying mean things to your daddy, and she wants you to be happy."

"Garrett . . ."

"Even a six-year-old knows you're unhappy."

"I am happy. I'm just really . . . going through a tough time with my parents and . . . and . . . surely you understand?" Olivia was at her wit's end. Sure, she had an awful moment. She was human. But that wasn't her normal mode of conduct.

"I wish I had both of my parents here with me. Imperfections and everything, and trust me, they were nowhere near perfect. My mom was too damn stubborn to get the vaccine. And now she's not here. My dad was not perfect. We bumped heads more than we got along, but I miss him. I want to hold them. Give them a hug. Most of all, I want them to be with Zora. She's missed out on so much. My parents. My *wife*. I grieve and I ache for them every single day."

Olivia's head snapped back. She knew he missed his wife, but damn, did it hurt to feel like a substitute.

"But they're gone. She's gone. And you." He pointed to Olivia. "Both your parents are alive. You may hate her, but you have a grandmother. You have a family with an amazing legacy. But you're too damn scared to reach for what you want."

"I'm not scared." She hated that her voice shook.

He leaned back, staring at her as if he were realizing just who she really was for the first time. "You are . . . or maybe you enjoy being unhappy. Living in constant drama."

Olivia shot to her feet. "You're being obnoxious."

"Oh, there she is."

"Yes. Here I am. I had a bad day. That doesn't mean I don't care for you and Zora. Or that I'm not serious about this relationship, o-or—"

"I've lost too much!" Garrett slapped his hand across his chest. "Zora's lost too much. And I can't have her get attached to someone like you."

Someone like me?

"What are you saying?" Olivia whispered, lowering herself to the couch.

"You're not good for her right now. She needs steady and positive role models. Someone who's going to stick around when the going gets tough."

"I am that person." Olivia sucked in a breath to steady her voice. "I'm good for her."

"Maybe you want to be that person. But I just keep thinking about what happened last summer, and what's happening this summer . . . and you haven't really changed. Not as much as you think." Garrett shook his head. "How long do I have to wait for the dream of you to come to life?"

She should've known he would ruin her. A man that kind and good-looking and loving wasn't real.

Don't break down. Don't cry.

She imagined an iron fist scrapping the pieces of her broken heart, then putting the pieces back together.

"Maybe you're the one who should look in the mirror, Garrett."

Olivia walked outside, shutting the door. She heard a rustling behind her that could have been either Garrett or a vicious animal poised for attack.

She didn't care. Nothing could make her turn around and look back.

Don't cry. Not yet.

Back at her house, she packed her bags and took a shower.

Not yet.

Olivia gathered a few other personal items to bring with her to Highland Beach.

Now you can cry.

She closed her eyes, already wet with tears and pain. A ding from her phone caught her attention. But she couldn't move. Her body and soul seemed to have been spun in a blender.

After little sleep, she rose just before dawn the next day. Olivia texted Cindy and CJ to let them know her plan to return later in the day.

Olivia did not call or say goodbye to Garrett. She didn't know how to say goodbye, or how to make up. Unfortunately, she'd realize much later, not saying goodbye was the wrong thing to do.

CHAPTER TEN

May 2022

MEET THE PARENTS

"Olivia! I'm so glad you're home."

Olivia locked her car door and stopped in her tracks, surprised to see an enthusiastic Christine hurrying down her father's porch.

Cindy, who stood near Olivia, moved to block Christine's incoming hug. "I told you to leave."

"I do not answer to you, Cindy." Christine's tone was fierce, yet she didn't drop her smile. "Besides, my son and granddaughter want me here. Isn't that right, dear?"

Olivia narrowed her eyes. *What does she want?*

"The issue isn't whether I want you around, when you've made it abundantly clear my presence is a nuisance."

"I was just . . . surprised. Taken aback by what that horrible person did to you, and I—"

Olivia swatted away her grandmother's protest with her hand. "If you were surprised, then you should have backed me up, not knocked me down."

Christine clasped her hands. "I'm truly sorry for my poor reaction to the news."

Olivia considered Christine's words. They didn't ring true. Deep down, she felt that Christine didn't regret her words or how they had made her feel.

Olivia gave her a serene smile. "As you said to my mother, we can't force you to leave. But I will no longer allow you to make me feel bad about how others react to my existence. Just so we're clear."

"Crystal. I respect your boundaries and would expect no less from a Jones."

"Setting firm boundaries isn't a Jones thing. It's from Amelia Vaux Tanner."

Christine sneered a bit and stepped aside to clear the way. CJ stood at the top of the steps.

"I'll get your bags," he told her in a cool voice.

He grabbed Olivia's bags, and Christine followed him inside, much to the supreme irritation of Cindy, if her long exhalation and low growl were any sign.

Olivia stood by the curb. "Is he upset?" she asked her mother for confirmation.

"Not upset. Just hurt."

"Did he tell you about our phone call?"

"A little, yes." Cindy nodded. "But it's not just that. He's mad that someone from his hometown violated your space. He's also mad at himself because he left you unprotected."

"I'm fine."

"Are you?" Cindy eyed her daughter. "You left with little explanation."

"I was simply resetting."

"And what does that mean?" Cindy held no recrimination in her voice but seemed genuinely curious.

"Between being followed around and the Facebook post, I was overwhelmed. I needed to find a safe space. CJ's home . . . this town isn't my safe space." Not yet. Maybe never.

"But Sag Harbor is? You didn't even go back to your apartment in the city."

"I . . . I love my apartment, but the waters calm me."

"Garrett calms you," her mother said in a matter-of-fact voice.

Well, he did, until he told her she wasn't good enough for him and his daughter.

"Sometimes he does." Olivia cleared her throat. "And then sometimes he wants more. More than I can give."

"Hmm. Preach," Cindy muttered. "Well, let's try to get Christine out of the house so we can have a conversation. A lot has transpired, and we want to make sure you're prepared."

"Is Alan in there?"

"Yes, though he tried to stay home to give you space. Ms. Christine here thought it would be best to face things head-on." She mimicked Christine's soprano tone.

She dropped her frown, grabbing Olivia's hand. "I can tell them to leave if you aren't up for this. But I would like for us to talk, at least the three of us."

Ama's powerful words about being up for the challenge motivated her decision.

Olivia gave a firm nod. "We can get it over with."

"We'll make it quick, then." Cindy squeezed her hand and then let go. They walked into the house and found Christine, Alan, and CJ in a whispered, but tense, conversation at the kitchen table.

"Okay." Olivia rubbed her sweaty palms against her jeans. "Let's talk."

Alan nodded. Christine looked proud.

CJ's face was carefully blank.

"Before we begin, how are you feeling? Do you need water? Coffee? Or something stronger?" Alan offered.

"I'll grab some water." Olivia thought it prudent to stay sober and hydrated during this conversation, lest she miss out on an important detail.

"I'll get it for you," Cindy offered.

Christine stared at her mother making her way around the

kitchen. She had to admit that Cindy looked like an elegant domestic goddess in her fitted tan athleisure wear.

She came back to the table with a glass of water. Olivia took a sip and returned her attention to Alan, who seemed to be the man with a plan.

"So, while you were away, we had a town hall meeting of sorts with concerned citizens. We kept it social, meeting at the pavilion with light snacks. CJ," he flicked a glance at her father, "took full responsibility for being an absentee father. He also mentioned that you had a stepfather, and that by the time he came to his senses it was too late. He stayed away, he said, because he didn't want to cause you any more harm or confusion."

Olivia's eyes stung with emotion. It must have been hard for CJ to admit his mistakes to the entire town and to be so vulnerable. Though it would not have been the first time.

"His apology was well received. Aneesa Leverette, who handles the newsletter and local paper, criticized your father. But then she said that what happened in his personal life in the past shouldn't affect his ability to be a good mayor."

Olivia turned toward her mom, knowing she likely had something to do with that positive outlook.

"But then there are a few of the elders who are old-school. And whew, they are thirsty for blood. They're disappointed that your father didn't 'step up,'" Alan said, putting the phrase in air quotes. "One of them started a petition calling for CJ's resignation."

Olivia gasped. "Oh no. How many people have signed?"

Alan took a deep breath. "Ten."

"Ten?" Olivia waved a hand. "That's nothing. We can wait until this blows over."

CJ finally spoke. "That's ten different households . . . 10 percent of the town. A few days ago, only three people signed it. You must remember we're small. And one person can easily convince another to sign the petition."

Olivia tapped her chin, running through the numbers and worst-case scenarios. "Are the people who signed it influential?"

Alan nodded. "A few are, yes. That's what worries me. Ignoring them will just unite the community even more."

Olivia nodded, conceding his point. "Have you all tried calling them individually?"

"Of course," CJ responded. "Most of them didn't take my calls. If they did, they said what they had to say and hung up."

She nodded. Most likely they were upset with him for having an affair with Riley and for not stepping up as a father. "So it's a morality issue for them?"

"For some, yes," Alan answered. "For others, they never liked CJ to begin with. They think the Jones family has run this town for too long. It's going to be a tough reelection for sure."

CJ looked miserable. And Olivia couldn't help feeling just a little guilty for all the horrible things she'd said to her father. She wanted to help. The wheels in her mind began turning.

"Okay, so CJ needs to reestablish trust. He can do that if I show he's a good father."

"No. I'm not lying to this town any longer," CJ growled.

"Charles," Christine admonished. "It sounds like Olivia is willing to help. So let her."

"No. If she trusted me as a father, she would've stayed."

The pain in his voice shook Olivia's heart. "I . . . it's not about you."

"Then what was it? Why didn't you trust me on this?"

She repeated what she had told Cindy. "I needed some time to think. And between what happened on social media and then the blowup with Christine, it was all too much. I just wasn't . . . I'm still not sure if all of this is worth it."

"What is *this*, dear?" Christine wiggled her manicured nails in a frivolous-looking gesture. As if she couldn't fathom the reason for Olivia's hesitation. For her distrust. They didn't even know each other.

"Aren't you going to answer?" Christine asked again, her tone sharp, when Olivia didn't answer her right away.

"Family." Anger surged in Olivia's dry throat. She stood, no longer able to contain the energy inside of her. "I know time heals all wounds and makes the young wise, but I can't simply drop my life to make you feel better for your poor choices."

She pointed to Christine. "You didn't want me to even be born. And you . . ." She turned her furious gaze to CJ. "You never claimed me, and you gaslit my mother because . . . why? Because you felt guilty? Because you were jealous of your brother? Well, you should feel guilty. He stepped up and took responsibility while you hid behind your mother."

The air crackled as if there were a gathering storm. Then thunder boomed.

Everyone turned to the door. It wasn't thunder, just a very loud knock at the door.

CJ stood, excused himself, and then opened the door.

"Lauren."

"It's me." Her voice was hoarse. She looked beyond CJ, her eyes stretched wide at the tense scene in front of her. "Hi, CJ."

"Hello."

"Christine." Lauren's tone went low. "How are you?"

Christine narrowed her eyes, but then her genial smile returned. "I'm well."

"And you." She sidestepped CJ and entered his home. "You," she said, looking at Cindy, "I haven't had the pleasure of meeting."

"No, you haven't," Cindy answered. "And you are?"

"Lauren Miles. Attorney-at-law, practicing in the DMV area. And you?"

"Cindy Marshall."

"Marshall?"

"Yes. Marshall," Cindy confirmed, giving Lauren her maiden name.

"I'm not sure if I'm familiar with your family."

"Oh." Cindy shrugged, looking unbothered by this information. "I'm sorry to hear that."

Christine jumped up from her seat. "Lauren, dear, we are in the middle of a very important meeting. You and Charles can set a dinner date later."

Cindy's attention snapped to CJ.

"We have nothing to discuss over dinner," he coolly replied. "But Christine is right on one thing . . . now is not a good time."

Lauren raised her hands in the air. "Now, I understand tensions are high, but I assure you my intentions are pure." She sighed. "I've convinced Danelle Lassiter to drop her signature. And she has convinced Eleanor Williams," she added with a wide grin.

Olivia assumed that these were the town influencers Alan had discussed earlier.

"That's wonderful." Christine clapped her hands.

"Yes," Lauren agreed. "But we'll still have to do something proactive. Something that conveys that CJ is steadfast and a solid choice. A man for the community."

Cindy looked nervous. Olivia knew what Ms. Miles was angling for: to be the one by his side, one half of the power couple. She had everyone on her hooks. Even CJ looked intrigued.

"Which is why—"

"I actually have an idea," Olivia interrupted, "if you don't mind." She raised her hand. "I am the one affected, after all."

"Go ahead," CJ encouraged.

"No more town halls, no more hanging our heads. We meet them at eye level. And nothing brings more people together than a community event. CJ, I saw on your calendar last week that you have the Memorial Day weekend event to kick off the summer, right?"

"Yes."

Lauren shook her head slowly and grinned ironically, as if she were interacting with a child. "Are you suggesting that he display you while he shakes hands?"

No, that's what you want, Lauren.

"No, if you'll allow me to finish. Janice mentioned someone needing a permit to take part in raising money for the pier. I know you already plan to give a speech, but how about we plan an event around it? Maybe we can do an art walk and then music, food, and dancing on the beach."

"It's a lot of work to do in such a short time. CJ, are you sure you have time with your busy schedule?" Lauren insinuated herself again. "Then there's the matter of you prepping for your debate with your contender, Harold Munroe. I think Pastor Stanley may throw his support for him."

CJ jumped up from his seat. "Lauren, I appreciate you checking in and helping to get Danelle and Eleanor to drop their names. But we have this under control. I'll walk you out."

Lauren stepped back, smiling. "Now, I hope you haven't forgotten about the deal?"

"I haven't." He smoothly slid his arm into the crook of her elbow. "We'll catch up later," he replied, leading her outside.

Lauren snatched her arm away from CJ. "I'm not some docile little girl you can manipulate, CJ. Keep your word or I *will* make things difficult for you."

"Now, wait a minute." Christine scowled. "I like you, but I won't tolerate you threatening my family."

Lauren gave her a serene smile that did nothing to hide the inferno blazing in her eyes.

"Oh, I bet you'd try. But this time you are out of your league, Mrs. Douglass-Jones."

Christine pointed her pink lacquered nail at Lauren. "Please don't think for one second—"

Lauren dismissed her with a wave and turned to CJ. "I'll be waiting for that call, Mayor Jones." She stormed out the door.

Cindy rolled her eyes. "So that's Ms. Lauren? The one who was so good for your son?"

"No one's good enough for my Charles, but—"

"Aren't you tired?" Cindy snapped.

Christine shook her head, as if she didn't understand her question. "Pardon?"

"Aren't you tired of butting into your children's lives? So far, it hasn't worked out for you. CJ barely tolerates you, and you're skating on thin ice with your granddaughter."

Christine looked at Olivia for confirmation. Olivia crossed her arms, nodding in agreement.

"Since I'm happy my daughter has returned, I'll give you some free advice. You are smothering. You smothered Chris, tried to make him fit into a mold that wasn't meant for him. Your son stood for what was right, even . . . especially . . . when things were difficult. He ran toward difficulty, toward danger," Cindy said, her voice breaking.

It nearly broke Olivia. She was nothing like Chris Jones. Chris wouldn't have run away to Sag Harbor. He would've faced things right away, embraced the problem, and solved it on his own terms.

CJ stepped back into the room, but only Olivia and Alan seemed to notice.

Alan cleared his throat, but Christine clicked her tongue.

"If he was so good, so brave, then why didn't he stay and fight for his family?" Christine snapped. "Chris left us right after his father died."

"No, Christine. No, you will face what you did: *you* pushed him away. It all started with the lies you told CJ, when you set me up to make it seem like I kissed another man. Back then, Chris was the only person who believed me . . . who believed Olivia was CJ's daughter. Chris stood up for me and made sure your granddaughter grew up in a stable household. Face it. Your lies backfired, and he chose us. And silly me, I used to carry this enormous guilt about him losing his family, but I see now," she looked Christine up and down, "he didn't have much to lose."

"Cindy." CJ grabbed her shoulder.

She shrugged him off. "Chris was a decision-maker. Indigo was too. And Christine, you did the same damn thing to your beautiful daughter. You snuffed out her light because she wasn't like you, she wasn't a stuck-up socialite."

"Cindy, stop this." This time Alan stood with his fist clenched.

"Maybe no one knows what really happened that night when Indigo died, but what we do know is that you and Indigo had a knock-down drag-out argument."

"Cindy, you don't know what you're talking about." CJ's voice was dangerously low.

Cindy twisted her neck to face CJ. "What I know is that Indigo came to me, telling me Christine was a hypocrite and she couldn't wait to get the hell away from Highland Beach. She begged me to take her with me when I told her I was moving away for college. And I should have. Maybe she'd be alive today."

Christine strode across the room and slapped Cindy.

"How dare you?" Christine's voice cracked. Her body shook as if she were freezing in the middle of a snowstorm.

Cindy didn't flinch, didn't touch the blooming red that spread across her cheek. She leveled her attention at Christine—aiming her eyes like a sniper rifle.

"Mom," Olivia said.

She shook her head, raised her hand as if to stop Olivia, and now CJ, from approaching.

Christine pointed her manicured pink nail at Cindy so close that it scraped her nose.

"You don't know anything. You want to talk about being a hypocrite? I know you let Olivia go off every summer to that . . . that vile woman, Amelia Vaux Tanner, at her home in Oak Bluffs. I know you could barely say a kind word to your own daughter. And yet you sit here and lecture me about pushing *my* children away?"

She turned to face her son. "This is the woman you want? A woman who would disrespect your mother and your sister's memory? A woman who allowed her precious daughter to be mentored by a woman who slept her way to the top?" Christine clamped her mouth shut, and the red of her lipstick spread just below her bottom lip.

"I won't support it." She shook her head. "I don't care how you feel about it, but Cindy is toxic to this family," Christine insisted, her voice ringing out an alarming pitch.

She finally looked at Olivia. "I'm sorry, my dear." She licked her dry lips. "I know we had a deal, but I can no longer be cordial to your mother. Maybe in time you'll still allow us to get to know each other."

His shoulders sloped forward, his face the picture of deep sorrow, Alan picked up Christine's purse and his hat.

They left the house without fanfare. Quietly, and with sadness, they shut the door behind them.

Cindy exhaled, grabbed the chair in front of her, and lowered herself into it.

"I'll get you some ice." Olivia dashed into the kitchen, found a large cloth, and packed it with ice cubes.

CJ took the pack from Olivia's hand, got down on one knee, and pressed it against Cindy's face. "Are you okay? Do you need an aspirin?"

Shaking her head, Cindy grabbed the cold compress and settled it onto her bruised cheek. "Is your mother usually violent?"

"No. I haven't witnessed it."

"And Chris? Indigo?" her mother pressed.

"No. She, umm, would hit my father a few times whenever she grew frustrated, but she would calm down after some time. She never . . . never hit us kids."

Cindy exhaled. "That's good at least. She must really hate me."

CJ didn't answer at first. His eyes swept the room before he returned his attention to Cindy.

"She doesn't know you."

"No, and she doesn't want to get to know me." Cindy sighed. "She thinks everyone is after her *boys*. It's truly unhealthy. I hope you know that."

"Trust me, I know. She's made it known how she's felt about my past relationships."

"How did you date over the years?" Olivia noticed the genuine curiosity in her mother's voice.

"I don't date much, and when I do, I'm discreet. What about you?"

Olivia hadn't met anyone over the years Cindy had dated, though she was sure her mother went on dates.

She snorted. "I'm a grown woman and free to do what I please, if that's what you're asking." Her eyes sparked with something.

"No. I'm asking if you are in a relationship."

"You . . . you're asking me this now?" Cindy's eyes went wide. "After your mother slapped me. Well, let me answer. No, I'm not in a relationship, and no, I'm not interested in a relationship, especially with a Jones."

Olivia grabbed her head. *What was her father thinking?* No way any person would want to be in a relationship with a man whose mother physically abused them.

"I understand." He finally stood up. "I'll be upstairs in my study if you need anything."

After he had left the room, Cindy turned to Olivia. "Do you think I was too harsh?"

"No. Christine just slapped you, and he looked like it was just a regular Saturday afternoon. Something isn't right about all of this."

Cindy removed the cloth from her face. "I'm going to sleep. I'll talk to your father in the morning once I get a good night's rest."

"I think that's a smart idea. I'm only a few steps away. Knock if you want to talk."

"I will, Olivia. Thank you for . . . for coming back."

"I shouldn't have run away."

Cindy shook her head. "But you came back. That's all that matters. That's more than what I did." She gave Olivia a sad smile and walked away.

The next day, on a bright Sunday morning, CJ, Cindy, and Olivia sat at the breakfast table. CJ had gotten up early to make them the fluffiest pancakes and crispiest bacon she'd ever eaten.

"This is really delicious, CJ," Olivia complimented her father.

"Thank you. One of our old cooks, Celia, taught me. She wanted me to be prepared for living alone in college."

"It's good, right, Mom?"

"Yes. It's . . . good." Her voice was light and noncommittal.

"Listen, Cindy, I'm sorry for my question last night. I just thought that, since you asked me about how I'm dating . . . that you wanted to open that door."

"I can understand why you misunderstood." Cindy bit into her bacon, staring out the window at the pool.

"I really don't have a chance with you, do I?" he whispered.

Cindy's eyebrows furrowed. "What?"

"What I did to you was unforgivable. I never fought my brother for you. But I wonder if you wanted me to fight. Was Chris so embedded in your heart that it would've made a difference?" He didn't look at Cindy when he asked. He seemed to speak to himself, as if musing out loud. "I'll leave you alone. I get that you don't want anything to do with my family."

"What are you talking about?" Cindy whispered.

"What you said about Chris not having much to lose with us.

About Indigo begging to leave with you. To you, Chris was a hero, but he was my brother. And my brother took the woman I loved away from me, knowing damn well I planned to pick you up that day."

Cindy shook her head. "Don't be silly. Of course, he didn't know. He wouldn't have—"

"He knew because I told him I was going to see to you. I was delayed because I went to buy you a ring. And all the while, I was trying to shake off my nerves and ask the woman I loved to marry me. He didn't know about the ring, but he knew my feelings, probably better than anyone. And later, when I called him out . . . when I called him and told him what I'd seen, he told me that you chose him, that you were happy. He told me to let you go because you'd already let me go in your heart."

He looked out the window. "Then I heard you in the background. You told him to get off the phone and come to bed."

CJ clenched his jaw, struggling to keep his composure, his eyes wet. "I don't know if Indigo was murdered or if it was an accident, or maybe she . . ." He cleared his throat. "Maybe she thought there wasn't a reason to stick around, either. Then I lost my twin and . . . you and Olivia. So if you can't see what I've tried to show you these past few weeks, what I've felt in my heart for thirty-five years, then I'll back off."

He stepped away from Cindy. "I'm leaving for a bit." He walked out the front door. Another quiet exit marked by sadness.

This time Olivia exhaled. She needed a drink, a bath, and a therapist, in no particular order. Maybe Cindy needed them even more.

"More coffee?" Olivia offered.

Her mother nodded her head. Olivia filled their mugs and brought them out to the back patio, her mother trailing behind.

"Did I make a mistake?" Cindy's voice was void of emotion, but Olivia could hear the sorrow. The worry.

"What do you mean?"

"With Chris? It's . . . it's hard to believe he would deceive me. He was so loving and so . . . so kind. Do you know how much work he put into making me love him?" She shook her head. "Which is hard to believe because he was so easy to love."

"He loved you, maybe beyond reason. He never once questioned you or my existence. If what CJ says is true, he simply fought harder for you."

"Yes, but according to CJ, he did it in an underhanded way," Cindy pointed out. "I still can't believe he would do that."

"Maybe, yes. But you can't ask him now. He's . . . he's gone. But you are here. CJ is here, and he's telling you how he feels. The question is, how do you feel about him?"

"I loved him to distraction. And now that we're spending some time together, I'm feeling . . . something more for him. He still looks at me the same way he did so long ago. And he's been asking about my favorite things and if I still enjoy reading. I told him about my favorite book, and now he's reading it."

"That's a good thing, right?" Olivia asked her mother. "The fact that he's not just relying on what he used to know about you."

"I like that he wants to get to know me, but I'm afraid," Cindy confessed in a tiny voice.

"Of what?"

"That he'll suddenly wake up and not love me anymore. He's done it once. He can do it again."

"He never said he stopped loving you."

Cindy lifted her coffee mug and paused before sipping. "Yes, but his actions proved otherwise."

After a pause, she went on. "You have to understand that my heart has been . . . simply beating since Chris died. But now that CJ's back in my life, it feels like someone's charged a battery inside my chest." She shook her head. "I'm too old to have these feelings. I can't risk it all for him again."

"You aren't too old for anything. But I think it's okay to be cautious, Mom. I think it's perfectly fine to protect your heart. But if I've learned anything the past couple of years, it's to trust your gut."

Cindy stared at the bottom of the mug as if it held the answers. "Okay, maybe, like you, I need some space to think. I could go back to New Jersey."

Olivia let out an audible gasp. "Don't leave me with these people!"

Cindy let out a sharp, surprised laugh. "I won't, don't worry. I can't let Christine think she's bested me. She's done that enough over the years."

Olivia swallowed. She wouldn't dare say it out loud, but spending time with Christine at lunch and on their shopping excursion had felt like her time with Ama. And something else that she would never, ever admit was that she admired the sacrifices Christine had made as a mother. She put her dream to be an attorney on a shelf and took care of her kids. Ama hadn't done that. And though Cindy had always been in her life, her mother hadn't provided her with the love and care she had so desperately needed.

"I say this without recrimination or judgment." Cindy's words broke into her thoughts. "But please . . . please be careful with Christine. As you saw last night, when things don't go her way, she gets bullish. Don't let your eagerness to reconnect with family allow someone to roll over your feelings. I didn't do much to protect you, and I have no right to try now that you're an adult. So I can only ask that you please protect yourself. Protect your peace."

"I can do that," Olivia assured her. She smiled at her mother.

"What is it?"

"Look at us, giving each other advice."

"It's nice, isn't it?"

The conversation was more than nice—it was a living miracle. Until the past few weeks, it was rare to see her mother cry or even raise her normally cool, even-toned voice. But here in Highland

Beach, Olivia had witnessed her cries and sharp words. Some might say that Cindy was experiencing a crisis, but Olivia would have argued the opposite. Just as Olivia had done the previous year, her mother was now becoming . . . blooming. Finding herself again after suppressing herself for years.

And she was falling in love.

CHAPTER ELEVEN

May 2022

WHAT THE HEART WANTS

"This is Garrett Brooks. I'm unable to come to the phone right now. Please leave a message and I'll reach out at my earliest convenience."

Olivia pressed the End button hard enough to crack the screen. She let out a long, exasperated sigh and paced the length of the patio. "Stop avoiding me, Garrett Brooks."

It'd been her third time calling since she left Sag Harbor. He checked in once by text to make sure she arrived safely. After that? Radio silence.

"He's the one who insulted me," she muttered under her breath.

"Are you having relationship troubles, too?"

Olivia screamed, holding the phone against her galloping heart. She relaxed when her brain kicked in and she recognized CJ, standing near the back door. She hadn't felt like she was being followed since she returned to Highland Beach three days ago, but then again, she hadn't been out and about.

"I . . ." She gave up the lie and simply nodded.

Yes, I most definitely have relationship troubles.

The sun set behind them, and the air cooled.

"You're home early," she said to her father.

He shrugged. "It's six thirty."

Olivia nodded. "That's early for you." Besides that, they were still preparing for the Memorial Day festivities, now only a few days away.

"You aren't avoiding your constituents, are you?"

"Not any more than you're avoiding my question." He lifted an eyebrow. "Are you having relationship troubles?"

Olivia crossed her arms. "I nodded, which means yes."

CJ sat on the bench. "You want to talk about it?"

Not really, she thought. But when she took in all of CJ's shadows—the five o'clock shadow across his jawline and the shadows under his eyes—she changed her mind. She sat across from him, hoping he wouldn't try to impart knowledge on a subject he'd spectacularly failed in.

He reclined into the cushioned seat. "I've heard from Mr. Whitt, but I'd like for you to tell me about your young man."

"His name is Garrett. He's in his early thirties and a widower. He's a real estate attorney, and he has a whip-smart six-year-old daughter, Zora, who's my goddaughter." Olivia couldn't help but smile when she thought of Zora. But the smile quickly turned to a frown. She hadn't said a proper goodbye to her goddaughter. How could she when Garrett obviously didn't want her around Zora?

Maybe I can convince him to let me speak to Zora to give her some closure.

Olivia immediately shook her head. Her goddaughter didn't need to be in the middle of a grown-up's mess.

"How did you meet?"

Olivia's gaze met her father's. His was a look of patience, of yearning, just like Olivia's.

How many times had she wished to relax into a conversation with her father? Something unlocked inside of her chest. Something sturdy, something brave. She didn't want to imagine any longer. She would try.

Olivia rubbed her palms against her shorts, working through her sudden shyness. She cleared her throat. "His mother was my neighbor. When she died of Covid last year, he moved in and . . . and I guess he never left. He and Zora now live in Sag Harbor full-time."

"Ah, so you fell for the next-door neighbor."

Olivia inhaled. "Eventually. I was engaged back then."

"Yes, your mother mentioned some other man. A comedian?"

"That's right. We ended our engagement last summer. He's an actor, too, with a comedy special coming out soon." Olivia sent up a prayer every so often that she would in no way be the brunt of his jokes. Anderson had done it before.

"Hmm."

Olivia could see him processing this information, then landing on the truth. She'd fallen for Garrett, cheated on Anderson, and later broke off their engagement.

"Things with Garrett are new, then."

"Not quite a year . . . but things got really serious." *Maybe too quickly. Just like my relationship with Anderson.*

Maybe Garrett was right about not knowing what I want? Her heart stuttered at the realization.

"Because you're neighbors?"

It would be so easy to blame falling for Garrett on the convenience of it. But Garrett was so much more than that. He made her laugh, made her heart beat out of her chest. Before Garrett, she'd had no desire to date a man with a child. Olivia fully accepted that her feelings about children had been selfish, but realistically, she knew she'd always come second to a man's child.

Though even if that was true, as it should be, she had never felt she came in second with Garrett.

But she'd made him feel that way.

"He's just an incredible man. With everything that's happening, I can't commit myself to a more serious relationship."

"What's your definition of a serious relationship?"

"Emotionally and physically supportive. Being emotionally supportive means talking daily, validating his feelings, spending quality time together, and loving him as he needs it."

CJ nodded. "Now, what's his definition of a successful relationship?"

"It's . . ." Olivia paused, drawing a blank as she realized she'd never asked him what he specifically wanted in a relationship. She had made assumptions. "I'm not entirely sure, but . . . I get the impression that he wants to marry me."

CJ lifted a hand. "My biggest regret with your mother was lack of honesty. I wasn't honest with myself until it was too late. And when I recognized my feelings, I allowed small things to get in the way."

"Okay, that means . . . ?"

"Don't repeat history. Don't assume things. Just ask the man what he wants. Then figure out if that's something you can and want to give him."

Olivia nodded. "What if he doesn't want me anymore? What if he's tired of waiting?"

Waiting for me to live up to this dream woman in his head.

"Then it's up to him if he wants to wait. And you'll have to respect his decision."

Olivia swallowed. She was too afraid to ask Garrett to wait. Anderson had asked her to wait, and it hadn't taken her long to realize that he wasn't the man for her. Garrett was only three years older than her. In his life, he'd fallen in love, married someone, had a child, and buried two parents. In contrast, Olivia had broken off an engagement, quit a lucrative job to start a nonprofit, and recently discovered that her biological father was not deceased, as she'd believed, but very much alive.

Garrett knew his feelings, his worth, and deep down she knew he was right about how she treated their relationship. Olivia had undergone many changes since last summer, but she still hadn't figured everything out. However, she wasn't ready to admit that she was the wrong role model for Zora.

"Okay. I'll try."

"I hope you will. And I hope you see what happens when you make assumptions and let the love of your life marry someone else. Don't be like me."

Olivia winced. "That was harsh. You should really stop insulting yourself."

"True."

Olivia gave him a sad smile. "I assume things haven't turned around just yet?"

"No. Not even a little." CJ shook his head. "Anyway, I just got a heads-up from Aneesa that they'll be doing a write-up in the paper."

Olivia nodded. According to Cindy, it had been Aneesa who deleted the photo posted on the town's Facebook page. She was also leading the search for the anonymous poster.

"Is she writing the article?"

"No such luck. The publisher feels that would be a conflict of interest, so Jackson Davis will take on the assignment. They're doing a little exposé on our family."

Dread filled Olivia's stomach. "Okay, outside of a secret love child, the young lover, your new lover Lauren—"

"She's not a new lover. She's just a partner."

"What kind of partner? A potential marriage partner or a business partner?"

"It's only ever been about business."

"What are the terms of this partnership?"

"She wants to be the next mayor. And I will endorse her after serving my term."

"An ex-girlfriend as mayor seems messy."

"Well . . . she wasn't supposed to be an ex so soon."

"So you've violated the terms of your partnership." *No wonder Lauren was upset.*

"We discussed it the other day, and she's fine with our breakup, so long as I keep my promise about the endorsement."

Olivia crossed her arms. "Fine. Do we have any *other* skeletons in our closet?"

CJ looked out at the pool. "When . . ." He cleared his throat. "When Indigo died, there was a lot of speculation surrounding her death. People spread rumors that either our family or a stranger had murdered her. Some even think that she took her own life. It just didn't make sense to anyone . . . to me . . . how she died. She was a Junior Olympian swimmer, and beyond that, the bay waters were calm. And I think Christine knows more than what she's let on. I think she and Indigo were fighting about something big . . . something regarding our family."

"What about the family?"

CJ shook his head. "It's just something about that day that didn't seem right." He stood. "I'm beat. I'm going to shower. Whatever comes out of that article, I'll deal with it, okay? You don't have to worry. You don't have to . . ." He let his voice trail off.

"I won't flee again. I promise."

He walked away without responding.

Olivia stared out at the pool with a question in her heart. Did the family secret die with Indigo?

"I'm leaving," Olivia blurted out loud to her mother as she paced the kitchen floor.

Cindy flipped the page to her book and then placed a bookmark between the pages.

"I'm assuming you mean you're leaving the house for a little bit, not Highland Beach?" her mother calmly responded.

"Correct. I'm just going out for an hour or two." Olivia hadn't jogged the beach for fear that someone would recognize her face from the social media post, or that the stalker would see her and start following her again.

Cindy nodded and reopened her book. "The town knows who you are now. You might as well venture outside."

Olivia stopped pacing and huffed. "Maybe I should jog later tonight."

"We'd prefer you not do that."

"But—"

"Please don't argue about that point. Indigo died on that very beach at night, and someone followed you and took your picture without your consent. You don't have to hide, but you need to be careful."

Now it was high noon and the locals, along with their visitors, flooded the beach.

But if I wear a hat, I can blend in.

"Aneesa wants to meet for dinner. How about you come with us?"

"Yes!" Olivia eagerly agreed. "When are we going?"

"Tonight."

"Oh good. I'll pick out what to . . ." Her voice trailed off when she realized she'd be crashing her mother's much-needed time with her best friend.

"Actually, I . . . need to call someone. I can't make it."

Her mother's face dropped into a dubious expression. "You need to call someone?"

"Yes."

"During dinnertime? At seven o'clock?"

"Yes. Perry and I are planning a visit to Billie and Dulce's place. They're going on an overdue vacation."

"Can't you reschedule your—"

"No." Olivia shook her head.

Cindy exhaled, and then, after a moment, smiled. "Neesa and I have caught up. We've been to dinner twice already, and we've spoken on the phone nearly every night since we reconnected. If you think you'd be a bother, you aren't. She wants to get to know you, too. She's pretty mad at me for keeping you away for most of your life."

"Are you sure?"

"Very. Now, go find something fabulous to wear, because we're going to a nice restaurant with the best wine, according to Aneesa."

Later that night, Olivia and Cindy met Aneesa at Café Normandie, a cozy French fusion restaurant. Even before they stepped inside, Olivia could smell the fresh baked bread.

The restaurant had a mix of old-world French and whimsical lavender decor. The round tables were small and arranged in the front near the window. Along the walls were partitioned booths with wood panels hewn from centuries-old trees. Aneesa, already seated in a booth, waved from her seat. A charcuterie platter and baked mussels sat in the middle of the table.

"We aren't late, are we?" Olivia stage-whispered to her mother.

"No. Aneesa's just always been that annoying 'if you aren't early, you're late' person."

Olivia smiled. Aneesa's time philosophy reminded her of how punctual her late godfather Omar was. She also imagined that it served Aneesa well as a reporter to settle in and observe her surroundings before someone else arrived.

Her mother slid into the booth beside Aneesa, and Olivia sat across from her mother's friend.

"Oh, this is nice," Olivia said, lifting the pink snakeskin Gucci purse from the seat. "Where should I place this?"

"Sorry, I'll take that," Aneesa responded. "I don't want any scratches on my baby."

It was then that Olivia noticed the cobblestone wall that led up to a carved archway with a hanging light.

"I ordered you that divine shiraz I told you about," Aneesa told Cindy, smiling. Staring at her friend, Olivia's mother said, "If I don't like it, I'm sending it back."

Aneesa rolled her eyes. "Girl, I know my wine. You'll drink it and you'll love it."

"We'll see," Cindy said in a grumpy voice, but her eyes shone with humor.

Aneesa turned her attention to Olivia. "I see your mom's still prickly."

Olivia was glad Aneesa found her mother's contrarian attitude endearing. Olivia certainly hadn't all these years.

The server quickly arrived and took Olivia's wine order. While they nibbled on appetizers and drank wine, Aneesa updated them on the happenings in town.

"I'm telling you, it's not as bad as you think. You should stop hiding, Olivia. Trust my reporter instincts on this."

"Alan and Christine say—"

"Christine is only looking out for herself," Aneesa snapped. "Sorry, I didn't mean to cut you off, honey." She leaned over and patted Olivia's hand. "But Christine has always looked out for number one—and that's her own hide." Aneesa whipped out a decorative fan. "Sorry. Hot flash." She fanned her face for a full minute.

Olivia wanted to argue, but it was true that Christine's initial reaction to the news had been off-putting. Though, since her return, Christine had been more than effusive with her compliments, telling her granddaughter how glad she was to have another woman of style around.

"Anyway, enough about that woman," Cindy jumped in. "Aneesa, tell me about your date last night."

"Girl." Aneesa waved her fan. "Snooze fest."

"No! You were so excited." Olivia had never heard her mother's voice so animated.

Aneesa turned to Olivia. "I've been divorced for three years, and I'm dating again. There's this silly app for old folks, and Richard, that's the guy's name, seemed nice enough. But he just talked about himself the entire time." She drank more wine. "He wants to meet up again."

Cindy leaned back. "So where are you meeting?"

Aneesa shrugged, tucking her fan into her purse. "I could go for some steak."

"Wait a minute, I thought you didn't like him?" Olivia asked.

"I didn't. But he kisses well enough."

Cindy laughed into her wineglass. "This is what she does. Complains, but then she'll end up doing the very opposite of what she wants."

"Who knows? Maybe he'll stop talking about himself on the next date," Aneesa said, with little enthusiasm in her voice.

Cindy tilted her head toward her old friend. "That's what I should've been doing all these years. Going on dates."

"Well, if you would've returned my calls, I could have imparted my wisdom." Aneesa laughed, then returned her attention to Olivia. "Speaking of men, how are you and Garrett?"

Olivia scrunched her face. She certainly hadn't spoken of her relationship with Aneesa. Cindy helpfully answered her unspoken question.

"Oh, I told her about your boyfriend Garrett and his sweet daughter."

Garrett. Olivia leaned back against the stiff, cushioned booth. Words hurt, and hearing his name was a reminder.

It hurt that he hadn't answered any of her calls.

It hurt that he didn't think she was good enough for his daughter.

But what hurt the most was that she wasn't all that sure he was wrong. "She told me about Anderson, too." Aneesa snorted, snapping Olivia out of crisis mode and into irritation.

"Mother."

Cindy winced. "Sorry."

"Sounds like you dodged a bullet there." Aneesa rolled on as if she had every right to know Olivia's business.

Olivia cleared her throat. "He's a good guy. We just didn't work out."

"Because he's white?" Aneesa fired off the question like the seasoned reporter she was.

"Aneesa . . ." Cindy's voice carried a warning.

Olivia raised her hand, halting Aneesa's oncoming questions. "No . . . because we didn't make each other better. Can you pass the bread, please?" Olivia could hear the desperation in her own voice. Aneesa nodded. "Sorry, sweetie. I realize I may have overstepped."

"It's okay."

"Speaking of incompatible, how about I tell you about my nutty ex-husband?"

She launched into a series of funny stories, and soon the tension from her earlier questions slipped away. She deftly moved away from talking about her ex-husband Jared to recounting childhood antics with Cindy, reminiscing about when they snuck out of their houses to wear two-piece bikinis.

"Honey . . . you couldn't tell either of us anything. I had the butt and hips. Cindy had the boobs. We were toddling around the beach—"

Cindy clicked her tongue. "I do not toddle."

"You did in those cheap platform sandals you insisted on wearing, remember? Not to mention you tripped and fell so hard you stumbled into the water."

Aneesa laughed, and soon Olivia joined in. She could not imagine her mother being a silly teenager.

Cindy gulped her wine.

"Whew. We had so much fun. Every summer felt like a turning point." Aneesa fanned herself again, in the throes of another hot flash.

"You're right. I think that's the last summer when things were fun."

"We were . . . what? Nineteen then?" Aneesa asked.

Cindy nodded. "The next summer, Indigo died and . . . you know."

"Yeah." The laughter fled Aneesa's voice. "I was thinking about looking into her case."

"Now, Neesa—"

"She was my friend, too." Aneesa turned to face Olivia. "Indigo was like our little sister, and I'm telling you, something's not right about what happened."

"So what are you going to do? Ask around town and hope that any persons involved will suddenly share new information about something that happened ages ago?" Cindy snapped.

"I'm going to have a conversation with my neighbors about what they think happened to Indigo." Aneesa snapped her fingers. "Hey, Olivia, do you want to join me?"

"Join you?"

"Once you're done with your dog-and-pony show with Alan and Christine, why don't you come with me and get to know the residents?"

"By asking them about the . . . the murder of my aunt?"

"No. We can simply say that you want to get to know the Jones family through the lens of the Highland Beach community. You'll also be assuaging their curiosity about you. A win-win situation, I say."

Olivia sipped her wine, thinking about the proposal. She wanted to help CJ with his reelection. And she would love to help him find peace about Indigo's death. "Okay," Olivia nodded. "Deal."

After dinner concluded, Olivia drove them back to CJ's home. Beside her, Cindy was so stiff, it was like she'd sprayed starch on her bones.

"All okay?" Olivia asked once she parked her car.

Cindy didn't move from the passenger seat. "Just thinking about things. About the past. I don't know if you should dig into the past with Aneesa."

"Why?" Olivia shrugged. "Indigo's death was probably accidental, and I'd love to hear more about her without causing pain to CJ or Christine."

"Because I'm very sure that something happened, and I don't know who may have done it," Cindy whispered. She opened the car door. "I think I may have drunk too much wine and I need to go to bed. My head is spinning."

"Oh, of course." Olivia hugged her mother, knowing something had rattled her.

"Maybe we can speak on it tomorrow?" Olivia asked.

"I would like that."

"To convince me otherwise?"

"Yes," Cindy confessed without remorse. "Your grandmother has too many enemies, and I'll be damned if you're going to get involved in her decades-old mess."

CHAPTER TWELVE

April 1991

THINGS BEST LEFT
IN THE PAST

CINDY

Cindy squeezed a dollop of sunblock on her palm and rubbed it into her skin. The sun was unseasonably high and hot, and if she and Aneesa sat out on their beach blanket for much longer, they'd turn into puddles.

"What's taking them so long?" Aneesa whined from beside her.

Cindy shrugged. "Chris said his mom wanted them to help break down some things after the parade."

"More like she wants to keep you two away from each other."

Cindy nodded. "Truth."

"Well, she's got the wrong twin," someone said from above them.

"Another truth." Cindy looked up, squinting into the sun. "Indigo." She patted the blanket, motioning her to sit. "You escaped Christine?"

"Oh yeah. Since I've got no prospects, she leaves me alone. Now, you . . . you better watch out."

Christine hadn't spoken a word to her, but Cindy had received plenty of dirty looks whenever she hung out with her sons.

Although she truly hadn't seen much of Chris lately since he joined the military. Cindy still couldn't believe her best friend had done something so impulsive without discussion. They talked about everything.

"I'll be fine. Your mother doesn't worry me." Cindy had more bravado in her voice than she felt. But she wouldn't give CJ up. Not after all the years of chasing him. From walking alone on the beach where she knew CJ jogged to making sure she ran in the same circles through invites to parties.

Back then, he didn't budge and in fact seemed oblivious to her affection. In that low voice of his, he'd say hello and find the farthest spot away from where she stood or sat.

She bitched and moaned to her best friends, Chris and Aneesa, about CJ ignoring her. Even though they were twins, Chris claimed to not understand his brother's surly attitude toward Cindy.

Then two summers ago, when he dated a rich girl visiting from California, Cindy gave up. CJ and the girl sat on a blanket at a beach party, and when she whispered something in his ear, he let out a low laugh.

With tears in her eyes, Cindy left the party and stayed close to her apartment. When Chris wanted to hang out, they avoided Highland Beach. But then Aneesa had convinced her to go to a party, because she needed Cindy to entertain her date's brother, Kevin. They talked and flirted, and soon the uneasiness Cindy felt about seeing CJ melted away.

Toward the end of the night, when they walked down the beach, Kevin tried to kiss her. Cindy liked him, but she wasn't in the mood to kiss a stranger. Even after she said no, he'd wrapped his large hands around her forearm and jerked her close. Out of nowhere, someone bumped him from behind. It had shocked Cindy to find

CJ standing there, his fists clenched, and with an angry scowl that reminded her of a thunderstorm.

Kevin was just about to make a fuss, but then a group of friends crowded around them. Kevin pushed past the group of locals, grabbed his brother, and left the beach.

But CJ wasn't done with his anger. He grabbed Cindy's hand and marched her away from their curious friends.

"How are you?" he grunted.

"Fine. Thanks for your help back there. I don't know what . . ." Cindy trembled. "I don't know what would've happened if you weren't there." She squeezed his hand. "I can't thank you enough."

He jerked his hand back. "Well, yeah. Chris wasn't here, so I had to step in."

"Where is he, anyway?"

"Sick. He's got a cold. You should be careful, especially if you two are kissing all the time."

"Kissing!"

"Yeah . . . because you're together."

"We are *not* together." She crossed her arms.

"You went to the movies last weekend."

"As friends. I think he's dating that Lacey girl, anyway."

He gave her that familiar look of disdain. "Trust me, Chris is not dating anyone."

Cindy shrugged. "Regardless, who your brother dates has nothing to do with me."

"Doesn't it?" His eyes narrowed. "You aren't jerking my brother's chain, are you?"

"Did Chris tell you we're dating?"

"No, never." CJ shook his head. "I just assumed since you're always together."

Cindy exhaled. "A boy and a girl can just be friends, and that's all we are. Don't be so old-fashioned."

He shrugged. "I guess so."

"You don't have to guess. I just told you, and it's a fact. Besides, I like someone else. Chris knows this."

"Does he?"

"Yeah. In fact, he's tried to help me from time to time. But I don't need his help anymore because the guy I like . . . well, *liked* . . . is too dense to notice me."

"I'm sure he noticed you."

Cindy snorted. *He truly is clueless.* "No, I'm very sure this guy doesn't like me. He's made it clear, and now I'm moving on." Cindy drove the point home by walking away. She needed to find Aneesa and get the hell out of Highland Beach.

CJ kept pace with her. "Who is he?" he asked in a small, soft voice. "Maybe I can help."

Cindy stopped in her tracks, then turned around. Suddenly bold, and definitely annoyed, she finally snapped. "It's you."

"Me?" He pointed to his chest.

"Yes, fool. But like I said, I *liked* you. Past tense."

"Why don't you like me anymore?" He had the nerve to look offended at Cindy's comment.

"You're a little rude. I understand you get annoyed with people who say harsh things and make mistakes, so I know you're not mean. But you're mean to me. I say hello, you mutter under your breath, wave, and then rush off like I'm contagious. And I know you told your brother that we hang out too much, because he told me."

CJ shrugged. "I stand by my statement."

"He's my best friend!" Cindy shouted. "You know what, you've made it clear you don't like me, and right now I really don't like you, either."

"I never said I didn't like you."

"You don't—"

"I like the way you look, for one. And I like it that your eyes spar-

kle when you're about to make a smart-assed comment. I like that
your smile's a little lopsided."

Cindy covered her mouth. "It's not."

"It is, and I like it." He pulled her hand away from her lips. "I
like that you always bring my favorite snacks when we have a party
on the beach."

To be fair, she brought things for Chris, too. Chris liked sour and
hard candy like Jolly Ranchers and Skittles. CJ much preferred salty
snacks like chips.

"I like that you listen before you speak. Mostly you do it to find
a fault in my argument, but you'll still hear someone out. I like how
your mind works, too. You know how to explain complex things
and break it down like it's natural."

Cindy clasped her hands. She'd gotten that trait from her mother.
Cindy noticed that sometimes folks with a little money—whether
they were Black or white—enjoyed sounding superior to their peers.
She could recognize someone with true intelligence versus someone
mimicking another person's intellect.

"I like it when you nibble your lips when you're thinking. Or
chomp on your bottom lip when you're pissed off. Right now, you're
thinking. Hopefully thinking about what I'm finally confessing to
you." He moved closer to Cindy, grabbed her hands, and wrapped
her arms around his back.

"W-what are you doing?"

"Showing you how much I like you," he whispered into her ear.
"Do you get me now?"

"I . . . I guess."

"I don't want you to guess. I want you to know. So I'll keep going." He pulled her closer and whispered a few more of his favorite
things about Cindy.

"I like how you treat my baby sister. She worships the ground you
walk on. And I . . . I like the way you look at me."

"You already said that," Cindy reminded him in a teasing voice.

"Because I *really* like it."

Cindy stepped out of his arms with heat flooding her cheeks. God, did he notice how much she stared at him? Aneesa told her she was doing it too much.

"How do I look at you?"

"Like I could sprout wings and hang the stars in the sky. Like I'm important to you."

Cindy's heart went *ka-thunk* in her chest. She shook her head. "It doesn't make sense. You've never made me feel welcome. You make me feel like a . . . a pest."

"Because I thought I was in love with my brother's girlfriend. I fought like hell to stay away from you. But now that I know you and Chris aren't together, now that I know how you feel . . ."

"Felt. Past tense," she lied to him—and herself.

"I feel confident in my ability to convince you otherwise." He pulled her back into his arms. "I want to kiss you. Is that okay?"

"I . . . I guess that's okay."

He lowered his lips to hers. Warmth flooded her. She knew from that moment on, she'd never be cold or alone again.

From that night on, they'd been inseparable. Well, except for the times when she and Chris hung out. It was important to her that Chris not feel like the odd man out.

"Earth to Cindy." Indigo snapped her fingers, bringing her back to the present.

"Hey, yes, sorry. What were you saying?"

"When is CJ coming back from Morehouse?"

"Should be next week Friday. Maybe Thursday if his last class lets out early."

Indigo twisted a trio of silver rings around her fingers. "Okay. That's good."

"What's wrong?"

"Nothing." Indigo shrugged. "Just family stuff."

"Do you want to talk about it?"

"Absolutely not." Indigo shook her head.

"I'm sorry if I'm overstepping, but you can talk to me about anything."

"I know that, trust me, but I'm just . . . embarrassed."

"Okay, fair enough. You can call him on his dorm phone if you need to speak to him sooner."

"No, I . . . I just want to see his face, you know?"

"Yes, I know. I miss him. I miss Chris, too, but I imagine it's hard for you not seeing your brothers every day."

Indigo sighed. "I feel like an alien, and nothing I ever do is good enough for my mom." She pouted, looking despondent.

"You're an accomplished athlete and you make straight As. You're the perfect daughter."

"Are you willing to write a testimonial for me?" Indigo batted her pretty eyes.

"I don't think my opinion will go a long way with Christine."

Indigo snorted. "True. But she'll have to get over it by the time you two get married."

"Married? Please, I've got too much going on."

"Well, it needs to be soon. Otherwise it'll look weird if I'm your flower girl."

"It would be weird now. Besides, I'll make you the bridesmaid. Aneesa gets maid of honor."

"Meh. I really wanted to throw flowers on the ground," Indigo insisted.

"You can hold them instead."

Indigo nodded. "Not as fun, but I accept."

"We've got some time yet." Cindy wouldn't deny that the thought had crossed her mind. She hoped, in another five years, she and Christine could have formed a healthy relationship.

"Oh, that's right. You're leaving me for college, too."

Cindy was just about to finish her associate's degree at Anne Arundel Community College. After that, she planned to get her bachelor's from the University of Maryland so she could teach middle school English.

Indigo glanced at her watch and then scrambled. "Oh, I've got to go meet my new friend Bree."

"Who is she? I've never heard of her."

"She's here for the summer to visit her dad. I met her at a . . . an event."

"You mean a party?" Aneesa called her out.

"Yes, but don't tell my brothers."

Aneesa waved off her worry. "Of course we won't. We partied with your brothers at your age, so why would we snitch? Besides, I believe in gender equality."

Indigo focused her large brown eyes on Cindy. "Please don't tell CJ . . . or Chris."

Cindy crossed both fingers. "I promise, so long as you aren't drinking."

Indigo rolled her eyes. "I'm not. I'm training for a swim meet, anyway. Now, I've really got to go. I'm ten minutes late."

"Okay, see you later." Cindy cupped her hand over her eyes and waved as Indigo stood up and then watched her leave.

"That girl is always running around," Aneesa said.

"Yeah, she is. It's good she's keeping busy. Things don't sound too good at home."

Cindy would talk to Chris and CJ about it, though Indigo would hate that she had talked about her behind her back. But sixteen-year-olds shouldn't have bags under their eyes. They shouldn't fidget or look stressed. Especially not rich sixteen-year-olds who needn't worry about their next meal.

"Dang, girl, you're eating all the popcorn." CJ moved to grab a handful, but Cindy slapped his hand.

"I bought you salt and vinegar chips." She pointed to her purse.

"But I'm in the mood for popcorn." His pout was so cute. She gave in and held the bowl out to him. He kissed her, then paused the movie on her television.

"Why are you pausing the movie?"

"Because I want to kiss my girl."

"Oh, well, then, you have my permission," she replied in a prim voice.

He flicked his attention to the door. "What time is your mom coming home?"

"Late."

"How late?"

"Overtime."

"Oh good." He grabbed her hand.

"Wait. Let me clean up, just in case." Cindy dumped the popcorn and washed the dishes in the sink. While she cleaned, CJ rearranged the sofa and moved the table back to its original position.

"Oh, I've been meaning to talk to you about Indigo." She'd already spoken to Chris about her concerns, but in the past week Indigo had seemed even more rattled. Chris had plans to come home in a week to check things out.

"What about her?"

"She seems a little . . . off."

"How so?"

"I think she misses you and Chris, and with her being the only kid at home, she's struggling with Christine." As she spoke, Cindy realized that CJ could have been spending time with his sister instead of with her.

"Maybe you should go home early and spend time with Indigo? Take her to the music store, or maybe just hang out on the beach."

CJ shook his head, a frown indented his forehead. "You know, I haven't seen her since I came home yesterday. She was out with a new friend." He crossed his arms. "Has she said anything to you?"

"We spoke a few days ago. She said there were some family things going on and she was too embarrassed to tell me about it. She said she would talk to you this weekend."

He glanced at his watch. "Yeah, maybe I should head back." His brown eyes glittered with worry. "You don't mind, do you? I know we were going to . . . lie down."

Cindy snorted. "Is that what they call it back at Morehouse?"

"I wouldn't know. I'm always studying."

Cindy rolled her eyes. Though CJ would never be the life of the party like Chris, he was social enough. "Please. I know those Spelman girls are all over you."

"No, not anymore anyway. They said I'm rude."

Cindy laughed this time. That she could believe.

"Now go home and take care of your sister. Tell her I said hi."

He squeezed her waist. "No matter what, I'll see you tomorrow night, okay?"

"Of course." Cindy nodded. "But if you need more time with Indigo—"

"Then she can be our third wheel. It'll be a pleasant change from Chris."

Cindy kissed him goodnight and closed the door. He was such a great brother to Indigo, and she knew that, whatever bothered her, he would fix it.

Between Chris and CJ, Indigo had the best brothers, but she often ran to CJ if she had a complex problem that needed solving. He also was the peacemaker between her and Christine.

The following morning, CJ called.

"How did it go with Indigo?"

"Well, good morning to you, too."

"Yes, good morning, Sunshine. Now, how's my Indigo?"

"Indigo . . ." He huffed over the receiver. "She didn't want to talk. She was being evasive. Said she had to figure out some things first, and that she wasn't sure if she was right."

"Right about what?"

"I don't know. I'm taking her to the music store today and then lunch at her favorite restaurant."

"Good idea."

"Yeah. Maybe she'll comb her hair and shower."

"What?"

"By the look and smell, she hasn't done either. I told her I was going to hold her down and spray her down outside if she didn't get her shit together."

"Something is definitely wrong." Indigo usually showered twice a day since she swam so much.

"Yes. And Christine is no better. She jumps at every little sound. She stares at Indigo like she wants to say something, but she hasn't said a word."

"What does your dad say?"

"He's so busy with his job, he's pretending not to notice. I confronted him last night, and he said she's just going through teenage drama."

"That's more than drama." Besides that, Indigo had experienced bouts of sadness even before her brothers left the house. She was extremely competitive, and on the rare occasion she didn't place in a swim meet, she would lock herself in her room and cry for hours. Then there was the time she broke up with her boyfriend. She barely ate for weeks.

"I think there may be a larger issue with Indigo. I know it's hard to imagine, but maybe she's depressed."

"That's what I said to my father, and you'd think I cursed at the man. He told me she's just sad about me and Chris, but she'll be just fine." CJ sighed. "I don't know . . . maybe I should transfer closer to home."

Cindy's heart soared at the thought. "Do you think it would help?"

"Someone needs to be around. Christine will never acknowledge

Indigo needs help. Dad is great, but sometimes he's so damn busy. And shit, Chris could deploy at any moment."

"Where would you go?"

"Maybe University of Maryland. With you."

"Christine would have a conniption."

"I don't care. Maybe that'll push her to take care of her daughter and stop worrying about appearances," he snapped. "Sorry. I'm not mad at you."

"I know."

"CJ!" someone called in the background.

"That's Indigo. She's out of the shower now."

"Good."

"All right, I'll see you later tonight."

CHAPTER THIRTEEN

April 1991

SECRETS NEVER DIE

CINDY

Cindy and CJ looked on while Indigo, who stood near the water, spoke in hushed whispers to her new friend.

"Do you know who she is?" CJ asked.

"Bree Miller. She's visiting some family this summer."

"Miller, huh?" CJ frowned as he stared out at the sea. "Maybe she's related to Jacqueline Miller, mom's old childhood friend, but I haven't heard anything about another relative."

Cindy shook her head. "You know they do the same thing to me? Who's that girl beside CJ? Who are her people?"

CJ bit into one of the sandwiches he'd bought for their impromptu picnic with Indigo. "They know full well who you are, as many events as you've attended with Chris."

"As friends," Cindy stressed. Despite the two years that had passed since she'd assured him that she and Chris were just friends, CJ was still bitter about having not known how she felt for years.

"I'm telling you," CJ said after taking another bite into his sandwich, "Chris knew I liked you."

"You never told him so how would he know?" She defended her best friend.

He grunted, then asked, "Have you talked to this Bree girl yet?"

Cindy shook her head. She watched the girls splash each other in the water, then straighten up when two good-looking boys strutted past them like peacocks. "And as far as I'm concerned, she's a wonderful influence. Look at her, making Indigo laugh." She pointed at the friends.

CJ sighed. "I guess."

"Don't go blaming whatever is going on with Indigo on that poor girl. Indigo's been through this before."

CJ rewrapped his sandwich. "You're right. I talked to Mom and Dad again about getting her some help. I found a few places in Annapolis, and even DC, if they need more distance." He shook his head. "They said she'll get through it. She's fine. She's just a teenager. But last night, when she took a long bath, Mom started banging the door down. She looked worried."

Fear struck Cindy's heart. "You don't think she tried to . . . to harm herself, do you?"

"No. I think we had a long day out and she needed to decompress in the tub. But if Mom is so worried about her being in the bath for a long time, then she knows damn well Indigo needs help. And there's no shame in that."

Cindy wrapped her arm around CJ's torso. "Maybe you should talk to Indigo. Ask her what she wants to do instead of deciding for her?"

CJ jerked back and studied Cindy. "Damn. Why didn't I think about that?"

"Because you're her overbearing big brother and you think you know what's best."

"Because I usually do." He nodded. "I'll ask her tonight before I hit the road."

"Good."

"Are you working tonight?"

Cindy shook her head. She worked at a laundry and dry-cleaning company in Annapolis. Most days she could bring her books and study in the back.

"Good. I'll pop by your apartment before I leave."

"All right," Cindy eagerly agreed.

After her friend left, Indigo walked over to their spot on the beach.

"What are you two up to?" Indigo asked just before she plopped onto the beach towel beside CJ and lay down flat, with her arms folded behind her head.

"Talking about you and your new friend," CJ said, getting right to his nosy point.

"Oh, Bree?" Indigo giggled. "She's funny, and she's really smart."

"She's smart, huh?" CJ gentled his voice.

"Extremely. Trust me, she's going to be the first female president."

"I'm not mad at that. Who are her people?"

Indigo played at the frayed bracelet on her wrist, avoiding his gaze and his question.

"Indigo?" CJ asked again. "Who are her people?"

She huffed like a dragon blowing smoke. "Who knows, who cares? Don't get all elitist like Christine."

"I'm not an elitist. I just want to know who you're with. The world is getting crazy."

"Yeah, well, I fit right in."

Cindy's eyes went wide. Did Indigo really feel that way about herself?

"You aren't crazy," CJ immediately insisted, his voice hard.

Indigo rolled over and punched his arm. "I know, I'm kidding."

"Anyway," she said, looking at Cindy, "I was thinking . . ."

"What about?" Cindy answered.

"I really would prefer to be your flower girl for the wedding.

'm much more flower girl material than bridesmaid. Aneesa can have it."

"I can have more than one bridesmaid."

"I know. But she's so . . ." Her hands carved out the shape of a mountain in the air. "Va-va-voom. I look like a kid beside her."

"Because you are a child. And what's this about you being a flower girl?" CJ asked.

"In your wedding, stupid."

"I'm not stupid."

"You'll be stupid if you don't marry Cindy."

He glanced nervously at Cindy, then focused his attention back on Indigo. Cindy's blood ran hot in her veins.

"I'm not stupid," he muttered under his breath.

Cindy released the breath trapped by the tension in her chest.

"Good to know." His little sister sounded pleased. "So when is it happening?"

"Are we really doing this?" CJ asked.

"Yes!" Indigo and Cindy shouted.

Cindy laughed when CJ jerked his head back.

"I've got to finish undergrad at Morehouse. Then Yale Law. Then I'll need to work for at least a year to save up."

"Save up? Sir, we're rich!" his sister argued.

"Our parents are rich. I'm my own man."

"Yeah, well. Now that I think about it, Christine ain't footing the bill for your wedding. No offense." She smacked Cindy on the arm. "Anyway, that's like six or seven years from now."

"Which is why you can't be our flower girl. You'll have time to grow into your va-va-voom," Cindy helpfully replied.

"I think you should get married right after law school, but that's just me." Indigo stood. "Anyway, I'm ready to head home. You can stop babysitting me now."

"All right." Cindy packed up, though CJ and Indigo would be

taking almost everything—the blanket, the umbrella, most of the food—back to their home.

CJ kissed Cindy's forehead. "I'll see you in a few hours."

"I'll be waiting."

A hard knock on the door woke Cindy from her sleep. She looked at her clock on the nightstand. It was near midnight. The knocking resumed, getting louder and impatient.

Must be CJ. He hadn't called, so she assumed he'd gotten caught up and forgotten to swing by before leaving for Atlanta.

She hurried out of the bed and opened the door. His eyes were bloodshot, his shirt disheveled instead of tucked into his khaki pants.

"What happened?" Cindy pulled him inside before a nosy neighbor complained.

"Indigo ran away."

"What?"

"After I took your advice about talking to her about getting help, she yelled at me. Told me I was clueless to what was going on around me, right under my nose. She told me she couldn't trust me, and she ran the fuck away."

"D-did you find her?"

He let out a long sigh. "She came back home. I think she was somewhere with her new friend."

He rubbed a hand over his face. "I shouldn't have said anything to her. I just made things worse."

"CJ." Cindy reached out, but he shrugged away from her embrace. "I'm sorry that happened. But the conversation had to happen eventually."

"Now she thinks I think I want her to go away."

"Of course she doesn't. Not deep down."

"Yes, she does. She told me as much."

"Sit down."

"I've got to go, it's a long drive, and—"

"Sit down, Charles Jones." Cindy hardened her tone. She knew if she dropped the matter, he would go back to Atlanta and ignore her calls. That's how he processed his feelings—stuffed them down so deep they hardened to stone. And if anyone tried to break through, he'd give them hell.

He sat beside her, staring at the floor. "I'll call Chris. She doesn't hate him."

"Chris will be home next weekend. Maybe she'll open up to him." Cindy patted his hand. "I know this is hard to go through right now, but what do you think would have happened if your parents got her counseling at *your* suggestion?"

"Same thing, I guess."

"Exactly. No kid wants to be viewed as different. They just want to hang out with their friends without worrying. They care far too much about other people's opinions. You know that."

"That's why I suggested we go to DC. No one has to know about it."

"She just needs time to think. I'm sure the idea came as a shock, but she of all people understands she isn't feeling her best. So let her sulk and let her vent to Chris, and then maybe he can leave some pamphlets for her to read. He's fantastic at convincing people to do things they don't want to do."

"Yeah, he is." CJ nodded. "I just feel like an asshole. I made her cry. Then I upset our parents for going behind their backs about counseling."

"They'll cool off."

He let out an unamused laugh. "It'll take a century. They're pissed right now."

"Well, they'll just have to be pissed. There's no crime in caring about your sister so much you want to help her. It's a lot more than what they're doing . . . going around pretending everything is hunky-dory."

CJ laughed. "And now you're mad."

"I am. I love Indigo, and I don't love the idea of counseling, but if she needs help, she needs to get it."

Cindy had seen her friend go from being on top of the world to crashing. Indigo had gone days without speaking, a dead look in her usually expressive brown eyes.

"Yeah, well, I'll keep at it. I'll let Chris have this weekend, and then I'm coming home the next week."

"Really? I thought you were busy with end of year tests."

He nodded. "Yes, but I can bring my books."

Cindy's smile spread wide. She was sorry about Indigo, but glad she would get more time with CJ. "Okay, call me when you get back to the dorms."

"It'll have to be tomorrow morning. They won't let me use the phone by the time I'll get back."

Cindy walked him to the door. The door lock twisted and opened, revealing her mom.

"Hi, Ms. Marshall, how are you?"

Though her mother was exhausted, she mustered a smile for CJ. "I'm good, young man. How are you?"

"I apologize for being over so late, but I had a family emergency, and I wanted to swing by before I left for school."

"It's no problem." This time Cindy's mother's smile was fake. It didn't matter that Cindy was nineteen years old. She did not condone him being in her home so late. Cindy knew her mother felt this way because she'd had her so young, at seventeen years old.

"I'll call you tomorrow." CJ bent over and kissed her cheek. "Bye."

"Drive safe."

She closed the door behind him, under her mother's watchful eyes.

"Now, I know you didn't have him up in my house so late."

"Sorry, Mama. But what he said was true. Indigo ran away from home, and he spent the better part of the night searching for her."

Her mother clasped her chest. "He found her?"

"She came back home. But he's worried, and so am I."

"Thank the Lord she's back home." Her mother let out a long exhale. "Well, I'm beat. I'm going to bed."

"Me, too."

After Cindy returned to bed, try as she might, she couldn't get to sleep.

Despite CJ's intention, he did not return home the following weekend. Or even the next. However, when Cindy checked in with Indigo, her young friend's sunny personality seemed to have returned.

But a few weeks later, Indigo disappeared again.

And this time she didn't come home.

When Chris called Cindy in a panic the following weekend, it was during her shift at the laundromat.

"Pumpkin Pie, I . . . I need you."

"What is it? What happened?"

"We can't find Indigo. She had an argument with Mom and then she just ran off. Have you seen her?"

Cindy glanced at her watch. It was just past midnight.

"N-no." Cindy gripped the cord of the phone and wound it around her hand. Her heart exploded in her chest. "Whenever she's mad, she's at the music store or the beach."

"They checked there already. Say, I know you're at work, but my parents are getting together a search party and—"

"Of course. I'll call my mom to see if she can cover for me."

"Thank you. I just can't . . . my gut is telling me something's wrong. We need all the help we can get."

After Cindy got off the phone, she called her mother, who quickly agreed to cover her shift.

As soon as her mother arrived, she dashed off and met Chris near Walnut Creek, where a group of over a dozen Highland Beach residents had gathered. Mayor Daniel stood in the center, giving directions and assigning people to search groups.

Cindy immediately spotted Chris and shoved her way into the crowd. He pulled her close and mumbled his thanks into her hair. She felt lasers on her back and turned to face Christine. Her expression looked murderous, but by the time Chris released her and turned to face his mother, she wore a mask of devastation.

I should be the least of her worries.

After two hours, the search was called off for the day, with promises to resume in the morning.

Chris and Cindy stood in the parking lot of her apartment complex. He'd insisted on following her home.

"CJ will be here tomorrow," Chris whispered to her.

"Oh? I haven't spoken to him today."

"CJ told me about his conversation. He feels guilty, but I keep telling him he did the right thing. He thinks he pushed her over the edge."

Cindy's throat went tight. "I hate to say it, but I think she was already on the edge. She's been unhappy lately."

"No, you're right. She's unhappy, and I think it's because of our mother."

Cindy leaned against her car door. "Did she tell you anything?"

"No. I just overheard some stuff. Indigo called her a hypocrite and a liar. And that she was tired of trying to be a perfect daughter when she's far from perfect."

A liar? "You know, she mentioned she wanted to talk to CJ about some embarrassing family stuff. Maybe that's related."

"I should confront Mom about this."

Cindy shook her head. "Your mom is scared witless. Let's resume the search in the morning and play it by ear."

"Hmm."

"Now you sound like CJ."

He cracked a small smile. "Guess that's not a bad thing since you're so in love," he said in a high-pitched voice.

"Hush." She nudged his shoulder with her own.

Chris tilted his head back and sighed. "I'm going to see if I can get leave, but I may not get permission." Tears filled his eyes. Cindy pulled him close and gave him a tight hug, wanting to protect him from the pain.

"Tell me it's going to be okay," he whispered into her hair.

"I'm praying for Indigo. Praying that wherever she is, she knows her family and friends love her. That's what she needs right now, more than ever."

"Okay, I'll call you tomorrow. We're meeting at the—"

"Coffee shop. I got it."

The next morning, Cindy couldn't sleep and left early. She found Chris seated in the back of the coffee shop, engaged in a heated discussion with a young woman. When Cindy came closer, she recognized her as Bree, Indigo's friend.

"Get up. Leave."

"I'm just . . ."

"What did I say?" Chris's voice went low.

With tears in her eyes, the young lady rushed out of the coffee shop.

"What was that all about?"

"Foolishness."

"What about? That's Indigo's friend, right? I'm sure she could help—"

"No. She doesn't know where my sister is. In fact, they got into an argument, which is probably why she's missing. So no, we don't need her help."

"O- . . . okay." Cindy had a lot more questions. For one, what were they arguing over? Was it over boys or something much more serious? Chris seemed like he was not in the mood for a calm review of the facts. His eyes were bloodshot red. His hair was uncombed.

"We'll find her, okay?" Cindy reached over to squeeze his hands.

But the search that day had been fruitless. Then Chris called her the following morning. Indigo's body had been found washed ashore.

CHAPTER FOURTEEN

May 2022

LOVE HURTS

Olivia woke up with the jitters.

Today she, CJ, and Cindy would face the town as a united front to kick off the Memorial Day weekend. The beach fest was organized with a local service-based organization for Black women called The Links, which included important figures like Kamala Harris. The chapter's goal was to raise funds to update the Pavilion, at the center of the neighborhood. Olivia knew a charity function with the town's who's-who roster would be the best way for the curious and the callous to get to know her.

The three of them sat around the kitchen table drinking their morning coffee. "The good news is, everyone is friendly, and no one is mad at either of you," CJ said.

Olivia knew his reputation had taken a beating. It was all over the newspaper, despite their ally in Aneesa. And social media—mostly the town's Facebook group, along with posts on Twitter—had blown up over the news.

"Are you nervous?" Cindy asked Olivia.

"I'm fine. How are you feeling?"

"I'm just worried about you." She spoke to Olivia as if she were the only one in the room. Cindy and CJ had come to some sort of weird arrangement when they were around each other. They would simply nod at each other and speak directly to Olivia—never to each other. It was truly nonsensical, but as she and Garrett were currently not speaking, she couldn't judge.

"I'll be fine. We'll all be fine," Olivia finally answered Cindy. She pointed a finger at her parents. "Though I will say that you two had better figure out something before tonight's events."

They looked at each other with various shades of guilt etched on their faces. Cindy forked her veggie omelet and chewed. CJ sipped his coffee, staring at her mother over the rim of his mug.

CJ cleared his throat. "We'll enter the front door. You'll be in the middle. Cindy and I will be on either side of you. Once dinner begins, Cindy, you can sit beside Alan and Olivia. Olivia, you will sit next to me, and Christine will sit on my left."

"Fantastic," Cindy responded, her voice Spanx-tight.

"Good," CJ said. "I wouldn't want to force you to sit beside someone you don't like."

Cindy's eyes flared with heat. "I never said I disliked you. I just don't trust you."

"Then why are you here?" he all but demanded.

"For Olivia, and thank God I came. It's been a month since we arrived, and someone has already splashed her face on the news. And now you're using her as a political scapegoat to salvage your campaign."

"I don't give a damn about this campaign. I only care about you and Olivia. Maybe one day you'll understand that you're the only woman that I've ever loved."

Olivia's attention darted between her mother and father. She wanted to leave, but something rooted her in place. Cindy attempted to stand, but Olivia reached for her hand, pulling her back down into her seat. After she settled, Olivia grasped her father's hand.

"I need you both to step away from the past and stay here with me. You're so busy looking behind you that you can't see each other."

Cindy's eyes, now wet, stared at Olivia. CJ sat silently, staring at the muted television.

"You can't see each other's pain. And look, both of you could have been more forthcoming about your feelings."

"More forthcoming?" Cindy scoffed. "I told CJ you were his. I told him I loved him. For hours, I waited in the rain and he—"

"Came for you," Olivia cut in. "But you chose Chris and made me believe he was my biological father. Now, I won't judge you for it. I get it, and I would've made the same decision if I'd been in your situation."

Cindy squeezed her hand. Gratitude shone in her eyes, wet with tears.

Olivia gentled her voice. "But, Mom, you had other choices you made that weren't the best. Like . . . you could've called CJ when Chris died."

Despite Christine's faults and CJ's lack of action, Olivia believed they deserved to have closure. Not knowing about Chris was especially cruel since Indigo had also died tragically.

Cindy finally spoke, her voice craggy with pain. "Chris was so mad at his family, and he never wanted to speak to them. I even . . . pressed him to reach out to CJ, but he refused. He told me to never bring up his name again. So I thought . . ." Cindy licked her lips. "I thought it would dishonor Chris to have them at the funeral."

Olivia squeezed her mother's clammy hand. "Even if there was a lot of bad blood between them, CJ should've had the opportunity to say goodbye to his brother."

"I know . . . I . . . I'm sorry, CJ. Back then, I was so hurt and humiliated by you. And I . . . I just couldn't face you. At the time, I wasn't in the best mental head space, and I couldn't handle the thought of seeing you. I couldn't tempt myself to be in your space."

She shook her head. "My heart was shattered, and I didn't want to love you or anyone else again because of what you did. B-because love hurts too much." Cindy lifted her eyes to meet his. "It seems like I never can make the right decision when it comes to you."

Cindy's shoulders shook. She pulled her hand away from Olivia's, covered her face, and sobbed into her hands.

CJ stood, moved past Olivia, and pulled Cindy into his arms. "I didn't make it easy for you. But I swear, this time you and Olivia will always come first."

He whispered something else that only her mother could hear.

Olivia's vision blurred. The tragic couple melded together like waves in an abstract painting.

Olivia stood, wiping tears with the back of her hands, and walked out the back door.

She hoped this would be one of many conversations for her parents. They needed to heal, and then maybe they could forge a new relationship—a stronger one, and one with more acceptance.

But first, they needed to forgive themselves and each other. Olivia knew all about self-loathing and was now consumed by her less than stellar communication with Garrett. Olivia could finally admit to herself that some of the cruel things he'd said held a few nuggets of truth. Such as her fear of committing to and loving someone again.

She pulled out her phone and scrolled to Garrett's name. Her thumb hovered over the green button.

"Should I call him?" Olivia mused out loud. She stared at his name, but then swiped it away. She needed reinforcements.

Addy.

When Olivia dialed her neighbor in Sag Harbor, she picked up after the third ring.

"Hey. What's cooking?"

"I need to speak to you about something sensitive. Something that must happen off the record."

"Of course," Addy readily agreed. "Whatever it is, your secret is safe with me."

Olivia sighed. "Garrett's not taking my calls right now."

"Hmmm." The phone went silent for long seconds. "So what did you do?"

"What did I do?" She shrieked her question.

"Garrett is a cinnamon roll."

That cinnamon roll had told her that she wasn't a good role model to his child.

"He's not without faults himself," she said.

"Oh yeah? Like what?"

"We had an argument, and he said some really harsh things."

"Like what?"

"I won't get into all the details, but he says I don't know what I want."

"You can't decide, can you? That's your problem."

"What's my problem?"

"You're so determined to make the right decision that you make no decisions."

"I made more than enough decisions last summer," Olivia responded, her agitation apparent in her voice.

"Yes, you did . . . *last* summer. I hate to break it to you, but as long as you're living, you will continue to make decisions. You don't get to hit the Pause button."

"I need to slow down and recalibrate."

"Okay, well, then you should understand why Garrett needs to slow down, too. Especially if he feels more for you than you do for him."

"I never said I don't have feelings for Garrett." Olivia had feelings. Deep, deep feelings. Garrett was her first thought in the morning. She worried about him constantly. Sometimes he worked so hard he would forget to eat, and she would often stop by with a packed lunch. And then he would burn out between the exuberant Zora and work. Often she shooed him out of the house and played with Zora. Or she would take Zora once a month for a girl's day in town.

Of course, she cared.

She more than cared. She . . .

"I love him." Olivia covered her mouth, looked around as if the government were recording her calls.

"Oh . . . Oh!" Addy chirped. "Does he know?"

"We haven't said the words just yet. I would also appreciate your discretion here."

Addy snorted. "Sure. I won't tell him."

Olivia shook her head. She knew that Addy would tell Whitney and Kara. In fact, it would probably give her friend pleasure to be the first to break the news.

"Just tell Whitney and Kara not to tell anyone."

"What about Mr. Whittingham?"

"Please don't tell him. Not yet." He was too close to Garrett, and she was sure he'd give obvious hints to his favorite neighbor, whom he viewed as an unofficial son.

"Bea?"

"Good God. Just keep it to Whitney and Kara."

She trusted Bea to be discreet, but if she somehow slipped the news to Billie, who would then tell Perry and Ama, then they would give her grief. She loved her friends and family, but everyone insisted on being the *first* to know things.

"Okay, fine, fine. Whitney and Kara will do. I'll tell them to keep it hush."

"How good of you."

"I'll do you one better. Tonight, I'll have a little chat with Garrett. I'll see where his head is at. Then me, Kara, and Whitney will call you and talk strategy."

"Do I really need to strategize about this?"

"I'm sorry. Did you not call me for help?"

"I did." Though Olivia was regretting it.

"Then don't question my methods, Ms. Jones. I'll call you back soon. Gotta go."

Addy hung up the phone before Olivia could say goodbye. She stared at the phone. Laughter bubbled inside of her chest. Olivia bent over, giggling at the ridiculous conversation with her former nemesis turned friend. On the surface, Addy was brash and often spoke before thinking. She'd been the neighbor who discovered Anderson's side job as an Uber driver and had spread the news far and wide. But after getting to know her, Olivia realized Addy deeply cared about her friends and community. When Olivia had broken her engagement with Anderson, Addy had been the first neighbor to come by with a care package, including wine and snacks.

She did, however, open the link to Dr. LaGrange's site and schedule an appointment for the following week.

Olivia wasn't ready to return to heavy. Sitting by the pool calmed her, so she sat on the edge and lowered her bare legs into the water. Smiling, she basked in the sunshine for a few minutes before returning to the house, where she found CJ by himself in the kitchen, pouring another cup of coffee.

But before she could ask for her mother's whereabouts, CJ said, "She's taking a shower, then we'll talk again about tonight."

He grabbed another mug and filled it with coffee, then added a third of a cup of almond milk and two tablespoons of brown sugar. He carefully handed the mug to Olivia.

"How did you know how I like my coffee?"

"You're not the only observant one in the family." He winked then sat beside her at the kitchen table. "You know, it isn't always the case that parents are smarter than their children, but they're supposed to be wiser. Thank you for your help."

Olivia dipped her head, weighed down by his surprise praise.

"It's no problem. I just want you both to be happy."

"Both?"

Olivia nodded. "Yes, of course I want that for you."

CJ nodded. "I wasn't sure if you wanted us together. In fact, I think you warned me to stay away."

"Back then, I wasn't sure you were serious about my mother."

Cindy had practically fainted when CJ popped by Olivia's house in Sag Harbor unannounced.

"What made you drive to my house last summer?" she asked.

Now that she knew her father a bit more, she knew he rarely acted on impulse. And if word had gotten around that he popped by some strange woman's home in Sag Harbor, that would've spurred rumors.

"Mr. Whittingham convinced me, though he probably didn't realize his influence."

"Really? How so?" Olivia blew on her coffee and waited for his response.

"He bragged so much about you. How brilliant you are, your career accomplishments. He said you looked just like me, which made me feel even guiltier because I . . . I said some unkind things to Cindy when she was pregnant with you."

Olivia sipped her coffee quickly, nearly burning her mouth. She sucked in air to soothe her scalded tongue.

"But then he told me about how nervous you were about Cindy arriving. And he insinuated that you two didn't get on very well. So, I . . ." CJ shook his head. "This entire time, I thought staying out of your lives was for the best. But then I realized maybe you aren't happy, and maybe Cindy isn't happy. And maybe I should try to make you happy. Actually, that's not totally true. I wanted to be happy, too."

"You weren't happy?"

"No." CJ laughed without humor. "In fact, I was at an all-time low. The town's opinions were divided about my relationship with Riley. Then I lied again when I pretended to date Lauren." He shook his head. "I did this all to myself, I know. Mr. Whitt asked me when was the last time I was happy. There were a few moments that I could recall. When I became mayor and when your mom and I were together are the strongest memories."

"You came after us to make yourself happy?"

"Absolutely. In my youth, my decisions were driven by the path of least resistance. Sure, I wanted to go to Morehouse, but I went because my father was alumni and that was the expectation. I did it because he had an impressive network, and of course, I formed my own over the years. Then I attended Yale Law because Mom, Dad, and even Alan influenced me. I enjoy practicing law, and I'm good at it. But it wasn't my first choice. The first time I chose something for me was when I asked your mother out on a date. And then next time after that was years later when I ran for mayor."

He sipped coffee after his confession. "Sure, Christine encouraged me to do so. She may think she put the idea in my head. But seeing my dad, the impact he made on our community . . . I wanted to give back to the place I love. To the people who had a hand in raising me. But more, I wanted to maintain the specialness of this place. This is a place where you can plant your roots. I wanted little boys and girls to grow up with a deep sense of pride in our history. I don't think I would want to be mayor anywhere else but Highland Beach."

"Wow."

"Yes," CJ said. "With all that's happening, I lost sight of my passion. When you're the mayor, people want everything from you, and for once I only wanted to be available 24/7 for you and Cindy. But now, with the threat of losing my office, I want to fight for it."

"Then we'll help you fight," Olivia readily agreed. She was good at being charming, and tonight she would act like a loving daughter.

But she wouldn't be faking it. In the past month, CJ had become important to her.

Her father. Someone she'd longed for ever since she could remember dads dropping off their kids at school.

Omar, can you see this?

She wondered how her godfather would react to . . . everything that had transpired in the last weeks. Would he have encouraged her to stay in Sag Harbor with Garrett? Or would he have told her to get to know her father?

She guessed he'd have given the latter advice.

"How about we watch a movie while Cindy relaxes?" her father suggested.

"Sure, what do you have in mind?"

"Your choice."

Olivia nearly groaned. Skipping through hundreds of titles reminded her of Garrett.

"What's wrong? You look unhappy."

"No, it's not that. It's just that . . . it may be best for you to choose. I'm terrible at picking movies. It drives my . . . my friend finds my indecision baffling."

"Who, Garrett?"

Olivia nodded. She hadn't spoken much about him.

"Mr. Whitt says he's a stand-up guy."

"He's just wonderful. Which is why I can't fully accept your praise for being wise when I'm screwing up my relationship."

"You still haven't spoken to him?"

"Not yet."

"He's more than welcome to visit. I have a spare bedroom."

"Let's get through tonight's festivities and make sure that our neighbors don't run me out of town with pitchforks."

"I'm telling you, the good folks of Highland Beach will love you."

"Maybe." Olivia's tone conveyed her unease.

"We'll see soon enough. And if we're not going to watch a movie, I need to prepare for tonight's events." He stood. "I'll see you later?"

"I'll be there." Olivia waved as he left.

For the next few hours, she sat outside and basked in the sun, but thoughts of Garrett kept demanding her attention.

She finally gave in to temptation and texted him once more.

Garrett, I really think we should talk. Can you call me?

After she clicked Send, she stared at her phone, fingers gripped around the case, hoping, praying he would call or at least text.

Dots danced across the screen for nearly a minute. She held her breath, waiting for the message to come through and then . . . nothing.

Just after she'd swallowed down the salty tears threatening to climb up her throat, the phone dinged.

I'm sorry, Olivia. I need more time.

CHAPTER FIFTEEN

May 2022

SOMETHING TO TALK ABOUT

Just as Alan had warned, many of the prominent families came to the gathering that evening—some to meet her and some to support the growing needs of the community.

Cindy wore a black-and-silver babydoll dress with spiked heels that made her legs look like they went on for days.

A Hervé Leger emerald dress with capped sleeves hugged Olivia's body. She paired the beautiful gown with gold Chanel sandals with bows that covered her toes.

When they entered the pavilion with CJ, everyone stared. Christine, who stood on the other side of the room, glided over to greet her family. The click of her heels cut into the acute silence.

"Charles, so good to see you, son." She pulled him into a hug. After stepping out of his embrace, she turned to face Cindy and Olivia.

"Cindy." She surprised her with a greeting. "You look good today." She reached for Cindy's hand. Her mother, who looked too stunned for words, simply stared while her monster-in-law squeezed her fingers.

"And there she is. My granddaughter," Christine said loudly and with pride. "Isn't she just gorgeous?"

Alan walked over to the group and pulled Christine to his side. "Absolutely." The crowd began speaking again. Some even formed a line to greet CJ.

"So this is the daughter." An old man with a snow-white Afro that looked like cotton balls spoke in a booming voice.

"Hello, Mr. . . . ?" Olivia offered her hand.

"Wiley. James Wiley. Nice to meet you, young lady." His loud greeting held warmth.

"Nice to meet you, too." Olivia gave him a winning smile. "Are you a full-time resident or are you just here for the summer?"

"Oh, full-time now. I retired some years ago." He wore an expensive gold watch, a tailored gray suit, and oak brown wingtip shoes.

"Oh? What industry?"

"I own a chain of boutique hotels called The Collections. I've passed it on to my daughter, Alyssa. She's just over there, with my wife, Wilma." Looking back at Olivia, he asked, "So what is it you do, young lady?"

Olivia told him about her work experience, from Array Capital to creating a nonprofit to protect historic Black neighborhoods. During her chat, Alan and Christine joined the conversation.

"We're proud of Olivia's accomplishments," Christine said with a wide smile.

James cut Christine a look that conveyed his doubt and then sipped the brown liquid out of a stout glass.

"Since you were in the finance industry, you have heard of Amelia Vaux Tanner?" A little twinkle sparked the handsome older man's eyes.

"Oh yes. She's my godmother." She missed Ama dearly and could really have used some of her pearls of wisdom right about now. Though everyone pasted on smiles and had been friendly so far, she could feel the undercurrent of tension flowing through the pavilion.

"Now, how were you lucky enough to have such an incredible woman in your life when you were growing up?"

Christine's eyes narrowed. "Oh yes, please do share that story with us. I'm curious how your paths crossed, especially at such a young age."

Olivia's knees buckled. There was no way she could tell Christine or James the true story. That Omar, her godfather, had erroneously caused her son's death by giving away the fact that Chris was a whistleblower for the police force. It had taken some time . . . years . . . for her to heal from the devastating news. She would never tell Christine or Cindy the truth.

Olivia inhaled and then relayed an alternate version of how she knew Ama and Omar. And one, she thought, that had been true most of her life.

"It started when Ama reached out to my mother. It seemed mysterious, at first, to get an invitation to spend time with such an accomplished person. She intended to start a mentorship program and had chosen me and my godsisters because of our academic performance and achievements. Well, she enjoyed our company so much that she decided against scaling out the program and focused on the three of us instead throughout the years. We truly feel blessed, and she has been one of the most important people in my life."

At one point, Olivia had literally wanted to copy every career move her godmother had made. She wanted to be the new Witch of Wall Street and was so far into being Ama's career twin that she hadn't given herself time to discover her own dreams. Last summer had been a gift, though at the time it felt like a curse. But now, knowing her own worth, she could stand on her own and would never let someone make her doubt herself again. Remembering this gave Olivia another mental boost.

Alan leaned in. "There're some refreshments near the beach. Or I can get you champagne."

Olivia squeezed Alan's arm. He was such a dear, and obviously giving her an out just in case she needed space. If memory served, James was the name Lauren had dropped as the person who wanted CJ to resign. It would be a boon to convince him otherwise, and without the help of CJ's ex.

"Champagne would be nice. James, how about I meet your lovely wife and daughter?"

James offered his arm, and together they walked over to meet his family. After ten minutes, Olivia had the trio eating out of her hand. She and Alyssa exchanged cards—the newly minted CEO wanted to figure out a way to partner with Legacy Alliance, the nonprofit that Olivia and Whitney headed.

Olivia continued to work the pavilion with a flute of champagne in hand, meeting a handful of full-time residents as well as a judge who summered every year in Highland Beach with her family and a former reality star turned talent agent who worked bicoastally between New York and Los Angeles. As CJ had already told her, many of those in attendance were older, with gray hair and wide smiles. And as CJ had predicted, there was no one there who was outwardly unfriendly toward Olivia.

Meanwhile, he was having a few whispered conversations in various corners of the room. Her mother stuck to CJ's side, though Olivia noticed that a few people had tried to move her out of the conversation. But anytime someone positioned themselves between the new couple, Cindy simply smiled, sidestepped, and put herself on CJ's other side.

Olivia also saw that her father noticed Cindy making this move, because he always smiled and pulled her closer. He was making a statement too: *Accept both of the new women in my life.*

"They certainly seem cozy," Christine's voice cut into Olivia's reverie.

"They *are* very cozy." Olivia smiled before she sipped her champagne. She was proud that she'd played a tiny part in her parents' romance, that she'd forced them to communicate. They had a long road ahead, but she could tell, between their heated looks and the way they moved around the room together, that they were prepared for the journey.

"Well . . . if he's happy, then we'll figure out a way."

Olivia didn't know who Christine's "we" included. Alan, for one, did not seem at all surprised or bothered by her parents' closeness.

As for the town's opinion? Well, that remained to be seen. Glancing around, she saw facial expressions that ranged from curious to downright furious.

Then, complicating matters, Lauren Miles strode in, wearing a fire-engine-red dress that hit just above her knees.

Her eyes scanned the pavilion, then narrowed when she found Alan, CJ, and Cindy laughing together near the back entrance. She smiled a bit, pulled back her shoulders, and sashayed to the back like a glamorous huntress preparing to slay her prey.

"Excuse me." Olivia turned to Christine. "I'm just going to—"

"Stay here with me." Christine grabbed Olivia's arm, as if that could stop her from leaving.

Olivia inhaled, pulling in oxygen and patience. "I really need to go help. That's what I'm here for."

"No. You're here to abate the curiosity of the residents of Highland Beach, and you do that beautifully. Do not engage Lauren. Charles or I will handle it, since she felt the need to threaten my son about revealing details of their little arrangement."

Olivia smoothly removed Christine's hand from her arm. "You knew about that?"

"Of course. I'm the one who planted the seed in Lauren's head when she told me about her interest in politics."

"And what about my mother?" She didn't want to see Cindy getting mangled in their power struggle.

"Your mother?" Christine snorted. "Please. Cindy can handle herself just fine. Unfortunately, we're forced to play this out, and you, their daughter, should not be in the middle of this. It simply won't do."

"It's not like I'll cause a scene."

"You want to protect Cindy, but I'm here to protect you. And for once, I intend to do my duty toward you. So please indulge me. Let's walk outside and refresh our champagne."

Christine slid her arm into the crook of Olivia's arm and navigated them outside. Christine held her head high, and not once did she spare a look in the opposite direction.

Olivia, however, was not so evolved. She stared toward her parents for as long as possible. Then her body language stiffened when she saw Alan moving to block Lauren and Lauren simply going around him to stand in front of the couple.

Christine waved at a woman who stood near the beach bar and called, "Judy, hello! I must introduce you to my granddaughter, Olivia."

Judy happily accepted Christine's invitation and launched right into a monologue about her own grandkids. A few minutes in, Christine excused herself to chat with a younger couple, and moments later, Janice, CJ's volunteer admin assistant, appeared.

Olivia's face flushed. Shame coursed throughout her body. The woman had called her twice since the news came out, but Olivia hadn't returned her calls. She was too afraid of what Janice would say and feared she would call her out for not revealing her identity that day she spent in the mayor's office.

Olivia graciously excused herself from Judy and whispered her thanks to Janice.

"That woman can talk to a tree and bore grass." Janice rolled her eyes. "How did you end up with her?"

"Christine wanted to distract me while CJ speaks to a few constituents."

Janice nodded. "I won't lie. The news really disappointed people. Especially after . . ."

Janice caught herself.

Olivia stiffened at Janice's statement. "CJ told me about Riley." Then Olivia looked away, sipped more champagne, and scanned the crowd.

"Don't get me wrong," Janice said in a low voice. "They don't blame you or anything. Folks are just curious about you, but disappointed in CJ. So am I, if we're being honest."

Olivia's attention jerked back to Janice. Alarm vibrated like a clanging bell through her chest. Janice had clearly adored her mayor before she discovered his daughter's existence. "You won't stop working with him, will you?"

Janice shrugged. "I'm here . . . for now." She tilted her head, a move that seemed to reflect her teetering loyalty to her mayor.

"I'll be honest, too," Olivia told her. "CJ wanted to tell everyone straight out of the gate."

Janice straightened her stance. "He did?" She looked around and then moved closer. "So why didn't he tell us the truth?"

"Because of me." Olivia didn't whisper. Knowing what her father faced and what he stood to lose had injected her with a big dose of bravery.

"I don't enjoy being the center of gossip. I didn't want people to assume things about me or treat my mother like a monster. It's all . . . very complicated."

Janice nodded. "You've got that right. Especially with Chris. He adored your mother, you know. And CJ loved her, too. So yes, there's been some speculation about all of that."

"That part, I'll leave to my parents. All I ask is that you give them a chance to explain. They were very young, and maybe they could have made different decisions. But here we are."

Janice gave her a soft, warm smile. "Thanks for speaking to me.

You didn't have to answer my Nosy Nettie questions, but I'm glad you did."

Though Olivia liked Janice well enough, strategically it was also advantageous to clear the air with a woman who was well connected and respected. Olivia understood that disregarding Janice's questions would not have pleased the other residents. Hopefully, she would do as Olivia suspected and spread the word.

"Whatever you decide, I do hope we can meet up to chat. I would like to get to know all the good places in town to go to."

"What do you mean 'all the good places'? Every inch of this place is a gem."

Olivia laughed at Janice's attempt to be a one-woman marketing machine.

"And we're only so big . . . but yes, of course. I hope you'll still learn from us and help other neighborhoods stay Black and thriving."

"I'm learning a lot, and some things we can incorporate to continue to protect Highland Beach. CJ and I have been strategizing." They hadn't exactly, but it wouldn't hurt to make Janice and the town think they were a package deal.

"Oh, I can't wait to hear more."

"Janice!" someone called from the other side of the road. She waved and mouthed something to her friend. She turned around and slipped her card into Olivia's hand. "You've got my number now. Call me sometime." She winked and then flitted away to her waiting friend.

Olivia tucked the thick beige card into her clutch and then navigated to where CJ and Cindy stood conversing with an older couple. The older man was speaking and tapping the tip of his cane on the ground to emphasize the points he was making in whatever they were debating.

"I don't know how you young ones get on now, but back in my day we took care of our responsibilities. Now, I know Christine and

Daniel brought you to church every Sunday, but I wonder if you listened to any of my sermons."

Oh Lord. Olivia snuck a glance at her mother, who rolled her eyes.

"Psalm 127: 3–5. Behold, children are a heritage from the Lord, the fruit of the womb a reward. Like arrows in the hand of a warrior are the children of one's youth. Blessed is the man who fills his quiver with them."

Olivia cleared her throat. "Excuse me." She raised her hand. "Fruit of the womb here."

"Oh, well, hello there. I'm Pastor Stanley."

"Nice to meet you. I hope you aren't giving my parents too hard a time for a mistake made so long ago. I'm sure you realize they have changed and grown since then."

"Well . . ." He straightened his shoulders. "It's my job to make sure my flock doesn't stray. CJ should've taken care of his responsibilities."

"I won't deny that." Olivia looked at her father. "But it's been such a blessing getting to know my father. If I can forgive him, the person who was wronged in the situation, then you can forgive him, too."

"It's not about forgiving. It's about character."

"I don't know about that." Olivia smiled kindly at the man. She could tell that he cared for her father but also wanted to give him a hard time. "There are quite a few Bible verses about forgiving, so I think it's important."

The old man laughed, and his wife patted his arm. "She's right, Pete."

Olivia leaned into the lighter atmosphere and the opening Mrs. Stanley had created. "You know, my godfather Omar used to have this conversation with me. When I was mad at someone for wronging me, he often told me, 'Do not judge, and you will not be judged. Do not condemn, and you will not be condemned. Forgive, and you will be forgiven.'"

The pastor smiled. "At least your mother raised you in the church."

Cindy nearly choked on her cocktail. Olivia blanked her face.

"My upbringing was excellent, and I never wanted for anything. I don't want to waste another moment of anger or guilt or fear. I only want to continue to get to know my father and this gorgeous town. Will you let us do that?"

CJ's eyes glittered with remorse. She didn't know if it was the pastor's words or her own, but something had hit him in the gut. He looked worn out.

The pastor offered his hand to Olivia. She quickly shook his hand. Then, in an entirely exaggerated fashion, he turned to CJ and opened his arms.

"I'll always be in your corner, CJ," Pastor Stanley vowed.

"Oh? I heard you were thinking of supporting Harold Munroe?" CJ asked with a teasing smile.

"Nothing wrong with talking to the man," the pastor hedged.

CJ stepped into the hug and patted his pastor on the back. "Good. I'll see you at the mayoral debate then?"

"You've got it, son."

The jingle of a bell halted the conversation. A hostess in a white shirt and black pants smiled at the guests. "Dinner is served."

The pastor and his wife said their goodbyes and walked away, headed toward the pavilion across the street. Olivia moved, but CJ grabbed her wrist.

"Can you give us a moment, Cindy?"

Her mother nodded. "I'll wait near the door."

"Good."

He leaned in and kissed her forehead.

CJ crossed his arms. "You've enchanted everyone."

Olivia chuckled. "Are they enchanted enough to want to keep you around as mayor?"

"I think I've got a fighting chance because of you and Cindy.

So . . . thank you. I don't want you to feel like I'm using you. It's not that I'm suddenly trying to be the family guy. I'm just a stubborn man who's made the worst decision he's ever made in his life."

"Well, looks like you're getting your second chance."

"I shouldn't have messed up the first chance." He shook his head, muttering something under his breath. Then he spoke loud enough for Olivia to hear. "This entire time, watching you . . . standing beside your mother . . . I'm really kicking myself."

"Your life isn't over yet," Olivia replied to her father. And, if she were being honest, neither was hers.

What was she waiting for with Garrett? Was she also missing out on the love of a lifetime and taking the risk of living with regret decades later? She needed to tell him, to show him, that she wanted to spend the rest of her life with him.

When they walked back into the pavilion, they saw that the seating arrangements were just as CJ and Alan had expected—with an exception, a very big exception that could not be ignored. Lauren Miles sat by herself at the round table, waiting.

Olivia strode toward her.

"Lauren?" Olivia spoke quietly enough to not startle the woman. "Will you join me outside before dinner is served?"

Lauren looked around, nodded, then followed Olivia out into the warm, dark evening.

"Was that your assigned seat?" Olivia asked her.

"No." Lauren shook her head. "No, it wasn't. Your father and I have been . . . partners for a while now. Maybe I didn't have an assigned seat, but I should have had a seat."

"You want to become mayor," Olivia acknowledged. "It's a fine goal."

"It's not some . . . some lofty goal. I deserve it. I've earned it. And Highland Beach needs new . . ." She cut herself off, laughing.

"New blood?" Olivia finished for her, remembering Alan's

comment about those who wanted to knock the Douglass-Jones family off their throne.

Lauren shook her head. "They need fresh energy. Someone forthright and brave."

"You don't think CJ has what it takes?"

Lauren arched her eyebrow. "You tell me. Was your father brave all those years ago when he let you and your mom go?" She waved her hand. "Now look at him, sitting there with his ready-made family. The town's forgiven him, and now I look like a lovesick fool."

"I'm sorry if my father hurt you."

"It's not your fault, Olivia." Lauren sighed, still not looking directly at her. "Trust me, my feelings have nothing to do with you."

"Then I'm sorry my father didn't hold up his end of the partnership deal."

Her eyes went wide. "He told you?" she asked with gale-wind force.

"I pushed him to talk about it after I met you at the boutique. Christine told me you two were dating. I wanted to make sure he wasn't playing the field while my mom and I were in his home."

She nodded absently. The steam of her anger seemed to fade. Slowly, she turned to face Olivia. "I'm going home now. I promise not to stand in CJ and Cindy's way. They deserve a second chance. They deserve each other."

"You know my mother?"

"Not well, no. I've just heard things, seen things. And deep down, when I saw her at CJ's home, I knew they had unfinished business."

"Thank you." The woman's easy surrender genuinely shocked Olivia.

"You're welcome. You remind me of someone I once knew. She was forthright and brave. To be honest, she's the reason I want to be mayor." Lauren began to walk away, but then halted. "And because you remind me of her, I'll tell you this: keep your eyes open and protect yourself, beautiful girl. There are sharks swimming among us."

Olivia had thought of the person who took her picture without permission as a nuisance. But if they meant to harm her . . . that was another matter.

"Is my life in danger?"

"No," Lauren said, shaking her head. "But there are other ways to hurt someone. Words, actions. Inaction . . . ask your father about that." With that, she walked away.

Olivia stood outside, the moonlight casting a beautiful silver glow over her skin.

Thoughts of Indigo flittered in her mind. She wondered if her aunt would have liked her. Maybe she would've pushed CJ to reach out to Cindy. And then they would never have missed Chris's funeral.

She hugged herself, forced a smile, and braced herself for the last leg of the night.

As Olivia reentered the room and scanned the smiling faces of the Highland Beach residents, she wondered about the sharks Lauren had warned her about. She knew just the woman who could help her find out.

MAYOR CHARLES "CJ" JONES AND FAMILY HAVE MORE SKELETONS

A person who has remained anonymous has reached out to this publication and provided proof that Indigo Jones, the daughter of the former mayor Daniel Jones and Mrs. Christine Douglass-Jones, lived with a mental illness.

The friend maintains that the Jones family, who were aware of her depression, did nothing to support their daughter. Indigo's friend, who has remained anonymous, has shared firsthand accounts and letters written by Indigo.

My mother is having an affair!!!! She tells me that people can't know I'm sad all the time, that I have to be perfect. But then she turns around and cheats on my dad!! She's such a hypocrite. And she won't even acknowledge the thing about our family line . . . I mean, who cares! We're still a part of the Douglass line. It doesn't matter about what happened in the past, right?

I still haven't decided whether to tell CJ. He'll be so pissed. He and Mom argue all the time about me and his girlfriend.

Chris will be upset, too. I think he ran away to join the military so he could get away from Mom's stupid expectations. I wish I could run away, too. If I could, I'd jump in that water and swim as long and as fast as possible. As soon as I turn eighteen, I'm out of here. I hope you were serious about us moving out west and being roommates. I don't think college is for me, since I'm an artist.

Well anyway, wish me good luck. But you're right. The truth is the best route to take. I'll talk to them tonight.

Your friend,

Indigo

The friend maintained that after the confrontation, Indigo's body was washed ashore.

Here is a personal quote from the source:

"I'll never forget that day the town came together to look for Indigo. I was sick to my stomach because I knew something had happened to her. I think Christine's lover may have had something to do with her death by suiãde, but I felt like I had no voice. Now, I do. And I'll be sharing Indigo's letter along with information that I know about the family. Justice will be served."

The publication has reached out to the Jones family and will await their reply to the allegations.

CHAPTER SIXTEEN

April 1991

SWEET LIES

CJ

"What are you doing out here, Charles?"

CJ found his father seated on the small porch facing the shoreline in the backyard with a cigar in hand. CJ didn't bother sitting down. Instead, he stood opposite his father, directly in his line of sight.

The orange-red light blazed from his father's cigar. It was midnight and CJ should've been on his way to Morehouse, with at least two hundred miles between them by now.

But he couldn't leave.

Not after what he saw. He quickly made plans to skip classes the next day. His line brother would help him smooth things over with his professors. Ever since the afternoon, he hadn't been able to calm his nervous energy or overcome the urge to vomit that clamped his stomach into a thousand nautical knots.

"I'm worried about Indigo."

"I know." His father's tone was somber. "But your mother feels it would cause a scandal. She's used to these kinds of things."

CJ shook his head. "So you're more concerned about the reelection?"

There were a lot of things he respected about his old man. He treated the citizens of Highland Beach with the utmost respect. No request from them was too large or too small, and he had a way of empowering people.

CJ also liked the way Daniel treated his mother. He never dismissed Christine and treated her like an equal. Though neither of them outwardly expressed their love, it was clear that his father nursed a steady flame of devotion to his wife. But it was times like these when he would lose himself in loving Christine, leaving his sensibilities behind.

Like now.

"What does Alan think?" CJ respected his father's adviser, who always observed things objectively.

Daniel snorted. "Alan thinks we should wait until after the election passes. Or go out of town to get . . . help."

"Then we'll go out of town." CJ jumped at the solution.

"We?" Daniel leaned forward, jamming the cigar into his ashtray.

"Yes, we. I don't mind coming back on the weekends. And like I said, there are programs where she could live on the grounds."

"Like an invalid?"

"No. Like someone who needs help around the clock. You and Mother won't bother to—"

Daniel cut him a sharp look.

"You and Mother *can't*," CJ amended, through clenched teeth. "You can't move your schedules around to support her."

He could understand his father, but Christine was another matter. Of course, she chaired foundations and had speaking engagements, but she could always quit. Her daughter should've been her top priority.

"Maybe your mother is right." His father shrugged. "Maybe it's all just teenage drama."

"She cuts herself, Dad."

"You know how kids are these days."

"Yes, I do." CJ crossed his arms. "And we weren't doing that shit growing up. She's not happy, and she hasn't been for a long time. She goes high and low, and we've always brushed it off as being high-strung, but that isn't it and you know it. Just like Mother does when she gets into her moods. You and I both know this isn't normal."

"Not normal?" He heard a pained whisper from behind.

Both CJ and Daniel snapped their attention to the back door.

"Indigo . . ." The regret was clear in CJ's voice.

"Y-you don't think I'm normal. I . . . you told me it was okay. You told me everything would be okay." Indigo's voice shook with recrimination.

"It will be. I'll take care of it, I promise."

"No. You're just running to Dad. And Dad's gonna run to Mom, and she's just going to make me feel even more defective."

She waved her gauze-laden arms.

CJ stared at the white patches covering up deep cuts on her skin. Some cuts were just a millimeter away from certain death. The sight left him raw.

"Maybe you're right." She swiped at the tears streaming down her face. "Maybe I'm not 'normal,'" she said, using air quotes. "I'm not the perfect robot like you. I can't pretend to feel something I don't."

"What are you talking about?" CJ asked. He moved closer, but she stepped away.

"You love Cindy, but you're too afraid of wrecking your perfect image. Not once have you introduced her to Mom or Daddy, even though they already know who she is. They keep tabs on everything."

Misery swirled in his stomach. He had never wanted Cindy to feel less than. CJ glanced at his father, who remained focused on Indigo. Daniel sat still, staring at his daughter as if she were a frightened deer who would dart off from any slight movement.

"And Daddy, maybe I'm not normal like you. Maybe I won't

pretend to not know what's going on around me. Maybe I should just pretend that ignorance is bliss, huh?"

Daniel pushed himself up from his seat and stood. "I don't know what you *think* you know, but before you point fingers," he said, pointing his own finger at her, "you damn well better know before you go off and ruin people's lives."

"Fine." Indigo nodded. "I'll get the evidence I need. All of you . . . all of you are hypocrites. But at least I'm honest." She thumped her chest. "And if that makes me not normal, then I don't give a crap."

She shoved past CJ and Daniel, running down to the beach. CJ stretched out his hands, desperate to catch her. "Indigo, I'm sorry. I didn't mean it like that," CJ called after her.

But Daniel grabbed his arm, pulling him back. "Leave her be, son."

"It's late. I'm not leaving her alone." CJ shrugged off his father's grip and ran down to the beach.

"Indigo!" he shouted, sprinting down the sandy pathway. His heart was beating as loud as his footsteps.

"Indigo!"

CJ returned to the house. Christine and Daniel sat downstairs.

"I couldn't find her." He answered their question before they could ask.

"Well, I'm sure she heard you. I'm sure that . . . that all of Highland Beach heard you shout her name," his mother croaked.

Christine's puffy red eyes betrayed her callous words. But CJ didn't have time for his mother's pretense game. Indigo was all alone—and she felt emotionally abandoned, too. CJ didn't know what to do, but seeing his sister calmly slice her skin with a razor made his blood run cold. What made things worse was Christine's prior knowledge that Indigo had been cutting herself, and her chalking it up to just teenage rebellion.

"So what if they heard me shouting?" CJ's voice rose with anger. "Then maybe someone will call if they find her."

"Calm down . . . please." Daniel's soft voice cut into the thick tension. Then he stood up. "I'm calling the police."

"Daniel!" Christine gasped. "You don't have to do that. She'll be home soon. I know it."

"Deputy Harris will be discreet. But we need to get ahead of this. If they don't find her, then we'll gather volunteers." He let out a weary sigh. "CJ, do you know any of her friends from school we can call?"

"Yeah, a few." CJ nodded, nearly kicking himself for not thinking of that sooner. But she'd complained that her friends were being weird and treating her differently. He thought they were jealous of her, but maybe not. Maybe she had pushed them away.

He also remembered her new friend, Bree. "She's got a new summer friend, too. I met her a few weeks ago."

"Oh really?" Christine sniffed. "Who are her people?"

CJ stopped himself short from making a sharp reply when he remembered that he'd asked the same thing. He'd snooped around and eventually figured out her last name, Miller. Who gave a damn about family? That was probably why Indigo called him out for hiding his relationship with Cindy from their parents. After they found his sister, he would apologize to Indigo and then formally introduce Cindy to his parents as his girlfriend.

"You two can sleep. I'll stay down here and listen out," CJ offered.

"My baby girl is out there. I'm not sleeping," Daniel replied.

"Neither am I." Christine clasped her hands together. Her normally crisp peach silk pajamas looked as if they'd been balled up in a corner for a century. "Besides, I want her to look us in the eye and explain why in the hell she caused such a ruckus."

"No, you won't." Daniel waved off her argument.

"Daniel, listen, she's just being dramatic."

"No, you need to listen." He slammed a hand on the table. "When she comes home, we will not argue, we will not yell. We're going to fix her some food, give her a hug, and talk. All three of us have told her what she needs to do, but have we once asked what she wants or needs?"

"No. She's a child. We're her parents," Christine argued.

Daniel nodded. "I understand that, but she's a smart girl, and she'll tell us what she thinks she needs. Simple as that."

CJ stared at his father with pride. "It's a good idea, Dad."

"Well, thank you for talking to me, son. Thank you for helping me see."

CJ couldn't get a minute of sleep all night. Fear and adrenaline made for potent insomnia. As an orange sun lit the sky, CJ rose from the sofa where he'd been lying awake through the night and turned to face his dad, who was standing near the door. Christine snored softly, her head resting on the cherrywood dining table.

"She never came back. She . . . she always comes back," Daniel whispered. He turned to face CJ. Worry had aged him a decade.

The cold that chilled CJ's skin seeped down to his bones as Daniel said, "Call the search party."

It had been twenty-four hours since they'd last seen Indigo. CJ's father went to the police station to shake down some walls.

CJ stayed with his mother at home, where they sat across from each other at the dining table.

"I . . . I just don't understand," she muttered for the millionth time under her breath. "Why would she do this to me?"

CJ, who hadn't slept in a little over a day, wanted to roar in his mother's face. The house phone rang. Christine glanced at her slim watch and stood.

CJ stood. "Sit down, Mother. I'll get it."

"No. I have a girlfriend calling me."

CJ nodded and rubbed the scruff of his neck. He could use a shave, and some space.

He could use a hug from Cindy.

"I'm going out for a drive."

"Sure you are," Christine said in a rough, low voice.

CJ didn't respond but grabbed his keys from the green glass bowl near the door and walked out the door toward his car. He marched across the porch and down the steps, stopping at the last one.

Guilt rooted him to the spot. He shouldn't put all the blame on Christine. Indigo had been furious with all of them.

And worst of all, she felt betrayed by CJ. He should've talked to his parents somewhere else, away from Indigo's ears.

It's my fault as much as theirs.

He sighed and turned around, determined to figure things out with his mother. She didn't need to be on nonspeaking terms with all her kids.

He opened the front door but didn't find Christine on the phone near the kitchen. He heard her distinctly soprano voice across the hallway in his father's study. The door had been cracked open.

"It's a damned mess," she hissed to her friend on the phone. "She's got it in her mind that we're monsters."

"I . . . yes. I told her it's her imagination. She's not thinking clearly, and it's no wonder what she's been up to." She sighed, dropping her head into her hand. "I worry about the rumors."

The rumors. His mother's words restoked the dying embers of his anger in the pit of his stomach. Her concern was always about the family's image, not her children's welfare.

"People will talk. And it'll ruin Daniel's—"

"Mother."

Startled, Christine jumped up, squeezing the green phone in her hand. Red splashed across her cheeks. "W-What . . . what are you doing snooping on me? I told you I needed privacy.

"Call you back, Al- . . . Elaine. Yes. I'm fine. Bye." She slammed the phone into the cradle.

"Who were you talking to?"

"None of your damn business." She stood with her closed fists on her waist.

CJ shook his head. "You're always so worried about other people. Not once during the phone conversation did you say, 'Where is Indigo? I miss Indigo.'"

"Because she's fine," his mother yelled through clenched teeth.

"How do you know?"

"Because I know."

"But how? How. Do. You. Know?"

"There's no other acceptable option!" Christine shrieked. "Don't make me imagine the worst. I won't allow the thought to seep in. I want to believe that all the hairs on my baby girl's head are safe and accounted for. Because if I let those dark thoughts take over, it'll destroy me!"

CJ shook from the deep, wrenching pain in her voice.

"Do you understand?" she panted, as if she'd returned from a sprint. She placed a hand over her heart and slid onto Daniel's office chair.

CJ swallowed. "Okay, I'm sorry. I don't want to stress you. You can call your friend back since I'm leaving now."

Before CJ could leave, the house phone rang again. "Hello, Jones residence," CJ answered.

"It's me," his father answered. "We found Indigo. I'm taking her out for breakfast. Can you let your mother know she's okay?"

CJ felt the tension drain out of his body. He bent over and took a deep breath. "That's great, Dad. How is Indigo?"

"She's fine. Sad, but fine. I think some food will lift her spirits."

"Can I meet you—"

"No." His dad cut him off. "I've got our girl, I promise. Tell your mother now."

"I will."

Christine stood by the kitchen entrance.

"Indigo's fine?"

"Yes. Dad or someone found her. They are grabbing something to eat."

Christine shook with relief. "Thank God. I'm going to bed. That girl, I swear she's going to be the death of me."

CJ waited until he heard her bedroom door shut before he returned to his car and sped to Cindy's.

When his girlfriend opened the door, he fell into her arms.

"It's okay. Come here. Come here," she said in a soothing voice. She somehow shouldered his weight and pulled him into her home. Her bed.

She undressed him, starting with his boots, his socks, and finally his pants.

When CJ lifted his eyebrows, she shook her head. "We're sleeping. Besides, Mama will be back in an hour."

"Will she be upset that I'm here?"

She shook her head. "She understands." Cindy wrapped her arms around his waist.

"Now sleep. It'll all be better tomorrow."

He thought Cindy was right when he saw his sister at home the next morning. But when Indigo ran away again, she never returned.

CHAPTER SEVENTEEN

June 2022

TELL ME LIES

Olivia showered, knowing that chaos would soon descend on the Jones household. By the time she showered and changed, the doorbell rang.

"I'll get it." Olivia opened the door, while a shaken CJ paced the floor.

She opened the door, finding Alan with his hands clenched behind his back.

"Oh, hello, Olivia," Alan said absently while staring over her shoulder.

"Hello, Alan." Olivia tried to temper her voice. Alan looked as if he had dressed in the dark. As soon as she greeted him, Olivia noticed that although his blue-and-white chambray shirt was ironed to a crisp, he wore a combination that did not match at all—teal shorts, brown leather belt, black shoes, and white socks.

"Are you okay?" Olivia stepped back, allowing him to enter.

He waved his hand. "CJ turned off his phone, so I stopped by. Christine, she's . . . not herself. I don't want to leave her alone for long. Could we move our meeting to our home?" Alan's voice shook. "She'll be upstairs, resting."

"Hey, Alan." CJ's tired voice boomed from behind.

Alan exhaled. "Can we speak for a moment?" He flickered his gaze to Olivia. "Alone?"

"Oh, of course. I'll just finish making my breakfast, Dad." Olivia jerked her head toward the kitchen to let them know where she'd be.

CJ gave her a wide smile. He did that whenever she called him Father or Dad, and she leaned into it—especially now with everything that was going on.

Alan made a beeline to the living room.

He waited until she rounded the corner to the kitchen before whispering, "We have a problem."

CJ groaned. "What now?"

"Christine is having an episode."

"An episode?" CJ shouted. "Christine hasn't had one of those in years."

Alan shushed him. "She has. I just didn't tell you."

"Why?"

"Because she asked me not to. It's . . . it's complicated, son. All of this is just so damned complicated." Alan's voice broke at the end.

"Okay, I'll come over and handle it."

"No. I've got my wife. You come over and we'll figure out your things first. That's what Christine wants. I've given her something to calm her nerves."

"Okay, we'll be over shortly."

"Can it be just you this time?" Alan asked. "Christine wouldn't want anyone to see her like this."

"No. Everything that's going on affects Olivia and Cindy, too. Mom's sedated, right?"

"Right."

"We'll come over for an hour, short and sweet, and then we'll get out of your hair. I'll make sure to check on her before I leave."

"There's no need."

"Yes, there is. You know I trust you, Alan, but I want to see her. And I'm mad as all hell that you haven't told me what's been going on."

"I know, I'm sorry. I wanted to, but your mother . . . she's proud, but she struggles. This type of thing doesn't just go away. You know that."

What type of thing? Olivia, who'd been trying to crack an egg for the past few minutes, tilted her head as if that would help her hear the conversation more clearly.

CJ grunted. "I'll see you in thirty minutes." She heard the door squeak open. "Thank you for taking care of my mother."

CJ entered the kitchen with his head low. He opened the fridge, skipped the almond milk and juice, and pulled out a Modelo.

It was Saturday noon, but even if it had been ten a.m. on a Monday, Olivia was not going to say a word.

"I'm not going to ask if you're okay," Olivia said in a gentle voice.

"Good. I promised myself I wouldn't lie to you or your mother again." He reached into a nearby drawer, pulled out a bottle opener, popped the beer open, and took a deep gulp.

"You heard Alan."

"I did." Olivia took the honest route, like her father.

"You have questions."

"I do. But you don't have to answer them now. I know we have more pressing matters."

He took another sip, this time a quick shallow one, swallowed, and then turned around to face her. He leaned against the counter.

"For as long as I can remember, at least back to when I was six or seven years old, Christine would have 'episodes,'" he explained, using quote marks. "That's what my dad called them back then. Now, of course, I realize it was just a euphemism."

"Did she . . . was she ever diagnosed?"

"I don't know . . . maybe? Anytime I broach the topic, she shuts me down."

Olivia released the uncracked egg and let it roll into the ceramic bowl, then settled on the barstool near the kitchen island.

"If I had to guess, I think she suffers from extreme depression. She'd have these high days, when she was a ball of energy. Cleaning the house, gardening in the yard, volunteering for every organization, be it community or something for me and my siblings. She was Superwoman. And that scared the shit out of us as kids."

"It did?"

"Because we knew what would come right after. She'd swing back low." He took another sip, his eyes miles away.

"So low, Olivia. Like . . . she couldn't move. She'd barricade herself in her room and wail. Dad would get us out of the way. Send us down to the beach or a neighbor's house, or off on some civic activity. Then, by the time we returned home, she was out of it. Knocked out by some sedative of the decade."

He rubbed his hand around the neck of the bottle.

"I didn't think she'd make it after Indigo's death. And when . . . when we got word of Chris, she didn't come out for months. No one ever questioned her depression back then. I mean, anyone else would've reacted the same way if their children died within a few years of each other. But then she and Alan got married. And she seemed to do much better. Or at least that's what I told myself. I didn't want to face the facts." He shook his head.

"I was angry with her for the things she did to us, but I didn't want to accept that it wasn't entirely her fault because it would make her seem more human. It wasn't fair of me to feel that way, but back then I needed someone else to shoulder the pain of losing our family. Because . . ." He inhaled. "Because I feel responsible for Indigo's death. For Dad's death, and for Chris."

The torture in his voice tugged at her heart. "Why Chris?"

"Because if I'd stepped out of the way and let him go after your mother, he wouldn't have joined the military, and later the police force. He joined the force because he felt like he had to figure out a way to take care of his family—*my* family. Or maybe I should've just stepped up sooner and this all would've been avoided. We could have done many things to avoid his death."

It's not your fault! Olivia wanted to tell her father as she wondered whether she should tell him the truth about Chris and Omar and their tragic fate. She was desperate to tell him what really happened, but would the truth comfort him at this point? They were both gone now, and CJ couldn't fight ghosts.

But his pain was so thick, she felt like she could drown in his misery.

Olivia stared at her father—his drooped shoulders and lowered head were the definition of defeat.

Not right now, she decided. It would be too much and too soon. She knew she had to tell him eventually, but she feared he'd hate Ama by association.

And worse, would he tell Cindy and Christine?

Can I trust him to keep a secret?

"I'm going to get your mother." CJ pushed himself from the counter. "We'll leave in ten minutes."

Alan opened the door and hurried them inside. "We'll be in the dining room," he said in greeting to Olivia, CJ, and Cindy, getting straight to business.

After they'd found their seats, Alan whipped on a pair of black-rimmed glasses and picked up his legal pad. "Okay, let's get started. We need to come up with a plan to counteract the lies printed in the paper. Now I have a few ideas—"

"Alan, wait." CJ raised his hand. "We don't know if that letter is a lie."

Alan removed his glasses and placed them on the table. "Of course it is, CJ."

"Indigo had a journal," he added. "She wrote in it all the time. You know this."

"Okay, then . . . whether it's true or not, it's extremely crude to publish a deceased teenager's personal letter."

"That person won't think that. Not if they're friends. Not if it's proving a point," Olivia argued.

"You're right." Alan nodded. "People aren't focused on decorum. They're focused on dragging the Jones family name."

"Not the Joneses. The Douglass family," someone said from outside the room.

All attention swiveled to the steps from the second floor. Though Olivia couldn't see who it was, she recognized Christine's voice.

Alan jumped up from his seat and went to the stairway. CJ followed suit, and so did Olivia.

"Sweetheart, what are you doing?" Alan called to her from the bottom step.

"They want to destroy us." Christine wasn't gliding down the steps as usual but leaning against the rail as she shuffled from one step to the next. Alan rushed to support her.

"Come now. We're going back to bed."

"I can't believe they're bringing this up again." She leaned into Alan's arms.

"It's okay. We're going to fix this," he vowed.

"Someone hates us," Christine said, gripping her nightgown. "Someone thinks they can be us, but they can't. It's all a lie."

"What's a lie?" CJ frowned. He was waiting at the bottom of the stairs. "What are you talking about?"

"It's nonsense," Alan snapped, his stern attention fixed on CJ. "Can you please go sit down? I'll handle your mother."

"I don't need a handler!" Christine shrieked. "He needs to know," she howled. Saliva streaks dripped from the sides of her mouth. "There are illegitimates about. Everyone wants to be like us, but they can't," she repeated. "So they lie!"

"Mom, it's okay. You can tell me later." CJ raised a halting hand.

"You must listen. You must . . ." she panted. Seeming to lose her energy, she drooped in Alan's arms and cried like a child. "I'm tired. I'm so, so tired. I . . ."

"Let's get your medicine. Let's get you fed."

"B-but I have to try—"

"Up to bed, sweetheart. You need your strength."

Alan lifted his salt-and-pepper eyebrows. His dark eyes were laden with sorrow. "I . . . I'm sorry, but I need to—"

"Go," Olivia cut him off.

"I'll call you later, CJ."

"You better. Either way, I'll be here tomorrow, bright and early. No matter what state my mother is in."

"She wouldn't want a . . ." He flicked his attention to Olivia and Cindy. "A crowd."

"I understand," Olivia assured him. "We'll stay at CJ's while you two . . . talk."

"This is the last time I walk away without answers regarding my mother," CJ warned Alan. "You understand me?"

Christine moaned in his arms.

"Yes. Lock up behind you." Alan gathered Christine in his arms and murmured something in her ear.

CJ, Cindy, and Olivia stepped outside.

CJ, who had a key, locked the door behind him. "Shit," he whispered under his breath.

They walked back to his house in silence. Once they arrived, went in, and closed the door, he let out a mighty roar.

"She's living with a mental illness, CJ." Cindy rubbed his back and hugged him. "Just like Indigo."

He hugged Cindy back. "I think the letter is true, and I need to understand why. But how . . . how can I ask my mother about what happened to Indigo? It hurts her too much to talk about her."

"I know, baby." Cindy hugged him tighter.

"I can't do that to her. It's not right."

"Aneesa wants me to work with her," Olivia said. "Find some people who were around back then and ask what they remember when . . . when Aunt Indigo died. We can try that way," she offered.

CJ looked over her mother's head. "I don't know if you'll get anything. But our town trusts Aneesa, and they seem to like you. It's worth a shot."

"Then I'll do it."

Olivia wasn't a detective, but she'd try.

She would try for her father, for her aunt Indigo, and even for Christine.

CHAPTER EIGHTEEN

June 2022

THE WATCHDOG

"Okay, so who do we speak to first?" Olivia settled across from Aneesa, who had brought a tripod, camera, and small clipped microphones to her kitchen table.

"Slow down, Inspector Gadget," Aneesa muttered under her breath while arranging her equipment on the table.

Olivia decidedly ignored Aneesa's comment and pulled out her iPad. "I have a list of questions, which I've also emailed to you. I think these will help us get to the core of what happened to Aunt Indigo." She slid the iPad just beneath Aneesa's gaze.

Aneesa read the questions and shifted her studious attention to Olivia. "You know I'm old enough to be your mother, right?"

"Certainly. You're my mother's best friend."

"And you know I've been a reporter for over thirty years."

"Yes, but—"

"I know what I'm doing, young lady. I do not need your questions, which are rather direct, given the difficulty of the topic."

Olivia's stomach clenched. She handled difficult topics well, but this one was especially challenging. The letter in the local paper was quite a setback for her family.

"Okay, that's fine and well, but how else do you expect us to understand who's harassing my family?"

"Porch Stories," Aneesa replied, as if those two words solved everything.

"I don't understand." Olivia grabbed her iPad. "You want them to tell a story on a porch?"

"*Porch Stories* is a video series in which the residents of Highland Beach are interviewed about its history. My friend started the series about a year ago, and it's posted on the Frederick Douglass Museum and Cultural Center's YouTube page."

Olivia searched for the series on the iPad. "Are there a lot of subscribers?"

"No, just around one hundred. It's a very niche audience, and most of our views are from residents and university students."

Olivia quickly found the channel with a thumbnail picture of the Frederick Douglass Museum and subscribed. "So how are we helping with the series?"

"My friend, the host, will allow us to interview one of his residents on his behalf." Aneesa tilted her head and folded her arms. "During the interview, we will observe, we will listen, and we will take in that resident's knowledge and wisdom. Once the interview concludes, I'll bring up old times."

"Old times?"

"Yes, baby, old times. Like, 'Remember that time when ole so-and-so pulled up that strange-looking fish out of the bay?' Or, 'You remember that time when Ms. Guthrie's granddaughter went missing, and we all came together and found her, and then . . .'" Aneesa waved a hand. "Then we'll talk about that time when one of our missing never came back. And they'll tell us what they recall. You live in New York, right?"

"Yes."

"So you know you don't ask a New Yorker about 9/11. You bring up something related, and then someone else will share their story about what they were doing the day that tragedy struck their community."

"Oh. I get it now."

"That's right. We aren't aggressive. People will share in their own time and as they feel comfortable. Or at least, that's how we *want* them to feel."

She pointed at Olivia's iPad. "If you come with a list of questions, and they feel like it's a formal interview, they're bound to get defensive. Just remember what you want out of the conversation, and a recorder is all you need. Trust me," she added. "I've won a few awards here and there."

Olivia nodded, tucking the iPad into her purse.

Aneesa flashed her a tight smile. "Now, once I broach the subject, and they tell us what they can recall, you can then ask them for a fond memory they have of Indigo. Bitter and sweet, but quick."

"Okay, absolutely. I will follow your lead."

"Whew, that's good." Aneesa mimed wiping sweat off her forehead. "I didn't want to fire my honorary niece on the first day."

She packed her equipment into a chocolate Tumi laptop bag. "Okay, for today we are interviewing the Francis family. Let's go."

Olivia followed Aneesa down the street as they walked toward the end of the run near Black Walnut Creek.

"The Francises are one of the oldest families in Highland Beach. They have a longer history than most families, so listen to their stories. They will also know where all the skeletons are buried."

Aneesa knocked on the door. Within a few seconds Olivia noticed a woman dressed in a peach sundress open the door to her screened-in porch. "Hey, Ms. Leila."

"Oh, hi, Aneesa. I forgot you're filling in for Matthew today."

"Yes, and I hope that's okay. He's off to visit the grandchildren."

"Oh, of course. I know you are more than capable of telling our story well." Leila smiled, but her voice conveyed: *Don't mess up.*

"Where do I set up?"

"We can place these two chairs by the screen door. Let's keep it open so we can film the yard. We can do some b-roll of Black Walnut Creek."

"You have a creative vision, Ms. Leila?"

"Oh you know it." She chuckled. Turning to Olivia, Leila said, "I know you've met a lot of us, but I'm Leila Francis. You are Mayor Jones and Cindy's daughter, correct?"

"That's right. I hope you don't mind, but Aneesa's asked me to help with the *Porch Stories* today."

"Oh, I don't mind at all." Leila smiled at Olivia. "I think it's a good way for you to understand your history and rich roots."

"Thank you. It's nice to meet you officially." Olivia offered her hand.

Leila took it without hesitation. "I have a good story that I think you'll enjoy about your ancestor Frederick Douglass."

Aneesa and Olivia arranged the chairs, then Aneesa sat down across from Leila. Olivia set the camera to Record, and Aneesa kicked off the intro for *Porch Stories*.

"Hello, this is Aneesa Williams with Leila Francis, for another edition of *Porch Stories*. Leila, thank you for having us this morning."

"Welcome, Aneesa. And I'm so happy we have time to sit down and talk about the history of our wonderful community. Highland Beach goes back to 1893, incorporated in 1922, and my family is one of the first families here. It's my extreme honor to share our stories with you today."

"That's right." Aneesa smiled. "And you are the reason I purchased a home in this wonderful community." Aneesa winked at her old friend. "Now tell me how your family came to Highland Beach."

"My great-grandfather was John Richard Francis Sr. He was a surgeon who owned and operated a hospital for Black folks in Washington, DC. He built a home in 1896. Now he and the Douglass family were friends," Leila said, briefly smiling at Olivia. "And they sold him a lot across the street from where we live now, which is now the Frederick Douglass Museum. Major Charles Douglass had selected this lot by the creek because of the views of Chesapeake Bay. But Frederick Douglass wasn't too keen on building a house at that location because he was afraid his grandchildren would drown in the creek. So he asked my great-grandfather, Dr. Francis, if he would switch with him, and he did. And we've lived here ever since."

Drown.

Unease moved quickly throughout Olivia's body. *Did Aunt Indigo drown in this creek? The very waters her great-grandcousin wanted to avoid to keep his family safe?*

Another interesting fact that Leila shared about her family was that she was related to E. B. Henderson, the grandfather of Black basketball, who'd been inducted into the Naismith Memorial Basketball Hall of Fame. But Olivia hardly took in that information. She was finding it hard to concentrate.

Twenty minutes passed quickly, and the interview concluded. Aneesa thanked Leila for her time, and soon the conversation transitioned from the past to the present.

"Are you okay, dear?" Leila asked Olivia. "Do you need any coffee, tea, lemonade?"

"Oh no. I'm sorry. I really enjoyed listening to your family's legacy. It's so inspiring."

Leila smiled. "We both have a lot to be proud of. Did you enjoy the story of the creek switch?"

"Yes! And I love that he cared enough for his grandchildren to be cautious about the water."

"Yes. I think he wanted to exercise caution considering his family had experienced enough tragedy with the deaths of his daughter and his wife, and then his house burning down. We have a book about it at the Douglass Museum if you want a copy."

"I would love that."

"Then I'll make sure that CJ gets you your own personal copy. He has one at home as well."

Leila leaned closer to Olivia while Aneesa took off her microphone and repacked her gear. "Are you sure you're okay?" the woman whispered. "You seem . . . distracted. Sad even. It's too beautiful a day for sadness."

Olivia stole a glance at Aneesa, who shrugged as if to say, *Go ahead.*

"Well, it's just that I find it tragic that my father's sister . . . my aunt Indigo . . . may have drowned in the creek. The very place Frederick Douglass tried to avoid for the sake of his grandchildren."

"Woo. You know I had that same thought, too, back when it happened. It was a tough time for our community. And Indigo, she loved the water. She asked me all the time if she could just sit on my back porch and stare at the creek."

"She did?"

"Oh yes. She was a good girl and didn't make a lot of fuss, so I didn't mind it. My children are a few years older, so they were off to college most of the time. I enjoyed having someone around the house, and she knew just when I wanted company." Leila smiled and rocked back in her chair.

"I liked that she found my house peaceful. She didn't seem to have a lot of . . . peace."

Olivia nodded, now knowing that her aunt and grandmother both suffered from depression.

"But she was smart, too. Loved history, like me. I would tell her stories about my family. Stories that were passed down about the Douglass family, too. She seemed curious about very peculiar things regarding her family."

Olivia leaned forward. "Curious about what exactly?"

Leila sighed. "Honestly, a bunch of rubbish, if you ask me."

"Well, I'm asking." Olivia softened her question with a smile.

"Frederick Douglass married his much younger white secretary, Helen Pitts, after his first wife died, and people criticized him for moving on too quickly. Frederick's kids weren't all that keen on having a white stepmother, as you could imagine, especially back then. And Indigo, well, she said she'd heard a rumor about Frederick and the second wife having kids. This was never documented, mind you." Leila waved a finger in the air. "In fact, it was documented that the second wife was barren. I told Indigo to hush. I didn't want to hear it." Leila dropped her hand. "Someone must've told her that lie, but I should've been kinder to her. She was just curious and . . . I didn't mean to crush her spirit."

"Ms. Leila." Aneesa stood and grabbed her hand. "You and I know it's not your fault. There was something much deeper going on with Indigo. But it's good to know she had a place of refuge when things got tough. Hold on to that memory. Not the memory of you checking her on unfounded gossip."

Leila nodded, but her eyes still held sorrow. She looked at her watch. "I can't believe it's already noon. I have a lunch date with an old friend. You all can sit out here for as long as you like."

Aneesa shook her head. "We're going to edit this wonderful interview, and I'll be sure to share it with you and Matthew before I post it on YouTube."

"I'm looking forward to it."

Aneesa and Olivia walked in silence back to Aneesa's home. As soon as she closed the door, Aneesa placed her things on the kitchen table.

"Did you catch what Ms. Leila said?" Aneesa asked.

"I couldn't miss it." Olivia crossed her arms. "You know, Christine said something the other day—that people wanted to be like the family, but they can't be *us*. I thought she was just being superior, but maybe there's something there."

"Someone is uncovering more skeletons in the Douglass-Jones closet. You should have another conversation with Christine and CJ."

Olivia let out a breath. It'd been only three days since Christine's breakdown. She didn't think enough time had passed to be asking her grandmother hard-hitting questions.

But I can check in . . . have lunch.

"I'll give Christine a call tomorrow."

"Good. You can get with your family, and I'll do some research. I'm sure Christine is on edge, so you'll need to be careful with how you frame your questions."

"Where are you going to do research?"

"The library, the internet. Not to mention I have a few historian friends I can tap. But for now, let's keep this little tidbit to ourselves."

"Including my parents?"

"Yes, even your parents. Cindy means well, but she's in that lovey-dovey stage where she'll tell CJ everything. Besides, there's no need to shake any tree until we know it bears fruit."

CHAPTER NINETEEN

July 2022

GONE SAILING

Olivia was in her bedroom when her phone rang. She was greeted by Ama's voice, lashing like fire, when she took the call.

"Have you been ignoring me, cher?"

"No, Ama, of course not. I've just been—"

"Busy dealing with the Jones family smear campaign and your aunt's mysterious death."

"How did you know?"

"I have a subscription to that lovely town's newspaper. And the newsletter."

"Isn't that only for residents?"

"You know the answer to that. As I'm sure you know that I have my ways to get information. Now, cher, are you in danger?"

Olivia shook her head. "No one's been following me, to my knowledge. I always jog during the day, especially since everyone knows me now."

Olivia had noticed some residents staring at her, but it seemed more as if they were looking out for her well-being than being nosy or stalking her.

"Someone doesn't like that Christine Douglass-Jones. Mark my words."

Olivia sighed. "My grandmother is complicated. She's living with a mental health issue."

"Oh well, I hate to hear that, but I have to say, that explains a lot about her behavior. Has she sought treatment?"

"I don't know, and honestly, I don't think it's my business to ask."

Ama tsked. "The way she's been acting, I would guess not. Maybe if she gets treatment, her behavior will improve and she won't be such an awful person to be around. Now, cher, I'm more interested in how *you've* been doing. How is that town treating you?"

The load on Olivia's shoulders lightened at just the thought of sharing her burdens with Ama. "Can you give me a moment?" Olivia stood from her bed, opened her door, and then checked out front to make sure Cindy was still out with Aneesa and CJ was at work.

She returned to her room and closed the door. "I'm back." She let out a shaky breath. "Ama, what I'm about to tell you will probably sound impossible."

"Go on."

"Right before she died, Indigo asked a historian if she knew about Frederick Douglass having a child with his second wife. She was—"

"White. I know all about Frederick Douglass, cher. And his two wives."

"I think someone insinuated he had a child with his second wife. And based on what I could piece together from Christine, I think someone had told Indigo this lie. She asked one of her neighbors about the rumor."

"And Christine handled it the best way she knows how . . . via blackmail. That woman has major control issues."

"Yes, but that theory is pretty damning. I'm sure she has a lot of pride in protecting her family."

"I know a few historians. I'll reach out to my trusted circle but not beyond them, to keep things quiet."

"Thank you, Ama. I would really appreciate it."

"Of course, my darling girl. I would have helped sooner if you only picked up the phone." Her tone was rich with affection.

Olivia's chest warmed. She knew she could always depend on her godmother.

"Do you want to know the truth? Or would you like for me to handle it?"

Olivia held her breath. Maybe she wasn't the best person to answer the question. She'd just discovered her roots, after all.

"H-handle it? Like Christine?"

"No, cher. I sting, but I'm always discreet."

"I . . . I don't know just yet. Can I think about it?"

"Of course. I'll be here. Now Carter and I are off for a walk. We'll talk soon, and this time you will call me, understand?"

"I do and I will. Thank you, Ama."

"Anytime. Bye for now."

Olivia ended the call and pressed her phone against her beating heart. The truth was always best, but she didn't know if Christine or CJ could handle the truth about Helen Pitts Douglass. They were so proud of their lineage through Frederick Douglass, a beloved Black historical figure.

She couldn't even find the courage to confess to them what really happened to Chris. Closing her eyes, she silently asked for strength and wisdom in making the right decision. But for now, she would remain quiet.

The Jones family could not handle another tragedy.

CJ had been quiet during the weeks after Indigo's letter was leaked and Christine subsequently had a breakdown. But he was still busy with his mayoral duties, serving his constituents with quiet dedication, despite their distrust, and prepping for the debate in a few weeks.

He'd surprised both Cindy and Olivia one morning when he shared his plan to take a half day off from work.

"I don't know about you, but I need a break before things get even busier. Would you like to go sailing today?"

"Do you have a boat?" Olivia asked her father.

"I've got a yacht and a license to sail." He grinned when Olivia pressed her lips together. That was the very next question she planned to ask her father.

He didn't have to twist Olivia's or Cindy's arm too hard. Mother and daughter packed sunscreen, towels, and snacks, preparing for a day of sailing. Then they drove to Annapolis, stopping close to the charming Eastport neighborhood, with its beautiful red-brick buildings.

"Let's go, beautiful ladies." CJ had a pep in his step as he walked them down the wooden plank with a maze of sailboats and yachts moored alongside.

Once CJ stepped into the boat, he assisted Cindy and Olivia into the cockpit area.

"The wind is good today." He raised his arm, his hand drifting with the wind. "We don't have to worry about going dead down-wind."

He smiled as he hurried about the boat, tying knots, taking the slack out of the sheet.

The yacht was spacious. Just behind CJ's pilothouse was an enclosed kitchen with a sink and oven. Two small booths on either side were separated by a long brown table in the middle. The entertainment area, located past the kitchen, had white leather seats, a table, and a TV with speakers.

"Safety first, ladies," CJ said, handing out two bright orange life vests. While they donned the vests, he sat on a padded seat in front of the helm, which had navigation equipment that looked like an old video game. He connected his phone to the Bluetooth speakers.

A fusion of heavy keyboards and soulful music blared through the speakers.

Olivia raised her finger in the air, trying to recall the artists. "Who's playing right now?"

"It's nice, right?" Her father smiled for the first time in days. "Fatima and Joe Armon-Jones. My line brother played it nonstop when I visited him and his wife earlier this year."

"I like it." Cindy bobbed her head to the music.

He turned the key, and the engine purred. The boat rumbled and jerked forward, easing them into the open water. Standing on the deck, CJ pulled up the sail in a rapid motion until the sail stood erect, flapping in the wind.

"And we're sailing," he announced, curving the joystick that steered them toward the wind.

A salty gust lightly whipped Olivia's tresses. She leaned into the breeze and smiled. Water droplets dotted her Dita sunglasses, but she didn't care. The megadose of vitamin D from the sun and the good music did wonders for her mood.

Cindy scooted closer to CJ, whispering something that, from his sly grin and affectionate squeeze on her thigh, made him happy.

Of course, she'd been sailing before, but never with her parents. And this was more than just the fantasy that would have made twelve-year-old Olivia ecstatic. Cindy had never looked so happy, or so free. Last year, Olivia had finally released her guilt over not being close to her mother and her secret fear that she'd ruined her mother's life.

Cindy's grief had shackled her to self-doubt, making her believe that she wasn't worthy of giving or receiving love.

Olivia knew that now. But watching her mother bloom in her self-confidence and fall in love was a sight to behold.

It's healing. Olivia frowned at the thought. Sure, it was Cindy's time to be healed, but Olivia had completed her own journey to healing last year, hadn't she?

Dr. LaGrange's voice floated in her mind.

Life is a journey. You hit a milestone and then you move on to your next goal. The work never really ends. Nor should it.

"And I'm my mother's daughter," she muttered under her breath, knowing the situation with Garrett was all the proof needed. Olivia exhaled and turned away to stare at the sea.

Why couldn't she just say how she felt?

She hadn't really loved Anderson, but she strung those three words together for him. Not to deceive him—she had thought she loved him, but she was never in love. Deep like? Yes. Heavy lust? Absolutely. But it wasn't love.

The way she felt about Garrett, in contrast, felt positively metaphysical.

Her heart ached for him. And during these weeks when they hadn't spoken, the silence felt like an enormous gaping hole in her chest. With each passing day, the pain only spread further.

I'll try again. I have to show him I'm serious, she vowed. *Will he accept my apology?*

"What are you thinking about over there?" Cindy slid into the open seat beside Olivia.

"That you and I are more alike than I thought."

"Oh . . ." Cindy's smiled faltered. "I hope I didn't mess up—"

Olivia shook her head. "No more apologies, okay? Today is a beautiful day. You're with the man you love," she whispered to her mother.

Cindy didn't answer, but she looked over at CJ with heart eyes.

"I just realized my feelings for Garrett are deeper than I've allowed myself to believe."

"For what it's worth, I like him for you."

Olivia smiled. "If memory serves, you also liked Anderson."

"I didn't like him for *you*, but he was likable." Cindy frowned. "Well, until he lied to you about his family, that is. I don't know what he was thinking."

Olivia had thought over and over about when she learned that ASK Developers' CEO was Anderson's father, and what she concluded was that he didn't believe that she would stick around.

He was right.

"We both hurt and lied to each other."

And now she was hurting Garrett with her inability to commit to something more.

"Well, no matter. You are now over your hump, and you're right where you need to be." Cindy patted Olivia on her knee.

It doesn't feel like it. Olivia felt an urgent need to return to Sag Harbor and speak to Garrett as soon as possible.

Her thundering heart confirmed her gut feeling.

Olivia didn't say anything more, just looked away and let the music dissolve the unkind thoughts rolling around in her head.

"Olivia." CJ motioned for her to sit beside him. She stood and walked to her father.

"What is it?"

"Can you go down to the kitchen and open some wine? There should be glasses in the cabinet."

Following his instructions, Olivia found the bottle of Ama's special blend, a rosé that wasn't yet available to the public. Olivia's heart surged with pride. Years ago, Ama had said in passing that she dreamed of creating her own wine, but Olivia would never have guessed that she'd buy her own winery—in France's Provence region, no less.

Bea had convinced Ama to use a recyclable bottle and add bees to the label design. The cream-colored label featured antique lettering and said: AMA'S BLEND. The back of the bottle carried the message: "I hope you enjoy, cher."

Olivia poured them glasses, and they toasted each other. CJ then set his glass aside, since he was serving as captain and had plans to work in the afternoon.

"It's been too long since I've gone sailing," Cindy said after taking a sip.

"How long?" Olivia asked.

"A decade at least, when I joined a few of my teacher friends on a weekend trip to Oak Bluffs."

Olivia frowned, not remembering a time when her mother went away for the weekend. "It was during the summer when you stayed with Amelia."

"Oh. I'm glad you had some time to enjoy yourself."

Cindy swirled her wine. "It wasn't easy. I had this unhealthy fear that Chris's pension would run out. So I worked myself to the bone. But that year was the fifteen-year anniversary of Chris's death, and it just hit me hard. I told a friend or two about it, and they rallied around me and finally convinced me to take a break."

Between the regular school year, summer school, and one after-school program or another, her mother typically worked yearlong. Back then, though, Olivia had assumed that her mother was doing everything in her power to avoid spending time with her.

"Anyhow, look at us now." Cindy smiled. "And in five years, I can retire early with my pension."

Olivia paused a moment before taking a sip of her wine. She glanced at CJ, who wore a soft smile as he navigated the yacht. She wondered if he would wait for Cindy to retire. He couldn't just up and leave his job as the mayor, and it wouldn't be fair for Cindy to move away from the New Jersey school district, leaving her hefty pension behind.

As "Purple Rain" blared from the speakers, Olivia thought back to a story Mr. Whittingham had shared about her father's goal of winning the Sag Harbor Talent Show with the Prince song. He hadn't wanted to perform with Chris and eventually took on Mr. Whittingham because of his guitar skills.

They won the talent show, and CJ forced Mr. Whittingham to split the prize money.

Back then, she thought CJ sounded incredibly stubborn, yet singularly focused and determined to do what was right.

And that was the key. Olivia's heavy heart lightened at the realization. CJ would always work hard to get what he wanted. Her parents could figure out a way to be together.

She smiled when she found CJ singing along with the tune. He shifted into autopilot and then waved her mother over.

"What is it?"

"Come here, Cindy."

Olivia helped by grabbing her mother's glass as she jerked her head toward her dad. Her mother finally stood, just as the guitar riffs began.

CJ pulled her close, dipping his nose into her hair. He spun her out, then pulled her back to his chest. Cindy let out a surprised yelp, threw her head back, and laughed.

But Olivia could clearly see that there was something in CJ's face that was all business—he was determined to win her over. As their mouths drifted closer, Olivia spun around to give them privacy.

I will not be joining them on the next sailing trip, she thought, laughing with joy as she observed her parents out of the corner of her eye. Yes, they would figure it out the second time around. They didn't need her help. Not at all.

After their sailing trip, her parents' budding romance gave Olivia the much-needed strength to call Garrett to apologize and reveal her true feelings. She set up her laptop outside, placing it on the wooden picnic table. Her hands shook, and she was sorely tempted to search online for tips on how to compose a love letter instead.

"Ah, this man," she growled. He hadn't taken her calls and responded to her texts only with terse messages.

I'm fine.

Zora's fine.

We're good.

Can't talk right now.

"I mean, how am I supposed to confess my feelings if the man won't answer his phone?"

She shook her head. But as quickly as her anger gathered, it rolled away. Garrett had gone above and beyond in courting her, from extravagant date nights in the city to picnics on the beach and weekly deliveries of flowers.

Admittedly, she was a failure at love. Her longest relationship had been with Anderson, and that, too, had been doomed from the start.

Olivia sighed. She wished she could call Omar. He was a master at penning letters, and he'd written Ama dozens of love letters.

Ama was no pushover herself in the letter department. Olivia cherished her godmother's written praise and words of encouragement that she'd received over the years.

Before she could overthink it, she called Ama.

It took only three rings for her to pick up the phone.

"Well, hello, cher. I'm glad you stuck to your word and called."

She heard a *whoosh* in the background.

"Where are you this time?"

"Oh, we're back on the Bluffs, visiting with Billie, Isabel, and Dulce," she said in a tone washed in happiness.

Olivia experienced a small pinch of jealousy. "Oh, sorry. I can call you back."

"If I couldn't speak, then I would tell you so," Ama gently chided. "If you're calling for an update on your family's origins, I don't have anything just yet."

"No, I'm not calling about the research."

"How are things at *that* beach?"

"That beach?" Olivia parroted.

Ama sighed. "Sorry. Highland Beach is a lovely place, but I can't stand that you're less than a mile from *that* woman."

Olivia smiled. She liked that Ama was a little jealous of her relationship with her paternal grandmother.

"Well, I've called for advice."

"One moment, cher. I'll need to move somewhere else for privacy."

Olivia could hear movement in the background before she heard a whisper. "Carter, I'll be just a moment. I've got Olivia on the line."

A minute later Ama confirmed, "I'm all yours, cher."

"Have you ever written a love letter?"

"Of course. Anytime I traveled without Omar, I wrote him about my travels."

Olivia shook her head. "No, not that kind of letter. A *love* letter."

"I wrote a letter to Omar, and I loved him. Is that not a love letter?" She could hear the laughter in Ama's voice.

"I'm writing Garrett a love letter to confess my feelings."

"Oh well, now that *is* different. Can't say I've written those kinds of letters."

"Not even to Omar?"

"Cher, Omar was head, fingers, legs, and toes gone over me. I didn't have to so much as pick up a pen. He loved me and told me *very* early in our relationship. I was the one who needed to catch up since I was so in- . . . infatuated with Carter."

"Well, we can't all be the gorgeous and brilliant Amelia Vaux Tanner."

"Nor can we all be the breathtakingly beautiful Olivia Charlotte Jones."

"I need help, not compliments."

"Well, I can't help you, cher," her godmother quipped.

"W-what?" Ama always offered advice, no matter the topic. "You don't like Garrett?"

"Oh, I like him just fine. He's a handsome young man, smart, and he is also head, fingers, and toes in love with you. Which is why I'm confused that you need to write this letter."

"I may not have made him feel secure in our relationship. Things have been so complicated with my family, and I've neglected him."

"Oh, I'm sure he's tough enough."

"I know he's tough, but . . . but no one puts him first. He's a great dad, and he makes lots of sacrifices."

Back when they were on speaking terms, Garrett had confessed his frustration with some of his male friends who never invited him out, assuming he'd say no because of Zora.

"I want him to feel special. I want him to know that he can be my number one."

"So long as he's making you his number one," Ama huffed.

"It's not like that, it's . . . he loves Zora, and he loves me. And he loves us in a way that's distinct. There's no competition because his capacity for giving love is massive. He's one of a kind, Ama."

"Well, it sounds like you already know what to say."

"I do?" Oliva thought about it, and then the realization went off like a light. "I'll tell him just how special he is to me."

"Bingo," Ama sang. "But it's not just the words, Olivia. You've got to *show* him. And don't ask me how, because you will know best. If you write that pretty letter, fill his head up with words but then don't follow it up with action . . ." She harrumphed. "Well, those words will just turn to ash."

Olivia nodded. "Okay, thank you, Ama. I'll keep your advice in mind."

"I know you will."

Olivia smiled. "I'll see you later. Hug Billie for me, and be sure to kiss little Isabel for me."

"Hugs? Kisses? Who do you think I am?"

Olivia laughed. Though Ama wasn't the most demonstrative, she showed her love in building a legacy, in words of affirmation, in just simply being.

"Fine. Just tell them I said hello."

"I can manage that, cher. Bye for now, and keep me posted."

"I will. Bye, Ama."

Olivia knew what to do. First, she'd write the letter. But she wouldn't mail it, she would hand-deliver it to Garrett. This weekend.

Olivia counted on the fact that he wouldn't slam the door in her face.

Garrett:

Right now, I'm sitting outside of my father's house, thinking of you and our first meeting.

I must admit that you scared me. You were wearing a striped blue-and-white shirt and khaki shorts. I didn't think I should have such a reaction to a stranger, even to a gorgeous stranger, but the pull was undeniable.

I chalked it off to attraction. Great chemistry. Nothing serious.

And now I realize my error and the lies I told myself. After all, how could I admit to myself that this stranger knew me better than my fiancé?

You noticed I ran so hard, I needed more shoes. You cared enough to buy me the best chess pieces to play my weekly matches with Mr. Whittingham.

You didn't judge me when I told you about my childhood issues growing up feeling unloved by my mother.

You were the catalyst to showing me my potential. And best of all, you let me shine.

But I wonder, who's protecting you? Who's loving you the way that you need?

It certainly hasn't been me . . . but that ends today.

Garrett, I love you. I love you because you are incredibly kind and strong and loving despite losing so many people in life. You take risks. It inspires me to take risks, too.

You make me better and I hope . . . I hope you can recall the times when I've made you better, too.

These past few weeks, without hearing your voice, have been agonizing. But yet, I am grateful because this is the swift kick I needed to appreciate you.

And I'm sorry that it's taken me so long. I'm sorry if I've made you doubt my feelings for you.

If you still feel the same about me, I promise you that I will:

1.   Be fully committed to this relationship. I want to be with you for the rest of our lives.
2.   Be the best stepmom to Zora—and if it isn't obvious, I love her, too.
3.   Love you how you deserve. I will show you my love every day in word and deed.

With all my love,
Your Olivia

Olivia sent a text to her SAG girlfriend group text.

I'm coming back to Sag for the weekend. I know it's last minute, but I have a few things to wrap up there. Would love to connect on Sunday for brunch?

Three dancing dots immediately popped up on the screen, showing an incoming text message.

Addy: Girl, you must have ESP because I was JUST about to call you. You need to come ASAP because that Francesca woman is making major moves on Garrett. The other day her "toilet" was clogged.

Olivia frowned at the text. Addy continued.

Addy: And I'm all like, Garrett, tell her to call a damn plumber. You're an attorney! Anyway, he helped, and then she just had to make him dinner.

Olivia: Oh great.

Olivia bookended the text with an eye-roll emoji.

Kara: Don't mind Addy. She's overreacting. Though Francesca is making her intentions known. So yes, good timing. But Garrett is solid.

Whitney: Well, I, for one, can't wait to see YOU. I'll set up reservations.

Olivia laughed. She was glad Whitney, who'd become a close friend, hadn't mentioned Garrett and Francesca.

Olivia folded her letter, with a plan to pack it before she hit the road in a few days. "Watch out, Garrett. I'm coming for you."

CHAPTER TWENTY

May 2022

THE WAY WE WERE

"Hello, Ms. Jones. Dr. LaGrange is ready to see you."

Olivia walked into her therapist's office, much calmer than she'd been the previous time.

"Hi, Olivia. Take a seat, please." Dr. LaGrange waved to the couch in front of her desk.

The therapist read something on her notepad. "According to your appointment notes, you want to focus on your relationship with Garrett today."

"I messed up the last time I was here . . ."

"The conversation with your father that Zora overheard," Dr. La-Grange confirmed, referencing the online meeting Olivia had with her a few days after her argument with CJ.

"I'm not sure what to do to convince him of how sorry I am. I've called, texted, I . . . I have this letter I've written him. I also plan to tell him I love him."

"Oh."

"You don't think I love him? Because I most definitely do."

"I believe you. But it doesn't matter what I believe. It's what Garrett believes."

"I can't convince him if he doesn't answer my calls."

"You're right." Her doctor nodded. "Olivia, do you believe Garrett loves you?"

"I do." Olivia nodded with confidence. "Not only has he told me, but I see it in the way he looks at me. Sometimes he stares at me like I'm this fairy tale come to life. And he's always encouraging me, he knows just the right words to calm me down. He takes time for me, which is a true gift since he's a single father. Buys me thoughtful gifts. He's also a . . . a very passionate man."

"He's shown you through words, which is what you need. You like letters and you like words of affirmation. Gifts, touch, and time. Have you done the same for him?"

Olivia thought back to her gifts for not only Garrett but his daughter. She, too, had given her time and was flexible if they needed to stay in when he couldn't find a sitter for Zora. She'd given him everything but the words.

She would give him that today.

"Yes. I've given him gifts, intimacy. I haven't given him the words just yet. And my time has been limited lately, because of my family. That's made it hard for me to call or see him. I . . . oh."

"Now you're saying, 'Oh.' What are you thinking?" Dr. LaGrange leaned forward, a glint of excitement in her eyes.

"The issue is my time. I've been inconsistent. What Garrett needs, and what Zora needs, is someone steady. Someone who won't walk away. And . . . and I fear between what he saw with Anderson, and my running away from Highland Beach, and now walking away from him when we argued, I think he may not trust me or trust my feelings."

Dr. LaGrange leaned back with a smile. "I think you may be on to something, Olivia Jones. Now . . . that's not to say that Garrett is totally blameless. He needs to be open to communication."

"H-how do I show him that I'm steady?"

"Steady takes time and also takes effort. Think about what he will need to feel secure."

"I . . . can back away from the relationship and be a good neighbor and be a good friend. I can focus on my relationship with Zora if he allows it. And if he truly loves me, I think time could help him heal. I do want to give him my letter."

"Then you should give it to him. You're also taking action, which is something else he needs to see."

"But is that enough?" Olivia muttered to herself. She felt like she should do something grand, like in the movies. Perhaps hire a skywriter or a band to sing a romantic song.

"You're putting your heart on the line, and that is enough. That isn't something you would've done a year ago. And if he can't see that, then he's the one who's missing out on someone amazing."

"Dr. LaGrange, did you just compliment me?"

She smirked. "You were due for one. You are so hard on yourself. I just want you to know you've come so far. Don't let this make you doubt how wonderful you are." She looked down at her watch. "I think we'll end it here. Do you feel confident about your next steps?"

"I do. Wish me good luck."

"Good luck. Call if you need me."

Olivia sailed out of the office with a smile on her face and drove home. She parked in front of her house, but then walked to Garrett's front door and knocked.

"You're here." Garrett opened the door. He didn't step aside to let her in or embrace her in a hug. He didn't give her that "light of my life" smile.

Oh no.

Olivia wound the strap of the Prada tote around her fingers and gave him a tremulous smile. "I told you I planned to visit on the voicemail I left you."

Garrett shook his head, staring at Olivia as if she were an apparition. "Sorry. I haven't checked my messages."

"You haven't checked your voicemail, or am I just the lucky one?" Olivia crossed her arms.

"Olivia." Garrett's voice was rigid and rough and frustrated.

She'd never heard that tone in the year that she'd known him.

"Are we ever going to speak about what happened?"

He stepped back and waved her to come inside.

"Thank you," she whispered before stepping in.

Olivia sat down, her hand now tucked into her purse. The love letter she'd penned was scorching the tips of her fingers.

Garrett didn't move to hold her, not even to touch her. He avoided full-on staring, as if she could burn holes in his eyes. After waiting for Olivia to settle, he sat on the opposite side of the room, silently making his position clear.

"Listen, I'm sorry for ignoring your calls. That was immature of me, and I apologize."

His apology stopped her racing heart.

"I appreciate that. But I'd like to apologize, too. I should have handled your feelings about marriage with more care. And I can admit that I shouldn't have taken that call from my father while I was half naked in your bedroom. That set a terrible example for Zora. I wasn't . . . I haven't been my best self, but being with you and Zora encourages me to be a better person."

She rubbed the envelope, silently seeking comfort. Silently seeking strength.

"The entire time we've been together, you've wanted more," Olivia began. "And I didn't give that to you. I was inconsistent with my availability and unclear about my feelings. I realize that now, and I apologize for not showing you how I truly feel."

"I . . ." He paused, as if weighing his words. "Yes. That would've been nice."

"I agree, and the only thing I can say is that I wanted to be sure. I didn't want to rush into anything again and hurt someone. I think you can understand my hesitation. But if the offer still stands, then I'd very much like to work toward—"

"I don't know how to say this," Garrett interrupted, "but I think we should stop . . . whatever we're doing."

Her heartbeat resumed its galloping speed. "You mean dating?"

"Is that what people call it?" Garrett chuckled.

Olivia didn't like his laughter. The unease that settled in the pit of her stomach morphed into irritation, then fire. "Yes." She narrowed her eyes. "Dating is when people spend time together, go out, do romantic things with each other. Have we not done all the above?"

"Yes." He nodded. "We spent some time together."

"We did much more than spend time together," Olivia whispered harshly. She hadn't meant to whisper, but she found it hard to force the words out of her mouth. "Is it . . . is there someone else?"

Garrett sighed. "No . . . not exactly." His voice trailed off.

"Oh my goodness. You really are dating someone else." Olivia shook her head. Thank God she hadn't given the letter to Garrett. That would have been entirely too embarrassing.

"I'm not dating anyone else, Olivia. But I . . . I think I'll start doing that now. I don't want to be dishonest with you."

Heat spread from the top of her head down to her toes. Her eyes throbbed and pulsed with pain, just like her heart.

He stood, pacing the floor, and proceeded to check off a very long list of reasons they wouldn't work out. He didn't realize her heart was crumbling.

"You're still sorting through your family issues in Highland Beach and starting up a new business with Whitney. You don't have enough space for—"

"That's just not true." Olivia cut him off. Her voice was tragic.

"It's not just me I have to protect," he rolled over her protest. "It's Zora's heart, too."

"You know that I'll always be here for Zora."

"But I don't think that is what's best for my daughter. It'll be too confusing for her if you stick around."

"Zora is a smart and capable little girl. Over time she'll understand if we're . . . just friends."

"She's only six, and everything is literal to her. Trust me when I say she won't understand."

"Garrett. I—"

"She views you as a mother figure. And lately she's already asking when you are coming to live with us."

Olivia's heart stopped crumbling, stopped fracturing, and exploded into a million little pieces. "I'm your neighbor, Garrett. What do you expect me to do when she says hello? I can't ignore her. I won't."

Zora was the daughter of her heart, and she would never willingly hurt or confuse her goddaughter.

"We'll play it by ear. For now, things should be fine, since you aren't here."

"I'm coming back home. For good."

"Then we'll make another game plan if you return."

"*When* I return. Do you expect me to live with my mother and father for the rest of my life?"

"I don't know. But what I know is that I've wasted too much time trying to figure you out."

"You aren't being fair, Garrett. I know what I want, and it's you and Zora." She had finally confessed her feelings. "I don't know what happened between now and the last time we spoke, but this reaction seems extreme. This isn't you."

Arms crossed, he sagged back into his overstuffed sofa. "I ran into Anderson."

"What?" Olivia perched on the edge of the chair. "When? Where?"

"He came by your place."

"But why—?"

"He wanted to see you, Olivia. It's clear he still loves you."

Olivia cleared her throat. "I don't think he loves me, for what it's worth. I was his safety net. You two didn't get into an argument, did you?"

"No. It was all civil. He even gave me advice and warned me to not allow you to drift away. That you were still trying to untangle the mess your mom and Omar had made. He said that you'd rather retreat so that no one could hurt you."

Not allow me to drift away?

She wasn't some fragile little flower who couldn't handle her emotions.

Not anymore.

"Look. The person I was last summer is not who I am today. And yes, I'm still figuring myself out, but I'm not going through an identity crisis. I have an amazing financial portfolio, and for the first time in years I'm doing mission-driven work. And now I want to take time to get to know my biological father."

Olivia stood, clasping her hands behind her back, pulling her shoulders together. "There are things I know I want. And Garrett, baby, I want you."

Garrett didn't look particularly moved by her impassioned speech. He looked contemplative. As if he were carefully weighing the pros and cons of building a life together.

He dropped his head, staring at the floor. "Olivia, you don't know what you want. You can't even pick out a show to watch."

Garrett's sharp words pierced the cloud of fog that danced around her head.

Olivia's head snapped back as if she'd been slapped. "You've thought this through."

"Yes, and for what it's worth, I'm sorry, Olivia. I really care about you."

Olivia laughed without humor. Here she was confessing her love, and now he only cared about her. Not only had the tables turned—they'd flipped and crashed. "I'm sure you think you do."

"Olivia . . ."

She reached into her purse and crumpled the letter in her fist. "Let's just leave it at that, Garrett." She waved with her other hand. "I don't want to say anything cruel. Goodbye." She stood from the couch.

"I'll tell Zora . . . ," Garrett began, but Olivia shook her head.

"When I return, please allow me to say a proper goodbye to Zora. I don't want her to feel abandoned."

"Of course. I wouldn't want her to feel that way. And maybe after some time and space, you can spend some time together."

She could hear the lie in his voice. After all, he didn't think she was good enough to be alone with his daughter.

The anger of the moment faded. Tears stung her eyes. "Goodbye, Garrett."

After the breakup, Olivia sent an SOS to her neighbors, who rushed to her home instead of waiting to meet up at the American Hotel for brunch.

"Wait a minute." Addy swirled the wine in her glass. "You're telling me that Garrett dumped you? Sweet, caring Garrett?"

Kara leaned over to smack her friend's knee. "Addy, please show some tact."

Olivia massaged her temples. "Yes. If it makes any difference, he wasn't rude when he broke things off. He was positively civil."

Whitney snorted. "I don't care how gentle he is . . . he made the wrong decision. It's clear you care about him. And listening to Anderson? That fool?" She snorted. "I wish I would've known he was in the neighborhood." Whitney was still angry at ASK, the real estate developers who tried to take over the neighborhood with their monstrous mansions.

Olivia shrugged. "Anderson is in my past, and Garrett knows it. I think he wanted to end the relationship, and this was his supposed nail in the coffin, so to speak. He says that I don't know what I want."

"What about that letter you told me about?" Addy chirped.

"It's in the trash bin."

"What? Why?" Addy stood.

"No, stop. It's trash, remember?" Kara tugged her hand, pulling Addy back down to the couch. She leaned over to whisper something in her best friend's ear. Addy rolled her eyes.

"More wine?" Whitney didn't wait for an answer and poured Olivia's portion to the rim.

"I'll be fine. It's not like I haven't experienced this before," Olivia reminded them, pushing through her lie.

"Experienced what exactly?" Whitney probed.

"Failure."

Heartbreak.

That was the word. But she had her girls staring at her, as if waiting for her to crumble. She wouldn't. Not yet. When they left and she turned off the lights, she'd allow the tears to fall.

It wasn't as if she were afraid of her feelings, or even of emoting in front of her friends. Dr. LaGrange had helped her process what had happened with Garrett, but she knew she needed the space by herself to grieve. She loved Garrett. And it would be hard to let him go.

"Why don't we go out for brunch? We still have time to make the reservation," Kara suggested.

Olivia shook her head. "No, thank you." She massaged her head again, feeling the ensuing headache. Faking it in front of strangers would further exacerbate the pain in her head and heart.

"Would you like to be alone?" Kara asked quietly.

"You know, I would like—"

"Of course, she doesn't," Addy interrupted, waving Kara's thoughtful question away. Olivia had just noticed Addy moving closer to the back door, seeming to scan her backyard.

Olivia took a deep sigh. "I do, actually."

Addy frowned. "Why? You shouldn't be alone."

Olivia shook her head. "I'm not afraid of being alone. And after all the things that transpired last year, I know I can't ignore my feelings."

"Otherwise, you'll explode." Kara nodded, understanding reflected in the depths of her dark brown eyes. "The school of Dr. LaGrange."

Therapy had been the best decision she'd made for herself, but right now she felt like a floundering freshman.

Whitney was the first to stand. "We will get out of your hair." She leaned in for a hug. Olivia took in her warmth. "Reach out to let us know when you're back at your substitute beach."

"Substitute?"

"Yes." Whitney's eyebrows snapped together like magnets. "First it was Oak Bluffs, then Sag, now Highland Beach. You better not move out there."

Olivia laughed. "Of course not. Besides, this is the only place where I have a home."

As soon as she closed the door behind her friends, she could hear their unintelligible whispers.

Let them talk. She mentally waved it off and grabbed her glass of sympathy wine, as Addy had called it. Grabbing her brand-new pink journal that was gifted to her by Dr. LaGrange at her last in-person session, she slid the back door open and stepped outside to her patio. The crashing waves pulled her into a trance so deep it temporarily soothed her hurt.

A light breeze danced with her hair, seeming to beckon her back to the present. She poured herself another glass of chardonnay, mentally reviewing all the things she could have done better to make things right with Garrett. He'd lost so much—his father, his wife, and last year his beloved mother. When his wife died, he had spiraled and drunk alcohol excessively.

Olivia sharply inhaled at her sudden realization. *It's not me who's afraid. It's Garrett.*

She wasn't sure if he was conscious of it, but he was afraid that Olivia would leave—be it willingly or unwillingly. Just like everyone else he loved.

She took another sip of wine. And another.

And another.

Her mind whirled through the possibilities. *How can I make him see?*

You can't, cher. She heard Ama's voice as if her godmother had sat beside her. Olivia's mind settled down. She knew that there was nothing she could do to "fix" the situation. At least not now. She'd attempted to share her feelings with Garrett, but he wasn't ready.

And maybe he'll never be ready. Fresh tears formed in her eyes. Garrett wasn't one of those guys she could write off. He was a good one.

But damn if it didn't hurt even more when the good guy broke her heart.

What he if dates someone else? What if . . . oh God, what if it's Francesca?

"I can't do it." She shook her head and drank more wine. Tears filled her eyes at the thought of leaving her newfound home.

"Hi, neighbor," a familiar voice called from the beach.

Olivia dashed away the tears from her eyes. "Mr. Whittingham."

He was doing the same thing he'd done when they first met— walking the beach, picking up trash or something else that didn't belong there. In his hand was a picker and a small brown paper bag.

He gave her a winning smile, climbed the three steps, and then crossed her backyard.

"It's good to see you." As soon as Olivia stood up, Mr. Whittingham embraced her in a hug.

"You, too." He sat across from her and crossed his legs. "How are things with CJ and your mother?"

"Actually . . . they are figuring things out." Olivia settled back on the cushioned seat bench.

Mr. Whittingham slapped his knee. "I knew he had it in him."

Olivia nodded. "I think he really loves my mother."

Mr. Whittingham leaned back and laughed. "Oh, I bet all of Sag Harbor that he loves Cindy. I'm glad he's taking advantage of life gifting him another chance with his first love."

Olivia stared at her nearly depleted wine. *Could she and Garrett have a second chance?* Or maybe they had never really explored their relationship the first time around. They'd both been too busy tending to their own wounds to recognize each other's pain. "Yes . . . second chances are nice."

"Oh, don't sound so down."

Olivia sighed. "Let me guess. Addy activated the neighborhood phone tree."

"That knucklehead who lives beside you told me what happened."

Olivia grabbed her wine and sipped it empty. "I'm glad he has someone to talk to about his feelings."

"Hmm." Mr. Whittingham shook his head. "Time is precious, and it waits for no one. And listen, both of you have wasted it."

"Tell me about it. I've seen the results of stubbornness and miscommunication. I hate it." Olivia shivered. "But, Mr. Whittingham, I can't force him to see me . . . to feel for me what I feel for him."

"He loves you, Olivia."

"Maybe he does." She shrugged. "But I want . . . I need him to take the leap." While they hadn't spoken seriously about marriage, it didn't mean that Olivia wasn't committed to their relationship.

"I think that's a fair expectation," Mr. Whittingham acknowledged. "But you can't tell me he hasn't shown you before."

Olivia thought back to the time Garrett had told her he could see himself spending the rest of his life with her. And when he gave her a key to his home. A key she needed to return.

He encouraged her to give CJ a chance to make things right for the sake of healing her inner child.

"Yes, he's . . . he's shown me his feelings. But are they truly genuine if he's willing to walk away so easily?"

"It's not as easy for him as you think, Olivia." Mr. Whittingham sighed. "Not at all."

Olivia nodded, glad that her neighbor was giving her a peek into Garrett's emotions. "And now I may have to move away," she confessed out loud.

"What for?" Mr. Whittingham's voice boomed.

"Because I refuse to pine over my neighbor." Olivia shrugged. "Or maybe I can just come here for part of the summer, and then Oak Bluffs for the second half."

Mr. Whittingham didn't look too pleased by her plans.

"Where are my manners? Would you like some water, coffee, tea . . . wine?" She gestured to the bottle.

"Oh no. But may I throw this away?" He lifted the small bag. "I'll be sure to put your trash out while you're away."

"Oh yes, of course. I already have some trash in there, anyway."

"I'll be right back." He stepped into the house and was back in under a minute. His chestnut brown skin held a pink flush.

"Well, I'll be heading off now," Mr. Whittingham said, suddenly turning to leave. "Don't be a stranger."

Olivia shook her head at his hurried exit. She returned inside the house and took a long bath with the spa kit Perry had given her last year. Soaking inside the tub, Garrett's words played on a loop.

"I can't believe it's over." Tears sprang up in the corners of her eyes. She didn't dare dash them away, not with her suds-soaked hands.

"I wish there was a way that he could see me . . . feel me," she whispered. But there was no answer from the universe, just silence. Her chaotic thoughts finally slowed down and her tense throat, neck, and back muscles were loosened by whatever magical essence Perry had sent.

The bath didn't magically heal her heart, but it gave her strength to drive to Highland Beach the next morning.

When Olivia arrived back in Highland Beach, she pasted on a smile and pretended everything went well. CJ asked her about Mr. Whittingham, and she told him they'd had a pleasant conversation. She made it seem like it was a friendly catch-up about the weather, not about broken hearts.

When Cindy asked her about Garrett, she replied that he was doing just *fine*.

But really, nothing was fine.

Olivia Jones was unraveling. She started to consider selling her home in Sag Harbor and going back to the comforting crowds of New York City.

CHAPTER TWENTY-ONE

July 2022

FIREWORKS

Olivia found that barbecues, picnics, and fireworks helped her more than ice cream to overcome heartbreak on the Fourth of July weekend.

Janice had *voluntold* Olivia to help with the festivities, although they had enough volunteers from the Highland Beach Citizens Association. Olivia served as liaison to the sponsors, making sure they had plenty of food and were enjoying the activities. She also reviewed the sponsored event request forms and made sure everyone who set up storefronts had correctly entered the details.

Though Olivia stayed busy, occasionally a wave of grief would crest and crash over her. When the feelings swelled, she skipped to another activity, giving it her full attention until the pain subsided.

"You're a natural at this," Janice complimented her, while setting up food on the picnic tables.

Olivia shrugged. "This time last year I helped organize a neighborhood block party."

Janice counted the cups and asked, "How are things different between here and Sag Harbor?"

"You all definitely have more civic-focused activities."

Olivia loved how Highland Beach not only embraced wildlife but fiercely protected the land. She was also impressed with how CJ showed people how to plant trees, perennials, and rain gardens on their own properties.

"This place is special." Janice surveyed the land around them, a small smile on her face. "So yes, we volunteer . . . a lot. Government, social activities, environmental . . . if you want to live in Highland Beach, you've got to roll up your sleeves and give it all you have."

Olivia nodded. That was the spirit of this place.

"Well, the picnic starts in an hour. You've got time to go home and get dressed. Mayor CJ is still meeting with some constituents, so I assume you'll meet him later during the festivities."

"Yes, that's the plan. Thanks for *allowing* me to help," Olivia joked. The woman would not have taken no for an answer when she asked for help the day Olivia stopped by to visit her father at work.

"Oh no . . . thank *you!*" Janice responded in kind, and with a smile.

Olivia walked back to CJ's place. When she opened the door, she found Cindy curled on the couch, a remote in hand.

"Hey. Why aren't you ready?"

Cindy shook her head. "I've been thinking . . ."

"Hmm?"

"And I think it's best I stay here."

Olivia shook her head. "I don't understand."

"Don't tell your father." She sat up from her prone position. "But I heard him working late last night. His reputation is still in tatters and, well . . . I think it's best that I don't attend. It'll just add more fodder to the rumor mill."

"Well, if that's the case, then I shouldn't attend either."

Cindy shook her head. "No, people are genuinely curious about you. And you've got this way of deflecting and diverting conversations. You're a charmer."

Olivia chuckled. "My charming personality didn't seem to do a bit of good on you growing up."

"You never showed me that side of you." Cindy paused, nibbling her lips. "Or rather, I didn't encourage it. I was a mess back then." She sighed. "Honestly, I'm a mess now."

"You did the best you could. But we can't move forward if you keep putting yourself down."

"My therapist says I have to apologize and acknowledge what I've done."

"You've done that," Olivia said. She sat down beside her mother. "Over and over. But now we move on."

Cindy frowned. "Aren't you mad? Aren't you bitter?"

Olivia leaned back. "I was . . . initially. I didn't understand you. No matter how many times I'd reached out, you just slapped my hand away. But last summer helped. Not just with CJ's arrival, but I've changed. I've done things I thought I would never do. Hurt people, lied, cheated." Olivia swallowed. "And all of that taught me to forgive myself, to accept forgiveness and to forgive others."

"So you really have forgiven me?"

Olivia leaned closer and squeezed her mother's hand. "Now, I'm no saint, and sometimes memories will surface, but yes. I forgive you." It was the truth. Holding on to all that pain was too heavy.

Tears leaked from Cindy's eyes. Olivia dashed them away. "I'd really like to get to know you, and for you to get to know me. Well, the adult Olivia."

Cindy sniffed. "I'd like that."

"How about we skip the picnic and stay in?"

A smile spread across her mother's face.

The fireworks started as soon as the sun set.

"Why don't we go outside and watch the fireworks on the porch?" Cindy suggested.

"Yes! Let me grab my shoes."

Her mother smiled. "I'll pour us some wine and meet you out-side."

While Cindy got the drinks, Olivia put on her sandals and changed into a fresh shirt. She paused when the doorbell rang, but resumed when she heard her mother open the door.

"Get out!" she heard her mother yell.

Olivia quickly shuffled on her shirt and hurried to the door.

Christine stood just inside, near the cracked door. "What's go-ing on?"

"Oh, Olivia, hello." Christine's eyes were clear. She wore a sim-ple mint green romper paired with pink bangles, halo pink dia-mond earrings, and a small pink clutch. If anyone else saw her, they wouldn't guess she'd had a breakdown a few weeks ago.

Olivia moved to her mother's side. "Hi. What do you need? Are you okay?"

Christine narrowed her eyes. "CJ mentioned that Cindy was un-der the weather. I wanted to check in—"

"No. You wanted to ambush me." Cindy's voice shook with rage. "And here I was thinking about you . . . feeling sorry for you."

"Why would you feel sorry for someone like *me*? I have money, class, and I've traveled to places you've only dreamed of." Arrogance seeped from her pores like perfume.

Christine shoved her way into the house and sat on the couch, perching on the edge as if she were Queen Bee.

"There's been a lot of buzz about Charles. People want to for-give him, though he has nothing to apologize about." She stared at Cindy as if she were a small insect.

"But if he can mend fences with our town, he has a really strong chance at running for Congress." Christine smiled, her stare seem-ing to come from millions of miles away. "Can you imagine my Charles, a senator?"

"Yes," Cindy whispered. "I can imagine it. He would be amazing."

Christine gave her a brittle smile. "On that, we can agree. He's done a lot for Highland Beach, from protecting our ecosystem to staving off commercial business in our area to keeping our place the best-kept secret."

"What are you getting at, Christine?" Olivia crossed her arms.

"I need you . . . the both of you," her attention drifted from Cindy to Olivia, "to back off."

Olivia laughed. "You think you can stuff us into the back of the closet, like we're some pair of unwanted shoes?" She shook her head. "CJ wants us here."

"Yes, he does. And now he's entirely unfocused. It's his dream to—"

"It's your dream. Not CJ's, not Alan's, *yours*." Cindy licked her lips. "I keep wishing . . . I keep hoping against hope that you'll change. That you'll see that you can't control a damn thing about CJ, let alone life. That one day someone could pierce through that selfishness you wear like a fur coat."

"Be reasonable, Cindy." Christine pretended to flick an invisible piece of lint from her romper. "He's going places. And you . . . you're going back to Tremont Middle School in New Jersey. You can't afford to leave your employer, or you'll lose your pension. Things won't work out with you and CJ. I'm just not sure why you'd put yourself through the uncertainty and pain."

"Please don't pretend you care about my feelings . . . or Olivia's."

Christine sighed and turned to face her granddaughter. "I adore you, Olivia. I want to build a relationship with you, and maybe once the dust settles from the reelection, we can figure out how to best address this situation."

Olivia's blood boiled. "Is that what you think I am? A scandal?"

Christine stood. "No. You're . . . special. And kind and gorgeous, and there is no getting around that you are a Jones. I'd just like for us to solidify the mayoral election, let the town settle their nerves without seeing . . ."

"Seeing what?"

"You just . . ." Christine's voice grew thick. "It's not just the fact that you're CJ's daughter. You remind people of Indigo." Christine lifted the corner of her lips, but pain seemed to weigh down her smile. "That's all people can talk about."

Olivia could only imagine how it would feel to look someone in the face who resembled a lost daughter. Olivia lowered the electrified fence around her heart. "Is that resemblance triggering for you, too?"

Christine balled her fist. "I loved my daughter very much. B-but . . ."

"Yes?" Olivia raised an eyebrow.

"There are things . . . that happened when she died. Things that are best left in the past. Even people you yearn to get to know." Her expression hardened. "Even people you love."

"I'm not in the past." Olivia walked backward to the door and pulled it wide open. The sky was lit in bright pinks, reds, and blues from the fireworks.

"You know," she said, "everyone warned me about you. But I gave you a chance. I tried to forgive what many would feel was unforgivable. And you proved them all right. You truly only care about yourself and your reputation. So . . ." Olivia waved her grandmother toward the door. "Please leave. And don't call. Don't secretly send Alan over to ask me out for lunch or dinner."

Christine's lips tightened. A flash of sorrow softened her glittering brown eyes. "You don't understand. You don't have children. Your life, your legacy, is just starting. But mine is crashing, and if I don't hold on tight . . ." Christine looked as if she wanted to say more, but she tightened her stance and strode outside.

Olivia slammed the door behind her. She leaned against it, her heart floundering in her chest, fighting against grief.

She had desperately needed . . . no, wanted . . . a relationship with her grandmother.

As in past tense. Now she knew she would never allow that woman into her heart.

Resting her forehead against the door, she pulled in painful breaths. One. Two. Three.

"Olivia?"

She waved away her mother's concern. "Just taking a breath."

Just saying goodbye to the woman who doesn't deserve my love.

"She really is terrible," Olivia whispered to herself. She pushed away from the door.

Thinking back to her conversations with Ama, Olivia felt like a fool, defending that woman to her godmother.

Cindy patted the sofa cushion beside her. Her eyebrows furrowed as she took in Olivia's distress.

"I'm sorry for what just happened."

"Why are *you* sorry?" Olivia asked her mother.

"It's disappointing when people let you down. Christine made you feel special, because you are, but she's always perceived us as threats since before you were born."

Olivia shook her head. "I want to be done with her, but I know that deep down she's struggling with her children's deaths. I know this has nothing to do with us."

Cindy sighed. "You're right. What are we going to tell your father?"

"The truth," Olivia immediately responded.

"The truth isn't so simple."

"Yes, it is. He needs to know what she did today. Maybe he can encourage her to get help. Otherwise, she'll never feel motivated to try."

Cindy lifted her hand in a defensive stance. "Trust me, I know. But your father . . . he loves his mother. She works his nerves, but she is his only living relative. It would be unfair to make him choose."

Olivia shook her head. Reining in her anger seemed like an impossible task. "*We* aren't making him choose. Christine is."

"CJ needs to draw his own conclusions."

Olivia refused to be abused while her father processed the realization that Christine did not have his best interest at heart. Christine wanted "first lady" status and wouldn't stop until CJ was the next Black president.

Cindy was rocking, hugging herself. She seemed years away. Her words echoed in Olivia's head.

CJ needs to draw his own conclusions. Those words blared in her mind as if they were on speaker.

"You're afraid he won't choose us."

Cindy stopped her rocking. "What's that?"

"Because he didn't choose us last time." Olivia sighed. For the past few months, her father had shown them in word and deed that he viewed Olivia and Cindy as his top priority. But her mother didn't see it that way. She still reeled from his earlier rejection.

"You still love CJ, don't you?"

Cindy looked around as if there were a secret camera. "I'm tired."

"Mom . . ."

"I think it's time I go to bed." She patted Olivia's knee and ran away from Olivia's question.

The next morning, Olivia ran around the small beach town, sticking to the sidewalks and road instead of the sandy beach. She spotted Aneesa in a hybrid Lexus.

Her mother's best friend gave her an exaggerated wave, signaling Olivia to stop and speak.

"Aneesa, hi." Olivia greeted her through deep breaths.

"Hey, so . . ." Aneesa closed her eyes, as if bracing for impact. "I haven't been able to get in contact with Cindy or your father."

Olivia nodded. It made sense. "CJ didn't come in until late. He's going to stay in for the morning and then go into the office. Why? What's happened?" Olivia leaned in.

"Someone else is entering the mayoral race, and I'm told this person plans to fight dirty."

"Who is it?"

"Lauren Miles. And she claims she's got all the dirt on your family."

"Like what?" A low thud started at the base of Olivia's neck. It was too damn early for bad news.

"I don't know. But she promised my colleague it's the scoop of the century."

CHAPTER TWENTY-TWO

August 2022

A NEW CHALLENGER

Someone banged on CJ's door.

"Can you believe it!" Janice marched into the house with a rolled-up newspaper tucked under her arm.

"Good morning, Janice. I suppose you've read the paper," Olivia said, greeting CJ's admin.

Janice stopped just in front of the sofa. "Yes. Haven't you?"

"We received the news last night."

Janice threw her hands in the air. "Then why are you so calm?"

"It's her right to run."

"Yes, but the current mayor's ex?" Janice shivered. "It's tacky. And she apparently has the support of Pastor Stanley."

Olivia sighed. She didn't know the pastor all that well, but he seemed to enjoy throwing his weight around.

"CJ's record speaks for itself."

Janice twisted her lips and her neck. "Please don't be dense."

"Dense?"

"Yes. Lauren, Pastor Stanley, or someone else clearly has a vendetta against your father. Let's see, we have the unsolicited picture of you, his daughter, posted online," she said, raising a finger to count. "The article about his sister Indigo revealing a personal letter she'd written, and now his ex-girlfriend plans to run against him, as a write-in candidate no less." She lifted her second and third fingers to count the remaining points.

Last night, when Olivia had discussed Lauren's candidacy with CJ, he'd said that as a write-in candidate, Lauren didn't have much of a chance to win, but her intentions were clear: to divide the vote.

"Will the town think she's a woman scorned?" Olivia drummed her lips with her fingers.

"Oh no. Lauren will make sure no one will land that low-brow narrative. She's a phoenix. She rises despite her adversity. Although Lauren has money, she didn't come from a prestigious family like some of our other residents." Janice snapped her fingers. "I'm telling you, there's something not right with that woman."

Olivia tilted her head. She wasn't all that sure Lauren was a complete monster. In fact, Lauren had warned her about someone being a shark. Unless that was all a front to soften Olivia's defenses.

"What do you have against Lauren?"

"I don't think she truly likes CJ. There's no light in her eyes. No passion when she's around him."

Olivia nodded, not surprised by Janice's observation. CJ and Lauren had been in a platonic relationship to rehabilitate his image after he dated his junior staffer. "Maybe she isn't into PDA."

Olivia had been the same way. *Until Garrett.* He didn't mind kissing her in restaurants, holding hands, and occasionally squeezing her ass when Zora wasn't around.

A tiny pinch of pain plucked her heartstrings.

"Trust me. For Lauren, CJ is just a means to an end," Janice said in a singsongy voice.

"How so?"

"He worked late nights, and she never seemed upset. Just only when they had plans to make an appearance. But a canceled movie or date night? Not a peep." Janice mimed locking her lips.

"Did you tell your boss about this?"

"No." She scoffed at the question. "We aren't close enough to discuss such matters. Besides, it's not appropriate for me to give him my opinion about his personal life." Janice dropped her voice as if they weren't the only two people in the house. "But . . . I'm not the only person who's noticed."

"The team?"

"Yes. Everyone. Now, don't get me wrong. I'm not here to bash another Black woman. But every time someone speaks of them as a couple, it's about their status. They're powerful, smart, and beautiful together."

And that was likely what CJ and Lauren wanted people to focus on—their status, wealth, and maturity. Nothing as passionate as an affair with a woman young enough to be his daughter.

"Yes. They were well matched," noted Olivia, repeating the words her grandmother had used when she first met Lauren.

"You get it."

Olivia stared out the window. In a place so rich in history, strategic partnerships and marriages made sense.

She understood why her mother had no choice but to walk away.

"Well, there's nothing we can do about it." Olivia sighed and said, "Lauren is running, and CJ could use the 'scorned lover' angle, but it won't be good for either of them in the long term."

Janice shook her head. "No, CJ wouldn't disrespect Lauren like that. He'll stick to the facts—his experience, the fact he's always lived here year-round."

"And then there's his contender, Harold Munroe."

"That's who CJ will need to focus his energy on," Janice agreed, with a decisive nod.

Olivia hadn't met Harold Munroe formally, but she'd seen him in passing. In his late fifties, Harold seemed to care about the community. He'd never served as mayor, but he had a solid background in political communications, much like Alan.

"How is Harold's relationship with the pastor?" Olivia asked, an idea suddenly sparking.

"Very cordial. He's a member of the church. Which is interesting. Why is Pastor Stanley throwing his support behind Lauren instead?"

"Maybe by supporting Lauren he's supporting Harold," Olivia mused.

"How so?"

"You said Harold is the one we should focus on. Maybe he's the one who's using Lauren to divide and conquer."

Janice laughed into her hand. "Have you met Pastor Stanley? That man isn't a mastermind. He can barely remember the points of his sermon these days."

"Aren't you a member of the church, too?"

"Yes. Which is why I know it's a snooze fest there on Sunday mornings and that man isn't a mastermind."

Is Lauren the mastermind?

Olivia narrowed her eyes. "Janice, do you know when Lauren will be hosting an event to drum up support? I imagine she'd want to do something before the mayoral debate at the Pavilion next week."

"Of course I know. Lauren's cohosting a picnic this Sunday after church."

"I guess I'll be dressing in my Sunday best this weekend."

Janice laughed. "Don't tell me you're going to pick a fight during the fish fry in the church parking lot?"

"Absolutely not." Olivia laughed with her. "I'm just going to have a friendly conversation."

Lauren didn't seem to love CJ. Even though CJ had broken their deal that he'd endorse her for mayor when he left office, Olivia needed to figure out why Lauren was running now, when she had little chance of winning. Was she the puppet or the puppet master?

When Olivia walked into the sanctuary Sunday morning, the churchgoers got their fill of staring at the mayor's daughter.

She hadn't told CJ and Cindy she planned to attend church. Otherwise, they would've thwarted her plan. And Olivia couldn't have that. So she endured the staring. In fact, she welcomed it. The harsh lesson she'd learned was that small towns abhor secrets. Hiding in her father's house and running away from feelings had led only to her being pushed to center stage. There was no such thing as hiding from the truth. Especially when Olivia was a doppelgänger of Indigo. She just hoped people were more curious than wary.

Pastor Stanley began his sermon. The first ten minutes were strong, but then he began recycling some of his earlier points—word for word.

Olivia sneaked a glance at Janice, who winked before she shook her head in disgust.

But when the service was coming to an end and she saw Lauren stand to deliver closing remarks and kick off the picnic, Olivia was alert with attention.

Lauren wore a bright blue shirt with a matching skirt paired with a small stylish hat and a pair of silver sky-high Louboutin heels. "Giving honor to God. Pastor Stanley, Deaconess Adams, members, visitors, and friends. Wow, that was such a great sermon today, wasn't it, family?" She clapped and the rest of the congregation joined in.

Pastor Stanley sat behind the pulpit, beaming from her praise.

"As you all know, I'm tossing my hat into the ring—I'll be running for mayor of Highland Beach as a write-in candidate. I want you all to know that I take this *seriously*. Let someone who is entirely focused on the advancement and protection of this beautiful historical gem of a town lead it. That's why I'm here . . . to serve the citizens of Highland Beach. I've got years of experience as a trial attorney and experience in environmental law that I believe will serve the community well. As we continue to grow, we must ensure that our community thrives environmentally, historically, and economically. Please allow me to usher us into the future while protecting our history. I'll be outside and I'm happy to answer any of your questions related to my vision for Highland Beach. And if I don't see you at the fish fry, I'll see you next week at the debate. Thank you."

She nodded to the congregation, who gave her thunderous applause, and then stepped down the aisle and out the door.

If Olivia hadn't been a Jones and the daughter of the incumbent, she would've clapped along with the congregation. The woman's brief speech was convincing.

Olivia left with the volunteers to set up the picnic before Pastor Stanley dismissed the congregation. She easily followed Lauren in her bright blue and found volunteers already outside frying the fish. The aroma coming from the combination of cornmeal, grease, and Old Bay seasoning made her mouth water.

Lauren moved closer to the shore. Olivia scanned the area before approaching her. Everyone else seemed either deep in their own conversations or focused on setting up the picnic.

Striding up to Lauren, Olivia called out, "Lauren?"

The woman didn't turn around. Not even when Olivia stood within touching distance.

"Lauren!"

Lauren whipped around, clasping her chest, her mouth open and ready to yell. When she finally noticed Olivia, she pressed her lips back together, as if swallowing her scream.

"You can't sneak up on people like that."

"I called your name several times. You didn't hear me?"

"No, I . . . I was deep in thought."

Olivia gave her a strained smile before she jumped into the conversation. "Listen, Lauren—"

"Don't tell me you're here to scare me off?"

"Scare you?"

"Yes. To protect your precious family," Lauren snapped.

Olivia shook her head. "I would never presume to tell you what to do. I just want to understand."

"So let me get this right. You wouldn't presume to tell me what to do, but you have no qualms about understanding my motives?"

Olivia nodded. "That's correct. And I . . . this may come out of nowhere, but did CJ hurt you?"

She didn't feel that CJ would physically harm a fly, but given his past with Cindy, she wondered if he had given Lauren too much hope. Men like CJ were like giants. They didn't know their own strength, but that didn't change the fact that they could squash you like a fly.

"Hurt me?" Lauren laughed. "He would have to give me the time of day to hurt me."

Her words and attitude seemed cavalier. She wore a sardonic smile and her arms hung casually by her side.

"You were partners for a while. You both are ambitious and have similar goals," Olivia probed.

"Listen, Olivia. I like you."

"You do?" She didn't know if she could believe Lauren. They hadn't had more than ten minutes of conversation.

Lauren nodded. "It's difficult being the new girl in a tight-knit community like Venice or Highland Beach. It's not easy to keep your head high when everyone has your name on their lips. Trust me, I know. But you've done an excellent job, and you don't seem to give a damn about what others think."

Olivia's cheeks warmed at the praise. She'd been so hard on herself for leaving town—for hiding away when the news of her lineage had been discovered.

"That's a rare trait in the infamous Douglass family."

"Infamous?"

"Listen, you don't need to understand my motives, but just know it doesn't have a thing to do with my feelings for your father. We were never meant to be. Besides that," she added with a nonchalant air, "I'm far too accomplished and easy on the eyes to worry about a man."

"Then what about the leaked photo that revealed my identity? The rumors about the family, and the letter in the newspaper?"

She pressed her hand to her chest. "You think I'm here to harass your family?"

Olivia didn't blink during the stare-down. She didn't want to point fingers—she wanted the truth.

Lauren slowly smiled. "The advice I gave you earlier still stands."

Olivia furrowed her brow. "That there's a shark about that I should be alert to?"

Lauren chuckled. "Honey, you're in shark-infested waters in your own backyard. Don't worry about me. Worry about yourself," she said, pointing now at Olivia. Then she stopped and began to turn away.

"And now, I've got some schmoozing to do."

"You're asking questions now . . . and that's good," she whispered to Olivia over her shoulder as she began walking away. "But you need to ask your family questions." She winked, turned, and greeted a waiting church member.

Olivia stood, stunned at Lauren's pointed advice.

Was someone in the family responsible for the leak?

But who?

CJ wouldn't do that to himself or harm his family. And Christine wanted CJ to run for Congress. She wouldn't dare sabotage her own son.

There was someone else in the family. Someone else she didn't know about.

She would take Lauren's advice. Olivia would start asking her family questions.

CHAPTER TWENTY-THREE

July 2022

THE RUMOR MILL

"I must admit, I'm surprised you asked me for lunch today." Christine's pearly whites beamed from across the table.

Guilt swirled in Olivia's stomach. After being confronted by Christine on the Fourth of July two weeks ago, Olivia had decided to never speak to her grandmother again.

But she couldn't shake the advice that Lauren had given her last week to ask her family questions, and those questions required privacy. That was the only reason she met up with her grandmother at her home rather than in a restaurant.

"I'll be honest . . . I have a lot of questions about the past. So if you aren't comfortable being asked some of those questions, I'll leave."

Christine took a deep breath. "It's fine. I knew the day would come when you'd want to know more about your father."

Olivia shook her head. "Whatever I need to know, I trust my parents will tell me."

"Oh, well, yes, I suppose so. But I meant Chris."

"I know a lot about Chris through my mother." And oddly enough, through Omar. "I want to know about Indigo."

"I-Indigo?"

"Yes. I know this may be tough to understand, but the letter in the newspaper is disturbing. And then there's the fact that I look just like her and someone is determined to use my face to stir controversy. So yes, I want to understand."

And perhaps Christine's memories held the key to figuring out who was behind the articles about their family's history.

Christine's thin lips curled into a sneer. "I don't think discussing my daughter will accomplish anything."

"There is someone out there who doesn't care for this family."

"This family?"

"The Douglass-Jones family. Otherwise, I wouldn't have had someone following me and taking my picture without permission. Someone wouldn't have posted anonymous comments to insinuate that the family is into illegal activity. Then there's—"

"We have broken no laws."

"Of course," Olivia quickly agreed. She believed Christine on that point. Her grandmother was far too smart, and too prideful about her family's legacy, to ruin the family name.

Christine stared at Olivia for a full minute. Olivia held her gaze, fully embracing the discomfort of the moment. She'd learned long ago that sometimes silence made people fold. Christine was no pushover, but Olivia needed to show her grandmother that she wouldn't back down.

"You're a Douglass-Jones, too," Christine said in an "admit it" tone.

"I am."

"Do you want to know the secret of success in being a matriarch in the Douglass-Jones family?"

Olivia nodded.

Christine grabbed her crystal glass. The look of longing on her face as she glanced into the glass made Olivia realize that she wished it were wine instead of water.

Christine sipped before speaking. "My mother told me the secret is to be the glue. To hold the family together, no matter what. If you must lie, so what? If you must suffer in silence, so be it. But you must never, *ever*, let someone threaten your family. It's especially important to lift up our Black men. No matter the sacrifice to your head and heart."

Christine returned her drink to the table and stared down at the place setting as if to gather herself. She finally refocused her attention on Olivia. "I was top of my class, I'll have you know. In undergrad and in law school. Higher than your grandfather, Daniel, for that matter. Higher than Alan. But I . . ." She meshed her lips together, shaking her head. "I had to seal the deal. Secure the line. Be with someone of my caliber." She wiggled her fingers.

"You see, Daniel was dating someone he really liked. What was that girl's name?" She pondered, then snapped her fingers. "Oh yes. Renée. She had his nose wide open. And we were all friends. But she was on a scholarship. And his family wasn't a fan. Mine was of the same accord. They all had plans for Daniel and me to marry, and they'd hoped we would come together naturally over the years. But that didn't happen."

"They just expected you to figure it out?"

"We ran in the same circles. We'd known each other since birth, so yes. They thought two attractive people who grew up together would want to marry." Christine rolled her eyes.

"What about you?" Olivia asked her grandmother.

"What about me?"

"You liked someone else, too, didn't you?"

"Hmm. Yes." She nodded. "But Mother told me I had to make that sacrifice, and so I did. To be fair, Daniel did the same. So we just sort of switched."

"Switched?"

"Alan dated Renée. A temporary thing, of course. Then I dated

Daniel. We decided to be mature and make the best of things. After a while, I didn't have to pretend with Daniel. I grew to adore him and eventually love him in time." She stiffened her lips, her shoulders, maybe even her resolve.

"When I became pregnant shortly after our marriage, I had to sacrifice my dream of becoming an attorney to take care of my growing family."

Olivia leaned back in her seat, letting her grandmother vent.

"So I had my two brilliant boys and then, four years later, I had my precious girl. And she was perfect. She had a will of steel that matched my own," she said in a tired, yet proud, voice.

"And secretly I rooted for her to have a different outcome than I had. I prayed my baby didn't have to sacrifice her brilliant light to prop up a man. I thought if anyone could escape the expectations for the Douglass women, it would be Indigo. She would figure out a way to make this life her own. One that honored her family but kept her individuality. A scholar and an athlete." Christine's eyes misted over.

"But then around twelve, during what I thought was puberty, she became *different*. Sullen. She wasn't the bright ball of energy that talked a mile a minute. She would go from the highest of highs to the lowest of lows. I . . . I couldn't reach her. I couldn't break through that dark storm that clouded her hearing and her sight." She shook her head and rubbed her forearm. "I didn't understand the self-harm, and I thought it was a cry for attention. So, I . . . I did what my parents did when one of us kids acted out. I froze her out. I had to ignore her so she could understand that her dangerous ultimatums wouldn't work on us." Tears seeped down her cheeks.

"But it wasn't a silent threat. It was a cry for help. I know that now. I know better now. And I didn't listen to my baby's cries."

She ducked her head into her hands.

Olivia stood, walked around the table, and sat in the seat near her. She grabbed and held Christine's soft, ageless hands.

"Did she have any friends?"

"She did until the beginning of high school. They just . . . they didn't really understand her, either. They couldn't swing with the highs and lows. Well, except that little girl from the summer she died. She was visiting family for the summer. I . . . can't remember her name."

"Hmm."

"Why the hmm?"

"Maybe she knows something we don't. It would be good to have a name."

Christine shrugged wordlessly until her eyes went sharp. "Alan may remember."

"Alan?"

"We were friends at the time, but he excelled in researching a person's background. I asked him to look into her background. He thought I was ridiculous, of course, and initially refused, but he promised he would look. But then with everything that . . . that happened, it no longer mattered."

"Of course."

"Did that . . . did I answer your questions, dear?" Christine asked, her voice exhausted.

Though Olivia wasn't totally satisfied with her grandmother's answers, she didn't want to overtax her with questions that could become triggering.

Christine exhaled. "Well, then. Now I'd like to eat." She seemed to gather up her usual regal air and cloak herself in it like an invisible barrier. She waved to the other side of the table.

"Then let's eat." Olivia returned to her seat across from Christine and cut into the Thai salad. When her phone buzzed, she pushed the Silent button.

"Are you visiting your sister this summer?"

"You know, I think I may," Christine answered in a measured voice. "And maybe absence will make the heart grow fonder for Alan."

"Are you and Alan having issues?"

"We're fine," Christine answered in a high-pitched voice. "But he seems distracted, and downright irritable lately. If it wasn't for him doing all of this for my son, I'd thwack him across the head."

Olivia laughed, despite the heaviness of the conversation. "Well, I'm sure it will pass over."

"Oh, it better, because my patience is running thin, honey." She flicked her hand. "And how are you and that man back in Sag Harbor?" She scooped some rice into her mouth and chewed. "Garrett, was it? I'm sure he's awful lonely without you."

Olivia cleared her throat and smiled. "He seems to do just fine." She didn't want to have this conversation with Christine, who probably had a nice and tidy dossier on Garrett.

She steered the conversation into safer waters and told Christine about her plans to visit London, Paris, and Greece.

"They're calling it 'revenge travel,'" Christine said. "People wanting to make up for all the time lost during the pandemic."

Just as they finished their lunch, Alan opened the door. "Christine?"

"In here."

"Good. I need some sugar. I ran all the way to DC for this . . ." His voice trailed off when he noticed Olivia.

He held a small brown package with a large RX label.

Is it her medicine? Alan stood too far away for Olivia to clearly read the label.

Christine exhaled. "We have company," she said through clenched teeth.

"Oh, I'm sorry."

She waved a hand, shaking her head. "Can you just . . . put that on my desk, please?"

"Of course."

"Oh, Alan, I'm glad to see you. Christine and I were having a conversation about Indigo, and she said you may know her friend from the . . . well, from the time before she passed."

Alan scrunched his face. He glanced at Christine, and a silent conversation seemed to take place between them. "Is there a . . . a reason you want to know?"

"Because she may have understood the circumstances behind Indigo's death and—"

"No." Alan crossed his arms and shook his head. "You don't need to drag Christine into that mess."

"But you investigated that girl?"

"I followed up. And I'm telling you, she's not worth the trouble."

Hands on the table, Christine pushed herself up. "Alan, I can't believe you."

"You told me to investigate it, and I did. But there were a . . . myriad of other things going on. We almost lost you to grief, and I'm not . . . dealing with that shit again."

Olivia's eyes widened at his exclamation.

"Is that what my grief is to you?" Christine demanded. "Shit?"

"That's not what I mean, my love. But you could not handle any more. Trust me."

"I can handle things just fine. The Douglass-Jones women have been doing so for centuries." Christine's eyes welled with tears. "Olivia, if you'll excuse me, I need to gather myself."

Then she stopped just before the stairwell and swung her attention back to Olivia. "Don't forget what I said. The secret to keeping the family together. Don't let anyone, especially a man, make you feel weak. You're stronger than you know."

Christine stormed upstairs.

"Oh God." Alan rubbed at his temples. "I knew this would come back to bite me in the ass."

"Then why did you lie?"

"Olivia, with all due respect, you just got here, and the issues in the Douglass-Jones family run deep. There are lots of people who will lie and drag your name in the mud. And this community, every single resident, has done their part in protecting what's ours. I am no different. Now," he crumpled the brown bag in his hand, "I need to see to my wife."

"Okay, Alan. I'm sorry if my questions caused you harm."

"It's not your fault. It's not anyone's fault," he assured her, ". . . but that woman." He muttered that last part to himself, but not low enough.

"I'll tell you what," Alan said. "Let me speak to Christine, and then I'll give CJ a call. I'll let him decide what to do next."

Olivia stood. "Sorry to leave this mess behind." She waved at the dirty dishes.

"Don't worry. I'll take care of everything. I always do."

Olivia had no doubt he was referring to more than the dishes. But then Christine's words echoed in her head. Maybe she didn't need Alan as much as he thought? Olivia had a feeling Christine could take on the world if she needed to.

CHAPTER TWENTY-FOUR

July 2022

AGREE TO DISAGREE

The mayoral debate was starting in just a few hours, and Olivia rushed to get ready. She wondered about the angle that Lauren would take that night. Alan thought she would leverage the negative news coverage and social media posts. Cindy thought she would bring up their relationship and secret baby.

Olivia didn't think either of them were right. Lauren gave her the impression that she had a secret agenda beyond that of a woman scorned, beyond mounting a response to mudslinging gossip. But that assessment didn't untwist the knots in her throat. In the past year, Olivia had begun listening to the little voice in her head. And lately, the alarm bells had been ringing.

Just as her senses tingled, her phone rang.

"Ama?" Olivia answered the phone.

"Hello, cher. Will you be at CJ's home for a while?"

"No. We are on the way to the debate."

"Oh, well, goodness. I feel like such a fool. I was popping by for a visit."

Those alarm bells started clanging.

"I'm sorry, Ama, but we'll be at the Pavilion. There's a nice restaurant in Annapolis that I can meet you at by . . . seven p.m.?"

"Don't need a recommendation, cher. I can find my way. See you soon."

"I . . ." Olivia bit her lip. "Is everything okay? Did you find more information about my family?"

Ama chuckled. "I have, and everything will be just fine. I look forward to our chat. And oh, I brought you some more of my special blend. I'm sure the debate will be one to celebrate."

"S-sounds good. Thank you, Ama. I'll call you right after."

"You do that. Take care of yourself." Ama ended the call.

Olivia looked at the ceiling and took a deep breath. *I don't know what her plans are, but Ama's up to something.*

Thankfully, Ama's meddling was *usually* benign.

Olivia opened the door to her room just as her mother lightly rapped her knuckles against the door.

"Ready?"

Olivia glanced at herself once more in the mirror and nodded. "Let's go support CJ."

Olivia and Cindy left the house and noticed a few neighbors were en route to the Pavilion, which stood in the middle of the neighborhood.

Cushioned folding chairs were lined up in neat rows. Cindy and Olivia opted for the middle row. Pastor Stanley strode toward the front, and his wife, trailing behind, gave them a sweet smile and small wave before she hurried after her husband.

"It's good to know she doesn't hate us," Olivia whispered.

"She's a sweetheart. Now, that pastor needs someone to knock the old-school out of him."

Olivia laughed.

The click of heels against the wood floor seized Olivia's attention. Lauren Miles walked into the room wearing a pale green dress with a smart collar, flared pockets, and yellow stilettos.

"Good afternoon, everyone." She smiled and nodded at those

already in their seats, but she didn't break her stride. Lauren's eyes were on the prize—three mic'd lecterns at the front of the room, where CJ and Harold were already standing.

Aneesa, who was serving as the debate moderator, surveyed the room. When she noticed Olivia and Cindy, she simply nodded. Olivia took no offense. She knew that Aneesa, as moderator, needed to maintain impartiality.

Christine strode in. She glanced at Olivia and Cindy, sighed, and sat down on the vacant seat on the other side of Cindy.

Cindy stretched her eyes wide but didn't utter a word. Olivia wasn't surprised. She knew it wouldn't bode well for her not to sit beside CJ's family.

Cindy reached for Olivia's hand and squeezed. When she didn't let go, Olivia covered her hand with her own. She stared at her mother, giving her the same "winning smile," as she called it, that she gave to her jumpy clients. She tried to convey a message silently with her eyes.

It'll be okay. CJ will do just fine.

Her mother nodded, then returned her attention to the three candidates. CJ stood in the middle, with Lauren to his right and Harold on his left.

"Good afternoon, everyone," Aneesa began. "Today's event is brought to you by the League of Black Voters. Each candidate has graciously agreed to take part in today's debate." She paused and looked at the audience of close to fifty residents, who took their cue to clap. Cindy still held Olivia's hand like a lifeline.

Olivia squeezed her mother's hand one more time and then pulled it away to rest in her lap. She didn't want to show nervousness or weakness during CJ's debate.

Aneesa ran down the rules of decorum and reminded the audience that she would be the only one asking the questions. Then she launched into the first question.

"The Highland Beach living shoreline project has been and continues to be a very contentious subject that has yet to be resolved. I want each candidate to share a leadership example that involves either taking a controversial position or bringing people together to solve a controversial issue. CJ, since this is your idea, let's start with you."

"Thanks for asking, Aneesa. When I first came to office, several residents quickly brought the shoreline erosion to my attention. I partnered with a biologist from National Centers for Coastal Ocean Science two years ago and received a recommendation for a cost-effective way to stabilize our ecosystem, also known as a 'living shoreline.' I'll admit that there are potential cons. Some scientists have highlighted that dunes and other beach features may migrate landward. The living shoreline isn't a guarantee and could fail with any sort of erratic weather. Many of you are concerned about maintaining our beachfront and views. We've heard your concerns, and therefore we canceled the project and did so democratically. Our goal is to avoid complete erosion at the beachfront, like at Venice Beach. So, Aneesa, to answer the question, I've listened to my constituents and deferred to their recommendations. We still have our task force in place, and we'll vet through workable options that will reduce the impact on the beachfront. I have and will continue to work with all of you."

A few people clapped.

Aneesa pointed. "Harold, you have the floor."

Harold smoothed his maroon linen shirt before he began. "Well, now, if my memory serves me, Mayor Jones, I distinctly recall that you didn't run this project by the fine people of Highland Beach, which is why we were upset."

Olivia scanned the crowd, noticing a few heads nod at his statement. "And it wasn't just about views. Let's get that squared away, Mayor Jones. It's not a guarantee with the sea level rise and increased rainfall."

More people clapped. She turned her attention to her father, who exuded confidence.

"Now, as far as what I've done to bring people together. As the former CEO of the largest textile company in the Northeast, I've had the exceptional responsibility of managing thousands of jobs while maintaining manufacturing safety with an eye on eco-friendly process." Harold continued to run down his résumé, citing examples of how he mitigated the pandemic by repurposing his factory to produce face masks.

Harold is definitely a top contender.

"Thank you, Harold. Now you have the floor, Lauren. Would you like for me to repeat the question?"

"No, thank you. And Harold has done an amazing job illuminating some of CJ's *opportunities* during the shoreline project. During my decade-and-a-half-long tenure as a trial attorney, we dealt in listening, in researching, in negotiations, and in going to court. The word 'contentious' feels hard. It feels belaboring." Her eyes scanned the audience, as if seeking to make eye contact with everyone there. "But sometimes things must be destroyed for new growth to come forth. We can't be afraid of hard truths." She leveled her stare at Christine.

"So as your mayor, I'll listen, I'll fact-find, and I will bring the truth to light." An eerie gleam shone in her eyes. "Thank you."

There were a few, markedly less enthusiastic claps.

"Actually," Lauren added, her fingers gripping the podium, "excuse me, but I have more to say about this thing called the truth. Some people," she said, staring at Christine, "would have you live in ignorance. Some people—"

"Ms. Miles, this is not the question I posed. I'll warn you that you need to adhere to the decorum of this debate."

"Screw decorum," Lauren growled, her voice low and guttural.

CJ turned to fully face his opponent. "Lauren, if this is about us, we can take this offline."

"It's about the Douglass-Jones family. Christine, in particular. Thirty-one years ago, my mother, Agatha, reached out to Christine in good faith. She told her that we, too, are descendants of the great Douglass family. But she just wouldn't hear of it because my mother is white."

Gasps filled the room. Everyone turned their attention to Christine, whose face had turned the color of a cherry tomato.

Olivia could feel a blush spread on her own cheeks like wildfire. Though her mother squeezed her hand, she couldn't quite feel anything but numb.

Aneesa leaned into her microphone. "Lauren, this is not the time or place for this conversation."

"Oh, I think this is the perfect time and the perfect place. You see, Christine paid off my mother."

"Mother?" Christine's voice shook with rage. "I didn't know that swindler had a child."

"Your karma has finally come." Lauren smirked. "And I'm so happy I get to serve it to you. You and your family have fooled Highland Beach long enough. You all deserve a mayor who doesn't use their family and connections to run this town like a Mafia boss."

Christine shot to her feet. "That's enough!" Her screech nearly popped Olivia's eardrums. Like everyone else, Olivia stared at her grandmother, whose body shook like branches in a windstorm.

With red-flushed cheeks and her shaking body, Christine was the picture of rage. "You think you know the truth, but you don't. Your mother is a swindler and has conned people several times over the years. There is no way . . . no way, the Douglass family has white descendants. I'll bet my life on it."

"Please," Lauren scoffed. "Everyone here knows the history. Helen Pitts *Douglass* married Frederick Douglass."

"They had no children. She was barren," Christine shrieked.

"Yet I'm standing here. Living. Breathing. Proof."

Olivia stared at Lauren as if she could visually piece together the clues of her lineage. Until just now, she hadn't realized Lauren was biracial. She had incredibly fair skin, just a shade darker than Ama's. Her hair was bone straight, likely the result of blow dryers and flat irons. Her eyes were a deep chestnut brown.

She'd seen the pictures of Frederick Douglass's second wife. In one she looked at him adoringly while he stared straight at the camera. Helen was twenty years his junior.

"You are nothing. A product of lies and nothing more."

Lauren narrowed her eyes, but her determination didn't waver. She crossed her arms and smirked. "Okay, then. If what I'm saying is a lie, why did you write my mother a check for $15,000 to leave town?"

More gasps and shouts and whispers filled the room.

"I can't believe they had kids!" someone who sat near Aneesa shouted.

"There's been no record. No, nothing. This is ludicrous," a woman who worked at the Frederick Douglass Museum argued.

Christine moved from her seat and stood in the middle of the aisle. "You little idiot."

"Answer the question, Christine. Did you pay my mother Agatha Pitts to go away?" Lauren taunted.

Aneesa ripped up her cards and threw her hands in the air. "I guess the mayoral debate is over now."

"I should have known Agatha's lies wouldn't disappear. And to think she deceived her own daughter." Christine shook her head. "Regardless, you have no relation to Frederick Douglass." Her voice shook with fury.

"My mother didn't lie to me. She told me the truth, and then I told your daughter, Indigo, the truth."

"What did you say?" CJ whispered.

"My mother wanted me to befriend Indigo." Lauren shrugged.

"Seeing as we're related and all. She wanted to see what Indigo knew about the Douglass line."

CJ stumbled away from the podium. He looked sick. Seeing her father's distress, Olivia stood, on wobbly feet, and tried to move to the front, but Lauren's shocking accusations had rooted her in place.

"No, we aren't," CJ said in a choked voice.

Lauren turned around to face CJ. "Yes, we are. Which is why we haven't so much as kissed."

She tossed her hair and turned toward the audience. "I told Indigo everything. But I . . . I also told her how my mom planned to blackmail the family. When my mother shared her plans, I warned Indigo because she had genuinely become my friend. I didn't want any money. I just wanted to get to know my family." A tear rolled down Lauren's cheek. "Indigo was real and raw and saw past the fact that I didn't wear designer clothes and shoes. And she treated me like a sister. She, above all, wanted people to know the truth. And the truth is, the Douglass family has—"

Loud banging interrupted Lauren's impassioned speech.

The door opened, revealing an older white woman who looked to be in her sixties.

"Mom?" Lauren gasped. "What are you doing here?"

Everyone's attention focused on the white woman gliding through a sea of Black faces. But Olivia noticed someone just behind Lauren's mother—Ama, wearing an ankle-length persimmon dress. Quietly, she settled in one of the few open seats near the door.

What is Ama doing here?

It seemed as if Ama heard her question, because she put a finger over her mouth, signaling Olivia to keep quiet.

Olivia nodded once. Her attention returned to the older woman, who wore a wrinkled olive-green blouse and equally wrinkled khaki shorts. "Why are you here, Bree?" she said as she shuffled toward her daughter.

Aneesa narrowed her eyes. "Is your name not Lauren Miles?"

Lauren huffed. "My name is *legally* Lauren Miles."

"But I gave you the name Breanne *Lauren* Pitts," the woman insisted.

"Wait a minute. Your name is Bree?" Cindy asked. "That's the girl who hung out with Indigo the summer . . . the summer she died."

"Bree, honey, I . . . I lied to you. I just . . ." Agatha Pitts wrung her hands as if she were drying a wet cloth. "We needed the money, honey. And I . . . we aren't descended from the Douglass family. We're just distant relatives of Helen Pitts's family."

"*What?*" Lauren snapped.

"Will someone tell me what the *hell* is going on?" CJ barked.

"I'll tell you." Christine's voice shook with rage. "This woman came to me and had the audacity to lie. She said that she was the descendant of Frederick Douglass and Helen Pitts. But they never had a child. As I said before, *Helen was barren.* All the women in our family know the true story. And when she came to me with these lies, I shut her down."

She turned to face Agatha. "And I told her to get the hell out of our town. But she threatened to sell her story to the media. And it doesn't matter if something is the truth or a lie. People believe whoever tells the story the best. And I couldn't have that. I couldn't have her lie about Anna and Frederick's legacy. So yes, I paid her to go away."

Olivia thought of her mother, and all the other girls and women Christine had paid to stay away from her sons.

That's what she does best. Pay someone to run away. But they always come back. Olivia had thought she couldn't think any lower of Christine, but it seemed her expectations didn't go deep enough.

"Mom, this can't be real. You told me . . . you swore we are descendants of the Douglass line." Lauren's voice shook.

"You aren't, my love. I'm sorry, but it simply isn't true. The truth is . . . I became sort of . . . obsessed with the family while I studied history in college. I had a particular interest because of her family as well. And as much as I wanted to believe it, it's not true."

"Why are you here?" Lauren asked. "Wait, let me guess, someone else paid you to show up. You must've run out of money again," she snapped. Though Lauren's tone was angry, her eyes showed her anguish.

Olivia looked at her godmother. Ama appeared innocent and unaffected by the chaos.

"I was made aware of your intentions," Agatha deftly avoided Laura's accusation. "I . . . I didn't know you were even here, sweetheart. You told me you were going to Singapore, but someone informed me otherwise."

"Someone, hmm?" Lauren scanned the room. Olivia exhaled when her attention skipped over Ama. Ama had seemed to know more than she let on during their last call. After the debate, Olivia would confirm her gut feeling that her godmother had been the "someone" who called Agatha.

"Well, I'm here," Lauren told her mother. "Fighting for my legacy. For a town that I hold dear to my heart. I'm fighting for my beautiful friend who died too soon."

"I'm not here to fight you. I'm here for you." Agatha reached out her hand to Lauren. "And I'm so sorry I dragged you into my lies. But it doesn't matter who your family is . . . you belong to me. Come home with me. Let's leave these people alone and in peace."

Lauren shook her head.

Olivia stood and walked to the front until she stood in front of her father. CJ, who'd been seated, held her stare. A look of devastation robbed him of his usual confidence.

"You have to get up. The town needs to hear from you." She offered her hand to pull him up.

CJ stood and cleared his throat. "Let's conclude today's debate. Our family needs privacy."

People nodded and began standing. But one woman raised her hand in the air.

CJ pointed to her. "Yes?"

"I don't want to leave. I want to hear it all. We deserve to know what's going on with that messy Jones family."

"This is a private matter for my family to discuss without the public listening," CJ answered. "We will resume the debate at a later date."

Janice stood up from her seat. "I agree with our mayor. We are better than this. Let them figure it out, and we'll wait for an official statement from the mayor. I'll make sure of it."

Janice not only stared at CJ but made eye contact with the entire Jones family, including Olivia. Her words encouraged the residents to leave, however, and they filed out, with some groaning and scandalized whispers. It took a full ten minutes for the room to empty out.

"I don't want to do this here, and there's bound to be some people listening in from outside. We will finish this conversation at my home," CJ declared to his family, Lauren, and Agatha. Then he lifted a finger in the air. "Once you step foot in my house, you tell the entire truth. We'll settle whatever's left at the end."

CHAPTER TWENTY-FIVE

July 2022

CONFESSIONS

Everyone was silent as they filed into CJ's living room. CJ, Cindy, Christine, Alan, Ama, Lauren, and Agatha took their seats, while Olivia remained standing near the entryway.

"We should begin now," CJ said, his voice still harsh with grief. "Lauren, why don't you tell us what you know about Indigo?"

Lauren sighed. Her eyes, now wet, avoided CJ's glare.

"I remember you now." CJ shook his head. "You're that girl who told Chris that Indigo killed herself."

Lauren sniffed. "I still think it's true. I—I'll tell you everything I know." She lifted her gaze. "I may have been off base about our . . . relations. But my bond with Indigo was real, and she was mentally ill."

Christine stood and went to Lauren, her hand raised in the air poised for an attack.

"Oh, you can try, Christine. But I hit back," Lauren warned.

Ama tutted. "Still the same old Christine."

"Still the same old Ama," Christine retorted, "sitting all pretty amid the chaos you've likely caused."

"I don't take kindly to false allegations. I'm here for my god-daughter. Since you clearly aren't ready to be her grandmother."

"Ladies," Olivia interjected, "let's please focus. Now, Lauren, Bree, or whatever you call yourself, you said that you were friends with my aunt Indigo?"

"I'm Lauren now. But yes. We were friends. Indigo was fun and sweet, but she felt like she was suffocating. She didn't feel safe to be herself at home."

"Don't you dare . . . don't you dare speak about my baby that way," Christine interjected. "She was perfect. Absolutely perfect." Tears lingered and dripped from her chin down to her collarbone.

Lauren shook her head. "Don't you get it? No one's perfect. Not you or me or my . . . scheming mother." She pointed to Agatha. "But you made Indigo feel less than just because of her depression."

Christine pointed a shaking finger. "*You* probably put those ridiculous thoughts in her head. You made her think that something was wrong with her."

"No, she knew. She just didn't think that you would help her. Even now you only think of yourself and keeping Highland Beach protected. But you wouldn't even protect your own daughter. You never validated her feelings."

"And did you?" Christine screamed.

"Yes! I encouraged her to talk to her father or CJ because I could already tell you wouldn't help."

"She tried to tell me," CJ said, his voice thick with grief. "And I messed it all up. I should've found a better way to talk to Dad in private."

"Don't listen to this charlatan," Christine sneered. "She doesn't know a damn thing."

"Oh really? I know you found her entry in her diary. You ripped it up and told her to never speak of it again."

Olivia stepped forward. "What did the diary say, Christine?"

"Nothing, just . . . nothing," Christine gasped.

"Mother, what did it say?" CJ's dulled eyes were suddenly alert. "What did Indigo need from us?"

"She wanted to end her life," Lauren announced. "And Christine told her to never share that with anyone."

CJ's knees buckled. He gripped the back of the chair. Olivia went to her father and shouldered his weight.

"Why would you say that?" Cindy whispered. "Why didn't you get her help?"

"Maybe I'm not your family," Lauren said. "And I'm sorry my mother swindled you for money. But I'm not lying when I tell you she wanted those waters to swallow her whole. Being in water was the only place she felt safe." She rubbed her cheek before dropping her hand. "So there's the truth."

"Get out." Christine's eyes were dark. "Just . . . go. Away from this house. Away from my town."

"You need to face the truth, Christine," Lauren said. "You need to accept that Indigo died by suicide."

"Get. Out." Christine's voice was ice cold. "Trust me, this is your last warning."

"Oh, what, are you going to pay me off? Or . . . let me guess. Get someone from your precious platinum Rolodex to ruin my life?"

"You have no idea how deep my networks run. Singapore won't be far enough for my wrath."

Ama stood and reached for Lauren's arm. "Let me walk you outside, cher." Lauren begrudgingly responded to Ama's tug on her arm. "You've shared what you needed to clear the pain in your heart."

When Lauren nodded her agreement, Agatha followed the duo.

Lauren stopped in front of Olivia, near the door. "I'm sorry. Following you around, I never meant for you to feel stalked. Indigo would've hated me for that."

"You were the one who took that photo?" Olivia finally realized.

Lauren nodded. "You were the most convenient way to topple the Jones family. But then the town came together and watched out for you. I am sorry. I never intended to cause you pain."

Lauren's eyes, still wet with tears, clearly reflected remorse. But there was one thing that Olivia couldn't understand. One thing she couldn't let go of.

"Did you even want to be mayor? Why . . . why go through all of this?"

Lauren closed her eyes. "When I returned five years ago, I had no intention of involving myself in politics. But I saw that Christine has done so much . . . things you'll never know . . . in the name of keeping this place safe. And to me, CJ just let her do it. I thought things could be better with me as mayor. They won't forget my behavior at the debate, so I will bow out of the election."

She opened her eyes and nodded her head.

"But your father and grandmother do not deserve to lead this town. I hope CJ does the right thing."

A lump formed in Olivia's throat. Her family had a mountain of skeletons in their closet, and there would be a long road to healing between them and the other Highland Beach residents.

"I apologize as well." Agatha's soft voice grabbed Olivia's attention. Lauren had the same large brown eyes as her mother. However, there was something else reflected in Agatha's eyes. Something that looked more like embarrassment than regret. "I shouldn't have encouraged my daughter to befriend Indigo. And I should have listened when she . . ." Agatha looked at Lauren, her eyes glistening with tears. ". . . when you told me that Indigo was hurting. Perhaps hearing this from another adult would have resulted in something different."

Christine didn't listen to her own son about Indigo, Olivia thought, but kept it to herself. "I accept both of your apologies. But Christine is right . . . you should go." Olivia looked at Ama and said, "I'll meet you outside in a few."

"I'll be waiting, my beautiful girl." Ama shut the door behind them, but Olivia could still hear the whispered conversation. "Indigo can rest now. And so should you."

"She was all alone . . . and those rumors. They were so bad."

Ama's soothing tone faded as the three women moved away from the door.

"I need you to leave, too, Mother." CJ's hard voice grabbed Olivia's attention.

"Charles, I—"

"There's nothing you can say that will change my mind."

Christine slumped into a chair. "You don't understand."

CJ slammed his fist against the coffee table. "She could be with us! Right now. She could meet my daughter. And she would've . . . would've forced me to chase Cindy to the corners of the world. Indigo was our heartbeat." He gasped for breath.

"P-people like her . . . like us . . . they don't treat us well. They send us away, shock us, until we tell them what they want to hear."

Shock? Olivia frowned at her grandmother's words, thinking she'd heard her incorrectly. They didn't shock people anymore.

CJ slapped the air with his hand. "I don't want to hear it."

"Dad." Olivia helped lower him to his chair. "Let her speak."

"Fine. But only for your sake." CJ clamped his mouth shut.

"You said 'send us away'?" Olivia asked, her voice gentle.

"They did that to m-me. My own father sent me away. Mother, she was hard, but she didn't want me far. She thought she could help me on her own. But Daddy said no. So they sent me to New York. They shaved my hair. They put this thing in my mouth, made me clamp down, and they h-hurt me. I cried . . . every day I cried for my mother and my father . . . but they'd never come."

Olivia's heart broke for the woman in front of her.

"So I couldn't do that to my baby. I couldn't let her go away from my sight. They do . . . a-all sorts of things . . . hurt you to make you feel good. Feel normal. But I still felt so bad. Until one day I didn't feel at all."

Alan passed her a tissue and pulled her into his arms. "It's not your fault, sweetheart. Like many others, you're living with a mental illness." When Olivia saw that he didn't seem surprised by Christine's admission, she realized her grandmother had at least had one person to confide in.

"You thought you were protecting Indigo?" Olivia whispered, almost to herself.

"Christine . . . Mom . . . why didn't you tell me?" CJ asked.

"Because talking about it makes me sad. And if I allow myself to be sad, then I can't get out of that dark place." She exhaled. "So that door must stay firmly shut. I can be angry, and passionate, and happy, but I can't let myself go there again. I . . ."

"I understand trying to make yourself numb the pain." Olivia stepped closer to her grandmother. "I'm sorry that you've been through so much." Especially with her parents.

Christine sighed. "There are medicines that help. I take them. And when they become ineffective, I go on vacation. Out of the country preferably. I manage just fine. You don't have to feel sorry for me."

"I don't feel sorry for you, Christine. But I am sorry for what I said to you about Indigo," Cindy apologized.

"I'm sorry as well. I should have never turned my anger on the two of you." Christine stood. "I think I'm going to need to take another vacation."

She stood and took a step toward CJ. He slid away from her touch. "Charles, I'm so sorry. I know now that I ruined your life. I ruined Indigo's, too, indirectly. But know that I love you . . . all of you . . . so much."

CJ leveled a stare at his mother. "I'm sorry about your childhood. I'm sorry about my part in what happened to Indigo. But I refuse," he said, looking at Olivia, "to live with regret. So I forgive you. And

I'm going to work on forgiving myself, too. And yes, I think it would be best for you to take that vacation. Right now, I need my family. My daughter and the love of my life."

Christine nodded, her tears silently showcasing her sorrow. Alan patted CJ's back, then took his wife's arm, and together they walked outside.

After the door closed, Olivia looked at her parents and exhaled. "I need to speak to Ama." She stepped outside to find Ama on the front porch sitting on a navy Adirondack chair.

Olivia nearly didn't ask her question. But she squared her shoulders, tilted her head back, and took aim.

"You called Agatha."

"Cher, can you grab my bottle of wine out of the car? In fact, bring the cooler."

"Ama . . ."

"This isn't a dry conversation. Trust me." Ama removed the keys for her rental and let them dangle from her pink fingertips.

Olivia followed instructions and grabbed the cooler before returning to a now-empty house for wineglasses.

She poured the wine, a beautiful pink rosé, and handed a glass to Ama, still seated on the porch.

"CJ and Cindy aren't inside. They're probably by the pool in the backyard. So we should have some modicum of privacy. So tell me, Ama: What happened?"

"I did find Agatha," she confessed. "When I discovered Lauren changed her name—Miles is her last name now, too—I grew curious. I found her people, which . . . wasn't much. It's been just her and her mother for a long time. But even lone branches have deep roots. So I followed those roots, and I found Helen."

"Frederick Douglass's second wife. Did she . . ." Olivia swallowed past the lump of fear in her throat. "Is it true?"

"Is what true, cher? If you want the answer, you must ask the question."

"Are they related to us?"

"Agatha and Lauren are related to Helen."

"Are they . . ." Olivia's throat closed. For some unknown reason, tears stung her eyes. She couldn't do it. She was afraid of the truth.

Ama leaned over and reached out her small brown hand to squeeze Olivia's hand. "I contacted some friends, but I also did my research. And you know what was the most interesting thing I learned?"

"What?" Olivia whispered.

"Anna Murray Douglass. That woman was strong. Resilient. Scrutinized in ways that I could never understand. For the color of her dark skin. Her illiteracy. Those white folks wanted someone *great* for Frederick Douglass. But he already had it in Anna." Ama sipped her wine.

"But then she died, and he married Helen. I understand loss. And heartbreak. But I also understand opening your heart to love again. And I'm sure she was a fine woman in her own way, but she wasn't Anna. Just like Carter isn't Omar.

"Anna Murray Douglass bore five children, some of whom moved on to do great things. Anna provided a refuge for slaves as they ran for freedom on the Underground Railroad. She took care of her family's house and money. Anna was the reason Frederick could gain freedom."

Olivia's heart soared with pride. "She was an abolitionist."

"That she was, cher. I don't want to give another minute of thought to conspiracy theories and secret babies and family lines."

Olivia refilled their glasses. "Let's have a toast for Anna."

Ama's laugh was deep and rich and absolutely perfect. "To Anna."

"To Anna," Olivia repeated.

People rarely celebrated or lauded the courage of Frederick Douglass's first wife in helping her husband to freedom. But Anna

Murray's story was a familiar tale for many women, especially Black women who endeavored to put their family's needs above their own and whose work and accomplishments were often diminished. But what made the disregard for Anna's accomplishments painfully ironic was that her legacy, which was always focused on the advancement of Black people, suffered because she could not read as well as her husband.

But at the end of the day, whose fault was that?

Olivia closed her eyes, silently thanking her ancestor.

"Her strength and her fierceness live in you, Olivia."

"I know. I feel it." Olivia scanned the horizon, only now noticing the setting sun.

"Ama?"

"Yes, cher."

"What if I wanted to know the truth about Lauren's family heritage?"

"I would've reached into my purse and handed you an envelope with the results from my trusted source. Even I don't know the truth." Ama sighed. "The sun is going down. I should get back to my hotel room."

"You can stay here."

"Oh no, cher. I don't think that would be appropriate . . . given . . . everything."

"Omar and Chris."

"Yes. It was hard enough to come here. The only reason I did was because I didn't trust that Lauren-slash-Bree character. But she's all right. Just a little lost."

"I'm just glad it's all over. I feel like I can breathe again."

"Well, take in all the air you need. I've got a feeling you'll be needing to brace yourself."

Olivia's hand shook so much she spilled her wine. "You've found out something else about my family?"

Ama patted her knee and stood. "No. Just some unfinished business. No harm will come to you, I promise," she said, walking toward her car.

"Ama, what did you do?" she called to her godmother's back.

She paused in her walk down the pathway and spun around. "What I've always done, cher. Made sure you have the best and brightest future. I'll always watch over you."

CHAPTER TWENTY-SIX

May 1882

ANNA MURRAY DOUGLASS

Washington, DC

"You need to go on over to Massachusetts, and tell him what it's for, you hear?" said Ruth, Anna's friend, who she'd met through the Anti-Slavery Society.

Anna rocked in her seat in the kitchen, humming as she shelled peas for summer. Her eldest daughter planned to visit her at their home, Cedar Hill, with the baby, and she wanted dinner to be perfect.

"Now, he's a good man," Ruth went on, "don't get me wrong. But you know how they are."

"I do." Anna knew all too well. Wasn't like she could go around blind. Everyone cut her a look as hot as an iron.

But what hurt the deepest, more than even what her husband did, was folks looking like it was her fault.

Anna kept humming. It soothed her nerves, her soul. The clopping of hooves outside caught her attention.

"Is Rosetta already here?" Anna muttered. She wiped her hands on her apron.

Her question was quickly answered even before she could welcome the visitor.

But it was no stranger. It was her husband.

"Well, hey, Frederick," Ruth said. "We was just talking about you. What you been up to? Giving those rascals down in Washington hell?" Her tone was jovial, as if she hadn't just called him a lying cheat five minutes ago.

Anna didn't make out what he said. His lips moved, and he muttered something about a speech to Ruth, but he was staring at his wife. His eyes glittered like a secret only the two of them knew.

Maybe it was gratitude that she'd sewn them sailor's clothes and made them fit just for him so he could escape to freedom. Maybe it was because she saved every cent to start a home for them.

He always looked at her like that, right from the first time they met. With dignity and awe and respect. Anna's cheeks warmed, and she hoped her friend could see the way he looked at her. She never doubted the love he had for her. Folks just liked to talk and gossip was all. He was an important man who made a lot of folks angry.

"Hey." Anna smiled wide and rushed over to greet him. Then she stopped when she noticed another woman standing just outside the inner door. She rocked back on her feet. The soles didn't have enough cushion to absorb her shock.

That woman, his *friend* and secretary, and their neighbor, Helen Pitts, strode in behind him. Sticking to him like molasses.

That woman looked around the house and then finally offered Anna a smile with too many teeth and too much familiarity.

"Hi, Anna. Very good to see you again."

"Hmm." Her friend snorted behind her.

"Wasn't expecting company," Anna whispered low to her husband. That company included him as well.

"Helen?" her husband's voice boomed. He looked at the woman with that same glimmer of something he had aimed at his wife. It wasn't as deep or as affectionate, yet it cut up little ribbons inside Anna's stomach.

"She isn't company. She is here to help me with my book."

Anna didn't reply. She couldn't hear nothing over her crumbling heart.

He's a good man. A smart man. He needs you, Anna. He says it all the time.

Anna dug deep and pulled out a smile. "Your daughter's coming home. I'll make an extra place for your guest."

Frederick smiled, inclining his head to offer his thanks.

"Helen, can you look over my revisions?" He reached into his vest pocket and pulled out a paper.

Anna's cheeks warmed again. This time from embarrassment. That was the one thing he didn't need from her, the one thing she couldn't do for him. She couldn't read a lick of what he wrote.

But ain't I done enough? His freedom? Taking care of our money, our kids, and our home? Making sure them slaves got they freedom, too?

She looked at his clothes. "I need to wash and press some suits for you." Anna excused herself and left the parlor.

"Anna." Her husband strode behind her. She kept walking. The tears were gathering, and she didn't think she could stop them this time.

"Anna." He gently tugged her elbow, dragging her to his chest.

He pulled her close, whispering in her ear. "Next time I come home, why don't we sit outside, and I'll read to you. Just like old times."

Anna rubbed her heart with one hand and squeezed his hand with the other. Her heart ached like the devil these days.

Another thing she was grateful for—he knew just what to say to soothe her. She guessed that's why folks paid him—to make them feel like they were special.

"Rosetta is coming over for supper. Will you stay?"

He shook his head. "I'm sorry. I've got a meeting, but I'll be home much later. We'll have guests in a few days—"

"How many?"

"Three. Two adults and a child. They'll need a room for the week."

Anna reached out, smoothing the wrinkles that gathered around his elbows.

"I'll take care of 'em."

"I know you will, and I thank you for it." His eyes filled with gratitude. "Now, I must leave, but I will see you soon. Tell Rosetta I will see her tomorrow."

"Sorry, Mama," Rosetta whispered while they cleared the table. "I'll clean up once I put them to bed." Her daughter's little ones sat with their toys in the parlor. They would make all kinds of mess, but Anna didn't mind so much. She smiled at her daughter. "No, you won't. You know I like to keep things straight on my own. Besides, we're gonna have some company soon."

"Who?" her daughter asked.

Anna shrugged while drying the dishes. "Your father said a wife, husband, and child. Don't matter to me if they Black or white, slave or the president."

Rosetta let out a long sigh.

"Didn't know you took up sighing as a trade," Anna quipped.

Rosetta laughed. Anna liked that she could be herself around her daughter once she became a woman.

"Mama."

"What is it?" Anna stopped her task.

"Aren't you tired of people dropping into your home? Aren't you tired of living in danger?"

"Long as there's hate in people's hearts, we all in danger. You know that. You used to read me the *North Star*."

"I know, but when my father writes about what's happening, houses burn down. Or he has to go into hiding."

"It's not just words from your father. He helps them people find freedom, find they own voice, too."

"So do you, Mama. You give them a warm bed, food, refuge."

Anna nodded. "Sure do."

Rosetta frowned at her answer.

"What's got you so upset?" she asked her daughter.

"I just hear chatter is all. And I get mad."

Anna placed her palms on either side of Rosetta's face. "I don't care about what them folks say, and if they are bold enough to say it to me, then I'll turn them out of my house. It doesn't matter that I'm not on that stage or traveling with your father. I've got my own life, too, and it's . . ." She struggled to find the right words to say to her daughter. "It's important to me that I keep things going. It's important that my children and grandchildren know where I am. It's important that the Underground Railroad keeps the doors open. Outside of helping your father, there is nothing wrong or low of me by keeping home. Do you understand me, little girl?"

"Yes, Mama. I do."

"Now, don't forget what I said."

"I'll never forget. And I'll make sure everyone else knows it, too."

Anna laughed. "You're gonna write it in the *North Star*?"

"I'll figure out something." Rosetta hugged her mother close. Anna inhaled the lovely scent of jasmine her daughter had dabbed on her neck. The grease that covered her scalp. She remembered nights of braiding her Rosetta's hair, holding her when she got sick, and tucking her in at night. She was so lonely when her children were young, but those hugs went a long way toward driving out the fear and anger. Seemed like it should've been the other way around, but her daughter, her children, smelled like home.

"Sometimes I forget that you're a woman. I know you don't need me anymore, but I will always be here for you."

Rosetta smiled. "You taught me to be industrious, and brave and loyal. I am who I am because of you. I want everyone to know how special you are to our family."

Anna didn't need those folks who circled around her husband to understand her. The same ones who rallied for freedom and equality while they looked down on her because she couldn't read. The very opportunity the world took from Black folks.

But Anna cared about what was in the heart and thoughts of her family. Her husband had always given her the words to make her feel that she was important. But Anna knew that her daughter, maybe more than anyone, understood her worth.

In her heart, she knew her daughter would see that the world understood, too.

CHAPTER TWENTY-SEVEN

July 2022

DECISIONS

OLIVIA

After Ama left for her hotel, Olivia returned to her mother and father, who were sitting in the backyard whispering to each other. She left them alone. They needed space to process all that had happened.

When she woke up the following morning, her father and mother were both seated at the table. CJ was typing on his phone, likely fielding messages from concerned Highland Beach residents.

"Good morning." Olivia stretched her arms.

"Morning. Did you sleep well?"

Olivia shook her head. "Not at all." It hadn't been entirely because of the stress of yesterday's events. She missed Garrett fiercely. She wanted to call him, get his advice, tell him all that had transpired with her family.

And soon she would return home to Sag Harbor. Potentially as just a neighbor he used to date. But she had another idea. Like Ama had said, she would show him her heart and properly apologize for her actions.

"CJ, you need to put that phone down," her mother admonished.

CJ shook his head. "Last night was a circus. I need to address what happened. It's the least I can do after what happened between me, Mom, and Lauren."

"Why don't I take a crack at it?" Olivia offered. "You can edit it later."

"Alan usually takes care of that as my campaign and communications manager, but I think he has his hands full."

"Yes. He didn't seem surprised by anything last night," Cindy agreed.

"Yeah, well, Alan knows everything. Though I can't see my mother ever telling him about the shock therapy."

Olivia nodded. She didn't know her grandmother as well, but her guess was that Alan had probably put two and two together. It was hard to hide depression from someone you lived with. Not only that, but as Olivia now also recalled, he'd come in with a small paper bag holding Christine's medicine when they had lunch the other day.

"Still, I think I'll draft something up. The town is probably out of sorts, and no matter what, it's my job to ensure everyone is okay." CJ placed his hands on his knees and pushed. He never looked a day over fifty, but in that moment he'd aged a decade.

"But, Dad, you should—"

"It won't take long." He leaned over and kissed Cindy's cheek. "I'll be back soon. And we'll talk."

"Aren't you talked out?" Cindy huffed.

CJ shook his head. "Not when it comes to you and me."

Cindy stared at Olivia, looking like the picture of confusion with her raised eyebrows and mouth slightly ajar. She snapped her mouth shut before responding. "Okay, if you're up for it."

"Sure am. I'll be back soon."

An hour later, her father returned downstairs.

"If you don't mind, I'd like for you to review my statement."

Serving the residents of Highland Beach has been one of the greatest honors of my life. However, I've come to the difficult decision to finish my term this year and not run for reelection.

I want to thank my staff and volunteers for supporting me and the town's initiatives. But now I want to be with my new family. I will remain a citizen of this beautiful place, and after some time I will find other ways to support Highland Beach.

I wish everyone the best of luck, and I hope you will do the same for me.

Sincerely,

Mayor Charles Jones

"CJ!" Cindy gasped. "Are you sure? I thought . . . I thought you really wanted another term?"

"Come here." He opened his arms, and Cindy stepped into his embrace.

"Yes, and no. This entire time I've been in agony, trying to figure out a way for us to be together. I know you have a life back in New Jersey, and I respect that. I can't make you give up your life to stay here. So this time, I want to chase you. I want to visit your home, stay a while if you don't mind, and figure out our future . . . together. Is that okay?"

"It's . . . it's very okay." Cindy sniffed into his chest. CJ smiled over her head.

"Come here, daughter of mine. I've got more than enough for you, too." He opened his other arm for her.

"I'd love to visit you at your home, too. I want you to show me all your favorite spots. We can visit New York together, too. I just want to create memories with my daughter. I'm unable to do that in my capacity as the mayor."

"I'm glad you made the right decision, Dad." Olivia joined her parents in a hug. This was always what she'd wanted—a relationship with her father. Three men in her life had loved her unconditionally— her godfather Omar, Chris, and now CJ.

"I struck gold when you two came back into my life. I won't ever let you go again . . . well, that is, until you get married. Even then, Garrett's going to make some room for me."

Olivia's heartbeat skipped for a moment. "Oh, well, Garrett and I aren't together, so you've got me for some time yet."

"I don't know about that, daughter of mine." She couldn't see his face, but she heard the humor in his voice.

A knock on the door grabbed their attention.

Olivia sighed. "I hope the good people of Highland Beach won't storm the house."

"They had better not. I'll handle it." Cindy walked briskly to the door and opened it wide. "We aren't receiving any guests . . ." She exhaled. "Oh, hello."

"Hi, Mrs. Jones. Is Olivia here?"

When Olivia heard the familiar voice, she rushed from the kitchen to the living room.

"What are you doing here, Garrett?" Olivia's heart clamored in her chest.

He waved a crumpled paper in his hand. "I got your letter. And then Ama called."

"Ama?" Olivia's confusion cleared once she remembered Ama's warning about settling unfinished business.

"Yes. She told me I was being a fool, but I'd already realized that when I read your note."

Olivia shook her head. "I didn't give you a letter."

Garrett cocked his head back. "Really? Because this is a dead ringer for your handwriting and you . . . what's on here are things that only you and I know." He glanced at Cindy, who made no pretense she wasn't eavesdropping.

"Oh . . . oh no," Olivia groaned after she remembered telling Addy that she threw the letter in the trash can. She was going to skewer Addy and then barbecue her friend. Slowly.

"Let's step outside." Olivia grabbed his arm and dragged him.

"Listen, Garrett, that letter—"

"Changed everything," he finished.

"W-what do you mean?" It took everything in Olivia to not look away. But she had to know. She was desperate to understand.

"You were right about what you said. I never felt like I was a priority, and after talking to Anderson, I let him get into my head. I leaned into my fears instead of remembering what you've been showing me all along."

"What did I show you?" she whispered.

"Your heart." He grabbed her hand. "And it's so big, Olivia. Big enough to love my little girl. Big enough to love Mr. Whittingham, and Kara and Addy and Whitney and your godsisters and Ama and your parents. Big enough to love me. I'm sorry I didn't realize it. I was so focused on my feelings . . . my fear of losing you."

Tears streamed down her cheeks. "Garrett." She lowered her head into her hands.

"Don't cry." Garrett pulled her close into a hug. "I'm sorry I made you cry. I . . . I caused us both a lot of pain, and I hope you can forgive me."

Olivia's throat became itchy and tight. She couldn't open her mouth. Everything felt like a dream, and she was afraid that, if she spoke, she'd wake up and realize she was all alone.

He tilted her chin. "Look, I know you didn't want me to see that letter. Mr. Whittingham told me he found it in the trash."

Mr. Whittingham! She couldn't believe her sly neighbor. Thank God she didn't go off on Addy like she'd planned to.

"But . . . do you still feel the same way? Do you still mean what you wrote in that letter?"

Olivia clutched at his hands cupping her face. "These past few months, I've been watching my mother and father. Judging them. Telling myself that I wouldn't let the past stop me from being with the one I love. But Garrett . . . I'm so scared."

"Why?"

"Because I love you!" She turned away from his heated gaze. "I've seen what love can do. And if you aren't careful, it has the power to destroy you." She'd witnessed it firsthand with not only Cindy and CJ but Christine. Her grandmother's motherly love destroyed her relationship with her children.

"No." Garrett shook his head. "Then that's not love. It's the absence of love. True love doesn't harm you, it lifts you up. I love you, too, Olivia, and I want it all with you. I hope I'm not asking for too much, too soon."

Olivia lifted her eyes to see him—to see his soul.

He loves me. I know he does.

She didn't even have to take one step. He came all the way to Highland Beach to confess his love and build a lifetime with her. Just like Ama and Omar. And Billie and Dulce, and Perry and Damon, and Cindy and CJ.

"No, it's not too much. I love you, too, and I want everything."

"More kids?" he asked, his voice hopeful.

Someone cleared their throat behind them.

Olivia turned to face her father. "Hi, Dad. Everything okay?"

"Why don't you both come inside?"

"Hi, sir. I'm Garrett Brooks." He offered his hand to CJ.

CJ took his hand, though his eyes narrowed. "Let's have a conversation, since you intend on doing 'everything' with my daughter."

When Garrett's eyes widened, CJ broke into a smile. He released it after a few extended seconds and stepped out of the entryway, where he walked over to stand by Cindy.

"He's intense," Garrett whispered in her ear.

"Relax. We'll be back home before you know it," Olivia replied in a low voice.

Garrett chuckled. "Speaking of which, where will that be? Your place or mine?"

Olivia, for once, didn't have a plan. She didn't care, either. "Wherever you are."

"That sounds like a brilliant plan, Olivia Jones."

EPILOGUE

Two Years Later

"I don't think the flowers are going to make it down the aisle," Billie whispered to Perry. Olivia stared at her reflection in the mirror. Years ago, three girls under the age of seven tossing blush pink rose petals in her dressing room would've sent her over the edge.

But to Olivia Brooks (soon to be Brooks in thirty minutes and counting), this was heaven.

"It's okay." Olivia smiled at Billie's reflection in the mirror.

"I knew Isabel wasn't ready for the big leagues."

"A three-year-old flower girl is a . . . choice, for sure," Addy added, while posing for the photographer who insisted on taking organic, behind-the-scenes photos.

"Well, I couldn't say no to that cute face," Olivia said, defending her position. "Besides, we can just pick up the flowers."

"And who is this *we*?" Addy teased.

"Maybe one or all of my seven bridesmaids."

Whitney laughed. "There are a lot of us."

"Yes, make that six of us on petal duty," Perry added. "There's no way Ama will pick up anything off the floor."

Olivia laughed. It took about a full week of begging to get Ama to agree to be her matron of honor. She argued that she was much too old to wear a dress in colors that matched those of her bridesmaids. But Olivia was adamant. She didn't want Ama just sitting in the audience. She wanted the woman who taught her to love and accept herself right by her side.

"Speaking of, where is my matron of honor?" Olivia scanned the room.

"Here," Ama said by the door. She waved at a server who held champagne glasses on a platter. Ama wore a beautiful sheer chiffon blush pink gown with sequin accents. The style differed from the other bridesmaid dresses, which were sweetheart chiffon gowns, but the colors were the same.

The server handed around glasses to everyone in the room.

"I'd like to make a toast to my beautiful Olivia. I know your mother and father will do the honors during the reception, so please indulge me in celebrating Olivia before the wedding begins."

Whitney, Addy, Kara, Billie, Perry, and her childhood friend Tanya lifted their flutes in the air.

"To Olivia. The woman who has it all. A beautiful and meaningful career. Strong friendships that I know will last a lifetime. A beautiful daughter, Zora. And now she's marrying the love of her life, Garrett. You've found yourself. You loved yourself through the difficulties, and that is why you have triumphed—because you've learned to love and trust yourself. And through this, all things flow. So let's raise our glasses and bask in my beautiful goddaughter's special day. To Olivia!"

"To Olivia!"

Oliva's heart burst with joy. She had found happiness, friendship, and her home.

She had finally pulled her brass ring.

ACKNOWLEDGMENTS

Thank you once again, Sharina Harris, for making sure we got it right. Thank you to my editor, Liz Stein, for making sure we got it done. Thank you to my friend and former editor Carrie Feron, who believed the Summer Beach Series would resonate. Thank you to my literary agent, Mel Berger, for keeping me on track and now, on to the next!

And finally to Erika Martin for being my steward into the world of Highland Beach. Janice Lloyd for your incredible knowledge of Highland Beach and your personalized tour of the Frederick Douglass Museum. The Newton family, for sharing your history. And to the families of Highland Beach, thank you for entrusting me with your stories.